MISS MARGARET RIDPATH

AND THE DISMANTLING

OF THE UNIVERSE

Novels by Don Robertson

THE THREE DAYS (1959)
BY ANTIETAM CREEK (1960)
THE RIVER AND THE WILDERNESS (1962)
A FLAG FULL OF STARS (1964)
THE GREATEST THING SINCE SLICED BREAD (1965)
THE SUM AND TOTAL OF NOW (1966)
PARADISE FALLS (1968)
THE GREATEST THING THAT ALMOST HAPPENED (1970)
PRAISE THE HUMAN SEASON (1974)
MISS MARGARET RIDPATH AND THE
   DISMANTLING OF THE UNIVERSE (1977)

Miss Margaret Ridpath and the Dismantling of the Universe

DON ROBERTSON

G. P. PUTNAM'S SONS

NEW YORK

SBN: 399-11925-6

Library of Congress Cataloging in Publication Data

Robertson, Don, 1929–
  Miss Margaret Ridpath and the dismantling of the universe.

  I. Title.
PZ4.R649Mi [PS3568.0248] 813'.5'4 76-51423

GIMME A LITTLE KISS WILL YA HUH?
Words & Music by Roy Turk, Maceo Pinkard & Jack Smith
© Copyright 1926 and renewed 1954 Cromwell Music, Inc. and ABC Music Corp., New York, N.Y. Used by permission.
© Copyright 1926 Bourne Co. Copyright renewed. Used by permission.

PRINTED IN THE UNITED STATES OF AMERICA

For Doris Fields and the late Arthur Fields

Contents

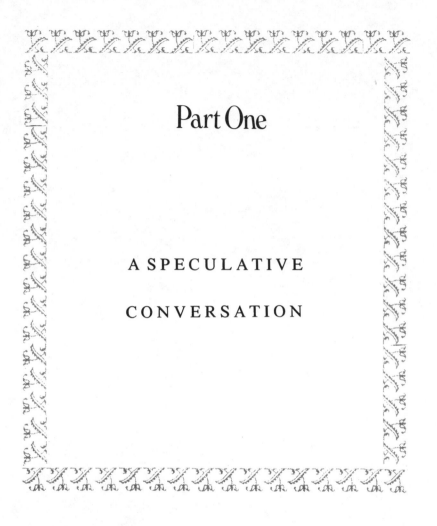

Part One

A SPECULATIVE
CONVERSATION

They are sensitive, and they are not unlettered, and they are not without a certain smalltown notion of what the world views as sophisticated behavior, but nonetheless they do occasionally spend a Saturday night drinking beer and eating limburger cheese in the white and spacious kitchen of the Saddler place. There are three of them: Pete Saddler; his wife, Sarah; their brotherinlaw, George Prout. They often discuss Miss Margaret Ridpath, who was Sarah Saddler's sister. They discuss Miss Ridpath's death . . . or, rather, the manner of her death. They swallow and munch, and their conversations are solemn, and it is as though they are seeking some way not to blame themselves. They drink perhaps five or six cans of Rolling Rock apiece, and they become a little slurred and disorganized, but they do know that they are splintering their fingernails against the surface of something horrifying and forever impenetrable. They do know that much. They are never *altogether* slurred or disorganized. They are perhaps accusing themselves of never having moved beyond childhood. Which is absurd, of course. Pete Saddler is a successful banker. Sarah Saddler is witty, fun to be with, quite lovely for her age. And, God knows, George Prout is Paradise Falls' most prosperous druggist. So why then do they commune with beer and the limburger? Why such a tacky escape? Why do they sprawl in that kitchen and mumble and dispute? What is it that they do not grasp?

"Myself," said George Prout one evening in the warm early autumn of 1975, "I think it was courage."

"She never had courage," said Sarah. "She was gentle, and she would not hurt a soul. Everybody walked all over her."

"Except Pauline Jones," said Pete.

"All right," said Sarah. "Pauline is the exception that proves the rule."

"No matter how far down you are," said Pete, "somebody else is a little farther down. All you have to do is find that person."

"That's a shitty thing to say about Margaret," said George.

"I apologize," said Pete.

"You didn't love her the way I did," said George.

"Are you proud of that?" said Pete.

"I had no control over it," said George.

"It was ridiclus," said Sarah.

"How's that?" said Pete.

"Ridiculous," said Sarah, slicing herself an uneven hunk of the cheese.

11

"Don't let your tongue get away from you," said Pete.

"I could almost take that as a dirty remark," said Sarah, gnawing.

"I certainly hope so," said Pete.

"If a person is gentle," said George, "courage can also be there."

"What?" said Pete.

"Sarah just said something about Margaret not having any courage," said George, "and she said it was because Margaret was gentle. Well, I say the two are not incompatible."

"I expect he has you there," Pete said to Sarah.

"It was all because of Otto York," said George.

"Maybe so," said Pete.

"She saw him lying there, and something flew apart," said George.

"There never has been anything like it," said Sarah.

"She should have stayed down," said Pete. "God knows, *I* stayed down. I was under Sam Elliot's desk with him, and I was glad to be there."

"I nair showed her I loved her," said Sarah.

"What?" said Pete.

"Never," said Sarah. *"I never* showed her I loved her."

"That's not true," said Pete.

"The way Ruth and I stuck her with Mother," said Sarah. "And me, I was the youngest. The spoiled one. The flibbertygibbet."

"So?" said Pete.

"So I should have done more. I should have stayed on longer instead of bailing out and marrying you."

"Do you regret it?" said Pete.

"No," said Sarah.

"I should of been the one to of married her," said George.

"We know that," said Sarah. "You have *told* us that and *told* us that."

"Maybe at the end I humiliated her," said George.

"Or maybe she was afraid of you," said Sarah.

"But why didn't she ever *seem* afraid?" George wanted to know.

"Seem is nothing," said Sarah.

"The *seem* is hardly ever the same as the *is,"* said Pete.

"Philosophy," said Sarah.

"More beer," said Pete.

"Say please," said Sarah.

"Please," said Pete.

Sarah fetched the beer. Pete popped open the can. George covered his mouth and belched. He drank. He said: "I wish she would of been able to speak."

"She wouldn't have told us a thing we don't already know," said Sarah. "It was all there in what she *was*, not what she would have *said*. Sixtythree years talk better than *words*."

George Prout drank. He is enormously respected in Paradise Falls. He poked at his eyes. "I came to see *Ruth* because I wanted to see *her*," he said.

"Yes," said Sarah.

Pete Saddler shook his head. He is also enormously respected in Paradise Falls. "There was too much noise," he said, "and I wanted to tear out the floor and drop to the center of the earth."

"Yes," said Sarah.

"I really loved her," said George.

"I really was afraid," said Pete.

"Yes," said Sarah.

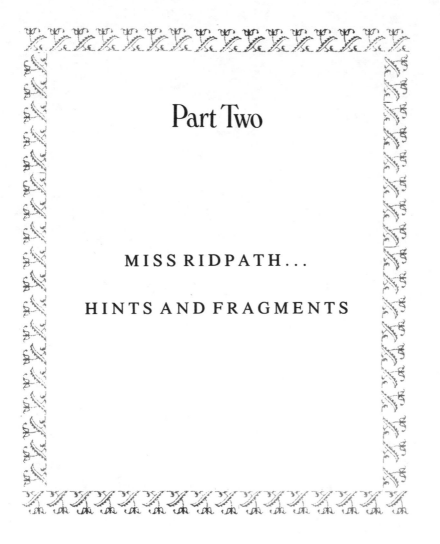

Part Two

MISS RIDPATH...

HINTS AND FRAGMENTS

When Margaret Ridpath was a little girl, there was a rich old woman named Bird who lived in a big house across the street. The woman was called "Madame" Bird, and she once had sung grand opera, or so it was said. She vocalized in her front room nearly every day until the day she died, and Margaret sometimes crept across the street to listen.

Mme Bird's voice was like flanges and broken crockery, but it thrilled Margaret. At the same time, though, it frightened her—but then so did just about everything else. Bees, for instance. Angry dogs. Lightning. Canoes. And even the taste of horseradish, which was altogether too intimidating for her.

She often saw herself as being puffy, flabby, incomplete. And her world was different. It abounded with iron people, and they all led iron lives, and they were *complete,* and sometimes they made her want to cup her hands over her ears, and sometimes she did just that.

Margaret's father was a veterinarian, and the first veterinarian in Paradise Falls whose practice was devoted entirely to small animals—house pets. He was a troubled and incoherent man, and he blamed everything on people he called criminal syndicalists. He drank a great deal of beer, and in 1926 he walked into the path of a Paradise Valley Traction interurban car, and that was the end of him, and Margaret never did learn exactly what a criminal syndicalist was.

Margaret was nicely formed. Sometimes her father called her "comely," and he warned her that she would have to be careful. "A comely girl must always watch her step," said Dr Ridpath. "Otherwise, she will be destroyed by the various temptations that will come her way."

Margaret loved her father, and she did not want to be destroyed, and so she said: "I promise to watch my step."

Dr Ridpath was holding Margaret on his lap. She was perhaps eight or nine. A Sousa march was playing on the Victrola. He kissed her chin and

17

her nose, and his mouth was moistly sour from his beer, his beloved beer.
"And you're the sort to keep a promise, aren't you?" he said.

"Yes sir," said Margaret.

    Promises occupied precious uncharted territory in Margaret's mind.
She grieved when she did not live up to them. She also became fearful. And so later, much later, when she entered into her agreement to play at slapping her poor dotty mother and inflicting on the woman a punishment that probably was neither logical nor right, she participated in that lunatic charade with a terrified earnestness that perhaps would have made her smile had she been the type. But she was not the type. The world was knives. The world was iron unyielding souls. Her heart was an army that had surrendered. Too many of her days had a way of wringing their hands. Therefore, she had to honor all promises. The alternatives were too hellaciously dreadful to contemplate.

    The word, *comely*, worked and scratched in the young Margaret's mind, and she kept it with her forever. Once, when she was eleven, she stood naked in front of the bathroom mirror and stroked herself. (She had, of course, locked and bolted the door.) She smiled and said: "Comely." She stroked her chest and her nipples (she had no bosom yet), and she stroked herself between the legs.

She was blond; she had large hips and shoulders. She never was stout, but at the same time she never would be called frail. She had fine strong cheekbones, enormous gray eyes, a good chin and a wide mouth. She had a slight overbite, but she already had learned to keep her upper lip pressed firmly against her teeth. That way, even though her smile invariably had a pinched and pained aspect, the overbite was not apparent.

Now, naked and fearful in the bathroom, she stood on tiptoe, and she continued to stroke herself, and she twisted this way and that. Tight-mouthed, she grinned into the mirror. The grin pushed back the fear a little. Perhaps her father was right. Perhaps she *was* comely, at least a *little*. She fluffed her hair. Wouldn't it be nice if she were?

In the summer of 1945, when Margaret was thirtyfour, she attended a party for a man named Herman Soeder, a local fellow who had gone west and had married a famous movie star. Now divorced from the famous movie star, he was back in Paradise Falls on a brief visit to attend the christening of his sister Anna Neumann's latest child. (Next to Captain Billy Ackerman, the famous World War I aero ace, and Miss Patricia Savage, the actress who had been born and raised as Patricia Timmons, daughter of the county sheriff, this Herman Soeder was probably the most noted celebrity Paradise Falls ever had produced—even though in the strictest sense he wasn't a *real* celebrity at all. But he *did* live in Hollywood, and he *was* said to be influential. He was head of Promotion & Publicity for one of the major studios, and his divorce from the famous movie star evidently had been amicable, and he was known out there as Henry Snow. It was rumored that he once had been Patricia Timmons/Savage's lover, but no one really knew about *that,* and anyway, it wasn't anyone's beeswax, was it?)

The party was given by a couple named Bert and Wilma Tazewell. They both had gone to school with Herman Soeder up in Lake Township. Bert Tazewell worked with Margaret at Steinfelder's Department Store, and last year, at a Christmas party in the back room, he had tried to kiss her and feel her up.

Now, tonight, for Herman Soeder, Margaret was wearing a green dress cut reasonably low in front. But only reasonably. After all, she did not seek to inflame anyone. She was sitting on a davenport, and Herman Soeder came to her, grinned and sat down beside her. His lower lip was loose, and cracker crumbs clung to the corners of his mouth. His breath was not good, and it reminded her of her father's breath. He said: "It's all a crock, isn't it?"

"I beg your pardon?" said Margaret.

"They want *me* to be the *godfather* . . . and *that's* what *I* call a *crock.*"

"But why shouldn't you be the godfather?"

"I don't believe I'm the type," said Herman Soeder. He was holding a glass of straight whiskey. It was a water glass, and it was nearly full. He sipped from it, and some of the cracker crumbs were washed away. Then: "I have evil habits."

"Well, you shouldn't *brag* about them," said Margaret.

"Sorry," said Herman Soeder.

"Perhaps you should *do* something about them," said Margaret.

"I have tried."

"Perhaps you should try harder."

"I don't want to try harder," said Herman Soeder.

"I didn't think so," said Margaret.

Herman Soeder was a tall man, quite blond and tanned. Margaret remembered him rather well. He was perhaps five years younger than she, and he had been something of an athlete at Lake Township Consolidated High School. He had left home in '34 or '35 (his departure had had something to do with the suicide of a sister . . . Margaret did not know the details), and *then,* the next thing anyone knew, he was married to *the* Diana Halvorsen, and he was living in Hollywood, and he had changed his name to Henry Snow. Now he reached forward, took Margaret by a shoulder and said: "It's a hard life if you let it get to you." His free hand still held his enormous drink. The liquid sloshed.

The man's hand was uncomfortable, and Margaret wished he would let go. "But think of all the *experiences* you've had," she said. She knew it was a stupid thing to be saying, but she could think of nothing else.

Herman Soeder did not seem to notice how stupid the remark had been. He released Margaret's shoulder and leaned back. He rubbed the glass against a cheek. Then he sipped from the glass, bared his teeth, blinked and said: "Don't give me too much credit. And don't think glamor. Glamor is a crock, too."

"But . . . I mean . . . Hollywood and all . . ."

"I don't want to talk about *Hollywood and all.* God's sake."

"All right," said Margaret.

"I'd rather talk about that dress you're wearing."

"Oh?"

"You are stacked. Hubbahubba and all that sort of thing."

"Now . . . now . . ."

"Now nothing. Do people call you Maggie?"

"No. They call me Margaret. In high school, my best girlfriend called me Peggy, but everyone else has always called me Margaret."

"I remember you," said Herman Soeder.

"You do? Really?"

"Yes. I remember seeing you in Steinfelder's. I remember I used to say to myself: Wow, is that girl put together."

"I bet you did. I just bet."

"I've always been interested in girls. Especially girls who are put together."

"Well," said Margaret, "that's reassuring."

Again Herman Soeder grinned. "I am many things," he said, "but a fairy is not one one of them.''

"I am very pleased," said Margaret.

"Ah, forgive me if I seem to be ungallant, but you *are* older than I am, and we both know that. But the thing is—how come you look so much younger?"

Margaret smiled tightly. "You *are* being ungallant," she said, "and I don't believe I *will* forgive you."

"All right, but answer my question."

"You're the only one who can answer that question," said Margaret.

"That sounds like a hint that I may have lived badly."

"I wouldn't know about that, of course," said Margaret.

"It's not all that important a question, is it?"

"That's not for me to say."

Herman Soeder shrugged. "I wish all these people weren't around," he said.

"Well, they are," said Margaret. "And I'm glad they are."

"If they weren't, I probably would make some sort of feverish pass."

"I doubt that," said Margaret.

"Don't underestimate yourself," said Herman Soeder.

Margaret folded her arms over her belly. Her hands were a little moist.

Herman Soeder looked at her arms. He frowned. "What are you protecting?" he wanted to know.

Herman Soeder drove Margaret home that night in a Pontiac he had rented. Gasoline rationing had ended the week before, and so first he took her for a drive up into Lake Township. It was a clear night, and he remembered the roads, and he said: "I think about dear old Lake Township just about every day of my life. You don't remember my sister Georgia, do you? Georgia and what happened between her and Tom Walls, who later went out out and earned himself a Congressional Medal, as I'm sure you know. Georgia who bled to death on 33-A. It was eleven years ago, and his father had it all hushed up, right? Ah, but none of that is here nor there. The thing is, though . . . it all drove me away, and if this sounds mysterious and fragmentary, I'm sorry, but there's no more I'm going to tell you . . ."

Margaret said nothing. She was sitting as far away from Herman Soeder as she could get. He was too drunk. She never should have accepted his offer to drive her home. Nothing good would come of it. She pressed her upper lip against her teeth. She kept wanting to hug herself.

Herman Soeder changed the subject. He spoke of some noted homosexual male movie stars, and the names made Margaret gasp a little. But Herman Soeder assured her he was telling the truth. Then he spoke of the malapropisms of a certain studio chief, and then he spoke of his former wife. Not looking at Margaret, he said: "You're everything Diana wasn't. Perhaps that's why there's the attraction."

"Which sounds like a fib of a *line,*" said Margaret.

"You're wrong," said Herman Soeder.

"But you barely have met me," said Margaret.

"Doesn't matter," said Herman Soeder.

"And you've been *drinking.*"

"Doesn't *matter.*"

Margaret coughed. "You shouldn't talk about attraction," she said. "I mean, if there *is* an attraction, it's all on *your* part."

"I never said it wasn't."

"All right," said Margaret. "Just as long as that particular fact is clear."

"Yes. It's clear."

"Fine," said Margaret.

"I'm lonely and frightened, too," said Herman Soeder. "Everyone is."

"Too?"

"Yes."

"What gives you the right to tell me *I'm* lonely and frightened?"

Herman Soeder squinted over the wheel. The farmland was black and gray, and the sky was clear, and the hills pressed against it like thumbs. Now, for whatever reason, Herman Soeder did not appear to be drunk at all. "Because everything is so rigid," he said. "Because we're all of us afraid to say what we mean."

Margaret did not reply. She wanted to fold her arms over her belly.

"My God," said Herman Soeder, "you're like some great untapped natural resource, do you know that?"

Margaret folded her arms over her belly.

"Do you realize what you just did?" he asked her.

Margaret nodded.

"Well, I just hope you know what you're doing," said Herman Soeder.

Margaret was silent.

"Not that *I'm* such a bargain," said Herman Soeder, "but I'd hate to think that you would . . ." He hesitated. "Oh, never mind . . . it's *your* life . . ."

"Pardon?" said Margaret. Now she was hugging her belly, squeezing it.

Herman Soeder said nothing. He drove Margaret back to Paradise Falls and walked her to her door. He did not attempt to kiss her. He walked back to the car, and he drove away, and she never saw him again. She was greeted in the front room by Wanda Ripple, her housekeeper. Wanda wanted to know had that been the great man *himself?* Margaret did not reply. She went to bed. She hugged herself and rolled from side to side. She was thirtyfour that year, and she was a virgin, and she didn't still really have much of an idea what went where. Herman Soeder died in 1969 of a stomach ailment. He died quite rich, and in his will he left one hundred thousand dollars to the Paradise Falls Public Library. It was Margaret's understanding that he once had entertained some sort of writing ambitions. Such people often did, she had been told.

At Paradise Falls High School, which Margaret attended from 1925 through 1929, there were certain boys who called her the bee's knees and such. By that time, her breasts had ballooned out, and she had grown to her full five feet, seven inches. Her principal beau was a boy named Eugene Pearson, whose father was rector of Grace Episcopal Church. Eugene was tall and muscular, and he always kept his fingernails clean, and he was an end on the football team, and he told Margaret she drove him crazy. She would not allow him to call her Peggy, but occasionally she did permit him to touch her breasts. Sometimes she had warmly salivary dreams about him, but she would not permit him any further liberties. He would now and then kiss her goodnight with his mouth open, and then he would attempt to insert his tongue between her lips, but she always pushed him away, and sometimes she scolded him, and he would stagger off, groaning.

Margaret was born on New Year's Day 1911. She had an older brother and two younger sisters. The brother, Paul, became a career Army officer and was killed on Corregidor in early 1942, thus becoming the first Paradise Falls man to die in World War II. The sisters, Ruth and

Sarah, both married well, and between them they had nine children. Margaret, who lived until the day Richard M. Nixon resigned the American presidency in 1974, never married. (It was as though she could *taste* the blood of poor Otto York, and her outrage was beyond measure.)

On Margaret's twentyfirst birthday, her mother ushered her into the front parlor, closed and locked all the doors, then sat down with her on the sofa and said: "It's time you knew about your father."

"All right," said Margaret. She had no idea what else to say. She supposed she was frightened. She wished she weren't, but she supposed she was. There was snow coming down outside, and the windows were spangled with ice ferns. She looked away from her mother. She looked at the ice ferns. She watched the snow.

"I told Paul on *his* twentyfirst birthday," said Inez Ridpath, "and I'll tell Ruth and Sarah on *theirs,* too."

"Fine," said Margaret, swallowing.

"Have you wondered why your father killed himself?"

". . . yes."

"You *do* know he killed himself, don't you?"

". . . yes."

"*How* do you know? Did somebody talk to you?"

Margaret sighed. All right, all right, all *right,* she *was* frightened again. This conversation was like bees and canoes. Still, she would show nothing. Her mother never would know. Never. (You could not afford to let iron persons know you were afraid of them. They would take advantage of you. They would destroy you, and Margaret did not want to be destroyed.) She said: "Nobody talked to me. Why should anyone have had to talk to me? A man just doesn't walk in front of an interurban car because he doesn't *know* any better. He walks in front of it because he *wants* to."

Inez Ridpath made a harsh noise in her throat. "It was because of a woman," she said.

Margaret looked at her mother.

"Yes," said Inez Ridpath. "She died, and he did not want to live, and so he drank a lot of beer and staggered out of here and killed himself. It was that simple."

Margaret studied the ice ferns. "Who was the woman?"

"Do you remember a woman named Dorothy Hall?"

Again Margaret looked at her mother. "Of course I do. Don't tell me it was *Dorothy Hall.*"

"You don't have to be so *casual* about it," said Inez Ridpath.

Again Margaret looked away, at the ice ferns and the snow. She supposed children were having fun with sleds and snowballs. Herself, she had never had all that much fun with sleds and snowballs. She had been afraid of falling, or hitting something, or being hit. She hugged herself. She spoke quietly. She said: "That's my way, Mother. You ought to know my way by now. I can't help what I am. Things just sit very quietly on the *outside* of me, and nothing much shows. But the *inside* of me is maybe a different proposition, you know? Maybe when I'm casual to *you,* I'm not casual to *me* at all."

"All right," said Inez Ridpath. She wearily shook her head. "I apologize. I didn't mean to make it out that you don't care."

"Thank you," said Margaret.

"But Dorothy Hall it was," said Inez Ridpath.

"Is that a fact," said Margaret. She moistened her lips. Bees came at her. Canoes were overturned. She sucked horseradish. Her sled hit a tree. She squeezed herself. "Is that a fact," she said. "My goodness."

Otto York had been an orderly man, and Margaret understood order and respected it. It made no sense for his blood to have been there on the floor. And it made no sense for those children to be yelling and laughing. It was all downright anarchic, and Margaret knew she would have to do something, and fear had nothing to do with what she did, and courage had nothing to do with what she did, and one of the children even asked her for mercy, but she refused mercy, and so not even *that* was a consideration.

Even though she was a veterinarian's daughter and even though other people's animals seemed to like her well enough, Margaret never kept a pet. And her world saw this as being something of a shame. Cats were forever jumping on her lap, and dogs seemed to enjoy nuzzling her and licking her. She always treated the cats and dogs kindly, and sometimes she spoke to them, and people told her gracious sakes, Margaret, you ought to get yourself a little doggie or kittycat; they certainly are dear company on quiet lonely nights. And surely you would take good care of an animal, what with your father having been a veterinarian and all.

She smiled when the suggestion was made.

She said: Maybe.

She wanted to hug herself, and perhaps she even wanted to fall down and scream, actually go and make a *scene*. She. Margaret Ridpath. None other than.

The truth of the matter of the animals was this: Margaret's father had refused to have pets in his home. "I am with animals all day," said Dr Ridpath, "and I simply do not want to be *reminded.*" And then, likely as not, he would pour a glass of beer from the pitcher his wife always kept in the icebox. (It was home brew, made by a man named Joe Masonbrink, who had a speakeasy over on Wells Street near the fairgrounds.) "I mean," said Dr Ridpath, "you become attached to them, and then they become sick, and you have to put them away, and it just does you in, right? So why bother with that sort of thing, right? I mean, the look in their eyes. They don't know any better, and they believe you're going to make them well, but all you can do is kill them. Which is sad enough when you're dealing with a *stranger's* animal. But your *own* animal, no . . . it's too much. Why bother with that sort of thing when you don't have to? The eyes and all. The way a cat's claws will work in and out when it's happy. A dog's tongue, the feel of it. No, I'm too sentimental to have a pet in this house. I know my limitations. I weep too easily. I always have."

Dr Ridpath's attitude was a comfort to Margaret. But it wasn't so much that she didn't want to become attached to animals and therefore grieve for them when they died. Rather, it was because she was afraid of animals. Oh, God, so many things frightened her. Then and always. So many.

In short then, she treated her friends' cats and dogs with kindness because she was afraid not to.

*

But at the end it was order and not fear that took command of her. And she almost smiled when she died. She figured she had won. She figured she had been successful in substituting her respect for order in place of her lack of iron. In her adult years she became one of the world's foremost bridge players, and surely bridge must be the most orderly of all games. There were those who said she had nerve and courage when she played the game. That was nonsense. Bridge did not require nerve. It only required a respect for arithmetic. And what was courageous about sitting at a bridge table and bidding seven no-trump when you knew the odds were seven to three in your favor, depending on the location of an adverse queen? No, Margaret knew she was not brave. Orderly, yes. Precise, yes. In love with arithmetic, absolutely. But courage barely nudged her, and probably not even at the end, when the blood and the laughter caused her to challenge those evil children. (Poor Otto York. Whom had he ever harmed? And beyond that, he represented order, and his death had been an affront to order, and it was time for somebody to do something, and Margaret was the somebody.)

It never fairly could be stated that Margaret often displayed her fears. She most assuredly did not. She worked at hiding them behind something she hoped her world saw as aloofness. She kept her voice dry, and her movements were small. Even though she was a large woman, and even though she had impressive breasts and a full round figure, her flesh betrayed nothing. As far as most of her world could determine, nothing lived within her rather splendid body other than a few twigs and stones— and an immense and astonishing capacity for playing bridge. Which really probably was more a function of her quick arithmetical mind, with her viscera having little to do with it. After all, viscera would have indicated courage, and courage was ridiculous. In there. In her. Ever. And so her world stood back at the end. Something had shoved aside the twigs and the stones. Or had it?

In 1974, when Margaret lay dying, she understood the question. She also finally understood that she was a human being. She said to herself: I may not have been brave, but at least I am not timid.

And she said to herself: But no one has the right to dismantle the universe.

꿈 That day when Margaret was twentyone and she spoke with her mother about her father's suicide, she simply could not sit there like a lump on the sofa. It was as though some thing were plucking at her flesh. She abruptly stood up. She went to a window. She rested a cheek against an ice fern. The sensation was pleasant, and it diverted her from her flesh. She opened her mouth and breathed warmly against the pane. The ice fern began to blur a little.

"I expect I must be boring you," said her mother.

"No," said Margaret.

"You look like you're about to fall asleep," said Inez Ridpath.

"I'm not *falling asleep,*" said Margaret. "I'm just trying to let it all *sink in.* I mean, *Dorothy Hall.* Are you sure it was because of *Dorothy Hall?*"

"Yes."

Margaret turned away from the window. She faced her mother. "Did he *tell* you he loved her—is *that* it?"

"Of course he did. He couldn't hide anything. You know the way he was, how open he was."

"But he hid it until she died, didn't he?"

"Yes," said Inez Ridpath.

"So he wasn't all *that* open, was he?"

Inez Ridpath said nothing.

Margaret turned back to the window. She ran a fingernail along the edge of an ice fern. She said: "Did he tell you he was going to kill himself?"

"No. Absolutely not."

The fingernail pressed harder, and it made a sort of squeak. Margaret looked straight out the window. "Did you have an inkling?"

"No!"

"All right. I was only *asking.*"

"Well, it is a terrible thing to ask. It implies that I —"

"I know what it implies," said Margaret.

*

Dorothy Hall, who died in the summer of 1925, was the wife of an embalmer at the Zimmerman Funeral Home. She was a large cheerful woman, and she had a daughter who was a year younger than Margaret. The girl's name was Rosemary, and Rosemary and Margaret were acquainted. They had adjoining lockers at Paradise Falls High School, and Rosemary allowed as how she was *consumed* by what she described as a *deathless* crush on Margaret's beau, Eugene Pearson. Rosemary was a tiny girl, but she had her mother's fair coloring, and she was considered quite pretty. Eugene was still a student at Kenyon when she married him in the summer of 1931. She was about four months pregnant.

But Margaret had barely known Rosemary's mother. Her acquaintance with Rosemary had been formed *after* the death of Dorothy Hall. To the best of Margaret's recollection, Mrs Hall had been a little flabby, a little loud and perhaps a mite pushy. It was impossible to believe that Papa had loved that particular woman. But Margaret's mother had some letters, and they pushed away all doubt. She showed them to Margaret that day in the front parlor. "I came acrost them in your father's papers when I was going through his things after the funeral," said Inez Ridpath. "Letters, I mean. Words that leave no doubt at all."

Margaret turned from the window.

"They were hidden away in the back of a desk drawer," said Inez Ridpath. She stood up and fished a small packet of papers from a pocket of her apron. She held out the packet. "Here," she said. "You can read them if you want to."

Margaret went to her mother and took the packet. She unfolded one of the letters. It read:

DEAREST DARLING LOVER,

I thought of you this Morning & I began to get all You-Know-What down There where you Thrill me so. When I saw you last nite coming out of the Ritz with your Wife & your Little Ones, the 6 of you all Smiley & Happy & talking about Mister William S. Hart, I could of fell down right there on the Sidewalk for the wanting of you. I kiss you. I love you. I kiss you wherever you want me to kiss you. I love you however you want me to love you. I adore you, Darling Lover, & I will see you Tues midnite in the (ha! ha!) "usual" place. For the "usual" thing. Which is NEVER a "usual" thing, not the way YOU do it! I love you & your "thing," and the hours of waiting are always too slow, like sick people with wooden legs.

Always Yours,

D.

There were only five of the letters, but they all were in that vein. Inez

Ridpath stood silently while Margaret read them. Then, when Margaret was finished, Inez Ridpath said: "I think I just about have them memorized."

Margaret nodded. She handed the letters back to her mother.

"I save Christmas cards," said Inez Ridpath. "You know that, don't you? Well, anyway, I found the Halls' Christmas card from 1923, and I compared the handwriting and it was the same. I am a regular Philo Vance, I guess."

"But Papa *had* told you about it? About how he felt?"

"Yes."

"And what did you do about it?"

"*Do* about it?" said Inez Ridpath. "*Do* about it? Why, what *could* I do about it? I did *nothing*—that's what I did. I did absolutely not a . . ." Now Inez Ridpath was weeping.

Margaret embraced her mother. Margaret stroked her mother. And she patted her mother. And she told her mother there, there, whatever it was, it all was gone now. But Margaret herself did not weep. She'd never been much of a weeper, and she never would be. But she was not insensitive. It never was *that*.

On Memorial Day 1951 Margaret and her sisters and their elderly mother visited Dr Ridpath's grave at Oak Grove Cemetery. They took fresh flowers, and Margaret helped Ruth and Sarah root up weeds. The three sisters tugged and grunted, and they did not speak, and after a time Margaret's back began to hurt. And she began to feel terribly thirsty. Finally she straightened, smiled a little and said: "I expect I'm not as limber as I once was."

"Well," said Sarah, looking up, "you just go on and take a little break."

The sisters had brought a folding canvas chair for their mother. She sat fatly in it, and she blinked at Margaret, and she said: "You don't want to hurt yourself." Then she spoke of Margaret's housekeeper, Wanda Ripple, whom she despised. She said: "That Ripple woman could of come to help. She hasn't got the decency the Lord gave a mouthful of sand." And here Inez Ridpath shook her head. She sat in a sort of spraddle, and Margaret could see her thighs, and they were purple. The canvas chair was the color of khaki, and years ago Wanda Ripple had printed the word *STAR* on its back in wavery red Glidden capitals.

Margaret rubbed a shoulder.

Inez Ridpath really was enormously fat. She probably was the fattest woman Margaret ever had seen. There was a bridge player from Waxahatchie, Texas, a woman named Marietta Tupper, who was perhaps fatter than Mrs Ridpath, but Margaret would not have wanted to bet her life either way. Surely both women weighed at least three hundred pounds apiece, and to Margaret it was a miracle that either of them was able to move around. But move around they did, and Inez Ridpath really was quite remarkable, all things considered, especially the fact that her brain was raddled and loose, and her words did not often make too much sense. Such as now, when she said to Margaret, "You're too precious. Precious people shouldn't hurt themselves. A bug can be squashed so very easy as it *is.*"

"Yes, Mother," said Margaret. She had not really listened. She stretched. She spoke to her kneeling sisters. "Would you mind if I took a little walk to get the kinks out?"

"Of course not," said Sarah.

Now Ruth looked up. "We're the gardeners in the family anyway. You go take your little walk."

"Thank you," said Margaret. She walked away. *They* could stay with Mother for awhile. It would no doubt do them a world of good. *They* could listen to her speak of Wanda Ripple or squashed bugs or whatever. *They* could listen to her and try to make some sense out of her. *They* did not have to live with her, and it would do them a world of good, all right. A world. Oh, yes.

Margaret slowly made her way up a shallow incline. She shook her head. Her legs were just as tired as her back was. She still was doing too much housework, and that was the truth of the matter, and some day she would have to speak to Wanda Ripple. All right, so Wanda *was* effective when it came to taking care of Mother, but she *also* had been hired to keep the place picked up, and she'd never really done *that* job. And so most of the cooking and cleaning had been left to Margaret . . . despite her job, despite her bridge tournaments. Oh, it just wasn't *fair*, and one of these days . . . oh, one of these blessed days Margaret would take Wanda aside and spell out some new rules. Not that Wanda was a bad person. Far from it. The only thing was, though—she leveled all her attention on Margaret's mother, and this despite the fact that she never had shown any sign of liking the old woman. It was all very, very strange . . . and one of these days Margaret and Wanda would simply have to have a nice long chat. One of these days. Oh, yes.

Still, despite her tiredness, Margaret knew she still was at least reasonably comely. She was forty, but there were those who said she didn't look a day over thirty, and she still had her figure. And she always was well girdled and brassiered. And her neck had not sagged. And her arms still were firm. Well, what with all the housework that her alleged *housekeeper* did not perform, plus the job at Steinfelder's, plus all the traveling to bridge tournaments, Margaret believed herself to be holding up quite well, even now, even with the pains in her back. And so, on serious analysis, she decided she was not quite *yet* the Face on the Poison Bottle.

She sighed, shook her head, chided herself for being silly. She grimaced. The wind was a little cold. She came to a pump. Her tongue felt muddy. She bent over the pump and seized the handle. She felt a new twinge in her back, but she tried to pay it no mind. She pumped, and after a time the water came. Quickly she cupped her hands under the spigot. She drank from her hands, and the water was so cold it made her gums ache. She swished the water in her mouth. The mud dissolved. She looked around. There was no reason for her to look around, but she did so anyway. She wished she could somehow reach around herself and rub her back, but she was not exactly a contortionist, and anyway, her hands were wet, and she would smear her dress. She blinked. She was wearing spectacles, and now she nudged them to the top of her head. It was then that she saw the Hall burial plot. She grunted. Still swishing the water in her mouth, she walked toward the graves. Stumbling a little (her heels were high and sharp), she involuntarily swallowed some of the water—but not all of it. She came to a tombstone that said:

HALL

DOROTHY S.	CLARENCE G.
Jan. 22, 1888	Feb. 17, 1885
Aug. 11, 1925	Mar. 27, 1949

The stone was bordered with intertwined wreaths and bouquets, and it was a flat pinkish color. Margaret walked to the foot of Dorothy Hall's grave. Again she looked around, and again there was no reason for her to look around, but she did so anyway. She looked up, which made just as much sense as looking around. Were photographers hidden behind the trees? Were television cameras hanging from the clouds? Had someone placed a microphone in that trash barrel over there?

Gracious *sakes*, Margaret told herself, just go ahead and *do* it. No one ever will know.

She nodded. She swished the water, and now it no longer was cold. She listened to some sort of bird, and she listened to the distant clatter and putt of a lawn mower. She rubbed a cheek with a wet hand. Then, with the terror pressing against her chest, the terror that came because terror always came whenever she tried to take arms against her particular troubles, such as they were, Margaret sent the water from her mouth in a white stringy jet, and it sprayed across Dorothy Hall's grave, and Margaret's ears slammed, and her face was warm. But she did manage á sort of smile. She kept her upper lip pressed tightly over her teeth. *"Patooey,"* she said. "All *right,"* she said. She grunted. She blinked. She pushed down her spectacles. She hurried back to her busy sisters and her vast spraddled raddled mother.

That day of the birthday conversation, after Inez Ridpath's weeping had subsided, Margaret said: "It's strange that you *found* the letters."

"What?" said Inez Ridpath. She and Margaret again were seated on the sofa. She dabbed at her eyes, blew at her nose, tucked her handkerchief inside a sleeve. "What do you mean strange?"

"Well, if he knew he was going to die, why didn't he destroy them so you wouldn't find them? Why didn't he burn them? He could have spared you that, couldn't he?"

"I don't know . . ."

"Leaving them behind meant he *wanted* you to find them," said Margaret.

Inez Ridpath shrugged. "All right. I expect so."

"He was bragging from the grave, wasn't he?"

"Margaret!"

"He was rubbing it in, wasn't he?"

"No!"

Margaret patted her mother's shoulder. "I don't mean to sound cruel, but isn't it better if we face the facts?"

Inez Ridpath's face was beginning to fall apart again. "You shouldn't say such things about him . . ."

"I loved him, Mother. I really did. And I believe I still do. But as long as we're talking about this thing, we might as well be thorough."

"Thorough?" said Inez Ridpath. Her bewilderment worked at the corners of her mouth. She snuffled, retrieved her handkerchief and again blew her nose. *"Thorough? Is that* what you said?"

"Yes."

"What is he? A frog under a microscope?"

"No," said Margaret. "Of course not."

"I've . . . I've forgiven him . . . and so can you . . . you have no right to talk about him this way . . . "

"But, Mother, isn't truth the best thing to find?"

"No."

"No?"

"The best thing to find is the thing a person can *live* with," said Inez Ridpath.

Margaret opened her mouth to reply. She closed her mouth. She was seeing too many bees and canoes again. She had brought this along altogether too far. She nodded. She patted her mother's shoulder. She cleared her throat. She stood up. She returned to the window. Now she pressed the tip of a finger against one of the ice ferns. She said: "All right."

"I've . . . I've forgiven him," said Inez Ridpath again, "and so can you."

"All right," said Margaret.

"It was the day after Dorothy Hall's funeral . . . " said Inez Ridpath, and her voice petered out.

Margaret turned. "How's that?" she said.

Inez Ridpath covered her mouth and coughed. Then she tucked the handkerchief back inside the sleeve. "Ah, your father was sitting here in this room, right on this sofa, as a matter of fact. It was after supper, and he was sitting here all alone, and I came in with a glass of his beer and I found him crying. And I said to him: 'John, what on earth is the *matter?*' And he said: 'I miss her.' And I said: 'You miss who? Who do you miss?' "

Margaret interrupted. "You don't have to tell me this. There's no reason I should know it, not if you don't want to tell me."

"But you're the one who is interested in being thorough."

"Well, I was wrong."

"I *want* to go on with this," said Inez Ridpath.

"All right," said Margaret.

"I *want* to tell you," said Inez Ridpath.

"Fine," said Margaret. She seated herself in a wing chair. She hugged herself.

Inez Ridpath resumed. "I didn't even know he'd gone to her funeral, but he *had.* Myself, *I* barely *knew* the woman . . . I mean, beyond saying howdo on the street, how's your little girl, that sort of thing . . . "

Now Inez Ridpath was staring brightly at Margaret. She twisted her apron, smoothed it, twisted it. "And so there he was, your father, crying like a little boy, and he said to me: 'Inez, the thing I did was: I put up the CLOSED sign and walked out of the office, and I went to Zimmerman's, and I stood in the back, and Clarence Hall was crying up there in front, and their little girl was crying up there in front, and the flowers were all yellow, and I was able to see Dorothy's face down there in the coffin, and do you know what it means to have your head pulled at by chains and hooks and barbed wire? I *loved* that woman, Inez. There was something large between us. I—' "

Again Margaret interrupted. "Mother, you don't really have to tell me all this. I don't know if I—"

"We have to be thorough," said Inez Ridpath.

"Now, look, you don't have to keep—"

"It's *all right,* " said Inez Ridpath. "It's been awhile now, and I've made my peace with it as much as I ever will, and I'm just telling you what I told Paul, no more and no less. And what I'll tell Ruth when *her* time comes. And Sarah."

Margaret nodded. She tried to force her arms away from her body, but they would not move.

"He told me they had been seeing one another for about ten years," said Inez Ridpath. "He told me he was sorry, but truth was truth. He said to me: 'Inez, it's possible for a man to love two women at the same time.' He said to me: 'Inez, I loved you all the time I loved Dorothy. And I still do love you.' He said to me: 'Inez, I don't suppose you'll ever understand that, but it's the truth.' " He said a lot of things, and I fetched him four glasses of beer altogether, and he put his head against my chest, and he bawled, and—"

"He really said all those things?"

"Yes."

"Did you believe him?"

"Yes."

Margaret stared straight ahead. "And he asked you to forgive him, didn't he?"

"Yes," said Inez Ridpath.

"And you did?"

"Of course."

"But you never did understand, did you?"

"No," said Inez Ridpath. "I never did. When a man says he loves two women at the same time, name me a woman who can understand that."

"I wouldn't be able to," said Margaret.

"But I *did* forgive him," said Inez Ridpath.

"Even though he left those letters for you to find."

Inez Ridpath looked away.

"He asks for your forgiveness, and he brags from the grave. The same man."

Inez Ridpath looked at her daughter. "You surely do have a fine analytical mind, don't you? Is it a comfort to you? Does it provide warmth?"

"Mother . . . "

"Yes?"

Margaret began to weep. Margaret who almost never wept. "I do . . . I do believe I still love him," she said, choking.

"That's very good of you," said Inez Ridpath.

"Please . . . please, Mother . . . "

"We have to live with what we have to live with," said Inez Ridpath. "An analytical mind is fine for *some* things, but not for *all* things."

Margaret poked at her eyes with her index fingers.

"Some parts of life are really very strong, aren't they?" said Inez Ridpath.

Margaret nooded.

"They go beyond analysis, don't they?" said Inez Ridpath.

Margaret nodded.

White lines had gathered at the corners of Inez Ridpath's mouth. She spoke tightly. She said: "Whatever it is you are but don't show, I hope it isn't weak. Because, if it *is* weak, and at the same time if you're so cold and remote on the outside that no one is able to penetrate the icicles and the concrete or whatever, then you are not in for much of a life. You should have gone to college when I wanted you to. The money was there. But oh *no*, you chose to stay on, where everything was *familiar*, and you wouldn't have to take any *risks*. Well, let me tell you—life without risks is life that is zero. Sometimes I'm almost ready to believe you are the most frightened person on the face of the earth. Otherwise, you'd stop *analyzing* and you'd begin to *feel*. Just once, Margaret, I'd like to see you do something *headstrong* or even downright *stupid*. Do you understand what I'm trying to say? Your father and I, so all right, so it all fell apart. But at least something was there *to* fall apart."

Margaret stared at her hands.

"At least you cried a little," said Inez Ridpath. "Maybe that's a start. You're an adult now, and maybe some things will start to open themselves to you."

"Could I hate her? Would that be all right?"

"Hate who? Dorothy Hall?"

"Yes," said Margaret.

"It would be all right," said Inez Ridpath, smiling a little. "You have my permission. It might be a nice little start."

"How did she die?"

"In pain, I'm told," said Inez Ridpath.

"I mean the *cause* of her death. The *disease*."

"Cancer," said Inez Ridpath. "Cancer of the uterus."

"That would be painful, wouldn't it . . . "

"Yes."

Margaret unfolded her arms. She stood up. She went to her mother. She seated herself next to her mother, and she embraced her mother. She kissed her mother's forehead and cheeks. Terror shouted at her. She closed her eyes, and she saw Dorothy Hall's uterus, and it was perforated and rotten, and then a sort of joy sliced through Margaret's terror, and her mind constructed an image of choristers and triumphant hallelujahs. It was as though she had found sunspots at midnight in a cave. She bit the inside of her mouth, and more tears came, but they were warm and comfortable. Later, though, when she was alone in her bed, she was ashamed of herself, and she drove away the choristers and the sunspots. It was not wise to endanger one's self so recklessly. The consequences were too large, and the dangers were enough to turn bones to chalk. And so Margaret placed hate in the same drawer with the bees and the barking dogs and the canoes. She slammed it shut. She locked it. She swallowed the key. It did not come up.

One night in 1955, while Margaret was with a friend named Irv Berkowitz, she told him of her father and Dorothy Hall. And she told him of the day she had spat on Dorothy Hall's grave. She said: "I was so frightened. You have no idea."

Irv Berkowitz smiled. "Did you have visions of a heavenly thunderbolt?"

"Yes. Absolutely."

"The life you lead, I have trouble relating to it."

"I know that," said Margaret.

"The woman had stolen your father, and she had damaged your mother. You had a right to spit on her grave. So why do you insist on whipping up some sort of *guilt* when by *rights* you ought to be *pleased* with yourself? My God, Margaret, hasn't there ever been a time in your life when you've been able to take it easy and not get yourself all involved in some sort of enormous and appalling Presbyterian morality crisis?''

"I . . . well, I guess not."

"Anybody else would have *pissed* on her grave."

"Irv. Please don't talk like that."

"Micturated," said Irv Berkowitz.

"Thank you," said Margaret, smiling.

"What's such a big deal about *pissed* anyway? Is the sky going to curdle?"

"I shouldn't have brought it all up."

"What am I?" said Irv Berkowitz. "Your enemy?"

"No," said Margaret. "I don't believe so."

"I want to schmooze your left tit."

"That would be very nice," said Margaret.

Chuckling, Irv Berkowitz leaned over her (she was of course quite naked), and his warm mouth sucked her breast.

When Margaret was a little girl, she usually played with her brother and sisters when they asked her, but otherwise she was quite content to be alone. No one hurt her when she was alone, and there were no disputes. She would hide behind a hedge for hours and listen to the smashed and terrible sounds that came from Mme Bird. She would close her eyes and see trolls and fair maidens. She would stroke herself. She would drag a stick along a picket fence, and her tongue would click in time with the sound. She even would imagine herself as being made of iron. The *world* was iron, and she wanted to be like the world. Sometimes she walked erectly and thoughtfully, and she held her breath, and she hoped and she hoped and she *hoped,* and she made not a sound, and she kept waiting to hear herself clank. But she heard nothing, and the silence made her want to cry. Yet she did not cry. She almost never cried. She knew she could not afford to reveal the feathers and marshmallows and all the other soft and rickety things that sat within her.

*

As a child, Margaret was considered to be just an absolute little angel, and so *pretty* to boot. Evenings, when the Ridpaths had guests for supper, some woman or other was forever saying to her: "Oh, what a *cunning* little blessing of God you are! I bet your mummy and your daddy are grateful to have you, aren't they?"

And Margaret's mother and father always laughed. And they said hush up, you'll spoil her. And Margaret's father drank beer. And her mother spoke of quilts and begonias. And neither of them said anything about being grateful.

Sometimes Margaret would spend an hour combing her hair. Her mother would josh her and tell her she was being terribly vain, and so she took to combing her hair in secret, sometimes out behind the hedge next to Mme Bird's house. And sometimes she combed her hair in rhythm with Mme Bird's music. It was foreign music, and it trilled, and Margaret got to combing so furiously that her hair gave off sparks. Mme Bird's voice was unable to keep up with the music. Margaret, though, loved it. Who had thought it up? No doubt very iron persons indeed.

Margaret's menstruations always were copious. The first time she menstruated, she had known nothing about the process, but she did not cry. It began while she was sitting on the toilet, and she thought she would die right there, and terror came up like a balloon. But she did not cry. She called for her mother, and she quietly told her mother she was bleeding to death, and she wondered whether perhaps her mother would fall down weeping and exclaim: *Yes, yes, Margaret darling! Now thát you are dying, the least we can do is tell you we are grateful to have had you this long!*

But Inez Ridpath uttered no such exclamation. Instead she smiled a little and showed Margaret how to take care of herself.

*

In August of 1974, when the dying Margaret was brought to the hospital, at least she was dressed well, and at least her undergarments were clean.

One hot day in the summer of 1917, when Margaret was six, she walked all the way to the Columbus, Paradise Valley & Marietta depot, which was a whole big long forever distance from her home. Her brother and some other children were playing War, and they had wanted to draft Margaret to be a Filthy Hun. But she ran away from them, and then she walked to the depot. The locomotives frightened her half to death, but better the locomotives than War, better just about anything. She walked slowly and erectly. There was a warm wind, and her hair kept getting in her eyes, and passersby smiled at her as she trudged along, and several women told her *my,* how *crisp* and *neat* she looked today. She smiled narrowly at the women, and she kept her upper lip pressed tightly over her teeth. She wondered whether Mother would worry about her, but she did not really think so. Most of Mother's time was devoted to Baby Sarah, who had been born just two and a half years ago. Baby Sarah had blue eyes, and she still gurgled a great deal for her age, but Mother called Baby Sarah the happiest baby she had ever known in all her blessed living days. Margaret had no particular feelings about Baby Sarah. Before Baby Sarah there had been Baby Ruth, and Margaret supposed there always would be a Baby Somebody in the house. (She herself probably had been Baby Margaret. And Paul probably had been Baby Paul. And so it went, and you did the best you could.)

Margaret wore a white dress that day of her walk to the C P V & M depot. And there was a white ribbon in her hair. She walked steadily, and she did not lollygag or moon. She did not know why she wanted to walk to the *depot* of all places, especially seeing as how the locomotives frightened her so desperately, but everybody had to have some sort of purpose, wasn't that so? A person didn't walk just for the sake of *walking.* A person walked because he was *going* someplace. A person fought a war because there was an *enemy* out there, because the Huns had done terrible things to women and little children and even those Catholic nuns. A person got up each morning and there were things he had to *do.* Idle hands were the devil's unholy sweatshop, and it was not proper to lollygag and moon.

And so perhaps Margaret really did not *walk* at all. Perhaps she *marched.* She had no desire to be fanciful or vague. The times demanded sterner behavior. Therefore, one *marched;* one did not *walk.*

She passed automobiles (which everyone called *machines*), and she passed horses and houses, and she passed little boys who carried sticks and wore scaleddown Sam Browne belts. She listened to shouts and birds, and she listened to warm leaves. Her breath came in dry gulps, and her hands were in fists, and the sunlight slammed down so hard it made her eyes water. Why was she away over here on some street she didn't even know? She could not read yet, and so the signs at the street corners meant nothing to her, and maybe . . . for all she knew . . . she had walked to China by now. Or at least Nelsonville. Or some such place. Oh, dear, she supposed she wanted to cry. What did the depot really matter? Why walk all this distance when oh, dear, oh, *dear,* the locomotives frightened her so much? Was she touched in the head? She had heard her mother and father speak of people who were touched in the head, and people who were touched in the head did peculiar things such as sitting in the attic and singing old hymns. Or conferring with chipmunks. Or making loose noises with their tongues. Or walking to the depot for no reason.

Perhaps Margaret should have cried, but she did not cry. Her eyes had watered, but she did not cry. She walked all that way to the depot, and her hands remained in fists, but she did not cry. (The distance was maybe a mile, but to her it was the belly of the earth.)

There were bells, of course, when she arrived at the depot. And she saw ankles and spats. Leggings. She walked out on the platform, and people were waiting there for a train. A locomotive stood chuffling on a siding, and its bell was incessant. Margaret seated herself on a bench. She arranged herself neatly. Solemnly she kicked her legs. She blinked, and she blinked again, and eventually the wetness went out of her eyes. She knew how frightened she was (if *she* didn't, who *did?*), and she could taste her fright. It was brassy, like from when occasionally she would chew on a penny or even . . . God help her if her mother ever found out . . . suck on doorknobs. (She had secret shames, no question about it. How many people *chewed pennies* and *sucked doorknobs?* Great day in the morning, perhaps—for all she knew—she was some sort of menace.) But right now the flavor of brass was better than War. Better to be a fearful little girl solemnly kicking her legs than to be a Filthy Hun killing people. (Paul had ragged her for refusing to play the game. He had called her My sister the sissy. Sis the sissy. So sis on her, Sister Sis the sissy.) Grimacing, Margaret fussed for a moment with her hair, adjusting the ribbon, tightening it. She hoped no one would notice her. She did not want to talk with anyone. She simply wanted to sit here and kick her legs and watch the people.

She saw moustaches. She saw teeth. She saw grand ladies in grand hats, and the hats had feathers. She heard laughter, and she saw two colored men, and one of the colored men displayed a gold tooth when he laughed. She enjoyed the sound of the laughter. It was better than War. It was better than the sandy trenches in the vacant lot out behind Babs Hamilton's place. She didn't like Babs Hamilton anyway. Babs Hamilton talked too much, and she played War too roughly; she bit and she punched, and it was as though she thought she were a *boy* or something. Poo on Babs Hamilton.

Margaret wished she had a feathered hat. And she wished she had a spangled and tasseled purse. She looked at a tall lady, and a tall man (handsome, wearing a gray cap, gray suit, spats and a flowered cravat) said, to the tall lady: "Now, Hazel, everything's going to be just fine. Wait and see." And the tall lady (she had red hair) smiled, but there was a sort of wobble in her mouth. "I love you," she said. And the tall man said: "Yes. Thank you. I know that." And then the tall lady murmured something Margaret couldn't catch, and the tall lady nuzzled the tall man's shoulders, and the tall man smiled with great kindness. It was a sort of kindness that made the corners of his eyes all soft and maybe wet and sort of narrow. He patted the tall lady, kissed her forehead, curled an arm around her waist and said to her: "It won't be all that long. We'll whip them quickly, and that'll be that. I'll be home before you know it, Sweetie." And the tall lady placed her hands on the tall man's shoulders and said: "You be careful now." And the tall man said: "That's an absolute certainty." And the tall lady said: "If you don't, then nothing will mean anything." And the tall man nodded. And he and the tall lady were silent, but the kindness kept working at the corners of his eyes, and for some reason Margaret had to look away from him and the tall lady. She supposed they were talking about the war. She supposed the tall man was going off to the war. A lot of men, tall and short and in between, were going off to the war. Margaret's mother talked about them a great deal. They all were Heroes, according to Margaret's mother, and a Hero was a grand person indeed . . . and no doubt so full of iron he just about sank through the floor because of it. There probably was a great deal of truth to what Margaret's mother said, but right now Margaret just didn't want to look at this particular Hero. She didn't like it when people had to go away from other people who loved them. She didn't like it when people's mouths wobbled, when they hugged one another so desperately. Why couldn't they just stay together? When Margaret grew up, would there be a lot of wobbly mouths and huggings and partings? Why did people have to live that way?

No one was looking at her, and so Margaret made a face.

She turned her attention to the other people on the platform. The two colored men were sniggering and nudging. A fat lady was scolding a little boy. The little boy had a pinched face, and his eyebrows grew together. He was hugging a wooden duck, and it had wheels. It was painted red and orange, and the wheels were green, and a string came from its beak or snout or whatever. One of the wheels was cracked, and the fat lady was saying something to the effect that if Kenny really wanted to take his precious *duck* with him, *he* would have to hold it and not keep trying to foist it off on *her*. After all, *she* had better things to do; *she* had better things to worry about; *she* had better things to carry.

"Yar," said Kenny, and he kissed the wooden duck's orange neck.

Margaret looked away from the little boy. She wished she had the nerve to go to him and offer to hold his wooden duck. Where would the harm be in that? Perhaps his arms were tired. Who knew? (If the little boy had been Margaret's brother, no doubt Mother would have trimmed his eyebrows by now. Mother valued neatness the way she valued truth and the Presbyterian church, and she would not have put up with those terrible eyebrows for a *minute*.)

Margaret looked in the direction of the Depot Hotel, which adjoined the platform. Men went in and out of the place, and they were jaunty men, and nearly all of them wore straw skimmers and striped shirts and rubber bow ties. These men were what Margaret's mother called Drummers, and they smiled a whole lot, and it was nice to see people who were so happy, whose mouths did not wobble. They shouted and grinned, did these Drummers, and their laughter was knowledgeable and profound. They seemed to know what they were doing, and they seemed to know why they were there, and they had an easy familiarity, and obviously they all were made of iron, and obviously they had no doubts. (They understood their lives. They must have. Otherwise, they could not have been so laughing and easy.) Margaret squinted toward the Drummers, and now she was looking directly into the sun, and she listened to the harsh sound the hotel's front door made when the Drummers slammed it behind them. According to Margaret's mother, the Depot Hotel had a reputation of being a terrible place, with *women* and all. Which puzzled Margaret no end. What was so awful about women? Wasn't Margaret's mother a woman? And wouldn't Margaret herself some day be a woman? Oh, the way her mother sometimes talked was enough to give Margaret a bad case of the frowns and the clucks. And anyway, why was it so awful that the Drummers laughed a lot and wore those jaunty skimmers? The Drummers walked with their arms around one another's shoulders, and they gesticulated grandly, and their suits were splendidly colorful, and their shoes gleamed brighter than noon, so what was so terrible about them? Oh, they frightened *Margaret,* of course, and she wouldn't have approached them for the world, but *that* didn't mean *they* were *terrible;* it only meant *Margaret* was a *fraidycat.* She wished she wasn't, but she was. She hoped some day she would learn not to be, but she was not exactly holding her breath.

She shook her head.

She was being a ninny, and she knew it.

Again she shook her head. She nudged at a nostril with a thumb. Nobody was looking at her, and so it was all right.

She smelled creosote and popcorn. There was an oily flavor to the air that was not all that unpleasant. She breathed with her mouth open, but she kept her upper lip firmly over her teeth. She let the oily flavor lie on her tongue. She sucked it. Then her attention again turned to the tall lady and the tall man. They stood so close together that their noses were just about touching. The tall lady was whispering, and Margaret could make out none of the words.

The fat lady and the little boy had gone off somewhere. Little Kenny with his wooden duck and his terrible eyebrows.

Then came the train, and Margaret stopped kicking her legs. She slid back on the bench, and she drew up her knees. She gathered her skirt around her thighs so her bloomers wouldn't show. The train came as though it owned the world, and Margaret put her hands over her ears. The locomotive spat and crunched, and Margaret closed her eyes. The locomotive gave off steam, and the steam rubbed her cheeks, and she squinched her eyes as tightly shut as they could squinch. If she didn't *see* the locomotive, maybe it wouldn't *be* there when she opened her eyes. But of course it *was* there when finally, cautiously, and only after the awful spit and crunch had subsided, she knotted up her face and timidly opened one eye a teeny *slit* and looked up and down the platform. A colored man (her third colored man of the day, by golly) hopped down from one of the coaches, and he was wearing a white jacket. He placed a little stool on the platform, and people came off the train, and other people began boarding the train. The locomotive was up ahead now, a safe distance away, and Margaret decided to open *both* her eyes, and *all the way.* She blinked, and a piece of soot smeared itself against her nose. She licked a finger and wiped the smear away, and she hoped nobody was looking. The tall lady and the tall man were hugging again, and the tall man said something, but Margaret could not hear his words over the din of the crowd of passengers jostling to step up on the colored man's little stool and board the train. Then the tall man kissed the tall lady on the lips, and she gave a sort of groan. Again he kissed her, and it was as though he were trying to swallow her. Her hands squeezed the back of his neck, and she was hugging him just as tight as tight could be. Up ahead, the locomotive gave a toot of its whistle. Margaret jumped. A man in a goldbuttoned uniform came along and hollered *"BOAARD!"* The tall man released the tall lady. She gave another groan. One of her hands came up and rubbed her mouth and pinched at her eyes. The tall man smiled, abruptly turned, then jumped aboard the coach without bothering to use the colored man's little stool. The man in the goldbuttoned uniform also jumped aboard the coach. Another toot, and the colored man scooped up his little stool and scrambled aboard. Margaret looked up at the coach windows and saw the fat lady and little Kenny. He was holding his wooden duck so it could see out the window, and he was talking to it in a confidential and knowledgeable way, and the fat lady was adjusting her hat. And now the locomotive spun its great drivewheels, and the train began to move, and the tall man was standing waving right smack at the top of the coach steps. And the tall lady walked beside the coach. And the tall man shouted: *"Don't you worry, Hazel! Don't you worry about a thing!"* And the tall lady stopped. The train was moving too fast for her. She was holding a handkerchief, and it was wadded. She unwadded it, and then she waved it. The train picked up speed, and now the windows were a blur, and the locomotive . . . distant now . . . gave two more toots, and the last of the coaches went past, and the tall lady waved her handkerchief and waved her handkerchief and waved her handkerchief. Margaret scooted down from the bench and went to the edge of the track and watched the train as it became smaller and smaller. Now it was a *nice* train, and it did not frighten her. And the tall lady still stood there. And the tall lady still waved her handkerchief and waved her handkerchief and waved her handkerchief.

Margaret looked at the tall lady.

The tall lady was wearing the most beautiful white hat Margaret ever had seen. It had white feathers.

Some of the people had not gotten abroad the train, and now they were drifting away in clusters and pairs.

The other locomotive, the one on the siding, still clanged its bell, but Margaret paid it no mind.

The tall lady's right arm was extended, but she had stopped waving her handkerchief. Now she was looking at Margaret.

Margaret decided she loved the tall lady.

"Well," said the tall lady. Her eyes were green, and her hair was the deepest red in the whole entire world. She was maybe the most iron person Margaret ever had seen.

Margaret pressed her tongue against the roof of her mouth.

The tall lady lowered her arm. She folded the handkerchief and tucked it in her purse. *"Well,"* she said, and she tried to smile.

Margaret coughed, swiped at her nose.

"Is . . . ah, is something the matter?" the tall lady wanted to know.

Margaret took a step toward the tall lady.

"Are you . . . are you lost?" the tall lady wanted to know.

It was as though Margaret were being pushed. It was as though some sort of grief were pushing her. She took another step, and then she stumbled a little, and then she scurried to the tall lady and pressed her face against the tall lady's skirt. She hugged the tall lady around the waist, but she said nothing. She closed her eyes, and not a word came out of her. Hot forks would not have pulled a *peep* from her. Not then. Not through whatever it was she was feeling.

"Well, goodness me," said the tall lady.

The tall lady smelled of heliotrope, and Margaret opened her mouth so as to taste the smell. The tall lady's skirt crackled against her cheek.

Then the tall lady hunkered down, and she said: "Please open your eyes."

Margaret's arms came away from the tall lady's waist. She jammed fists against her eyes.

The tall lady pressed her hands against Margaret's shoulders. "Have you lost your mommy and daddy?"

Margaret took away her fists and opened her eyes. She shook her head no.

The tall lady was smiling. "Good," she said.

Margaret nodded.

"You have very pretty eyes," said the tall lady. "Nice and big and gray."

Margaret said nothing.

"What is your name?"

No reply.

"A pretty girl like you, in such a pretty white dress, surely you have a *name.* Let's see now, what could it be Susie Q. Prettyface? Is that it? Or maybe . . . ah . . . Princess Grayeyes of Paradise Falls? That's a *fine* name, isn't it?"

"I'm . . . " said Margaret, hesitating.

"Yes?"

"I'm . . . my name is Margaret . . . ah, Margaret Ridpath . . . "

"Oh! Say now, I expect you're related to the dog and cat doctor, aren't you?"

"Yes. He's my daddy."

"I've never had the pleasure, but I understand he's a nice man."

"Yesm."

"My name is Mrs Muehlbach. Mrs Hazel Muehlbach. And that was my husband Fritz I saw off on the train."

"Yesm."

The tall lady straightened from her hunkered position. Her knees popped a little. She still was smiling. "*Listen* to me," she said.

"Yesm," said Margaret.

The tall lady's smile widened. "You aren't much of a talker, are you?"

"No ma'am."

"Are you here all by yourself?"

"Yesm."

"Oh? Do you come here very often? Does your mommy know where you are?"

"Yesm. I come here a whole lot."

"Aren't you afraid of all the trains?"

" . . . yesm."

"But you come here anyway," said the tall lady. "Which means you're brave."

"No ma'am," said Margaret.

The tall lady made a distracted movement, smoothing the brim of her hat, sort of tugging at it, as though perhaps it had done something bad. Then, frowning a little, she said: "If I say you are brave, you are brave." She reached down and fussed a bit with the ribbon in Margaret's hair. "There," she said. "Now you're so pretty it's just about a crime . . . "

Margaret looked at the tall lady and did not blink. Margaret the liar. Margaret who had fibbed about coming to this depot a whole lot.

"What's the matter, child?" said the tall lady.

"Nothing," said Margaret, trying to smile.

"But why did you do what you just did?"

Margaret did not understand. Did the tall lady already know she was a liar?

"I *mean*," said the tall lady, "why did you come to me and hug me, a perfect stranger? Not that I'm so perfect, but oh well, you know what I mean. But what I'm *trying* to say is—people just don't go around hugging strangers, perfect or otherwise. I mean, we hadn't even been *introduced* or anything."

"I'm sorry . . . "

"Oh, now, *now*," said the tall lady, "there's nothing to be sorry *about*.

I'd just like to know *why* you did what you did.''

Margaret shrugged.

"Well," said the tall lady, "if you don't beat all, I don't know who does." She tried to make her words stern and reproachful, but she was not very successful. Her voice was too light. Not even Margaret was frightened by it, which meant it wasn't hardly frightening at all. The tall lady shook her head. She expelled breath in a sort of puff. She asked Margaret whether an ice cream would be nice. Margaret nodded, and so the tall lady took her by a hand and marched her into the depot. The tall lady bought two vanilla cones, and *nickel* vanilla cones at that, from a man who wore a white apron and was working inside a little booth that was covered by a red and white striped awning. She and Margaret seated themselves on one of the waiting room benches. She handed Margaret one of the cones.

"Thank you," said Margaret.

"You're very welcome," said the tall lady.

Margaret began to lick.

"Is it good?" the tall lady wanted to know.

"Yesm," said Margaret. She licked fastidiously, did this Margaret, this Margaret the liar. She was a licker, not a biter. She seldom made a mess. Paul always made a mess, but Margaret seldom did.

The tall lady began to lick her own cone. "Ahhh," she said, "it surely tastes good on such a hot day."

"Yesm," said Margaret, licking.

"Won't you *please* tell me why you hugged me?"

Margaret shrugged.

"*Pretty* please?"

Margaret shrugged.

"I . . . I mean, we . . . my husband and I don't have any little children," said the tall lady, "and I expect we just don't understand why they do the things they do . . . "

Margaret looked up at the tall lady. Some of the ice cream had pasted itself against the roof of Margaret's mouth, and so she pressed her tongue against it to make it melt faster. She did not know what to say to the tall lady—and even if she had known what to say, she would not have known how to say it.

The tall lady licked at her ice cream in circles. Then: "Some day, when Fritz comes home from the war, perhaps we'll have a little child or two. We both want children. We really do." Her tongue removed a smear of ice cream from her upper lip. She swallowed. "He didn't *have* to go, you know. He is thirtytwo, but you see, with a name like *Fritz Muehlbach,* he felt he had to prove something. It seems men all the time have to prove things. He didn't want people to think he was a slacker or anything like that, what with his name being what it is. I mean, we've been receiving mail that's . . . well, I shouldn't rattle on this way. It can't be of any possible interest to *you*. I should just lick my cone, isn't that correct? And perhaps we should talk about the weather. But I can't. I *can't*. He's . . . he's on his way to Columbus to enlist, and he wants to be in the infantry; he wants to go to France. Our mail has been just . . . you would not believe our mail . . . well, he's as good an American as *anyone*, and probably better than most, and it's not fair that he be made to think that he has to . . . oh, what do *you* care about any of this? I certainly have no right to . . . oh, never mind . . . I'm very sorry . . . "

Margaret had only the most shadowy idea what the tall lady was trying to say, and she wished she could help the tall lady, but how? The tall lady was an iron person if there ever was an iron person, and how was *Margaret* supposed to help *her*? Did the horsefly help the elephant?

The tall lady apparently was out of words. She worked on her cone.

Margaret listened to the sounds the tall lady's lips made. She listened to the sounds her own lips made. They were just about the only sounds in this waiting room, which was almost deserted now. The train had come and gone, and most of the people who had been here were off about their business, and finally Margaret coughed a little, looked away from the tall lady and said: "Maybe I was ascared? Do you think maybe I was ascared?"

"So you said. The trains, you said. But that doesn't really explain why you came to me the way you did. I say you're brave, and so it doesn't explain a *thing*. If you *weren't* brave, if you really *were* ascared as you put it, you wouldn't come to this depot in the first place. Can you follow that?"

"No ma'am," said Margaret.

The tall lady placed a hand on Margaret's shoulder.

Margaret looked at her.

"I'm sorry, but I'm the sort of person who always has to look for explanations," said the tall lady.

Margaret nodded.

"So?" said the tall lady.

Margaret began to speak, and she began to speak quickly. "I just wanted to *be* with you," she said, and now the words came in a rush. An edge of her cone began to drip, but she caught the drippings with her tongue. "I . . . I love you . . . "

"What?" said the tall lady. Her great green eyes enlarged themselves, and she gave her cone a ferocious lick. "How's that? What did you say?"

Margaret wanted to *die.* She concentrated on her cone. She never had said those words to anyone except her mother and her father, and here . . . right now . . . they had sounded so *dumb,* and she just wanted to curl up and wither away.

"Now," said the tall lady, licking, "correct me if I'm wrong, but didn't you just tell me you love me?"

Margaret concentrated on her cone. Her tongue was fastidious. She did not blink. She concentrated on her cone. She concentrated on her cone. The devil could reach up and seize her by a foot, but she still would concentrate on her cone.

"It's nothing to be ashamed of," said the tall lady. Now all *her* ice cream was *gone,* and she began nibbling at her cone's crisp sugary edges. "I am very flattered," she said, crunching. "It's not every day someone as nice as you tells me she loves me." She rummaged in her purse, found her handkerchief, then carefully dabbed her lips. "I . . . well, let's just say you've made a bad day a lot more bearable . . . "

Margaret did not believe a word of it. Iron persons did not need the likes of *Margaret Ridpath* to make their bad days bearable. Iron persons were iron persons, and besides, they never even *had* bad days.

The tall lady was silent for a time. Clearly she was waiting for Margaret to say something, but of course Margaret said nothing, and so finally the tall lady spoke up. "Well now," said the tall lady, "if the cat's got your tongue, I expect there's nothing much I can do about it—but there *is* one thing *I* want to say, all right?"

Concentrating on her cone, Margaret nodded.

"Margaret, I love you, too. I really do. You are a lovely little child."

Margaret blushed. Ice cream or no ice cream, she blushed, and again she wanted to *die.*

"Yes," said the tall lady. "Absolutely."

Margaret concentrated on her cone.

The tall lady crunched down the last of *her* cone, then wiped her mouth and returned the handkerchief to her purse. "Such things aren't easy to say, are they? The world makes them difficult, doesn't it?"

Now Margaret finally was down to the cone part. She said nothing. She crunched. Her face was still away far too warm.

The tall lady patted one of Margaret's knees.

Margaret nibbled and crunched.

The tall lady looked away from Margaret. She cleared her throat, started to say something but then apparently thought better of it. Her hands worked at the edges of her purse, which were fringed. Her fingers poked through the fringe. Her fingers twisted the fringe. She did not look at Margaret. She looked at the walls, and she looked at the floor, but she did not look at Margaret.

But *Margaret* looked at *her*. And finally, swallowing, Margaret said: "Ma'am, I don't . . . " She hesitated. Perhaps she was dying. It would have been nice to have known.

"Yes?" said the tall lady, still looking away.

Margaret finished the cone part. She swallowed. It scratched going down. Now it was *her* turn to clear her throat. She rubbed her face. Then: "I don't . . . I fibbed to you . . . I don't come here alone *ever* . . . the only reason I came here *today* was because I didn't know what to *do* . . . Mother was in the house with Baby Sarah, and Paul and the rest of them wanted me to play War with them and be a Filthy Hun and kill those Catholic nuns or whatever . . . and I . . . so I came *here* . . . but don't ask me why . . . I just got to walking, and when a person walks he has to go *someplace* . . . and that's all I know . . . only that I fibbed to you . . . Mother doesn't know where I am . . . nobody knows where I am . . . " Here Margaret's words expired. She looked down at her knees. Her mouth hung open, and her tongue lay against her lower lip, and some of the crunchy part of her cone was lodged in her throat. She coughed a little. She covered her mouth. Her mother had taught her always to cover her mouth when coughing, not to mention yawning. Now Margaret closed her eyes. She did not want to see the tall lady. She did not want to see anything. She had said too much, and she had been too reckless, and there was no iron in her, no iron at all.

"Oh *dear*," said the tall lady. "Oh my *goodness*." Then her arms were around Margaret, and impulsively she pulled Margaret to her and pressed Margaret's face against her breasts, and the odor of the heliotrope was all soft and warm, like Mother's soap chest. Margaret did not open her eyes. She breathed the heliotrope, and then the tall lady's hands were stroking her hair and fussing again with the ribbon, and then the tall lady kissed her on top of the head, and then the tall lady said: "I . . . I teach Sunday School, if you can imagine such a thing . . . and anyone who teaches Sunday School is supposed to believe in God—wouldn't you call that a pretty important qualification? But, well, *myself*, sometimes I'm not so sure. I look at all the drawings of The Gentle Jesus and the saints and all the rest of them, and I sing the hymns in a voice that is loud and clear and strong, and every Sunday morning the little ones such as yourself sit at their little desks and look at me with such . . . such *belief* . . . and oh I don't know . . . sometimes I'm not so sure about *any of it*. Sometimes it's all too much for little old Hazel Muehlbach, you know? I mean, what with the war and all, what with Fritz going away because all of a sudden

he's some sort of *devil* in the eyes of most of the world around here
. . . can you understand that?"

Margaret opened her eyes and looked up at the tall lady.

The tall lady was smiling a little. She pressed her thumbs against the
corners of her eyes. "But now," she said, "*right now* I do believe I know
He's there. I . . . and I . . . well, and I can thank *you* for that. I really
can. Honestly. It's the small things, Margaret. It really is. The small
things, and the small honest words. You . . . do you have any idea the
sort of person you are?"

Margaret did not reply.

"That's all right," said the tall lady. "You don't have to say a thing."

Margaret burrowed into the tall lady. She wriggled. The tall lady
hugged her. The world was heliotrope and sugar and ice cream. And then,
a little later, Margaret and the tall lady were outside again, and the sunlight came in smacks and speckles and great golden dots. The tall lady
lived up on Hocking Street, and so she walked Margaret almost all the
way home. They walked slowly, and they held hands, and the tall lady
chatted of children and hats and summer flowers and her pet cat, which
was named Solomon. Margaret breathed earth and sun. She smiled. The
tall lady smiled. People nodded at Margaret and the tall lady, and some of
them even said howdo. Everyone smiled.

Fritz Muehlbach survived the war just fine, and he and his wife had
two children. Margaret saw the Muehlbachs on the street and in
Steinfelder's from time to time, and they always smiled, and so did she.
Fritz Muehlbach died in 1956, and Hazel Muehlbach died in 1962, and
Margaret attended both the funerals. She never had been invited to their
home, nor they to hers.

When Margaret died in August of 1974, there were two public elements of her personality that set her apart from everyone else in
Paradise Falls. One was, quite simply, the *way* she died . . . which was
melodramatic and certainly uncharacteristic. The other was her skill as a
bridge player. Or probably genius. Her mind clicked and slid and rejoiced
in the game's mathematical purity. Sometimes, when she walked along

the street, her manner was so bemused and distant that one *knew* she was counting trump, or calculating the odds for a triple finesse or a double squeeze or whatever, Obviously, she was the best bridge player in Paradise Falls. And she was one of the best in the state of Ohio. And she was one of the best in the nation. And she was one of the best in the world. In the years from 1938 through 1974, she competed in more than one hundred fifty major state, national and world tournaments, not to mention perhaps fifteen hundred to two thousand duplicate games of lesser importance, and she was of course a Life Master, and the Ridpath home was full of cups and plaques and medals. She dusted them every week without fail. Otherwise, her mother complained, telling her: "Tacky, tacky, tacky . . . we mustn't be tacky, else we all shall go to hell, and the devil will throw away the key . . . " Margaret listened to her mother's demented ravings for nearly forty years, and it was a shame she was not an iron person. Had she been one, she no doubt would have pounded her mother into the ground like a tent stake.

Margaret's closest chum at Paradise Falls High School was a belligerent little blond girl named Lexie Musser, whose father was a motorman on the Paradise Valley Traction cars. Lexie's favorite expression was: "You want to bet?" She used it all the time when she discussed her family and her boyfriends and whatnot. She was the only person who ever addressed Margaret as Peggy. She said: " 'Margaret' sounds too much like some awful *pill* of an *oldmaid schoolteacher,* and so to *me* you'll always be Peggy, and you just might as well not fuss at me about it. And anyway, people who fuss at me they sometimes wind up with a knot on the head, you know what I mean?"

Lexie grimaced a great deal, and she would as soon punch a boy in the stomach or clout him across the head as look at him, yet she was nonetheless quite popular with them. Her face was too small and too pale, and it had too many freckles most of the time. But her figure was good, and her legs were excellent, and she was an outstanding dancer. She was not reluctant to shimmy, and she was not afraid to show her thighs. "From the neck down," she told Margaret, "I ought to be preserved in bronze. From the neck *up,* though, I ought to ask the Lord for a recount." Then, grinning: "So *all right.* So I'm not afraid to show my thighs. I got to *divert* their *attention,* don't I? And anyway, letting them *see* a little isn't about to get me into any trouble. And you know as well as I do—the girl who gets into trouble is the girl who *wants* to get into trouble. And so, well, I mean, all right, I have a good time. I mean, the other night, when Leo Van Zandt took me home from the Senior Mixer, he sort of *patted* me *above* the *knee*, you know? And he told me my God, he said, but you got good legs, he said, and I just can't hardly keep my eyes off of them when you dance the way you do, he said, and then he said I want you real bad, Lexie, and he got to breathing through his teeth, you know? Like sucking maple syrup through a paper straw, you know? And then he said Lexie, he said, you're going to be my girl ain't you? And I said you want to bet? And then he sort of got to acting like he was sick to his stomach, you know? And then I said you want I should go into the house and get you some good old bicarbonate of soda? And he said I love you, Lexie. And I said you don't *either.* And he said I do *too.* And I said you want to bet?'' And here Lexie laughed, and she nudged Margaret, which meant it was all right for Margaret to laugh, and so Margaret did laugh . . . a little. And Lexie was delighted, seeing as how Margaret laughed so seldom, which she had known for a long time. And, oh, how Margaret did love Lexie Musser. The girls were inseparable from the ninth grade through the twelfth. They walked to and from school every day, and often they held hands. Lexie always walked with her chin out, and sometimes—just for the fun of it—she pushed boys or tripped them. She liked to watch them sprawl. She enjoyed their anger. Margaret was of course frightened by Lexie's mischief, even when Lexie told her: "You got to let them know who's boss. If you don't, they'll kick you around like you're an old tin can. And you'll wind up laying on your back all the time, and first thing you know you'll have about umptyteen babies, and you'll be asking yourself hey, where did all the years go? Can you understand that, Peggy? Please try. It's very important. This is *old Lexie* speaking, and she is not talking through her hat.'' And Margaret nodded. And Margaret told Lexie yes, yes, she *did* understand. But there was no way on earth Margaret could behave the way her friend did. Yet she loved Lexie nonetheless. Who clamored with more iron than Lexie? Who moved with more confidence? Who was braver?

Lexie and Margaret shared a locker at school, and Rosemary Hall's locker was next to it. Rosemary had her locker all to herself, which evidently gained her the substantial enmity of the implacable Lexie. "I wouldn't trust her any farther than I could throw her," said Lexie to Mar-

garet, "and neither should you, Peggy my girl. The way she comes sucking around you all the time with her *sweet* and *gushypoo* talk about Gene
Pearson, her *deathless crush* and all, you'd just better watch your step. I
don't know how serious *you* are about him, but *she's* serious about him
and *then* some, and that's the God's truth. You got to watch out for those
fragile little buttercups like our sweet precious Rosemary, or she'll just
steal old Gene out from under you before you can blink an eye. Out from
under you . . . ah, that's only a *manner* of *talking*, you understand. Ho,
ho, Lexie the comedian. Well, anyhow, she'll just whisk away old Gene
in about ten seconds if you don't watch out. She'll just wrap herself
around him and go ohhh *my,* isn't the big *mans* so *cute* and *sweet,* and
poor little *me* could make him so happy if the *situation* weren't that he
was going with *Margaret Ridpath,* who is a *nice girl* and all *that,* but *really*
now, is Margaret Ridpath *truly* what big mans *wants?*" And Lexie invariably made moist simpering sounds when she imitated Rosemary, and
Margaret would smile and tell her: "Oh, Lexie, for heaven's sake—you
just don't like Rosemary because she has a locker all to herself." And,
grimacing, Lexie would say: "You want to bet?"

People forever strayed from Margaret. They did not flee her,
though. They were never that open. They simply strayed. Hazel
Muehlbach was a good example. Lexie was another. In October of 1929,
less than four months after she and Margaret were graduated from Paradise Falls High School, Lexie went and got married. The boy's name was
Eddie Stribling, and the newlyweds moved to Columbus, where Eddie
took a job with a wholesale sausage firm. Lexie and Margaret correspond-
ed for about four years, and Margaret visited the Striblings several times
in Columbus. But the visits were not successes. Lexie was as snappish
and belligerent as ever, but somehow she had been drawn apart and reas-
sembled. The snappishness and the belligerence were no longer uncon-
ventional, and she told Margaret: "We're working hard, and Old Man
Depression isn't about to get the best of *us,* no indeedy *ma'am.* Mister
Blumenfeld has kept on only his *best* men, and *Eddie's* one of them,
which means *he's* still working, drawing his pay regular as you please,
and we're going to buy us a little house soon as times get better, just you
wait and see. Maybe a little place somewhere near Groveport, down in
that area, you know? Where maybe I could grow my own vegetables, and
we could put up swings and a sandbox for the kids." And Lexie smiled,

and her voice was the same as it always had been, but she kept her skirt pulled down, and it was as though she were daring Margaret to remind her of the old days. So Margaret did not bring up the old days. Lexie did occasionally, but Margaret never did. Lexie had become pregnant within six months of her marriage to Eddie Stribling, and by 1933 she had given birth to three babies, all boys. She said: "All right. I guess I lay on my back a lot. I guess people change. And what's wrong with that? What kind of person is it who stays the same all his life? A person who stays the same all his life might as well not be alive at all, right?" A thin smile. "I mean, what do you want from me—consistency?" Then: "I mean, here I am, and I *know* where I am, and it's a *comfort,* all right?" And it was as though Lexie were waiting for Margaret to say something, but what was it Margaret was supposed to say? She had no idea . . . and she certainly wasn't about to remind Lexie of all the brave old high school words. She never laughed at Lexie, or scoffed. She simply sat in Lexie's cluttered front room and nodded from time to time. And Eddie Stribling, a squat young fellow with dark curly hair, smiled blankly at both of them and drank home brew. He was one of Mister Blumenfeld's very best men, and sometimes Margaret noticed shreds of gristle under his fingernails. One time, while Lexie was in the kitchen, Eddie set down his glass of home brew and went to Margaret and tried to kiss her on the lips, but she managed to turn her face aside. Grunting, he returned to his chair, sat down and sniggered. He briefly cupped a hand over his crotch, gathering up the bulge of his penis and testicles. He scratched himself, hummed a little, then reached for his glass of home brew. Speaking perhaps to himself, he said: "Bad Eddie. *Baaad* Eddie." And so the visits were discontinued, and Margaret never again saw her friend Lexie.

Margaret's sister Ruth was married in 1936, and her sister Sarah was married in 1938, leaving Margaret to take care of their mother, who already had begun to behave strangely. Ruth married a man named George Prout, who owned Vance's Drug Store, and Sarah married a tall handsome chap named Pete Saddler, who was a teller for the Paradise Falls State Bank. Both men thrived—and Pete Saddler, as a matter of fact, was elected president of the bank in 1958. In any event, Margaret never had any money worries, and her sisters and their husbands always contributed generously to the upkeep of the house and the custodianship of Mrs Ridpath. (Paul, her brother, was off in the Army from 1926 until his death in 1942, and he never was asked to contribute. He did make the offer, but his sisters told him pshaw, the Army didn't pay enough to keep a flea healthy, and so he was not to worry about Mother. They would take care of her, and they bore him no grudge. And Paul never argued all that strenuously over the issue. He was too preoccupied with soldiering. He had enlisted shortly after his father's death, and it was probably the best thing he could have done. Surely God had placed him on this earth to be a soldier. Margaret and her sisters could not *imagine* him being anything else.)

At any rate, the generosity of Margaret's sisters and their husbands enabled her to save a great deal of the money she earned keeping the books at Steinfelder's. At the time of her death in 1974, her personal worth was well in excess of one hundred thousand dollars.

Margaret had trouble with her teeth throughout most of her adult life, and in 1970 she had them all removed. Her appendix had been removed in 1940, and her female organs in 1966. She was farsighted, and from 1935 until her death she wore spectacles for reading and other close work. She bathed at least once a day, and she used Nair on her legs, and she lost her virginity in the late summer of 1951, when she was forty. At the end she killed three persons, and one of them was a girl. She was a Presbyterian and a Republican, and she never masturbated. The chances are she did not know how.

She could have gone to college, of course, and her mother was upset when she did not. But Margaret was afraid to go to college. Instead, she took the job at Steinfelder's immediately after her graduation from high school in 1929, and in 1936 she became the store's head bookkeeper. Her mind for balances and statistics was remarkable, and clearly this was what made her such an outstanding bridge player. She always remembered what cards had been played, and she had no trouble calculating odds. To her, it all was as simple as breath, but she never was altogether happy with any of it. After all, how could one be comely and mathematical at the same time? (Oh yes, she knew she was being silly, and her friend Irv Berkowitz often told her she should stop all her goddamned *picking apart* of everything that happened to her and everything she was, and she told him yes, yes, she *knew* she was a dumb bunny, but she just didn't know what to *do* about her condition. And Irv Berkowitz told her nuts, she was no dumb bunny; all she needed was to relax a little. And *Margaret* told *him* all right, show me how. And *he* told *her* fine, give me time.)

Margaret never hated her sisters, and to say such a thing would be an exaggeration. Still, she did resent them at least a little . . . but at the same time she tried not to delude herself into believing that she would have been some other sort of person (an iron person perhaps?) if Ruth and Sarah had not gotten married, leaving her to take care of Mother. As a Presbyterian, Margaret subscribed to the doctrine of predestination. God and the elements had deprived her of iron, and God and the elements had willed that she be the one to remain imprisoned with Mother, cooking Mother's meals and laundering Mother's clothing and sharing Mother's clouded and indistinct and sometimes downright mendacious memories. There were two housekeepers who helped out—first a woman named Wanda Ripple and then a woman named Pauline Jones. But the ultimate responsibility was Margaret's, and she was aware that she could not avoid it. And she never did. Not really. And so for about forty years she carried her mother on her back like a sack of rocks. Inez Ridpath's decline began in about 1934, when she was not even yet fifty. First she fell into great florid rages. Then she began to weep for no reason. Then she became careless about her cleanliness and appearance. She forgot to take baths, and she forgot to comb her hair and brush her teeth, and she became fat and mottled. By 1936 or so, she spent entire days in her nightgown, and sometimes she even prowled naked through the house, and she became the topic of more frontporch and backyard gossip than even your King of England and your Mrs Wallis Warfield Simpson. And all the time she talked. Of love. Of animals. Of her late husband. Of hollyhocks and antimacassars and Dorothy Hall and Pullman cars and the 1904 St Louis World's Fair, when she was eighteen and her name was Inez McClory and she had a smile that would have brought tears from a pile of coal. Which was when she met John Ridpath, a young veterinarian who was a friend of her brother's, and this John Ridpath persuaded her to marry him, and they came to Paradise Falls, and Baby Paul was born in 1908, and Baby Margaret was born in 1911, and Baby Ruth was born in 1913, and Baby

Sarah was born in 1915, and it all was a very nice life, thank you very much indeed, and she supposed she was grateful she knew nothing about Dorothy Hall until it all was over and Dorothy Hall was dead and in the ground with her perforated uterus, may the elements curse her forever. And Margaret heard this sort of talk for forty years, but at the same time she developed a talent for not *listening* to it, and so at least *she* remained sane. At least there was *that* much good to be said for it. And yet, even though Inez Ridpath's days were ringed with nonsense and inaccurate memories, and even though she became a great flabby soursmelling grotesque, she nontheless retained some notion of the proprieties, and she insisted that Margaret keep the house clean and picked up. "A stranger could drop in at any time," said Inez Ridpath, "and we just don't want the world thinking the wrong thoughts, do we? It wasn't a bit easy for your father and me, the obtaining of this house and the accumulation of these worldly possessions, I mean, and it would be indecent if we let everything go to your proverbial pot. So we must have a place for everything, and everything must be in its place. The pussycat does not live in the owl's house, and poodledogs don't lie down with hummingbirds, now do they? That man may be rotting in his grave and corrupting the earth, but he was a *presence,* and we should *respect* him; we should keep his house *picked up.* If you and those *friends* of yours want to *play cards* and *smoke* and *chatter* until *all hours,* that's *your* business of course—but the *least* you all can do is clean up your mess, all those tacky old cigarette butts and whatnot. We have to pay attention to your father's memory. He courted me very sweetly, have I ever told you that? His hands always were clean, and he always took care to scrape the dirt out from under his fingernails. And he liked to kiss my hand. He really did. He said to me: 'To me you'll never just be Inez McClory. To me you'll always be some sort of princess in disguise.' Oh, I *know.* To *you* and *your brother* and *your sisters* he never really said all that much, did he? And maybe you thought he was just this side of being tonguetied. But that's all incorrect, believe me. And I should be the one to know. Today we perhaps think of him in a way that is I suppose not altogether full of praise, but are we really being fair? Shouldn't we perhaps devote more attention to the gentler memories of the times before the time that did him in? Just because some stupid woman wrote him mash notes and spread her legs for him, is that any reason to mark him on the tabernacle wall as the world's worst villain? Oh, yes, yes, I can indeed see him now, working her open, and maybe he even kissed her hand, but I can forgive him; I really can. Do you think he kissed her hand? Oh, working her open, working her open *indeed,* with fine words that *you* and *your brother* and *your sisters* never re-

ally heard uttered in your presence, what with his beer and his silences
and all, but *believe me,* the fine words *were* there. Yes. Absolutely. And he
stroked her and he kissed her: *Dorothy Hall.* My goodness, who would
have thought such a thing? But, well, you have to give *me* credit for one
thing. I waited until *all* of you were old enough to face the world on your
own. Or at least *Paul* and *you.* When I told Ruth on her twentyfirst birthday, and when I told Sarah on *hers,* maybe I wasn't really that much on
top of my game, but at least I came close, didn't I? I held on as long as I
could, didn't I? And even then I at least *put on a dress,* remember? For
Ruth and then for Sarah—a bath and a girdle and a dress. I have respect
for the truth, and I could not be tacky when I *told* it. And, ah, beyond all
that, what about the years between the time your father killed himself and
the time I, ah, gave up? I did mend your clothing for all of you, didn't I?
And I did cook your meals, and I was there on the bad days, and I did not
shirk a thing. *Now,* though, *now* it doesn't matter. The only thing is—you
just *have* to keep this place picked *up.*" And Inez Ridpath's voice raled
and crackled, and sometimes she shook a finger in Margaret's face, and it
all was ridiculous, but Margaret did keep the place picked up. Or her two
housekeepers . . . first Wanda Ripple, then Pauline Jones . . . kept
the place picked up. (Pauline was a great deal better at it than Wanda had
been.) And Inez Ridpath talked and talked and talked for forty years, and
her words disintegrated but they never diminished. She had a favorite
chair, and antimacassars were pinned to its arms. She had crocheted
those antimacassars, and she fussed with them while she talked, sometimes even bending the pins all out of shape, and naturally she even talked
when she was alone. She would blink like a frog and smile at the wallpaper and say: "The world is hollow and you go inside and you get lost and
there should have been a better way than an *interurban car.*" She smiled
at generations of wallpaper, and she said: "The best part of anything is
the dream you have of a thing before the thing comes to you. Before the
dance, the girl dreams of fiddlers and a warm mouth. He kissed my hand;
he bowed and scraped like a Hapsburg count. He said: 'Miss McClory, I
have been exalted.' That was the exact word he employed—*exalted.*
Where is the book that shows us how to fail well? What are the words?
Well, all right, so Dorothy Hall died, and along came that interurban car,
and I did my duty by Paul and the girls. Fine. Hip, hip, hooray for Inez
Nancy McClory Ridpath. Perhaps a medal should be struck: *Inez Nancy
McClory Ridpath did her duty.* Fine. Fine. Fine. But where is the girl who
dreamed? Where are the fiddlers? Where is the girl who was courted by a
Hapsburg count who allowed as how she exalted him? The blood be-
comes oily and slow, doesn't it? The flesh no longer glistens, does it?

Cells rot, don't they? Can I help it that I was born not smart enough to understand?" And sometimes Inez Ridpath made faces at her invisible audience, and it was as though she were summoning a list of particulars against the air she breathed, and in forty years it became quite a list, and its implications certainly were more than Margaret could grasp. And so Margaret did not follow them through. Oh, occasionally she would *try* to *listen* to her mother's words. But there were so *many* of them, and Margaret was only human, and finally she simply let them pass unheard, like distant automobile traffic or the hollow basement roar of the furnace. After all, a person had only so much strength. And yet, even though she was the one who was stuck with the old wreck all those years, it cannot fairly be said that she hated her sisters. She did not. She did not. She did *not*. Matters of rightness and decency aside, hatred was far too iron an emotion for her, and it would have punched her full of great bloody holes.

In July of 1971, when Margaret was sixty, her sister Ruth collapsed and died of an embolism. Ruth was barely fiftyeight, and the death came as an enormous shock to the family. Ruth's husband, George Prout, the druggist, was so distraught he had what perhaps was a mild heart attack, and at any rate he was unable to attend the funeral.

Margaret was in Chicago (where she and a woman named Imogene Brookes had gone to participate in an invitational Life Masters tournament) when she received the news of Ruth's death. It came via a longdistance telephone call from her sister Sarah's husband—Pete Saddler, the banker. "Ruth was talking with Mildred Oates," said Pete. "They were sitting on Mildred's front porch, and they were discussing Senator Muskie."

"What?" said Margaret. She was standing at a house telephone in the lobby of her hotel. The tournament was being conducted in the hotel's grand ballroom, and she had been paged. She and Imogene were in third place, and the final round was about to begin. She stared at the telephone, then: "What was that? Did you say *Senator Muskie?*"

"Yes," said Pete. "According to Mildred, Ruth had just told her something about Senator Muskie being Polish, and then Ruth sort of gave way."

"Gave . . . what? Did you say gave way?"

"Yes. Ruth said something about not feeling very well, and then she slid off the glider. She spilled iced tea all over herself, Mildred told me."

"Iced tea," said Margaret. "Well. Iced *tea*."

"The funeral is Friday," said Pete.

"All right. Ah, what day is this?"

"Wednesday," said Pete.

"No," said Margaret. "It's Tuesday, isn't it?"

"Oh. Yes. Right you are. Tuesday."

"Have . . . ah, have the children all been notified?"

"Yes."

"How did they take it?"

"Just fine, I guess. Sarah was the one who called them."

"How is George doing?"

"Not very well. He doesn't *look* well at all. We're worried about him. He's over here at our place, and we have him resting in Virginia's room. He has bad color, if you know what I mean. And he keeps saying his life is over."

"Well," said Margaret, "he loved her very much."

"Sure," said Pete.

Margaret nodded.

"Are you there?" said Pete.

"Oh," said Margaret. "I was nodding. On the telephone, a nod doesn't register very well, does it?"

"No," said Pete. A hesitation. "Ah, when do you think you'll be home?"

"Well, I'll catch a plane to Columbus first thing tomorrow morning. My car is at the airport, and so I should be home I don't know, an hour and a half or so later. Make it noon. I should be back by then, counting the driving time and all."

"Fine," said Pete.

"Has anyone told Mother?"

"No," said Pete. "Not that I know of."

"Well, you tell Sarah I'll take care of it when I get back."

"Fine," said Pete.

"Oh . . . and how is *she* doing?"

"She's holding up. She's keeping herself busy, what with George here."

"Good," said Margaret. "And another thing—I wish you would call Pauline and tell *her* to be sure not to say anything to Mother."

"All right," said Pete. "I'll take care of it."

"I'm the only one who can handle Mother anymore. Pauline is no Wanda Ripple, and she never has been."

"Yes," said Pete.

"You tell Pauline just to behave as though nothing has happened. I'd call her myself, but she'd just get to weeping and carrying on too much, and Mother might ask a question or two. It's possible. I mean, she *is* rational from time to time. So you just call Pauline, and you tell her *I* said mum's the word, and you tell her *I* said she is to stay in control of herself. Sometimes I honestly don't know which one is worse—Mother or Pauline. I hope that doesn't sound too cruel. I hope you understand what I mean."

"Yes," said Pete. "I understand."

"Well, expect me at about noon. Good—"

"Wait a minute," said Pete.

"What?"

"There's one other thing. George keeps asking for you."

"For *me*?"

"Yes," said Pete. "I just came from being with him. He's lying down on Virginia's bed, and he keeps saying his life is over, but at the same time he keeps asking for you. He keeps saying when's Margaret coming home. And a little while ago he said something to me about . . . well, something about maybe you would hug him . . ."

"I beg your pardon?" said Margaret.

"Well," said Pete, "I don't know exactly how to put it, but you see he was crying, and he . . . well, he got to saying something to the effect that he needed you because you would *hug* him, and then somehow that would make it better."

"Well," said Margaret.

"I'm just telling you what he said . . ."

"All right," said Margaret. "Fine. I'll see you tomorrow."

"I suppose it sounds stupid . . ."

"Yes," said Margaret. She hung up without saying anything more. She frowned. So George Prout wanted her to hug him. She shook her head. The very idea was insane. She wished Irv Berkowitz would have been there to explain it. She sucked saliva. She swallowed. She returned to the ballroom. She said nothing to Imogene Brookes about Ruth's death—not until after the tournament was concluded later that night. Margaret and Imogene took tops on the final three boards and finished second, missing the championship by only one and a half points.

*

Imogene Brookes was a slender woman in her late fifties, and she wore too much lipstick. She was the wife of a prominent Cleveland banker, and she and Margaret had been partners in major tournaments for about ten years, since shortly after the death of Irv Berkowitz. She was a more aggressive and chancetaking player than Margaret, but her game nonetheless was quite sound. She understood Margaret, and Margaret understood her, and they played very well together. Charles Goren had written flatteringly of them in his column, and the Jacobys also had expressed admiration for their play. Imogene talked a great deal, and she flirted with all the men players, and she was forever fluffing her dyed black hair and calling herself an overthehill Loretta Young, and she insisted she was a superficial human being, and she hoped to *God* her husband and her children never learned just how superficial she was, especially now in her declining years while she was doing what she called the aging glamorgirl bit, having what she called her last spavined and asthmatic flings (such as they were, what with her . . . ah . . . decreased stamina), and she said she thanked heaven she had a talent for bridge, because at least it got her *out* of the *house* and made her aware that some ruined fragment of herself still was able to take nourishment from life, and then she invariably laughed, and she told Margaret that nothing in this world was more pitiful and absurd than the clacking pointless ramblings of a menopausal prom queen. And Margaret invariably did some laughing of her own (a little, never too much), and she told Imogene you hush now, you sell yourself far too short. And Imogene invariably touched Margaret's hand and squeezed it and told her thank you; God love you.

At the close of the final session, most of the players went into the hotel bar for a last drink before calling it a night. Sometimes this last drink became four or five or six last drinks as the players rehashed the hands, but Margaret was a teetotaler and did not much care for rehashing, so she usually retired early. The night of Ruth's death, though, she did accompany Imogene into the bar. They seated themselves in a booth, and it was then that she told Imogene what had happened.

Imogene was lighting a cigarette, and she nearly choked on it. The cigarette dropped from her mouth onto her lap, and she furiously beat at her lap, finally managing to brush the cigarette onto the floor.

"Oh, dear," said Margaret, "did you burn a hole in your dress?"

Imogene still held the match, and it burned her fingers. "Oh my God," she said. She shook out the match and dropped it into an ashtray. "Oh my God in *Heaven*," she said. "*What* did you just say?" She sucked her fingers and blinked at Margaret.

"I asked you did you burn a hole in your dress."

"*No*. I meant *before*. I meant *about your sister*."

"I'm sorry," said Margaret. "The phone call came tonight. It was what the page was about. It came from my brotherinlaw, Pete Saddler, the banker. You've met him."

"Yes," said Imogene. "I've met him." She bent over and picked the smoldering cigarette off the floor. She stubbed out the cigarette in the ashtray. "I . . . yes . . . he is her husband, right?"

"No," said Margaret. "He is *Sarah's* husband. *Ruth's* husband is a man named George Prout."

"Oh," said Imogene.

"I'll be going back first thing tomorrow morning."

Imogene nodded. She lighted another cigarette. A waitress came to the booth, and Imogene ordered a double Chivas on the rocks. Margaret ordered a 7-Up with a twist of lemon. The waitress went away, and then Imogene said: "You should have told me right away."

Margaret did not reply. She looked around. She watched the bartender pour the Chivas.

Grimacing, Imogene drew on her cigarette. "Don't you have anything to say?"

Margaret shrugged.

"Please say *something*," said Imogene.

Margaret cleared her throat. "Well," she said, "I just . . . well, you are my friend, and I didn't want you to be . . ." A hesitation. Margaret's tongue rubbed a corner of her mouth.

Imogene persisted. "You didn't want me to be *what*? Please, Margaret, whatever it is, you can tell *me*. This is *Imogene Brookes*, and she *loves* you."

"All . . . all right," said Margaret, nodding. "We were . . . ah, I just didn't want you to be disappointed . . . I mean, we were up there in third place, and I know how you'd have felt if we'd dropped out . . . and so, well, I just thought I might as well hold up on telling you anything until . . . well, *you* know . . ."

Imogene was wearing eyeglasses that had sequined rims. She pushed the eyeglasses to the end of her nose. She had brown eyes. She blinked at Margaret, and her eyes were small and tight. "Just what do you think I am?"

"Pardon me?"

"Do you think I am a *monster*? Is *that* it?"

"Monster?" said Margaret. "No . . . no . . . of course not . . ."

"Then you must think I am *so* trivial and *so* without dimension that I would . . ." Imogene's voice petered out. She shook her head. "A *bridge tournament*," she said. "And *you* don't want to upset *me*."

"That's right," said Margaret. "What I mean is—would telling you and spoiling your evening have changed anything?"

"Jesus help me," said Imogene.

"Pardon me?" said Margaret.

Imogene leaned forward on her elbows. The waitress came with the drinks. She was young, and she had red hair, and she wore a black blouse, black miniskirt, black fishnet hose and black spiked shoes. Imogene glared at her, and so she quickly set down the drinks and went away. Then Imogene said to Margaret: "How long have you hated me?"

"Pardon me?" said Margaret.

"Stop saying pardon me. Just answer my question. *How long have you hated me*?"

"I . . . I don't hate you."

"Don't say that when I know differently," said Imogene.

"What?"

"You *have* to hate me," said Imogene. "Otherwise, you wouldn't see me as . . . oh, I don't know what . . . some sort of *creature* that would be *put out* because of a stupid *bridge tournament*. Look, I admit it; I am a trivial human being . . . but even *I* have my *limits* . . ."

"Did I insult you?"

"Yes," said Imogene.

Margaret embraced herself. "I didn't mean to," she said. "I didn't mean to *at all*."

"Oh my *God*," said Imogene. She sipped at her Chivas on the rocks. Then: "Please forgive me for being so emotional about it, but you might as well have *thrown up* on me and been done with it."

"Thrown up on you?"

Imogene took another sip of her drink, then fussed with her eyeglasses, pushing them back. "You see the entire world as being terribly cruel, don't you?"

"No," said Margaret. "Not at all."

"I'm supposed to be your *friend*, remember?" said Imogene. "I mean, I'm certainly not your *enemy*. So why do you treat me like one? I mean, *look*: I happen to be very fond of you. Don't you *know* that? And don't you know I wouldn't give a damn about *bridge* at a time like this?"

Margaret stared down into her 7-Up with the twist of lemon. A white plastic swizzle stick poked out from the ice in the glass. She removed the swizzle stick and bent it, breaking it in half.

"I know," said Imogene. "I know. I *know*. I am made out of string and waxed paper. I flirt too much, and I talk too much, and I try to make out that I still am thirty and I wouldn't know a hot flash if it kissed me on my firm but pliant lips, and . . . and . . . *all right* . . . so I'm no bargain . . . but how could you have sat through that entire session and not uttered a peep because you thought I would what? pout? have some sort of tantrum?"

Margaret set down the halves of the swizzle stick. She sipped at the 7-Up, and the coldness hurt her gums. She said: "I . . . I was just trying to do what I thought was right . . ."

"Dear God," said Imogene.

Margaret looked away.

George Prout's seizure, which may or may not have been a heart attack, was reasonably mild. It took place the next morning, a few hours before Margaret returned from Chicago. He was sitting in the Saddler kitchen, and he was drinking coffee, and he was talking with Pete and Sarah about the funeral arrangements. He abruptly set down his coffee cup and said something to the effect that he felt a thinness in his chest. Pete and Sarah drove him straightway to the Paradise Valley Memorial Hospital, where he was given sedatives and placed in a private room. He called for Margaret. He wept. He told Pete and Sarah he wanted Margaret to come hug him. He told them it all was too much for him. He wanted Margaret simply to hug him, that was all, simply to hug him so he could feel her warmth and concern. He said it didn't matter whether any of his five children came to see him—all he wanted was Margaret. He had been given ten milligrams of Valium, and after a time he began to yawn, and finally he dozed off.

Pete and Sarah's oldest daughter, Olive Streeter, met Margaret at the Saddler front door and told her what had happened. Margaret nodded, returned to her car and drove to the hospital. After parking the car in the hospital lot, she checked her appearance in the rearview mirror and made sure her hair was neat. She did not *look* sixty; she really did not. She looked perhaps fifty at the most, and a comely fifty at that. She grimaced into the rearview mirror, baring her dentures, checking to see whether they were stained. She hoped Imogene felt better today. She had apologized to Imogene, and she had *apologized* to Imogene. She did not want to lose Imogene as a friend. She did not want Imogene to drift away. Shaking her head, Margaret decided she passed muster nicely, and so she got out of the car and went inside the hospital. As she walked, she smoothed down her suit. It was a warm morning, but she was not perspiring. The suit was a heavy gray, yet it was cut nicely, and it flattered her full bosom and hips. A long time ago, commenting on her appearance, Irv Berkowitz had called her *ageless*. Which was almost as nice a word as *comely*. It was good to be suppressing sixty so well, and that was the shameful truth of the matter. Margaret shook her head. She entered the reception room, and the nurse on duty told her oh yes, Miss Ridpath, you're to go straight to 137; everybody is waiting for you. Margaret nodded. She walked briskly to Room 137, where she was met by Pete and Sarah, who were standing at the foot of George Prout's bed and whispering with a Dr Frank Groh, who had been the Prout family physician as long as Margaret could remember. Margaret glanced at George, and he appeared to be asleep. He lay on his side, and his hands were tucked under the pillows, and he put her in mind of some plump frightened child that had cried itself to sleep. Pete and Sarah came to Margaret, and they embraced her. Dr Groh nodded. He quickly filled Margaret in on the details. George apparently had suffered a sort of anxiety attack. His EKG was reasonably normal, and he appeared to be in no danger. The sedatives had done a good job of work, according to Dr Groh—especially the Valium, which probably was the world's opium of tomorrow, unless he missed his guess. Margaret thanked Dr Groh for the information. She glanced around the room. She was aware of what seemed to her to be too much sunlight. It came rioting in the window, and the yellow somehow was artificial, too bright, too hard. It was as though the morning's high rigid sky were some sort of bald and stupid hoax. Then Pete and Sarah began whispering at once, and at first Margaret could make little sense of the words—they were too quick and too salivary. Finally, frowning at Pete and Sarah and telling them to hush down a little and talk one at a time, she squinted intently at them in that crisp little room with its urgent spattered sunlight, and first Sarah and then Pete told her how George had been asking for her over and over again. And Dr Frank Groh nodded. He wet his lower lip with a gray tongue, and the terrific sunlight glinted off his spectacles. He had been one of her first bridge partners . . . back in the '30s when she had just been learning the game. He had been an awful overbidder and not much on defense either. Still, she did like him. Sometimes he was a little gruff, and he surely was not the most patient person on the face of the earth (no pun intended), but he'd never been anything less than honest and direct. And so she paid attention to him when he suggested that it *would* be good if she stayed with George for awhile. "He'll be coming out of it soon," said Dr Groh, "and he *did* ask for you, and I honest to God think you're needed here." And Margaret said: "Of course I'll stay. I'll do whatever I can. I like George very much." And she blinked out the window at the relentless plastic egg of a sky. And she said: "Did he *really* ask for me?" And Dr Groh said: "Yes. That he did." And Pete said: "He keeps saying that he wants you to hug him." And Sarah said: "*I* tried to hug him, but he told me it wasn't the same." Sarah's voice was a little edgy, and she stared down at her hands. Margaret did not reply. The sky smacked at her eyes. And Dr Groh said to her: "He'll be waking up any minute now. We're going to leave you with him. We'll be right out in the hall." He patted one of Margaret's arms. "All right," she said. He ushered Pete and Sarah out of the room. Margaret seated herself next to the bed and waited for George to come out of it, whatever *it* was. And he finally did. His eyes came open, and he saw her, and his hands came out from under the pillows. She leaned over him and hugged him. His breath was dry and papery. He said: "Good Christ, Margaret, can you believe what's happened?" And Margaret stroked her brotherinlaw's bald head and said: "No. I can't." And George pressed his face against Margaret's strong gray bosom and said: "I love you." And Margaret looked away.

It turned out that George Prout became the second man in Margaret's life—as far as The Physical went. It also turned out that he was the last man in Margaret's life—as far as The Physical went. He eventually went so far as to propose marriage, but she of course resolutely declined. She saw it all as being unspeakably demented and grotesque, and she was frightened, and she never really enjoyed it, or at least not the way she had with Irv Berkowitz.

*

George constantly spoke to Margaret of what he called his Need, which perhaps should have placed him on a subordinate level, but it did not. Instead, his words, weak and weasling as they might have *seemed*, actually showed him to be still another of the iron persons who populated Margaret's days. They were really such *relentless* words, and she knew of no way to stuff them away, and so she allowed him to do what he wanted. In weasling lay strength, and no mistake.

When a woman of sixty yields herself to a man of sixtytwo, and when they even go so witlessly far as to couple like two adolescents on a couch in the darkened back room of a drugstore, or in the commodious back seat of the man's gleaming magenta 1969 Cadillac El Dorado, or in the bed that he shared with his wife (her sister) for more than thirty years, their behavior surely must be considered demented, or grotesque, or more than likely both. And Margaret was sorely ashamed of herself, and no mistake. Occasionally she would read in some magazine that there was nothing wrong with older persons engaging in such behavior, and the writer would go on to explain that it all was *normal* and *natural*, but Margaret nonetheless was ashamed of herself, and no mistake. It was disgusting, and no mistake. (The magazines meant older people who were *married*. Margaret was not stupid. They certainly did not mean *this*.)

Oh yes, she was comely enough for her age, and her figure still was splendid, and her world found it hard to believe that she was as old as the calendar said she was. (Incidentally, she never was hesitant about telling her age; she really did not have the courage for any sort of coyly girlish beating around the bush.) But did her attractiveness explain anything? Was it any sort of excuse? And what about the undoubted fact that she and George Prout were committing what a great deal of the world would define as incest? Dear sweet heaven, was it her final destiny to be the silent guilty elderly mistress of a plump whimpering pharmacist who kept insisting each time that she tell him how *strong* he was and what a *man* he was and how *fully, deeply* and *richly* he *satisfied* her? "Who's that all big and fat inside you?" he would say. "Who's your bestest lover, huh? You love me? You like the way it feels? It's the best you ever had.

right?" And Margaret nodded. She told George he was excellent. But she also told him he should try to relax. She told him she did not want him to have another of his spasms or whatever. He, though, told her *he* would be the one to worry about *that*. He told her he was her big old *stud*; he was a *real man* again; he was not about to be laid low by any goddamned spasm. He said: "The last ten years with Ruth, well, we were brother and sister, you understand? I'm not blaming her, you understand, but it was like there had just been too many days for us, you know what I mean? Too many flat days with only *words* and *politeness* and nothing much else. We could of gone on. We could of kept sleeping together. And I could of got it up for her. But we just ran out of . . . oh I don't know . . . I suppose maybe you'd just have to plain and simple call it *interest*." But now everything had changed, and George Prout told Margaret he felt better than he had felt in at least twentyfive years, which meant he was in complete control of the situation, and no mistake.

He told her he had wanted her all his life. He told her she made him want to dance on the ceiling. He told her better late than never.

Some time in 1972, or perhaps 1973, Margaret's mother said to her: "Oh, of course, I'll admit it, yes, when the moon comes over the mountain and you add up all that's happened, maybe you'll blame your father, or maybe you'll blame me, or maybe you'll blame Ruth, or maybe you'll blame Sarah, or maybe you'll blame *all of us*, but I expect you'll *really* blame *yourself*, won't you? *I* said to you, *I* said: 'Margaret my girl, you should go off to Ohio University.' But *you* said: 'No, I want to stay here.' *You* said: 'Mother, I just don't want the aggravation.' And then *I* said to you, *I* said: 'All *right*, but don't come whining to *me* in forty years.' I really did say those things, didn't I? Oh, I *did*, and I *know* I did. And so maybe now, yes, I'll admit it, I'm choking on my own spit, and you and that Pauline think I got nothing in my head besides broken fingernails and maybe some old pencil erasers, but I *know* what I *know*, so don't come crying to *me*, my girl. Enough is enough."

*

The inevitability of the George Prout thing curled over Margaret like some sort of awful stinking cloak, and she knew it was there right from the beginning, right from that day of his seizure and his tears and the hideous sunshine. Her sister Ruth was stretched out naked in Zimmerman's Funeral Home, and the embalmers and cosmetologists were pumping her full of liquids and plumping her cheeks and applying their powders and rouges, and right *then*, right as all that dreadful busywork was taking place, Margaret and George were moving into position for the mad ritual that after a time would resolve itself in the back room of his drugstore, and in the back seat of his magenta El Dorado, and in his (and Ruth's) bed.

George Prout—good heavens. George Prout—of all people.

Even though he was a successful businessman (his closest competitor, a man named Ferd Burmeister, did barely seventy percent of George's volume), and even though hardly anyone in Paradise Falls considered him anything less than a consummate good fellow, George Prout never was what one would call physically prepossessing. He was short and globular, and he had lost all his hair by the time he was thirty, and most of the time he talked too much. In addition, he had a curious way of moving around, and it put some people in mind of the way Groucho Marx moved around. It was a kind of lope, with the trunk of his body bent forward, giving him a sort of lunatic crouch, like a parenthesis. It was lucky for him he did not smoke cigars. Had he done so, the Groucho Marx aspect of his movements would have been irresistible . . . at least in Margaret's opinion. As it *was*, his urgent curved gallop had a taut and sorefooted absurdity that seldom failed to embarrass her. (She sometimes even wished she had the strength to laugh.)

But Ruth had loved him, and no mistake. Of the three Ridpath girls, Ruth had been by far the most aggressive (but at the same time the homeliest), and oh how she had *loved* George Prout, and so she had *seized* him, and he had stood not a chance. It was a love that was a *love*, yes indeedy *bob*. Broad of bust and beam, with a flat pugged face and sturdy pink legs, Ruth had pursued George Prout relentlessly, pressing her loose overfed flesh against his loose overfed flesh and allowing him to talk all he wanted, telling him the world did not stand a chance against him; oh dear, oh goodness, he could move all the proverbial mountains if he wanted; he could shoulder aside the sky. So they were married in June of 1936, and it all was as inevitable as death and cornflowers and frogs in the mud. The phrase was Ruth's, and she used it one night just a week or so before the ceremony. She and Margaret were sitting on the back stoop, and the sky hung crisp and warm, and there was a sound of insects, and Ruth said: "It had to be, and so I made sure. I mean, marrying George is to me like death and cornflowers and frogs in the mud—without it happening, there would be nothing, and so it *had* to happen, do you follow me? Ah, it's either him or nobody. Jean Harlow I'm not. It's not like *regiments* are *pounding* at the *door*, right? Anyway, it just so happens that I love him. I'll be a good wife for him. I'll hear him out, and I won't make fun. He's never had a chance against me, the poor dear. I mean, he's Jonah, and I'm the whale, ah hah, if you get what I mean. Yum yum. Chomp chomp."

In the first nine years of their marriage Ruth and George had five children—three boys and two girls. They came in just that order, first the three boys, then the two girls. They were homely children, all of them, and the girls were downright dumpy to boot, yet they never were defeated by their lack of beauty. They had great respect for their mother, and she would not permit such a thing as defeat. She would not *hear* of it, and so she clothed her children well, and they were good students, and they were active in school, and they won class elections. And they all turned out well. George Jr, the oldest, was an associate professor of history at the College of Wooster. Raymond was the sales manager of a toy manufacturing firm in Bergen, New Jersey. Frank was the owner of a thriving Chevrolet agency in Coshocton. Nancy married a man named Earl Watts, who had several successful Arthur Treacher Fish & Chips franchises near Erie, Pennsylvania. And Kathleen's husband, Lloyd Gorsline, had inherited from his father a prosperous chain of auto wash establishments in and near Youngstown, Warren, Niles and Boardman.

In addition, Ruth's five children had produced thirteen children of their own, and she was immensely proud of her grandchildren. Nothing ever had come easy for her, and she knew nothing ever had come easy for her children, and so she figured she had a right to be proud. "After all," she once told Margaret, "it's not as though they are *golden* and *beautiful*; it's not as though things were handed to them because of their . . . ah, their *charisma* or whatever it's called." And then, laughing a little, Ruth said: "Good grief, your sister's, ah, loins have produced a *population*, can you beat that? Um, when I was a bride, little did I realize that every time George and I pleasured ourselves we were working toward the creation of a *trend*, ha ha, a sort of, oh I don't know, like a whole *township* or whatever . . ."

But all that was then. All that was ago. All that was gone. Now there was no more Ruth. Her liquids were being replaced by the embalmers' liquids, and her flat pugged face was being dabbed and painted by the cosmetologists, and her pride and her laughter had ceased to exist. And Margaret should have been mourning her that morning in George Prout's hospital room, that morning of the hideous sunshine. But all she did was sit there, and George Prout's face was pressed against her bosom, and he kept telling her he loved her, and it was a wonder to her that they both were not struck dead by a bolt of fire flung down from the sky. It was a wonder to her that God did not reach down and squeeze her until she popped open, squirting, like a melon past its prime. But nothing happened. The sky and God apparently had better things to do. Nothing came except George's words, and she had no idea what to do about them. And so finally she stroked his lumpy veiny hairless head, and she tried not to look at him, and his words came hollowly against her chest, blathering and dribbling like a torn drainspout: "All my life I've loved you . . . it's been you all this time . . . if you weren't here, I would have withered away and died . . . please believe me, Margaret darling . . . oh, the *feel* of   you . . . my   God . . . bless   you . . . I   want   you *so* . . . I . . . oh, my darling precious . . . you just don't know what it's been like . . . all these years, all this feeling inside me . . . don't turn away from me . . . please."

Margaret shook her head. Finally she was able to interrupt. She said: "Now, George. *Really* now. Just a minute. You don't know what you're *saying.* Please. I understand what you must be going through, but *please* . . ."

George's face came away from Margaret's bosom. His eyes were splintered. He wiped at them with a corner of a sheet. He lay back. "Don't be mad at me," he said.

"I'm not *mad* at you," said Margaret. "Don't talk so childishly. It's just that I don't want you saying a lot of things you'll regret later."

"I can't help the way I feel . . ."

"All right," said Margaret. "All *right*."

"It doesn't mean I think any less of Ruth . . ."

Margaret said nothing.

"I loved her too," said George.

"Please, George. Please stop this kind of talk. And keep your *voice* down. Pete and Sarah and the doctor are right outside in the *hall*."

"I loved her very much," said George. "Just because I love *you*, that doesn't mean I didn't love *her*."

Margaret wanted to hug herself. She thought of her mother. She thought of her late father. She thought of the late Dorothy Hall. She said: "I am going to leave." But she did not move. She weighed a million pounds, and besides, she had been nailed to the chair.

George paid no attention to what she had said. He closed his eyes. He groped for one of her hands. He found it and squeezed it. "There was no warning at all," he said. "Who'd have thought such a thing? It was Pete who called me. I was fixing a tin roof sundae for old Howard Amberson, and we were talking about the war. We don't do enough soda fountain business anymore to keep a sparrow alive, but now and then an oldtimer will come in, and I'll wait on whoever it is just like it's 1940 or whatever. Well, I was about to slop on the whipped cream when the telephone rang back in the prescription department, and it was Pete, and he said to me: 'Ruth's dead. She was drinking iced tea and she was talking about Senator Muskie and she had an embolism.' That's what he said, and he said it flat out."

"I don't suppose there is really any other way to say it."

George opened his eyes.

"I mean," said Margaret, "no matter how it comes out, it's bound to come out cruel."

"Yes," said George. "Nicely put. You've always had a way of getting to the heart of a thing."

Margaret frowned at him.

"I didn't mean that sarcastic," said George. His hand was wet. He squeezed her hand more tightly, and then he began to knead her fingers. "I love you too much for that. I wouldn't hurt you, and I wouldn't insult you. Not for anything."

"Please," said Margaret.

"I always have loved you. That is the absolute truth."

"This is ridiculous," said Margaret. She thought of her mother. She thought of her late father. She thought of the late Dorothy Hall. She thought of Memorial Day 1951 when she had spat on Dorothy Hall's grave. She shook her head. She tried to pull her hand free, but George would not release it.

"No," he said.

"This is . . . this is not proper . . ."

"All right," said George. "So it's not proper. What am I supposed to do? Jump out the window?"

Margaret jerked her hand free. She hugged herself. "*Ruth* is *dead,*" she said.

"Yes," said George.

"Then stop talking this way. Stop embarrassing me. You don't know what you're saying."

"I was two years ahead of you in high school," said George, "but you never even *saw* me, did you?"

"What?"

George leaned forward a little. He plucked at the covers. Now his face

was close to Margaret's. "But *I* saw *you,*" he said. His breath was sour.
"I used to dream about you. And all the times I came to call for Ruth, if
you were there it made the evening for me. Otherwise, there was just
Ruth, and it was no great event. I mean, she *always* was there. And she
always was telling me what a fine kettle of fish I was . . . the same old
stuff, over and over again. She built me up so much, it was as though she
thought I was Alexander the Great or Thomas Edison or I don't know
who. And all right . . . *all right* . . . I got so I loved her. And anyway,
in case you don't remember, I wasn't exactly a beauty, and I was
. . . well, I was human. I still am, for that matter. You're with a female,
and she keeps telling you're the greatest thing since the invention of the
wheel . . . and sure, maybe *she's* not all that much of a beauty *either* . . . but after awhile you *do* respond . . . *if* you're human.
Which I was. And still am. So I got to seeing her in a pretty good light.
And then the love came. So we got married. And the kids came along.
And fine. Sure. All right. She was a good and loving wife. She worked
hard, and the kids turned out well. She was a good cook. She took care of
me when I was sick. She never laughed at me because I lost my hair so
early. She was fine, all right. She was excellent. And I loved her. But I'll
tell you something—*you're* the one I've always—"

"No," said Margaret. "I don't want to hear any of this."

"Do you think silence will kill the truth?"

"You're . . . ah, you're filthy . . ."

"Filthy? Who's filthy? Is truth filthy? Since when? My God, Margaret,
I'd give five years out of my life just to see your tits. Don't you know
that?"

Margaret stood up. Somehow she was able to tear loose the nails that
had kept her in the chair. She felt faint.

Whimpering, George reached for her.

Margaret blinked into the hard relentless sunlight.

"I'm not filthy," said George, scrabbling toward her, twisting the
sheets. Margaret looked at him. His mouth was loose, and she was able to
see his tongue and his gums. "Look," he said, "maybe I'm falling to
pieces. I don't know. But I *do* know I'm not *filthy.* Look, I *loved*
her . . . I really *did* . . . but my God, *I love you too* . . . what's so
filthy about that?"

Margaret shook her head. She turned away from the bed.

George threshed in the bed.

Margaret started toward the door.

"You'll see," said George. "You just wait."

Margaret stumbled out of the room. Pete and Sarah and Dr Groh were standing in the hall. She went past them without saying anything. She tripped over her feet, and she almost fell down. She lurched and she flailed. Pete came to her, but she pushed him away. She told them she was very sorry. She hurried from them. Dr Groh said something she did not catch. Her legs were loose, and she hugged herself. She staggered out of the hospital and crossed the parking lot to her car. Her foot was too heavy on the accelerator when she tried to start the car, and so she flooded the engine. She had to switch off the key and wait for the carburetor to drain off. She stared at a sign over a door. It said: EMERGENCY. She shuddered. She thought of bridge hands. She worked theoretical problems. She calculated odds. She hugged herself. After a time, the carburetor did drain off. She drove away, and terror was in her throat like gas.

Otto York was order. Otto York was faultless teeth—all his own— and a quick smile and a uniform that always was pressed and creased just so. To Otto York, it always was a nice day, and his hand always went to the bill of his cap when he saw Margaret. A frown meant disorder, and so Otto York never frowned. He was a childless widower, and he had lived alone for more than thirty years, but he liked to say Paradise Falls was his family. He never harmed a soul in his life, and the town was fond of him, even though sometimes people would joke with him, telling him God save us all if John Dillinger should walk in.

People had strayed from Margaret all her life, and she was used to that. But in July of 1971, without warning and certainly without her permission, her sister's widowed husband was inflicting himself upon her . . . which meant he was moving against the flow, so to speak, and Margaret did not know what to do. And she had no Irv Berkowitz to advise her. And so, because nothing had prepared her for such a thing, she yielded. There was what one could laughingly call a decent interval, but she did yield, and it was as though she had been pushed, careening and clutching, inside some sort of feverish smear of lights and sounds and flesh. George Prout's naked words tongued at her and pulled out her insides, and there was nothing she could do about anything. He was made of iron, and no mistake.

She visited George the next afternoon, and of course he was expecting her. He was sitting up in bed, and he was wearing striped orange and green pajamas, and he smiled and said: "Well, look who's here . . ."

Margaret walked to the foot of the bed. She was wearing a white blouse and a green plaid skirt. She folded her arms across her belly, and then she said: "Now, George, I'm not here for the reason you think."

"Oh?"

"There are some things we have to get straightened out."

"That so?" said George. He spoke jauntily. His *wife* had *died* two days ago, and he spoke *jauntily*.

Margaret nodded. She had thought it all through. She knew what she had to say. "It's about our conversation yesterday," she told him. "It was a ridiculous conversation. You know that, don't you?"

"No," said George. "I don't."

"Well, it was. You were in an emotional state, that's all. You didn't know what you were saying. The way Ruth died and all, you were upset. The suddenness of it and all. You *had* to be upset, and I can *understand* that, but I don't want you to have any sort of notion that I would—"

"Margaret, I love you."

Margaret spoke quickly. "No," she said. "Incorrect."

"You're talking like a schoolteacher grading papers."

Margaret began to tremble. "What's the *matter* with you? Your *wife* has just *died*. How can you *talk* this way? Have you no *feelings*?"

"'Incorrect,' she says. What sort of word to use is that?"

Margaret unfolded her arms. She leaned against the rail at the foot of the bed, and that way she no longer trembled. "I try to use words I think are appropriate," she said. "I'm here because I want you to understand for once and for all that I have no intention of letting this—"

George's jaunty smile had not diminished. "Why don't you unbutton your blouse?" he said.

Again Margaret stumbled out of the room. Again she hurried to her car. Her legs and armpits were damp, but this time she managed to start the car without flooding the engine. She drove erratically, though, and she almost sideswiped a milk truck and a plump girl on a bicycle.

Talk about grotesque. Talk about ridiculous. Talk about downright evil. There she was, the stately and unapproachable Miss Margaret

Ridpath, sixty years old there in 1971 and just as rigid as rigid could be, just as unsmiling, just as remote, with all sorts of statistical calculations clattering within her skull, and yet at the same time she was being pulled apart by that clownish and *jaunty* George Prout with his Groucho Marx walk and his refusal to accept his obscene behavior and his dreadful suggestions. To listen to *him,* one would just about believe he *meant* what he *said.* Good gracious sakes, what sort of animal *was* he? To *proclaim* his indecency as though it were some sort of great ennobling *truth,* to loll grinning in such loud and unseemly pajamas, to carry on that way while his wife lay all powdered and painted in Zimmerman's Funeral Home— how could Margaret show such a man how badly he was conducting himself? How could she get through to him? And, at the same time, what about her late sister? Didn't she owe that much to poor Ruth? And so wasn't it incumbent upon her to show George how terribly he was dishonoring Ruth? Yes. Yes. *Yes.* It *was.* Margaret visited Zimmerman's later that afternoon, and she barely recognized her sister. Ruth never had been much for makeup, since all it had accomplished was emphasize the flat pugged plainness of her features, and she had been intelligent enough to know this. But the cosmetologists hadn't been that intelligent, and so there Ruth lay, her lips moistly crimson, whorish crimson, her cheeks glowing like a virgin's, and Margaret turned away. A sour taste came to Margaret's mouth, and she flooded it with saliva. Ruth's daughter Kathleen Gorsline, the one whose husband operated the auto wash establishments, came to Margaret and asked her whether she was feeling all right. Margaret said nothing, and so Kathleen led her out of the viewing room and down a hall to a little kitchen. Kathleen gave Margaret a glass of water. Margaret drank. Kathleen asked her whether she felt any better. Margaret nodded, smiled a little and told her niece yes, yes, thank you, she felt a great deal better now, thank you very much for your attention. And the words were of course untrue. The water had not even removed the sour taste. Margaret closed her eyes for a moment. She saw George Prout, and he was pleading with her to open her blouse. Quickly she opened her eyes. Kathleen was frowning at her. Margaret pushed past Kathleen and returned to the viewing room. It was called Parlor B, and the name RUTH RIDPATH PROUT was displayed on a discreetly small easel at the door. The letters were white pressed against black felt. Margaret shook her head. She went to the open coffin. She stared down at the corpse, and she took several large breaths, and she did not blink. She swallowed some of the sour taste. She leaned over her dead sister. "Now you hear me, Ruth Ridpath Prout," she whispered. "I'll try. Honestly I will. After all, who does he think he is? And who does he think *I* am?"

Then Margaret quickly straightened and looked around. This place, this room, this Parlor B . . . mourners were everywhere, and they murmured, and a few women smiled at Margaret. Kathleen was standing nervously at the door, but apparently no one had heard a thing.

And so Margaret moved through the room, and she was clasped by some of the mourners, and she was embraced by others, and she accepted soft kisses on the cheek from several of her woman friends, and she told everyone thank you for coming, thank you so much; yes, it has been a shock; you are very kind. She swallowed more of the sour taste, and she said to herself: I'll tell him in no uncertain terms that he is behaving very badly. And that'll be the end of it. Yes. (She smiled. She pressed her upper lip against her upper plate.) But it did not turn out that way. And later she told herself, or *admitted* to herself, that she had known all along it would not turn out that way, and never mind her whispered promise to that pinkly prettified cadaver.

The next day, the day of Ruth's funeral, George told Dr Groh he did not feel up to attending. The minister, Mr Ordway, devoted much of the eulogy to expressing sympathy for poor Mr Prout, and how profoundly he (Mr Prout) had been prostrated by the death of dear Mrs Prout. The church, St Mark's Presbyterian, was crowded, and Margaret was squeezed between Sarah and Kathleen. She had some difficulty breathing, but she did not let on. Sarah wept, and so Margaret held one of Sarah's hands. Pete held the other. Sarah pressed her face against Pete's shirt. Margaret leaned forward and tried to listen very closely to Mr Ordway's words. Pete and Sarah actually were Methodists, and a first cousin of Pete's, a man named Wesley Saddler, was the pastor of the First ME Church, and later Margaret overheard Sarah tell Pete something to the effect that when it came to eloquence, this Miller Ordway was no Wesley Saddler, not by a long shot. And Pete nodded, but at the same time he motioned with a finger for Sarah to shush. Margaret rode with Pete and Sarah to Oak Grove Cemetery in a limousine driven by a young man named Stroup, and he told them he was sorry if the ride was a little rough, but the engine had been idling badly the past day or so, and there really wasn't a filling station in town that had a mechanic who was all that qualified to work on your typical Cadillac. Pete nodded, smiled at young Stroup and told him not to concern himself. Mr Ordway developed a frog in his throat during the final graveside prayers, and he had to cough several times, and once he even sneezed, and Margaret said to herself: There is nothing more aggravating than a summer cold. The coffin was bronze, and it was enormous, and Margaret sat on a folding chair that pinched her buttocks.

She visited George in the hospital later that afternoon. She had changed from her funeral black, and now she wore a rather tight green dress that just about matched his pajamas. Or at least they did not clash. She opened the dress for him and allowed him to stroke and kiss her breasts. He wept, and she kept expecting a nurse to come into the room, but none did. She leaned over the bed so he would not have to strain himself. Finally he got to licking and gnawing her breasts, and she moaned a little, and she perspired quite a lot . . . which had not been typical of her yesterday and was not typical of her today. She grimaced, and her arms hung loosely at her sides, and George mumbled and grunted, and his tongue anxiously circled first one nipple and then the other, and she felt them harden, and she could have died, and whom was she trying to fool? So finally she kissed his head and his nose and his forehead and his cheeks, and finally she kissed his mouth, and she told him yes, yes, all right, oh God forgive us, and she embraced him, and then it was that she got around to describing the funeral for him . . . Mr Ordway's words and Sarah's tears and the large turnout and all the rest of it. And she buttoned up the front of her dress. And George smiled. And his mouth made kissing sounds. And the room was a proclamation of iron.

But surely George would not stray. Surely he was too old to stray. And surely nothing better was obtainable for him. And anyway, he did say he loved her. He said it, and he said it, and he said it right up to the day she died. He and Margaret slept together an average of two or three times a week for more than three years, and he never tired of saying it, and he never showed himself to be bored with her, and he never showed himself to be impatient with her, and he kept nuzzling her breasts and telling her he was her big old stud. And who else was there for her? What was she supposed to do? Flail around in a vacuum? Play bridge twentynine hours a day? If he really loved her, and seeing as how Ruth was *dead* and *gone,* where was the harm in any of it? Was there to be nothing for the rest of Margaret's days beyond bridge tournaments and her crazed mother and poor cowering Pauline Jones, the housekeeper? Would that have been fair? After all, did Margaret deserve such arid final years? What had she ever *done*? Whom had she ever *harmed*? So yes, she accepted George

Prout and his mouth and his words and his insistence that he loved her. And after a time it got so that the fact that *she* was to *Ruth* what *Dorothy Hall* had been to *Mother* was not all that important. And all right, perhaps some day someone would come spit on Margaret's grave, but was it all that dreadful? Would the spittle cause her to sit up screaming in her coffin? Good heavens, such nonsense. And so Margaret Ridpath opened herself to her late sister's husband. And he promised her he would not stray. And he did not stray. And he was with her when she died, although she did not know it. He leaned over her, and he spoke to her of courage, and she heard not a thing.

Dying, blind, unaware of voices, Margaret said to herself: If I only ever was able to describe the ecstasy, the rewards of simple order, of consistency, of behavior that did not fall apart because of whim or laughter or weakness. The blood of Otto York was the final outrage, and those children had no right. I did not hate them, though. I resisted them, and I punished them, but all I sought was to erase the outrage and set things back in order. It has nothing to do with iron; it has everything to do with propriety. We have laws. One drives on the right side of the road. One stops when a traffic light turns red. One lines up at the Kroger checkout counter and takes one's turn. Rules and patterns must be honored. Either we are civilized or we are not.

So then at the end, by her own estimation, Margaret Ridpath did not behave so badly. And in a sense she behaved according to the image she had presented all her life—the image of erect dauntlessness, of the coolheaded genius at bridge, of the neat and still comely Presbyterian maiden lady who never masturbated and who appeared to have immense resources. With the exception of Irv Berkowitz and perhaps George Prout, no one really suspected her lack of iron, and no one really knew how frightened she was most of the time. (*Canoes,* for heaven's sake. *Bees,* for heaven's sake. *Horseradish.*)

*

In Margaret's mind, the word *sex* was simply an indicator of gender. She would have preferred that its use have been confined to government forms and census statistics. Its other meaning was always referred to by her as The Physical or Sleeping With. Her friend Irv Berkowitz had on occasion used the word *fucking*, which had appalled her, and she always had been quick to tell him so. She was sensitive about what she considered to be propriety (and in fact she died because of it), and so she was genuinely angered when people made scenes or used offensive language. Faced with a choice between style and substance, she invariably chose style, and Irv Berkowitz had pointed this out to her. And she had agreed. Her mind may have been mathematical and precise, but it was quakingly romantic. And so . . . to her . . . *comely* was a prettier word than *fucking*, and no mistake.

Margaret never had much of a sense of humor. As a result, she was forever tormented by the paradoxes and inconsistencies that her world—her *iron* world—seemed to have no difficulty accepting. For instance, she never really understood how it had been possible for her chum Lexie Musser's rebelliousness to have changed so quickly to such blandly conventional ambitions as happy children, a little house in Groveport and a garden. And she never really understood how it had been possible for her father to have loved two women simultaneously. And she never really understood how George Prout loved both herself *and* the memory of Ruth. Or why she, Margaret, had yielded so quickly to George (and kindly dismiss loneliness; it was not really enough). Romantic mind or no romantic mind, Margaret could not grasp behavior that moved in an unplotted and illogical direction. (That tall lady, for instance, that Hazel Muehlbach. Margaret had *loved* that lady, and the tall lady had loved her, and they had uttered mutual confessions of their love. But nothing had come from that fine summer day in 1917. No visits ever had been exchanged. No logical progression ever had taken place. For decade after decade Margaret and the Muehlbachs had exchanged smiles on the street, but there never had been anything more than the smiles, the fleeting and vacant courtesy, and how come?)

*

So, since she did not understand paradoxes, Margaret never really stopped to examine her own inconsistencies. How could she have? How can one examine something one does not know exists? As an example, take the events that followed Ruth's death. On the one hand, Margaret was permitting the impassioned George Prout to suck her breasts. On the other, though, she had no difficulty whatever functioning coldly and firmly in her own home. The very first day, when she arrived home from Chicago, even though she was aching over the death of Ruth (she *had* loved Ruth, and of that there was no doubt), and even though she was further depressed because her friend and bridge partner Imogene Brookes had scolded her the night before, Margaret took charge immediately, and she did what had to be done. She was greeted by a weeping Pauline Jones, the housekeeper, who embraced her and made wailing noises. This was typical of Pauline, and finally Margaret had to shake Pauline and tell her there, there, all right, please *get hold* of yourself. And Pauline promptly cut off her tears. Snuffling a little, fingering her eyes, she said: "Yes, Margaret. I'm sorry. I know I shouldn't act this way."

"All right," said Margaret, disengaging herself from Pauline.

The two women went into the front room, and Mrs Ridpath was sitting in her favorite chair. She was eightyfive years old there in 1971, and she plucked at an antimacassar and smiled at Margaret and said: "So good of you to come here to my apple tree, Sidney."

Margaret looked at Pauline.

Pauline was holding Margaret's suitcase. She set it down. "I didn't tell her *anything*," she whispered, nodding toward old Inez Ridpath. "I did just what you told Pete Saddler I should do . . ."

Margaret nodded. She went to her mother's chair, leaned over and kissed Inez Ridpath on a cheek.

Again Pauline fingered her eyes. She fished in her apron for a handkerchief. She blew her nose.

"When you feel like a fish in a bowl," said Inez Ridpath, "then you have to watch yourself at all times. The world sees you naked, so you have to be careful."

Margaret wanted to wipe her mouth. Her mother's cheek had tasted dusty. But all Margaret did was smile and nod. Then, after a hesitation, she squatted next to Inez Ridpath's chair and said: "Ruth is dead."

Inez Ridpath was not so fat any more. She wore a pink robe and pink slippers, and the robe hung loosely. It was as though most of the fat had been sucked out of her, leaving great blots of drooping aimless flesh—on her neck, her arms, her legs. "A fish in your typical bowl," she said, "cannot afford to behave like a dirty beast. There are too many witnesses, and they would carry the news too far." A small cough, and Inez Ridpath fastidiously covered her mouth. "In my apple tree, Oscar, the world glistens so finely, do you know that?" Her voice had a quality of ragged cloth; it no longer had the crazed strength it had carried in her fifties and her sixties and even her seventies. In those days, she had *shouted* her lunatic nonsequiturs, sometimes while waddling splayed and nude from room to room. Now, though, she barely was able to walk at all, and her voice had diminished to this ragged croak, and perhaps some day she would die, but Margaret for one was not altogether certain of this. (In 1974, when Margaret died, her mother still lived, still plucked, still talked . . . a serenely incoherent eightyeight.)

"Mother," said Margaret, "I'll say it again: *Ruth* is *dead.*"

"You take care of it," said Inez Ridpath, patting Margaret's cheek. "Perhaps a spray of violets. A soft aspect is necessary, don't you think?"

Behind Margaret, Pauline flopped on the sofa and again blew her nose.

Margaret looked briefly at Pauline, then turned back to her mother and said: "I don't want to have to hit you."

"Well," said Inez Ridpath.

"I hardly ever hit you any more. You know that."

"Well," said Inez Ridpath, "perhaps marigolds. Perhaps something gay and sentimental at the same time, if that can be arranged."

"I hate it when I have to hit you," said Margaret.

"Get the beans all in order in the beanbag," said Inez Ridpath.

"*Mother,*" said Margaret.

"You first have to get the animal's attention," said Inez Ridpath. "John used to say that. I mean, when he had time for me, when he was able to tear himself away from that Dorothy Hall. Ah, but he never was needlessly cruel. Not like people nowadays, your Nazis and your Hitler and the rest of them."

"*Mother,* " said Margaret.

"Actually," said Inez Ridpath, "fountain Coke is better than bottled Coke. Sweeter. Perhaps we can arrange for a reception, and perhaps that George Prout will supply us with fountain Coke from his drugstore. He has a peculiar way of moving around, but he's not as bad as I thought he would be, do you know that?"

Margaret raised her right hand. She and her mother had gone through this ritual for more than thirty years, and most of the time it worked. It had to do with engaging Inez Ridpath's attention—and the thing was, Inez Ridpath herself welcomed it. "If you don't listen to me," said Margaret, drawing back the hand, "I am going to hit you smack across the face, and it'll put a big fat *mark* on your *cheek* . . ."

"With pretzels," said Inez Ridpath. "We all love pretzels."

Margaret sighed. Behind her, Pauline moved uncomfortably on the sofa. Margaret brought the open hand in a quick chopping movement directly toward her mother's cheek, but she pulled back the hand just before striking the cheek. Nonetheless, even though it had not been touched, Inez Ridpath's face jerked back, and the old woman let out an enormous shriek. It was as though her former shout had returned; her mouth was open, and her tongue protruded, and she writhed.

"Well," said Margaret, "was that a good one?"

Inez Ridpath's writhing stopped. She smiled. "That was a *good* one," she said, and the frenzy was gone from her voice, the pain or grief or guilt. She rubbed her cheek where it had not been struck. She rubbed first with her right hand, then with her left hand. "Did I holler good?" she wanted to know. She grinned down at her hands. She grinned so widely her dentures slipped. Noisily she sucked them back into place.

"You hollered just fine," said Margaret.

Inez Ridpath tongued her dentures. "I wouldn't want you to think I didn't *like* it," she said, winking.

"Ruth is dead," said Margaret.

"The average can of tunafish, if you don't drain off the oil, you can get sicker than a dying cockroach," said Inez Ridpath.

"You want me to do it again, don't you?" said Margaret.

"Yes," said Inez Ridpath. "Do it again."

"All right," said Margaret. She raised the arm.

"No," said Pauline, snuffling.

Margaret looked back at her.

"It's cruel," said Pauline. "She . . . she really doesn't like it . . . and she never has . . . she only goes along with it because she thinks it pleases . . . ah, because she thinks it pleases *you* . . ."

Margaret had been squatting too long, and her knees were giving her pain. She stood up. She glared at Pauline.

Pauline scrootched back on the sofa.

"Why would it please *me*?" said Margaret.

Pauline studied her knuckles. She shrugged.

"So don't talk nonsense," said Margaret. "You weren't living here when it all began. You don't know all that much about it. You never have. You see it for one thing when it's really another." Then Margaret bent over her mother, raised her arm and delivered another mock slap. And again Inez Ridpath shrieked. And again Inez Ridpath writhed. And Margaret said to her: "Mother, *Ruth* is *dead*. It was an embolism. It came while she was drinking iced tea with Mildred Oates, and they were talking about Senator Muskie."

Inez Ridpath rubbed the second place where her face had not been slapped. Again she smiled, and again she was calm.

Pauline shuffled her feet, and the sound was like a mouse in straw. She had always despised these mock slapping rituals, but she always watched them. This made little sense to Margaret; it disturbed her feeling of consistency. Pauline once had been quite beautiful in a slender and graceful way, but that had been a long time ago. She had fallen in love with the wrong man, and the experience had done away with her good looks. Oh, it was possible to see where the good looks had *been*, provided one looked carefully at her eyes and perhaps her cheekbones, but now she was skinny, leathery and veinylegged, with gray hair that was too thin. Her romance had been ridiculous, and Paradise Falls had laughed at her, and so her girlish beauty had been peeled away, and now she shuffled like a mouse in straw—yet she always was present when the mock slaps were delivered. She was a devoted watcher of television, and to her the ritual apparently was just as enjoyable as NBC Saturday Night at the Movies— if not more so. Perhaps she also felt the nonexistent pain from the nonexistent blows. Perhaps some day Margaret would take the time to ask her.

"Well?" said Margaret to her mother.

Inez Ridpath still smiled. "One more ought to do it," she said, sloshing spit between her dentures and the insides of her lips. "Until then, though, I reserve the right to watch the blackbirds howl in the fireplugs and listen to the little worms clamor in the asphalt—you know, the way they do when the roads are bad, full of pits and cracks and whatnot. And mark what I say . . . your average fountain Coke has it over your average bottled Coke by all the miles in Creation. John and old Mister Vance used to *argue* about it, do you know that? It was after Edna Vance had married Bill Light, and her being his fourth wife I think it was, and she'd serve tea, and we'd sit in the old Vance place with its cupola and its *purple wallpaper* in the *parlor*, if you can *imagine* such a thing, and for all I know maybe Dorothy Hall was hiding outside in the bushes and making eyes at my poor John, and he and old Mister Vance would talk about Coke until I'd finally stop them by laughing and saying silly silly silly, the two of you are just making a silly silly fussy old *fuss*, like *bees* in *glue* or whatever."

Margaret reached back. (When had this stupid charade begun? 1933? 1934? And how come, if on the one hand Pauline Jones *despised* it so much, she *enjoyed* it so much at the same time? Which was true. Which was *absolutely* true . . . and some day Margaret just would *have* to take the time to rummage around for an answer.)

"Just one more time," said Inez Ridpath. She removed her dentures and snapped them in Margaret's face. She sniggered, and her nose began to leak.

Pauline mewled.

Inez Ridpath returned her dentures to her mouth. She adjusted them. "Sometimes I get so *happy* I just want to *bite* your *nose* off," she said to Margaret.

Margaret's slap pulled up just short of her mother's left ear.

Inez Ridpath screamed.

Margaret nodded.

Inez Ridpath twisted and grimaced. She rubbed the ear.

"Now?" said Margaret.

Inez Ridpath smiled. "All right," she said.

"Who is it who's dead?" Margaret wanted to know.

Inez Ridpath thoughtfully rubbed the ear. "Ruth?"

"Ruth. Yes. Ruth. That is correct. And how did she die?"

Inez Ridpath swiped at her nose with the back of a hand.

"Get her a Kleenex," said Margaret to Pauline.

Pauline hurried out of the room.

"Now," said Margaret to her mother, "how did Ruth die?"

"She was drinking iced tea with Mildred Oates," said Inez Ridpath, "and they were talking about some senator or other, and then she had an empirism."

"Embolism," said Margaret.

Pauline returned with Kleenex. She gave some to Inez Ridpath.

"Now you blow," said Margaret to her mother.

Inez Ridpath blew her nose. She sucked mucus, and she blew and blew.

"Very good," said Margaret.

"Thank you," said Inez Ridpath. She handed the soiled Kleenex to Pauline, who went out of the room with it. Then Inez Ridpath rubbed the ear. She nodded in the direction Pauline had gone. "A real nambypamby," she said. She rubbed the ear, and she rubbed the ear. Then she winked, and she smiled a little, and she said: "Correct me if I'm wrong, but isn't Ruth the one with the homely face, sort of flat and all?"

No, on second thought, the ritual of the blows that were not blows began later than 1933 or 1934. It began in 1936, which was the year Margaret became head bookkeeper at Steinfelder's, and her life more or less fell into the design it would follow until her death—and the deaths of the three persons she took with her. (It must be emphasized: Margaret Ridpath preferred design to disorder, and design did indeed far outweigh disorder in her days, even when George Prout is taken into consideration, and even Irv Berkowitz, and even those three final accompanying deaths, and even the ritual of the blows that were not blows. To Margaret Ridpath, design was order, and they had the power of earthquakes and avalanches and fear, and no mistake.)

Oh, it *had* to be 1936 at the *earliest* that Margaret's fraudulent slappings of her mother began. That was the year Inez Ridpath began prowling naked through the house, and one evening she came flopping into Margaret's bedroom and said: "Don't you think maybe somebody ought to punish *me*, too?" She was naked except for a pair of fuzzy slippers.

Margaret had been combing her hair. She turned from the mirror and said: "I . . . I'm sorry, Mother, I didn't get what you just said."

"The world is going to punish *Roosevelt* some day," said Inez Ridpath, "so why shouldn't it punish *me*, too? I mean, ah, it'll take something *large* to punish *Roosevelt*, and I grant you *that*, but couldn't something *teeny* be found to punish *me*? A teeny *person* maybe? A teeny person who would come along and say to me: 'Inez McClory Ridpath you old rip you, a marshmallow lay down with a pickle, which was very stupid.' Ah, do you follow me? Do you follow what I'm saying?"

Margaret sighed. Nodding, she said: "The terrible thing is—I think I do."

"Really?" said Inez Ridpath. She seated herself on the edge of Margaret's bed. She scratched her crotch, and there was an odor.

Margaret put down her comb. "Really," she said tiredly. She did not want to look at her mother's crotch, but she looked at it anyway, and it appeared to be trailing thread, or perhaps something more substantial, perhaps yarn or string.

"Maybe you could be that tiny person," said Inez Ridpath, smiling.

"Maybe so," said Margaret. "If I only knew how to go about it." (She was just twentyfive there in 1936, and Ruth already had left home, off married to her precious George Prout, and Paul had been in the Army for ten years, and Sarah was chasing all the boys in Paradise County, plus portions of Hocking, Vinton, Athens and Fairfield, and Margaret was prettier and smarter than either Ruth *or* Sarah, and so how come it was *Margaret* who had to have that thread or yarn or string thrust in front of her? Where was her iron? Why was she unable to repel all this sort of thing? *Thread,* for heaven's sake . . . *yarn* . . . *string* . . . perhaps Mother was saving up a supply for some sort of insane emergency . . . a fire perhaps . . . Rapunzel . . . oh, dear God.)

"You could do me just fine," said Inez Ridpath.

"You mean punish you?"

"Yes," said Inez Ridpath, blinking down at her hands. Her flesh was in gray folds.

"I can't see why you have to be—"

"We could make it a game," said Inez Ridpath.

"How's that?"

Inez Ridpath bent down, reached inside one of her slippers and ripped some loose callused skin from a heel. Using a thumb and forefinger, she rolled the skin into a ball. Then she flipped the ball on the rug. "Tacky tacky," she said. "You'll have to clean it up. Mother's been a bad girl." She smiled at the tiny wad of skin, then looked up at Margaret and said: "In all my life, the best thing I ever did was take each of you aside on your twentyfirst birthday and tell you the truth about your father—first Paul, then you, then Ruth, then Sarah. Paul took it the worst, you know that? He had some sort of large idea of his father, the way boys do, some sort of beau ideal notion clapping around in his head . . . *you* know, like the way he'd go to the office every chance he had and hold the little doggies and kittycats so their temperatures could be taken. And he spoke softly to them, and they never fussed at him, and half the time they cuddled against him, you know? And his father called him a good boy. And they did a lot of hugging and kissing . . . for a father and son, I mean . . . now *you,* maybe *you* saw Paul as being *loud* and full of *fight,* but he never was all that much of a—"

"Yes," said Margaret, "I *know* all that."

"I loved your father very much," said Inez Ridpath. Her smile was gone, and the corners of her mouth had turned down. They were brown, perhaps from something left over from supper. She licked at one corner, then the other. "There was nothing I wouldn't have done for him . . ."

"So why should I be the teeny person who punishes you?" Margaret wanted to know.

"I . . . I made a mess . . . I dropped that tacky old *ball* of *skin* on your *rug* . . . I mean, bold as you please I just went and *did* it, and *you're* going to have to clean it up, and I am *shameless* . . ."

"So that means I should punish you? What do you think would be appropriate—a nice visit to the electric chair?"

Inez Ridpath sprawled back on the bedspread. She cupped her hands over her crotch. She spoke to the ceiling, and she said: "Listen to me, Mister Ceiling. Listen to my story. Two years ago, when I took Ruth aside on her twentyfirst birthday, even then I'd already begun to chip a little at the edges, right? But I did take a bath, and I did wear a girdle, and I did wear a dress. But that was two years ago, and a lot more has been chipped away, but I made the effort again *this* year, didn't I? With Sarah, right across the hall there, in February, when she was the Birthday Girl. And it was *more* than an effort. Really it was. It was a determination on my part that I would not allow anything more to be chipped away. How does the phrase go— *take hold of yourself?* Well, that's what I wanted to do. I wanted to *take hold of myself.* John has been dead and buried more than ten years, and *enough* is *enough.* Enough ruination is enough ruination, right, Mister Ceiling? It was about time I pulled myself away from all that heartache, right, Mister Ceiling? I had done my duty by my children, and they were *good* children, and now it was my turn to do for myself, right? And forget about Dorothy Hall and John and her letters and the way he died, right? So the thing I did was—I again took a bath, and I again wore a girdle, and I again wore a dress. And it was a nice blue dress my sweet Margaret had got me on sale at Steinfelder's. And so I marched into Sarah's room . . . Sarah the Birthday Girl . . . and I told her all about her father and Dorothy Hall and the letters and all the rest of it, and I said to Sarah, I said: 'You are twentyone, and you are the last one to know, and now I have done my duty.' Well, Mister Ceiling, do you know what Sarah did? She *stood* there—*that's* what she did. She stood there and stared at me, and it was as though maybe I had been talking about the price of a peck of pickled peppers. She was all gussied up, getting ready to go out on one of her *dates,* all blue and white she was, all rouged and perfumed and lipsticked like maybe she was *Claudette Colbert,* and she said to me: 'Mama, I know all about it. Ruth told me two years ago, right after you told her.' And then Sarah came to me, and she hugged me, and oh she *meant* well all right, and she said: 'Mama, *sure* it hurts, but it's all water under the bridge after all this time, isn't it? And, well, Mama, to tell you the truth, I don't even remember him all that well. I was only ten years old at the time, and my memory is sort of foggy . . .' " Here Inez Ridpath abruptly sat up. Her hands came away from her crotch, and she made fists, and she beat the fists against the bedspread, and she was speaking to Margaret again, and she said: "I was going to *try,* you know what I mean? I was all *bathed* and *fresh* and whatever, and I'd said to myself, I'd said: Inez, you can't go around like a pig all the rest of your days. You've got to put on a nice *girdle* and nice *hose* and nice *clothes* and not let yourself go to pot just because your responsibilities have been, ah, fulfilled. But then, when I talked with Sarah, it came to me in a big filthy rush that I had done *nothing,* that it didn't *matter,* that it all was *water* under the *bridge,* that none of you ever will be able to share with me the real and awful fact of *how* he died and *why* he died . . . and . . . and why should you *want* to? What concern is it of *yours?* Sarah was right, you see. Oh, she hit the old nail on the old bean, she did. Which means that I never can share it—the burden, the knowledge, the feeling. And so what I *do* is, you see, I think and I think and I think, and I wander around, and how could he have loved me and her at the same time? what was it I could have done that I did not do? how could I have helped him? should I have given him less beer that night? should I have hugged him? should I have taken him to bed? For more than ten years I've told myself that I could purge myself by seeing to it that you and Paul and your sisters at least were raised decently and knew all the facts . . . but now it turns out that the facts are water under the bridge. And so the burden cannot be shared. And so here I am, and I need to be punished, and excuse me for all this talk, with it all coming from my mouth like old *spit,* blah blah blah, but it's just that I want you to make it so I—''

''*Can't you leave me alone?*'' said Margaret. She pressed her upper lip against her overbite. She embraced herself. She was wearing a chaste flannel nightgown, and she was tired, and all she wanted was to finish combing her hair so she could go to bed and get some sleep, and then tomorrow she would be efficient with her balances at Steinfelder's, seeing as how Mr Wolf trusted her so completely, seeing as how he was convinced her mind was the finest arithmetical instrument he'd ever encountered, and no decent person betrayed all that trust and respect, and it had been *Mr George Wolf himself* who had pleaded with her to take the position of head bookkeeper when old Rudy Kingman had died so suddenly in February . . . and so why didn't . . . why didn't her mother just get out and stop all this *talk,* this eternal *blabber* of guilt and grief and bewilderment?

''You're afraid,'' said Inez Ridpath, speaking quietly. ''You're telling me: 'Bad Mother, go away; you scare me.' ''

''No.''

''Then punish me,'' said Inez Ridpath.

''How?''

''Think up a way,'' said Inez Ridpath.

''What do you want me to do— *hurt* you?''

''That's not a bad idea,'' said Inez Ridpath.

''I can't do that.''

''But I *deserve* it,'' said Inez Ridpath. ''I think too much about water under the bridge, and I wad up tacky old skin and throw it on your rug, and you don't like it when I take off all my clothes, now do you? Tell me the truth— *do* you?''

''You know I don't.''

''So all right,'' said Inez Ridpath. ''Then hurt me.'' She stood up and came toward Margaret. She licked the corners of her mouth. ''Bad deeds must be punished,'' she said.

Margaret abruptly stood up.

Her naked mother smiled. Then Inez Ridpath worked at her crotch, plucking out the thread or the yarn or the string or whatever. She let it float to the floor. She was like a child playing with thistledown. "More bad," she said. "More bad *mess* for *Margaret* to clean *up*."

Margaret grimaced.

Inez Ridpath smiled. "You told me the truth about him, didn't you?"

"What?"

"Don't you remember what you said after I showed you the letters? You said he left them behind because he wanted to brag from the grave."

"I did?"

"You did. The words came out all clear and sharp."

Margaret shook her head. "I don't remember saying such a thing."

"It was your analytical mind at work," said Inez Ridpath. A frown. "And I don't want you to call me a liar. I don't lie. I do a lot of bad things, but I don't *lie.*"

"Then *I'm* the one who ought to be punished," said Margaret. Perhaps she would be able to divert her mother.

"No," said Inez Ridpath.

Margaret's arms moved forward a little, and she almost wanted to embrace her mother.

"*No,*" said Inez Ridpath. Her face knotted. "No. No. No. *I* am the bad one. I am so bad he went to someone else. I am so bad he went to that terrible frumpy *Dorothy Hall,* and the two of them they—"

"*No,*" said Margaret. "*Be quiet with all that.*" She moved forward and brought an open hand straight toward her mother's cheek. But it struck nothing. At the last moment Margaret's arm froze. Her palm was so close to her mother's cheek that she was able to feel its warmth, but it did not touch flesh . . . then or ever.

But none of this mattered to Inez Ridpath. Only the *punishment* mattered. And so she wailed. And her face waggled with a great flabby joy, and she cried: "*Yes! Oh yes! I love you, and I thank you!*" The words came clearly; the wailing did not get in the way. She hopped on one foot, and then she hopped on the other, and her flesh flabbed and slapped, and her eyes ran, and her mouth was sopping and askew, and she cried: "*Do it all you want!*" And she cried: "*Do it any time you want! I don't care if it's three o'clock in the morning!*" And she cried: "*Bad girls must be punished!*"

Margaret opened her mouth. She stared at her palm. It was not pink. She stared at her mother's cheek, and of course *it* was not pink either. For a moment she almost had been ready to believe she *had* struck her mother. But that was nonsense. She had not. She tried to smile. "Mother," she said, "what are you talking about? I didn't hit you . . ."

Inez Ridpath moaned happily. "You did too hit it me," she said. "You hit me for a faretheewell . . ." She wiped at her mouth. Her nipples were distended. "I . . . I thank you . . . " She moved to embrace Margaret. "I had it coming to me . . . "

Margaret backed against the dresser. Up came her arm again.

"Yes," said Inez Ridpath. "*Please.*"

Margaret spoke quickly, desperately. "It'll be like a game—a little *game,* all right?" Her arm shook and again she tried to smile. "Just a dumb little playact?"

"*Please,*" said Inez Ridpath. "*Pretty please.*"

"A game?"

"I don't care what you call it. You can call it ham and eggs. You can call it Alf Landon. I don't *care.*"

"What?"

Inez Ridpath moved closer. Her nipples touched the front of Margaret's nightgown. Her hands moved on Margaret's waist, arms, chest, thighs.

"All right," said Margaret, shuddering. She brought down the arm, and again it froze just short of her mother's face.

Inez Ridpath shrieked. She staggered back. She rubbed her face. She rubbed her breasts, her swollen nipples. "*That's the ticket!*" she bleated. She jigged. Her arms moved in frenzied circles. She wept. Now she was sweating, and her sweat dripped on the rug. Some of it ran down her cheeks, and she licked at it. She grinned. "*The Birthday Boy knows!*" she hollered. "*And all the Birthday Girls know!*" She beat the sides of her arms across her breasts. "*Oh, that man . . . that man . . . he could take the most miserable and mangy little puppydog and work on it with those . . . with those soft hands of his . . . those soft loving HANDS . . . and that puppydog it would THRIVE . . . and some little boy or little girl would wind up with just the PRETTIEST and the HAPPIEST and the HEALTHIEST puppydog you could IMAGINE . . . and when he was with ME, and it was a WHOLE LONG TIME AGO . . . why, he would KISS MY HAND and BEHAVE JUST AS NICE AS YOU PLEASE . . . and it all means that there was so much GOOD in that man . . . and . . . and I want to ask you something, Margaret my girl . . . I want to ask you something REALLY IMPORTANT . . . I want to ask you—suppose I had been the one to die from the cancer of the uterus . . . you think he'd have thrown himself in front of that interurban car THEN—because of ME? You think he was telling the truth when he said he loved us BOTH? None of you Birthday People ever asked me THAT question THAT way, did you? IN OTHER WORDS, YOU TAKE THE SHOE AND YOU PUT IT ON THE OTHER FOOT, AND WHAT ANSWER COMES UP?"* Now Inez Ridpath's mouth was leaking again. She paused, sucked spit. Then, quietly: "Just think about it . . ." She nodded. "I thank you kindly for my punishment . . ." She gave a sort of despairing snort. Rubbing her breasts, she turned and waddled toward the door. She placed a hand on the knob, and then she hesitated. She turned. "I mean," she said, "just let it work at your mind." Her voice was cold. She went out. Her buttocks were gray. She closed the door softly behind her.

Margaret went to the closet and dragged out her carpet sweeper. It sucked away her mother's detritus . . . the wadded skin and the thread or the yarn or the string or whatever. Then Margaret removed the bedspread and stuffed it inside the closet. She lay down on top of the bed blankets. An odor of her mother still was there. Margaret closed her eyes. She tried to think of soap and flowers. She did sums in her head. She concentrated on multiples and balances and other clean things, and they were just as effective as soap and flowers. It was perhaps an hour later that she began to weep. But she made no sound. She was not known as a weeper, and surely she did not need to be noisy about it. She became cold, and so she slid under the blankets, and she embraced herself.

At the end, on that warm August day in 1974 when Margaret died and took those three children with her, it was as though she were attempting to reassemble the universe. Otto York was such a terrible *mess* there on the floor. Talk about your *detritus.* But bravery had nothing to do with it. Neatness, though, had everything to do with it.

The slapping charade was never *quite* as wretched as it might have been. It certainly never was gratuitous or immoderate, and it took place only on those occasions when Inez Ridpath's behavior moved altogether too far out of bounds. Ordinary misbehavior received ordinary scolding from Margaret (or, more often than not, simple silence), and so the fraudulent slappings really were infrequent . . . reserved for felonies, never misdemeanors. Such as those times Inez Ridpath wet herself at the table. Or the times she insisted President Franklin D. Roosevelt had wheeled himself into her bedroom for the purpose of ravishing her. Or the times she uttered foul words about God and the Commandments. But really, those times were not all that frequent—and usually her madness was most apparent in her talk, the river of lunatic blabber that came from her day and night, year upon year, whether she was naked or clothed, fat or thin, angry or contemplative. And Margaret came not to hear it, or at least Margaret came not to hear most of it. A point arrived where very little of it mattered. And, beyond all that, consider the situation this way: If a *charade* fulfills the same function as the *real thing,* is it not just as true and honest? Especially when there really is no other choice. In Margaret's case, she saw herself as being made of tinfoil in a world that was made of iron. Therefore, she was incapable of striking her mother, of bestowing on her mother the precious gift of punishment. And so Margaret did the next best thing—she gave the *illusion* of punishing her mother, and her mother's lunacy was the illusion's happy collaborator, and her mother's tears and wailings never failed to erupt, and so where was the harm? And in fact weren't the daughter and the mother sharing something that was necessary for both of them? For Margaret, it was the illusion of strength. For her mother, it was the illusion of punishment. And it was their particular precious secret.

Margaret never even told Irv Berkowitz about it. And she *certainly* never told George Prout about it. Oh, Pauline Jones knew about it, but Pauline never really had mattered. And yes, a woman named Wanda Ripple had known about it, and she had appeared to enjoy it, but in her case the appearance had not been all that close to the truth. She had died in 1960, but her presence remained in Margaret's home, mainly because Inez Ridpath would not relinquish it. Wanda Ripple was dead and gone, as the saying went, but not all *that* dead, and not all *that* gone. The mind preserves. Even the raddled mind. And Inez Ridpath, who had hated her (and whom she had hated), heard from her forever.

Part Three

WANDA RIPPLE

It was in 1938, when Sarah went flibbertygibbeting off to marry a young bank teller named Pete Saddler (and a handsome and industrious fellow he was too, with a fine dimpled chin and a quick unexpected smile), that Margaret was left alone in full charge of the raddled and hortatory Inez Ridpath. But of course, since Margaret spent her days working as the head bookkeeper at Steinfelder's, it was necessary that someone come to the house on a permanent basis and care for Inez Ridpath, keep Inez Ridpath at least partially clothed, clean up her detritus and make sure she did not wander into the street to be struck down by an automobile. Also, by that year Margaret was already an experienced and popular tournament bridge player, and sometimes she went out of town for tournaments, which meant someone had to care for her mother overnight. This had been Sarah's job, but now Sarah was gone, and Margaret had to find someone else, and the someone else was Wanda Ripple. George Prout and Pete Saddler helped with the expense of Wanda Ripple (as they later did with the expense of Pauline Jones), and it all really worked out quite smoothly. Wanda was a gray and stringy woman, widowed twice and childless, and she had a sinus condition that gave her voice a hollow, disjointed and rather clownish aspect. It was as though she were forever speaking through a fragile and tattered paper bag. (Her maiden name, incidentally, had been Carper, and her first husband's name had been Harper, which made her full name Wanda Gwendolyn Carper Harper Ripple, which amused even Margaret, which is saying quite a lot.) At any rate, Paradise Falls abounded in those days with such women as Wanda Ripple, widows who lived alone in tiny frame houses and seemed to spend half their waking hours scrubbing linoleum and pincurling their hair, sitting silent and invisible behind muslin curtains at their front windows and waiting for the bread man to come along, or the ice man, or some spent and spotted survey taker . . . or broom salesman . . . or anyone . . . *anyone at all* . . . anyone who would provide another voice, whose presence would tell the silent Wanda Ripples of the vacant Wanda Ripple afternoons that yes, yes, yes, you *are* here, Wanda; you *are* real; the linoleum *is indeed* spotless, and your muslin curtains *are indeed* a glory, and you really *do* look fine when you take care of your hair. (You never spent ten dollars more wisely than when you bought that curling iron.)

That was the Wanda Ripple whom Margaret hired as housekeeper. But there was more to Wanda Ripple. She had a history. It governed her, and in a sense it governed Margaret, and surely in large measure it governed Inez Ridpath. And surely it explained why Wanda hated Inez Ridpath so desperately. She had to. It was quite literally a matter of life and death. She needed to remain *necessary.*

Wanda's husbands had both been yard conductors for the Chesapeake & Ohio Railway. The first one, Tim Harper, drowned at the age of forty after suffering an apparent attack of cramps while swimming in Paradise Lake. Wanda was only twentythree, and she and Tim had been married less than a year. His best friend, banty little Vance Ripple, a brakeman, visited her a week after the funeral and told her: "God'll make it right with you, and that's a fact. Things got a way of working out." Vance Ripple was wearing green suspenders that day, and he snapped them as he spoke, punctuating his words so they came out: God*snap*'ll make it right*snap* with you*snap*, and*snap* that's a fact*snap*. Things got*snap* a way of working out*snap*. And Wanda, bewildered and aching, stared numbly at Vance while he told her that effective the following week he was being moved up a step to take Tim's job as yard conductor, such being the perquisite of the brakeman at the top of the seniority list. Then Vance grinned a redfaced banty grin (but at the same time he tried to keep it properly respectful, considering her recent widowhood), and he said: "Hell, and please excuse the French, I won't never be the man Tim Harper was, but by God, Wanda, I'm sure going to give her a try." (What was he saying? What sort of try did he mean? Why was he telling *her* all this? Why didn't he just get up, snap his suspenders a few more times for the sake of emphasis or good manners or whatever, and then march out the door and leave her alone? He was *ridiculous*, and that was a fact. He was skinny; he was beaked; he was barely five feet tall; he'd always put her in mind of some ravaged and spindled bird staggering around in search of an inconspicuous place to flop down and die. And his breath, when he came close to her, was like creosote and wet grass. And his hair, plastered down in speckled reddish ringlets, had a drenched and foolish look that reminded her of the oafs and buffoons she saw every afternoon in the Columbus *Dispatch* funnypaper section. And so why didn't he go away? Why didn't he pay more attention to her grief? And why did *she* simply *sit* there and *tolerate* him? The nerve of him! Bragging on coming into Tim's job! Some people had no sense of rightness at all!)

Wanda Gwendolyn Carper Harper and Vance Ira Ripple were married in the autumn of the year following Tim Harper's death. The groom was thirtyeight, and the bride was twentyfour, and fortysix days after the ceremony he died of a heart attack. He bent down to throw a switch, and that was the end of him. The year was 1922, and the man who replaced Vance Ripple as yard conductor did not attend the funeral. Mutual friends told Wanda the fellow was ashamed of himself for not paying his respects, but it was just that he valued common sense over courtesy. The man's name was Ewald Silger, and he happened to be a bachelor, and so he and Wanda earnestly avoided one another, crossing to opposite sides of the street, zagging like implacable enemies, never nodding, never speaking, lest somehow a contamination be passed. (Both Wanda and Silger understood this, even though they never discussed it. He eventually married a girl from Logan, and the girl was the first of four wives, and he lived to the age of ninety-one, and Wanda never bore him the slightest grudge. He'd have been crazy to have behaved any other way.)

Wanda saw that year 1922 as the largest of her life. And perhaps she was right. For it was in 1922, after the death of silly homely Vance Ripple (her second husband to expire in little more than fifteen months), and even though she was just twentyfour that year and certainly still in possession of a certain bony prettiness that in the past had brought her a reasonable share of interested young men, and even though most people (with the exception of the prudent Ewald Silger and a few others) were too sensible and realistic to accuse her of inflicting some sort of baleful *spell* on her hapless husbands (after *all*, she was only *Wanda Ripple,* for heaven's sake; she was *not* something that had *crawled* out of a *hole*), that Wanda retreated. And voluntarily. In that year, she saw silence as being desirable. It was only later that she lurked behind her muslin curtains and waited for anyone . . . *anyone* . . . to come along.

But in 1922 she was more astonished than she was lonely; she was more grieving than she was lonely . . . and she kept wondering whether she had *done* something. She had loved both her husbands, and she had loved them dearly, but she gave all their photographs to a sister, and she tried not to think of them. She gathered silence around her, and she treasured it. Her days were without breath. She said to herself: If I do not think about Tim and Vance, maybe God will not harm them. (Did she perhaps believe in some sort of curse after all? Was this why she understood how Ewald Silger had felt? Perhaps so, although she did not know for certain. Granted, most people do not believe in curses, but Wanda Ripple was not most people, at least not in those days.) Ah, but hold on . . . 1922 was not forever, and Wanda began to understand that she had a great many more days remaining to her, and so she endured, and after a time she even was able to put together a sort of frail and jerrybuilt structure that surrounded those days—all of it small and tentative but nonetheless as real as she could make it. She lived in a small house on Roundhouse Street; it had small rooms and a small outhouse; she kept a small garden of tulips and begonias and daffs out front; she subsisted on two small C & O pensions and two small insurance policies; she walked in small steps; she took small bites; she aged with small wrinkles, and eventually (in small stages, to be sure) she was able to think back on her husbands (small men, both of them), and she finally was able to ask her sister to return the photographs (which were in point of fact quite small). That was about 1928 or so, but Wanda still never really *pored* over the photographs. She simply gave them small glances. She did not want to press the luck of Tim and Vance, wherever they were.

If 1922 was such a large year, why did such smallness come out of it? This is perhaps an interesting question, but unfortunately it never occurred to Wanda Ripple, and so it has no real point here.

In a sense, Wanda was like Inez Ridpath—she had begun well. Her bony prettiness had attracted all the young men any girl could have wanted. Although never really what anyone would have called a chatterbox or a flirt, and certainly not hailing from anything approaching a Better Family (her father, a tired and inconspicuous little man, had been a printer for the Paradise Falls *Democrat*), Wanda nonetheless had a capacity for popularity, and she had many school chums, both girls and boys. She had a certain shy and sometimes even downright foxy charm that reinforced the bony prettiness, and she was skillful at disarming people with the things she said. One time, when she was perhaps seventeen, she told a boy named Bob Bittermann that she didn't mind his being in love with her *at all,* but she *did* wish he would stop gnawing at her *ear* as though it were a piece of *licorice.* Grinning, she said: "Licorice is one thing, and Wanda Carper is another, and I tell you what: I just happen to have an extra penny here in the pocket of my dress, so why don't we go to the store and I'll treat you to a whole big penny's worth of licorice so next time you'll know the difference?" Which is precisely what they did. She insisted on paying for the licorice, and she made Bob Bittermann eat every smidge and sliver of it. She stood with him at the corner of Main and Mulberry, and he gnawed on that licorice, and he sucked down every last black drop, and Wanda giggled like a squirrel. And after a time he also giggled . . . this Bob Bittermann, of all people, who played football for Paradise Falls High School and was six feet two inches tall and as a general rule giggled about as often as he became pregnant. And he was not the only victim of Wanda's foxiness. There was a young man named Howard Reese, for instance, who was all of twenty when he began sparking Wanda (she was sixteen) and for whose twentyfirst birthday she knitted what appeared to be a white muffler but really was a long white artificial beard, complete with string that wrapped around his ears and the back of his neck, giving him the look of a brilliantined and embarrassed St Nicholas or Smith Brother or Father Time. And Howard Reese, who sold burial vaults for a firm in Lancaster and normally had about half the sense of humor of, say, a Bob Bittermann, nonetheless took just one look at himself in the Carper front hall mirror and actually managed to laugh. The sound came as a sort of stony grunt. Wanda rewarded him with more of her giggling, and she jumped around, and she tugged at the great knitted beard until she just about bent poor Howard Reese's ears in two, and then she permitted him to embrace her and kiss her—through the beard, of course. (And she told him she had worked *so* many long clicking silly hours. Your average person had absolutely no *idea* how much *time* was necessary for the successful completion of such a project, especially if that project was to be done *right,* and of course if a person didn't do a thing *right,* why do it at all, *right?*) And so laughter and the foxiness governed a great deal of Wanda's girlhood, and she never was able to take the Bob Bittermanns and the Howard Reeses as seriously as they would have liked. She enjoyed being with them just fine, but that was all. She teased many of them, yes, and she played foolish little games with many of them, yes, but she certainly never meant them any *harm,* and she certainly never meant to be *malicious.* And she certainly never *talked* about any of them (or at least not *too* much, and then only to her closest and/or most trusted friends . . . there can of course be a difference). But all her beaux just seemed too young for her. She saw them more as playmates than as suitors. Tim Harper, though, was a *man,* and she rejoiced in his maleness. She had promised nothing to her young beaux, and she had relinquished nothing, and so she was a virgin when she lay down on her first marriage bed. Tim Harper received fresh goods, and that was the God's holy truth, and it made Wanda proud. It was worth all the planet's licorice. It was worth a happy eternity of knitted beards.

Timothy James Harper always was polished. He crackled as he walked. He was barely five feet four inches tall, and he weighed barely one hundred twenty pounds, but his shoes always squeaked heavily and with a sort of mucky authority, as though he were striding across fresh wax that had not quite hardened. He and Wanda's father were members of the same Masonic lodge, and Wanda's father brought him home for a chat nearly every Tuesday night after the meetings, and they would sit in the kitchen and drink tea and murmur darkly of what they called the Papist Menace. Wanda had known Tim Harper just about all her life, and so she was astonished when she abruptly fell in love with him a little after her nineteenth birthday. She got into the habit of waiting up for him and her father, fixing them cookies and sometimes little cakes and sometimes even a *big* cake or a nice fruit pie. Tim was nearly thirtyseven when Wanda began seeing him as something more than a fastidious and courteous little fellow who sometimes did not speak too highly of Catholics. And then it was, to be sure, that she began to understand why she had been unable to take her young beaux very seriously. Had she ever known a Bob Bittermann who crackled as he walked? *Young* men simply did not know how to *carry* or *comport* themselves; they lacked the rhetoric to speak so knowledgeably of the Papist Menace and the Perfidious Democrats and other such profound issues. And, beyond their lack of rhetoric, the young men lacked the *proclamations* of *time* that sat so jauntily and with such glamorous weariness on the face of Tim Harper . . . the lines behind the ears, the lines in the forehead and the neck, the windburned cracks at the corners of the mouth, the sense that here was a *man* and not a *boy*, a *lover* and not a helpless fumbling haywagon and porch swing *adversary*, a person who understood the nature of *flesh* and how it was different from *licorice* and stupid clownish *knitted beards.*

And at the same time this man was never anything less than warmly considerate of her. He always held her chair for her those Tuesday nights when she joined him and her father after serving them their tea and cookies or whatever. It was clear to her that he sensed the blossoming of her interest in him, but he did not try to take any cruel or corrupt advantage of it. He was the old family friend, nothing more . . . until, that is, one Tuesday night when he sat alone in the kitchen with her (her father had gone off early to bed) and said to her: "Wanda, I have a few things to say to you, and I'd be grateful if you didn't interrupt." He was sitting across the table from her, and he had just put away a second enormous slab of her peach pie. For such a little fellow, he ate like a starving mountain lion, and that was a fact. One of his hands moved to touch one of hers. He said: "I see something in your face that is very dear to me. I have never seen it before in anyone's face, not ever, unless maybe it was the day my sister Mae married Harvey Haggins. And even *that* I don't think was the same. Not as strong, I mean. Ah . . . that is to say . . . look . . . and please, like I said, please don't interrupt . . . look, I am just what I have always been, and I have a distinct recollection of holding you on my lap when you were maybe four or five years old . . . certainly you were no older . . . and you sort of bounced up and down, kaploop, kaploop, you know, like that? Kaploop, kaploop. Oh yes, you'd be surprised how clear I remember all of it . . . you and your grin, the sort of quiet mischief of you . . . kaploop, kaploop . . . yes indeed . . . *but that's all different now, wouldn't you say?* I mean, if I was to do such a thing right now, the bouncing and the kaploop, why, none other than County Sheriff Allen B. Rohr would come rushing in here, or *rohring* in here, if you follow my meaning, and he'd lock me up and throw away the key, and I'd be the first one to admit he was doing the right thing. So here I am, pushing forty like the devil was breathing up my nose, a man who'll never be anything more than a plain old C & O yard conductor don't matter if he lives to be a thousand, and by God you darling girl you, it would honor me if you became my wife, and if you say yes, don't fret about your daddy. I mean, why do you think he went to bed so early tonight?"

Wanda said yes so quickly she caught something harsh in her throat. Tim came around the table to her and clapped her on the back. She coughed and sputtered. He laughed. He hugged her, and he kissed her, and then he got to weeping a little, and so did she. He smelled of soap and hair oil, and he was vested and buttoned, and he squeaked and he gleamed, and his mouth tasted like the peach pie, and she told him *yes,* oh *yes,* and she told him *yes* and *yes* and *yes,* and then her father and mother—scamps and sneaks, both of them!—came grinning and footdragging into the kitchen, and Daddy winked at Tim, and Mama clapped the heels of her palms together.

"So it's settled, eh?" said Daddy.

Tim looked at Wanda.

And *Wanda* looked at *Tim.* If he thought *she* was about to utter as much as a *peep,* he had chipmunks in his old belltower.

So Tim dug at his eyes with his thumbs and finally said: "Yes."

"What's wrong?" said Daddy. "Got bugs in your eyes?"

"I expect so," said Tim.

Wanda still was hugging Tim. She grinned at her father and said: "Me too. I got bugs in my eyes. Wet bugs."

"My goodness," said Daddy.

"Dear *me,*" said Mama.

"Now don't you fun at me," said Wanda to her parents. She squeezed Tim. Then, to Daddy: "*It is settled.* He couldn't get out of it *now* if he was to hit me on the head with a *club.* I'd sue him in a court of law."

And Daddy and Mama, both of them waxen and slatted in their long flannel nightclothes, happily shuffled forward, and hugs were exchanged all around, and small fragmented words were spoken, and then Wanda and Tim and Daddy sat down at the table, and Mama clucked around the kitchen and brewed up an immense pot of tea, and Wanda kept squeezing one of Tim's hands, and she would not release it (as long as she could touch him, then he was real, and the night was real, and all his words had been real, and he had meant what he had said, which meant that she would be the *wife* of a *man,* which meant that her days of foxy girlish maneuverings were forever over and done with, thank the Lord), and everyone seemed to want to speak at once, and their voices all became jubilant and operatic, and the tea steamed and steeped with what to Wanda seemed a sort of hot brown joy, and Mama broke out the rest of the peach pie, which was immensely enjoyed by one and all (Tim had his *third* piece, the scallywag!), and Tim told Daddy and Mama he would marry Wanda just as soon as he was able to buy a house. But the house would be unencumbered by a mortgage, and this was important to him. He quickly went on to say, though, that he had more than three thousand dollars in the bank, and so it wouldn't be long at all before he would have enough of the old wherewithal to buy a house free and clear, and he said to Wanda: "I'm real sorry but I can't abide the thought of a debt. If a person wants something but he can't pay for it, he either ought to save his money until he *can* pay for it, or he ought to do without. But you and me . . . we just have to have a little patience. The money, it's almost all been gathered together. It's not like I'm asking you to wait until we both topple into our graves. Only just a *little* patience, all right?"

"Surely," said Wanda.

"That's the right attitude," said Daddy.

Mama's words were muffled by a mouthful of the peach pie, but she managed to say: "The peepul wih their fee on the groun are the peepul who geh aheah."

Wanda smiled at the sound of her mother's words, and she squeezed Tim's hand more tightly, and all right, if Tim said wait, they would wait. If Tim said cut bait, they would cut bait. If he said fish, they would fish. Whatever he wanted, it was fine. He was a *man,* and he was maybe a miracle, and she was not about to argue with him. She said: "Mr Harper has his feet on the ground, and so do I."

"Tim," said Tim.

"Yes sir," said Wanda.

"Say it," said Tim.

"Tim," said Wanda.

"Excellent," said Tim.

Everyone laughed. Daddy and Mama nudged one another.

Later, when Wanda and Tim were alone again and her father and mother had gone off to bed *for real,* Tim said: "It won't take all that long. I promise you. A year, maybe a little more. Soon as it gets to thirtyfive hundred or so, I know of a nice little place on Roundhouse Street we can have, and you know something? Roundhouse Street is not exactly your Main Street or your Cumberland Street, but it's so near to the tracks you can stand on the porch and wave at me every day, long as you aren't all that fussy about cinders. That'll really be something, way I see it. I mean, there'll be *your husband,* hanging on some boxcar ladder, and he'll be just waving back at you like he's fit to *blow up* on account of he is so *proud* of you and like he's saying to the world: *Have I got me a princess or have I got me a princess?"*

Wanda's eyes filled. "You . . . all I thought was . . . well, *you* know, that you were like an old friend of the family, you and Papa and the lodge . . . but then it all sort of got to changing . . . you got to be more than that . . . "

"Thank you," said Tim.

"It'll be all ours. The house, I mean."

"Yes," said Tim. "Like I told you, I don't care for debts."

"You are a good man," said Wanda.

"Thank you," said Tim.

"I love you," said Wanda.

"Mutual," said Tim.

*

But the engagement was longer than Tim had anticipated. A maiden sister of his died penniless, and he had to spend some of his money for her funeral. And later he had to come up with nearly five hundred dollars for the treatment of a painful rectal infection that finally had to be attended to surgically in a Columbus hospital. And so it wasn't until three years after his abrupt kitchen table proposal that he and Wanda finally were married. The little place on Roundhouse Street was theirs all lock, stock and clear as the old barrelhead, as Tim said, grinning, waving the deed in front of Wanda's face, waving it so close that it tickled her nose and made her giggle. They went to Cincinnati on their honeymoon, where they dined on knockwurst and kraut (which were acceptable again, now that the Great War was over), where they took trolley rides and ate ice cream and kissed a lot and visited the zoo and saw gnus and baboons and other unusual critters, and Tim was tender with Wanda, telling her he always would try to make it, the You Know, easy for her, and whatever she wanted or didn't want was fine with him, and she shouldn't aggravate herself about it, and oh dear, oh God, could anyone doubt that she loved a man who would talk to her that way? Could anyone doubt that anyone was happier than Wanda Gwendolyn Carper Harper?

"That's quite a name you got on you now," said Tim.

"I'm proud of it," said Wanda.

"It sings like the birdies in the trees," said Tim.

"That's a sweet thing to be thinking up," said Wanda.

"Old *geezer* like *me* getting a *girl* like *you*," said Tim, "I ought to be strung up like a dog."

"Hush," said Wanda.

"The night I popped the question, it surprised you, didn't it?" said Tim.

"What *ever* gave you the first *hint*?" said Wanda.

"And we bawled, both of us," said Tim.

"And then down came Daddy and Mama, and Mama made tea, and we ate the rest of my peach pie," said Wanda.

"Correct," said Tim.

"I seem to recollect that I didn't talk a whole lot," said Wanda.

"Correct," said Tim.

"I seem to recollect that I said just one word," said Wanda.

"Do you recollect what that one word was?" said Tim.

"I seem to recollect it was *yes*," said Wanda.

"Correct," said Tim.

"That's me," said Wanda. "Some talker."

"It's a wonder my ears don't fall off," said Tim.

"Just think," said Wanda, "I used to sit on your lap when I was a real little girl."

"Kaploop," said Tim.

And then Timothy James Harper went and drowned in Paradise Lake. He was a fine swimmer, and everyone knew it, but he went and drowned anyway, and Wanda's astonishment was even larger than it had been the night he had asked her to marry him, and sometimes she would say to herself: What *was* it? I mean, we were *happy*, the pies and the cakes I fixed for him, the way he'd wave at me from those boxcars or gondolas or whatever, the sweet nights we had together, the Brotherhood picnics, the good *smell* of him, the way he was forever *cleaning* himself and *polishing* himself, the *squeak* and the *crispness* of him, the times we'd sit and hug in the front room and talk of maybe a little baby coming along, the times he'd fetch the deed home from the bank deposit vault just so we could spread the paper on the kitchen table and read all the small print and grin over the words because what they meant was we *existed* . . . because what they meant was *him* and *me* and *ours* . . . and so how *come*, I mean, how *come* a man who was such a good swimmer would go jumping and flopping into Paradise Lake after eating four frankfurters (him and his mountainlion appetite) and drinking three bottles of Joe Masonbrink's green beer? Frankfurters and green beer and all, a man who was such a good swimmer should have had more sense. I mean, a man who was a Mason of the Thirtysecond Degree . . . I mean, he should have just laid there in the sun until the *green beer* had wore off at least, not to mention the frankfurters. And maybe I could have made more of a fuss. All I did was say to him: *Maybe you ought to wait a little before you go back in the water.* And he said: *There's nothing to worry about.* And that is as far as it went. I did not make any more of a fuss. His hair (beach or no beach, wind or no wind, green beer or no green beer) was combed just so, and he patted me on the knee (I was laying on a towel, and there were freckles on my shoulders), and he went off jumping and flopping, and then came his cramps or whatever, and he sank to the bottom quicker than it takes me to tell it, even though Vance Ripple and Henry Packer and Fred Hart went in after him, and how come it had to happen, huh? Had some kind of book been written, huh? Is some sort of score being kept? If so, *how* is it kept? What's a hit and what's a run and what's an error? Is it like maybe there's such a thing as *too* happy, like eating too much or laughing so loud you get to choking? I mean, how did old Cousin Cyrus die? Well, he happied himself to death. I mean, is *that* it? I mean, is there a point where a person tells himself he's so happy there's no way he can be happier, so he goes out while the going's good and while it's all still sweet? There they are up there—Cousin Cyrus and Tim Harper, happied to death. Smiling. Strumming their harps. I can see teeth and clouds and angels, and it's all crazy, and so am I, and a lot of comfort *that* is.

Tim Harper was of course dragged out of the water. And he was dried, stuffed, coffined, viewed, mourned, eulogized and buried, and Vance Ripple (who had been the best man at the wedding of Tim and Wanda) naturally was one of the pallbearers, and Wanda watched the poor banty clownish little fellow quite honest to God sure and certain *stagger* from his share of the weight of the coffin. He actually nearly fell down, and Wanda had to clap a hand over her veiled mouth so no one would see her smile, and the taste of the veil was dusty. A knot of silent laughter was like a clutch of worms in her belly, and they were disrespectful worms, to say the least, and she supposed her grief perhaps had made her a little strange in the head. Part of the veil became pasted to her lips. Quickly she plucked it loose. She concentrated on the cemetery and its stone angels and obelisks and sleeping lambs, and the worms had the decency to go away. She managed to weep well and honestly. She uttered high splintered cries when the moment came to pray over Tim for the final time and lower his coffin into the earth.

And then Wanda went home to the place on Roundhouse Street, and she read and reread a letter of condolence (all three paragraphs of it) that had come from the division superintendent, none other than Mr H. C. Boston himself. It was typed *just so* and centered on the page *just so*, with Mr Boston's signature all spidery and precise, and the two words *terrible tragedy* lay hellacious and scarifying in the second paragraph, and what a wise man was Mr H. C. Boston, him and his neat letter and his fine signature, his words as flattened and spiritless as a collection of embalmed frogs spread under dusty sunstreaked glass in a museum. And Wanda thought: Yes, Mr Boston, a *terrible tragedy;* you said the God's truth. And after a time, and not too long a time, she got to twisting and kneading Mr H. C. Boston's splendid letter (all three calm and considered paragraphs of it), and then she began tearing off little corners of it, and finally one afternoon she carefully bit into the paper, her teeth coming down on both the hellacious *terrifying* and the scarifying *tragedy,* coming down on them *just so,* and the taste of the words was as dry as the taste of her veil had been, and she shook her head and said to herself: Well, here I am—eating paper. It's all over with me now. I might as well give up. I mean, what's going to come next? Am I going to get down on my hands and knees and eat the carpet? Or maybe I can make me a sandwich out of that chair over there. Or, hey, how about my hair or an elbow or maybe a toe or two? Maybe I can *eat myself up* and *get cramps,* like maybe I was made out of frankfurters and green beer. Eat myself up and vanish, presto chango, like the woman the magician made disappear that night when I was a little girl and I wore the green dress with the white collar and Daddy and Mama took us to the Aeolian Temple for I think it was called THE DOCTOR WIZARD APOCALYPTIC NECROMANCY EXTRAVAGANZA. I mean, will I disappear too? What's going to happen now? Should I ought to be locked in somebody's attic? (Hey, now that I've bitten into that letter and torn it, dear old Mr Boston's dear old fancy letter, do you suppose now I could be called a Boston tearer? Oh, how funny.)

Well, as it turned out, Wanda Gwendolyn Carper Harper did not devour herself, and so she did not vanish, and neither did she go mad. Instead, she had to rush about putting up barricades against the insistent attention paid to her by that absurd little Vance Ripple, with his green suspenders and his drenched ringleted hair and the dumb banty way he augmented his voice by snapping his suspenders, and by God, pardon the French, he absolutely would not take no for an answer. He told her he knew he was not the man Tim Harper had been, and he told her he knew he never would be, but he said he loved her, and by God, pardon the Hottentot, he would make her believe him or he would die in the attempt. And Wanda couldn't seem to be able to do anything about the situation. No matter what she said to this Vance Ripple, he would not vanish, and she was not DOCTOR WIZARD, and anyway, such a thing as APOCALYPTIC NECROMANCY or whatever was only for crazy people, and she had decided she was not crazy, and it was for this reason (along with an amused and wearily baffled sort of love, or at least fondness) that she finally told Vance Ripple all right, *all right,* have it *your* way; if you really want to marry me, if you really think I'll be able to do something for you, then good enough; that'll be just fine and dandy. The words, accompanied by an exasperated but not unkind smile, came after nearly a year of backing and filling with Vance Ripple, him with his dumb old hair, with the bones sticking from his dumb old wrists like maybe somebody had pierced them with broken sticks, him with his creosoted grassy breath and his by Gods and his pardon the Armenian. The words, sighed almost like a confession, came only after Wanda knew that she could rag Vance Ripple whenever she wanted, that she could holler at him whenever she wanted, that she could tell him his hair looked like something the junkman's tomcat had thrown up, that she could tell him he had his dumb banty *brass* visiting her all the time and sitting in her front room and making his indecent suggestion when all along he was supposed to have been such a close friend of her late husband, that every time he snapped those galluses of his she wanted to *scream* and *throw herself in the cistern*. But none of this seemed really to matter to Vance Ripple. It almost was as though he welcomed the insults and the ridicule and the threats. He told her insults and ridicule and threats really did not matter when a man was in love . . . when he truly was in love. And so nothing discouraged him. He would not withdraw. And he waved at her every time he happened to be clinging to a boxcar or gondola that rolled past the little place on Roundhouse Street, the place Tim had paid for in cash money, that *small* place with its *small* outhouse and its *small* rooms and its smaʟʟ ɡarden and all the rest of it, and so all right, *all right*, Wanda finally up and *admitted* it; she needed another husband to come into her life; she had to do more than clasp silence; she had to do more than munch on dry words. Oh yes, marriage to the likes of Vance Ripple probably was foolish . . . but was anything ever perfect in a world where people could happy themselves to death? So she finally accepted Vance Ripple—and, on hearing the good news, he dropped to his knees and seized both Wanda's hands and covered them with desperate little kisses.

She was sitting on the sofa in the front room. She smiled down on his damp little head. She stood up. She gently pulled him to his feet. "I expect we'd better kiss *the right way* so it's *official*," she said. She took him in her arms (she had to bend down a little), and she kissed him, and he tasted of the creosote and the grass. The taste of him was not as unpleasant as she had anticipated. This was the first time she had kissed him on the mouth, the first time ever, although Lord knows, *he* had been trying to kiss *her* on the mouth for *months.* But all she had allowed him had been pecks on the hands and cheeks and wrists. Now, though, *now,* well, a decision had been made, and Vance wheezed and even groaned a little, and she patted him on the back, and then she opened her mouth for him, and he shook and chattered like a frightened puppy floundering in a snow-storm, and perhaps she should have laughed, but laughter would have been indecent and unkind, and anyway, there was a certain slanting and unhinged *love* within her feeling for him, and this time she would work very hard to make sure everything came out fine. Vance Ripple was no Tim Harper, but then who ever would be? The world went on, and there were kinds of love and kinds of love, and a person's first responsibility was to survive.

Wanda and Vance honeymooned in White Sulphur Springs, West Virginia, and the water gave them both severe distress in their bowels. Fortunately, Vance had obtained a room in one of the better hotels, and the room had a private lavatory, and he and Wanda contended for that lavatory like two children playing King of the Mountain, sometimes even sniggering and grappling over the commode like wrestlers (she was larger, and she usually won, or at least he usually let her win), and they brayed and they clutched, and occasionally one or the other of them would release an inadvertent flatulence, and later Vance allowed as how this would all of it make quite a story to tell their friends, *quite* a story *indeed,* if only somehow they could get it to come out (so to speak) fit for the ears of decent company. And Wanda shook her head. And she felt tears. And she came looping into Vance's skinny arms. And whatever she felt no longer was slanting or unhinged. And she told him all right, *all right,* she hadn't thought it could happen twice to the same woman in the same lifetime, but she *loved* him, and he would have to make the best of it, him and his dumb hair and the sticks in his wrists. And Vance, who was standing roosterish and preposterous in his BVDs, knelt in front of her and embraced her belly. She shook her head no. She pulled him to his feet. She told him no, he did not have to *pay court* to her any longer; it was not *necessary.* And Vance nodded. He barely appeared to be breathing. He escorted her to the bed. He carefully spread her there, and his hands were gentle, and then he climbed atop her, and she was damp, and he was enormous, and he said: "I never *have* done it with a woman who *loves* me."

"Well, now you're about to," said Wanda.

"Honest to God?" said Vance.

"Yes," said Wanda.

"*You* love *me*?" said Vance.

"Yes," said Wanda.

"*Me*?" said Vance.

"You," said Wanda.

"Great day in the morning," said Vance.

"Kindly get a wiggle on," said Wanda.

So down came the BVDs, and Vance's sharp bones dug into Wanda's arms and even against her ribs, him and his dumb sharp old bones, but he was getting a *fine* wiggle on, and Wanda grinned, and she bit one of Vance's shoulders, and she bit one of her own arms, and she grinned, and she knew there weren't all that many people in the world who received second chances, and she reached down and stroked Vance's dumb damp old hair while he sucked and licked her breasts, and he wiggled to beat the band, and Wanda grinned to beat the band, and away they went, away they both went, aflopping and aroaring, and their bowels be damned, and she was so moist she could have been the source of the Paradise River plus all the lakes and all the other rivers of the earth, and Vance slid hugely, and oh my, oh my, oh my oh my oh *my*, and then it was done, and they were silent for a very long time, and neither felt constrained to visit the commode, and someone whistled *Alexander's Ragtime Band* outside in the hall, and finally it was Vance who spoke, and he said: "What with one thing and another, this here has been some honeymoon."

"That is a fact," said Wanda.

"I expect I'll remember it all the rest of my days on this here earth," said Vance.

"I surely do hope so," said Wanda.

And he unquestionably did—since all the rest of his days on the earth came to precisely thirtyseven (they had been married nine days when the conversation had taken place), and the morning of the day he died he sat at the kitchen table and said to Wanda: "I know I ain't much, and I know I'm sometimes like a clown in the Ringling Brothers, but whatever it is I *got* to give you, whatever it is I *can get* to give you, it's yours." There was a smear of egg at a corner of his mouth, and he was wearing *brown* suspenders that particular day, but there really was nothing clownish about him any more, at least not to Wanda, at least not by then. Not even his drenched ringleted hair was clownish. Not even his wrists. She loved him hugely, astonishingly, and so she ran around the table and kissed him on the mouth, and of course she tasted creosote and grass and egg, and dear Lord, everything was just as fine as fine could be, and some day perhaps she and Vance even would be able to figure out an inoffensive way to tell their friends about White Sulphur Springs and the water and their bowels; some day even *that* miracle would be accomplished, and then of course *nothing* would be impossible. So Vance went out that day and set off a boxcar on one of the Paradise Falls Clay Products Co sidings and died while throwing the switch. Cinders and gravel scraped his face, and the bridge of his nose bled a little.

Vance Ripple was of course scooped up off the track. And he was patched, stuffed, coffined, viewed, eulogized and buried (and Ewald Silger was of course nowhere to be seen), and Wanda again concentrated on the cemetery and its stone angels and obelisks and sleeping lambs, and this time she felt no clutch of worms (although she did kind of wonder whether maybe the Lord had put her on this earth to pay periodic visits to this place, perhaps like a soldier on guard duty). She managed to weep well and decently. She uttered high splintered cries when the moment came to pray over Vance for the final time and lower his coffin into the earth.

And then Wanda went home to the place on Roundhouse Street, and she sat by the muslin curtain at the front window. And sometimes she saw Ewald Silger riding loose and easy on a boxcar. But she did not wave at him. She always looked away. She fussed with her hair a great deal, and her bones became sharper, even though she was not a light eater, and even though she used up a great deal of her empty time in the preparation of enormous meals that she ate alone. She was especially fond of cakes and eggs and potatoes and fruit pies and noodles and limburger cheese. She often heard squeaking noises in her dreams. Sometimes she even saw damp ringleted red hair. She would not acknowledge the squeaking noises, nor would she acknowledge the damp ringleted red hair. She clutched at silence; she embraced it; she piled it around herself like blocks of heavy pitted tile. She worked in the garden when the weather was warm, but she fled indoors whenever anyone approached her. She kept the house clean and picked up, and from time to time she read a second letter she had received from the one and only Mr H. C. Boston, the division superintendent. This letter (also three paragraphs) was just as neat, and the wording was precisely the same, right down to the hellacious *terrible* and the scarifying *tragedy*. Oh, the *name* had been changed, of course, from *Mr Harper* to *Mr Ripple,* but the words were in exactly the same embalmed frog sequence, or at least as closely as she could recall from the first time. The first letter no longer existed. After biting away the *terrible tragedy* part, she had torn up the rest of that letter and had burned it in the kitchen stove. The second letter, though, she for some reason retained.

Margaret Ridpath found that second letter in Wanda's effects after Wanda's death in 1960. It was in a small cloth bag together with printed invitations to Wanda's two weddings, plus two ticket stubs from the Cincinnati Zoo dated June 11, 1920, plus a brochure describing the therapeutic benefits to be derived from the wholesome mineral water at White Sulphur Springs, West Virginia, plus numerous pins, plus some pennies, buttons, nickels, pincurlers, and a slim and tattered book, bound in cardboard, having something to do with Grief and the Master's insistence that it was necessary for all of us to assume our fair burden of it. As executrix of Wanda's estate, Margaret saved the pennies and the nickels, but she threw out the rest of the stuff. She did, however, glance through the book, and some of its words made a sort of shriekingly farcical sense to her. There was one passage she found especially impressive. The author, a man named F. F. Geer, of Ottumwa, Iowa (but otherwise unidentified), wrote: *By its very nature, the essence of inevitability denotes the invalidity of appeal. There, we must bow to His will. To do otherwise would be an act of the most gross and obscene sacrilege.* The passage was so moronically accurate and true that it actually made Margaret smile whenever she thought back on it. Had she been the sort to laugh, she might even have guffawed. But she was not that sort. Still, she *did* smile. Her friend Irv Berkowitz had died of a myocardial infarction the year before, while he and Margaret had been in London on a vacation that had really been a search for peace, for gentleness, for quiet days. That journey . . . oh, that blessed journey . . . had been the first time in Margaret's life (and it turned out to be the only time) that for once she had not been all that aware of her fears of iron persons and this iron planet. And so naturally Irv Berkowitz had had to go and die, and Margaret (fine obedient tinfoil Presbyterian that she was) had bowed to His will with precisely the sort of submissiveness urged by the shadowy Mr F. F. Geer, of Ottumwa, Iowa. And the raddled and blathering Inez Ridpath said to her: "Now see here, God comes like a celestial Burglar over the back fence, and He steals Jews like He steals all the rest of us, and don't think I don't know about that Jew, you and all those letters and all that running off to New York City while *I* got to sit here like an *owl* and watch Wanda hate me like she's been hating me all these years, her the hungry Miss Pussycat sitting at the foot of the tree and looking up at old Mrs Owl and telling her: *You're going to die some day, and you're going to fall down from that tree, and then I'm going to eat you up real quick before you stink.* All these years, and I get gas and the sweats just from *looking* at her and watching her hate me, and me not having done a thing to that woman in all my days. And it's a good thing *you* do the cleaning, or the dust'd *never* come off all those trophies, and *then* where'd we be, huh, you tell me? Up to our bellies in dust and fuzz and I don't know what all, and *your friend* Wanda wouldn't even bestir herself *then*. It's to distract her from hating me, and *that's* the clear cool water of the real story and *that;* I'll bet you a nickel on it, or a fountain Coke at Vance's Drug Store . . . whichever you prefer. When I was a girl, little old Inez McClory of St Louis, Missouri, a fountain Coke was called either a Coca-Cola or a Dope. A woman was more likely to call it a Coca-Cola. A man was more likely to call it a Dope. Don't ask me why. You might as well ask the moon to roll across the sky on railroad tracks."

Wanda Gwendolyn Carper Harper Ripple took her dear sweet time coming to the realization that she no longer required the silence she had gathered around herself. For sixteen years she lived alone in that little place on Roundhouse Street, and gradually she pushed back her grief and her bewilderment and the taste of the embalmed words. But not altogther. Never altogether. The grief especially never really disappeared. She could not have been that obscene. But she did finally say to herself: I am human. What am I supposed to do? Take on burdens I don't see how I deserve? I mean, if I want to look at their pictures from time to time, don't I *have* that right? (I mean, just as long as I don't look at them *too* long. I mean, just as long as I sort of *blink* over them real quick so nothing is disturbed.) And so, in 1928, Wanda asked her sister, a vague and dewlapped woman nameed Muriel Hesketh, for the return of the photographs. And Muriel smiled and said: "Ah, now you're getting your senses back, and thank the Lord."

"Maybe so," said Wanda, nodding. It was a Saturday night, and she had invited Muriel and her husband, old Fritz Hesketh, for limburger and beer. The odors were enormous and splendid.

"You're still not a badlooking woman," said Muriel. "You're not done with the world, not by a long shot. I wish *I* had your looks."

"I second the motion," said old Fritz.

"That'll be enough out of *you*," said Muriel, grinning.

"I meant about your sister still being a goodlooking woman," said Fritz.

"I *bet* you did," said Muriel.

"I *did*," said Fritz.

Wanda held up a hand. "Truce," she said. Then: "Look if you two

think I'm a goodlooking woman, I thank you very much. And you can talk
like that all you want. You can stay here until a week from next Tuesday.''

"Well, we mean it," said Muriel.

"Yes ma'am," said Fritz.

"Thank you," said Wanda. She drank some beer. It came from Joe Masonbrink, and it was a little green, but some time had passed since she had
borne him all that much of a grudge. She smiled at her sister and her brotherinlaw. She said: "You know, I sometimes go through an entire
day . . . and sometimes an entire *two* days . . . without talking to a
living soul. I mean, I keep fixing my hair and working in the garden and
scrubbing linoleum and ironing curtains, and it's like I'm getting ready for
a visit from *Mister Calvin Coolidge himself* . . . but, ah, the thing is
. . . nobody comes . . . nobody . . . and that Ewald Silger, when he
goes rolling past here, hanging onto some boxcar or whatever, he won't
even *wave* at me, even though he's *got* to be seeing me sitting at the curtain or squatting over my daffs, filling the time however I can fill it. Do
you think it would *hurt* him to *wave*—*now*, after all *this* time? I mean, he's
not single any more; he's all married up real good to that Erlanger girl
from Logan, so what difference does it make *now*, what with him having a
wife and all? It's not like I could hurt him *now* . . .''

"I don't quite understand what you're talking about," said Muriel.

"Me neither," said Fritz.

"Never mind," said Wanda. "Here. Come on, you two, take some
more of this limburger. Can't let it sit around. Couldn't afford the fumigator.''

And so Wanda came to *despise* the silence that she once had held so
valuable and had seen as so utterly necessary. And she had to do
more than simply push it back. It had become a malignancy—and when it
did, there came a purpose to her vigil at the front curtain, and the bread
man, the ice man, the spent and spotted survey takers and broom salesmen all became immense to her, punctuating her days like great claps
from the sky. Not that she *did* anything with them. Lord, *no*. There never
was any of the You Know involved in it. Vance Ripple was the last man
who ever touched her. But she surely did *talk* with everyone who came
along. And her fruit pies surely were delicious. And many were the flabbergasted survey takers and broom salesmen who came belching away

from her place, bowing and grinning and picking their teeth after listening
to Wanda speak to them of Clara Bow and Mister Hoover and hard times,
of Communists and the bonus marchers, saying: "Now just what would
you have done if you were the President of the United States and a million
red agitators just went and squatted on your front lawn? Agitators. How
come so many people got to agitate? The way *I* was brought up, you *did*
with what you *had*, and maybe then some day you got *more*, or maybe
you *didn't*, but you thanked the Lord for what you *did* have, and you sure
as Sam Hill didn't go around making a mess out of Our Nation's Capital.
Here. Have another piece of this pie. A spoiled pie is a waste of the
Lord's bounty, and it smells funny, too. Can't let it sit around. Couldn't
afford the fumigator."

Wanda's ridiculous sinus condition didn't really come all abloom
and take command of her voice until about 1930 or so. At first she
was not aware of it, but then one afternoon, while she and the bread man,
Julius Purdue, were sharing some banana cream cake in the kitchen (it
was *her* banana cream cake, out of *her* stove, not *his* banana cream cake,
out of *his* truck), she said something having to do with the weather, and
Julius found the remark very funny. He turned his face away, but not before she saw that he was grinning. And then she saw his shoulders shake.
And then there came from his throat a series of suppressed hollow noises,
almost like whinnying horses heard from a substantial distance. Wanda
frowned. What had she said that had been so funny? Julius Purdue was a
sober and hardworking family man, the father of five strapping sons, and
he simply was not the sort to grin and whinny for no reason, and so the
first thing Wanda asked herself was: Do I talk so stupid as all that? I say to
the man that the weather's been awful cool for August, and so he has to
turn his head away because I'm so stupid—is *that* it? (When a person lives
alone for a number of years, this sort of concern becomes enormous.) So
Wanda put down her fork. She made fists. She spoke stiffly. She said: "I
was not aware I said anything all that funny."

Julius tried to gulp down his laughter. His neck reddened.

"Well?" said Wanda.

More gulps. Julius looked at Wanda and attempted to speak but could
not. The corners of his mouth were smudged with cake. He wiped at
them.

"I surely must be a real sketch," said Wanda.

Julius shook his head no. He was sweating now, but why should he be sweating on such a cool August day?

"Then what's so *funny*?" Wanda wanted to know. "You ought to see your *neck*. You could take it to George Froelich's grocery store or the A & P and *sell* it like it was a *tomato*. Or a *radish* or a *beet* or some such thing."

Julius held up a hand. He cleared his throat. He swallowed. The color drained. He wiped his face with a handkerchief. He swallowed, nodded. Now the grin was gone, and he said: "I'm sorry. It's just that lately . . ."

Wanda waited, but apparently Julius could not continue, and so she asked him straight out: "It's just that that lately *what*?"

"Ah . . ."

"Ah *what*?"

"Ah . . . well . . . Wanda, you see, your voice . . . "

"My voice *what*?"

"It's like . . . ah, it's like something is . . . ah . . . trying to stuff your voice up your, ah, *nose* . . . "

"Up my *what*?"

"Your *nose*," said Julius. "Up your *nose*."

Wanda looked at Julius Purdue. She looked through him.

Julius made an apologetic movement with his hands and arms and shoulders.

Wanda nodded.

"I'm sorry," said Julius.

"Surely," said Wanda. Now the taste of the cake was sour. She opened her mouth. She closed her mouth. She snuffled. She did not *want* to snuffle, but she did snuffle. She softly cleared her throat. Then she said: "Now do I sound better?"

"No," said Julius.

"This isn't some sort of joke, is it?"

"No," said Julius.

"I didn't think so," said Wanda. She snuffled more loudly. She coughed. She swallowed. She cleared her throat more loudly. "*Now* maybe?" she said.

"No," said Julius, and then he again was forced to make noises. They came this time as a series of knotted bleats and mewlings, soprano and demented, and he stood up, and his belly danced with mirth, and he said: "I mean oh ha ha ha . . . I'm really sorry, Wanda . . . but ah ha oh ha ha sometimes when a person gets on a laughing jag . . . I mean, oh ho ho ho . . . dear sweet Jesus . . . the least little things set him off, if you ha ha ha know what I mean . . . Wanda, you're a ha ha good woman, and you'll hate me oh ha hor hor hor hee hee for saying this, but ha ha, oh my oh *my* . . . your voice has turned into the goddamnedest funniest . . . oh ho ho . . . the . . . well . . . I ho ho ho hee hee got no words for it . . . ''

Wanda stared at him. She could not move.

Julius shook his head, and tears ran down his face. He lurched out the kitchen door, and she heard him laughing all the way around the house as he stumbled back to his truck, which was parked out front. A locomotive hooted, and somewhere someone's radio was saying something flattering about Cliquot Club. Wanda stood up and went into the bedroom. She walked to the mirror and opened her mouth and studied her teeth and her tongue and her throat. She moved her tongue this way and that; she reached up and pulled back her lips. She saw nothing unusual, but then it hadn't been her teeth and her tongue and her throat Julius had been *talking* about. It had been her *nose*. Up your *nose,* he had said. Up your *nose.* So now, using her thumbs, Wanda spread her nostrils. She blinked at them. They appeared no different than they ever had. They were nostrils, nothing more. She pinched them together. She shrugged. "So I god a fuddy voice dat's like id's comin oud my *mou* buh somebody's stuffin id bag up my *node,*" she said. "Well, aid tha grad?"

Wanda did have a sense of what was right and what was important, and so she did not weep over whatever it was that had happened to her voice. She had wept over her *husbands,* of course, which had been *right,* which had been *important.* But her tattered and silly voice was a much smaller cross . . . oh, a *cross* certainly, but not of the most profound rank. And anyway, it wasn't all *that* terrible, once a person became used to it, and it certainly didn't have any adverse effect on her cakes or her fruit pies or her daffs. After all, one did not *talk* a pie into being tasty, correct? And so, even after his pained and reluctant hysterics, Julius Purdue always was welcome in her home. It was several weeks before he returned, but return he did, and she said nothing about his laughter, and she fed him two pieces of apple strudel, and he told her it surely was better than anything his own company offered (he worked for the Snowden Bakery Co of Columbus, Lancaster, Newark, Zanesville, Logan, Athens,

Nelsonville and Paradise Falls), and then he made what could have been a choking noise. Looking away from her, he said: "You're a goodhearted woman, and you got a generous, forgiving soul."

"Bushwah," said Wanda.

"Don't you bushwah *me*," said Julius. "I know what I know."

Wanda smiled.

Julius looked at her. He saw the smile. He nodded. He allowed himself a smile, too.

She very nearly reached across the table and touched one of his hands.

"Thank you," he said.

She told him pshaw, he was thanking her for nothing at all. She went on to say that she'd had hearttoheart chats with her sister Muriel and a number of friends (including the ice man, old Lloyd Box, and a fellow who collected every month for some encyclopedia firm located in East St Louis, Illinois), and they all had agreed that her voice had indeed acquired a new and peculiar sound to it, and Muriel even had said that it sounded as though Wanda were trying to suck words up her nose. Yes indeed, up her *nose*. Then, shaking her head, she told Julius she certainly didn't want him to think that he stood alone. Julius nodded, and he told her he was grateful for the information. It was unclear to him, though, that some *encyclopedia fellow* from *East St Louis, Illinois,* would have been able to know anything about the difference between the old Wanda Ripple voice and this shredded new Wanda Ripple voice. *How* would he have known? Was he a regular visitor or what? And could he really be called a *friend*? What sort of life was it *Wanda* led when she thought of *herself* as a friend of a man who was in *that* line of work? Julius finally asked Wanda precisely that question, and she told him: "Oh, why, Mr Donaldson has been stopping by for *years*, and I've never even bought an encyclopedia set from him. I guess it's just that he likes to sit here and eat cake or pie or whatever and take a load off his feet. Which for *him* is probably a relief. He tells me he was wounded in the leg at Belleau Wood, and I can *believe* it, seeing as how he's got such a bad limp and all. The poor man, not exactly the youngest rooster in the barnyard but real nice, if you know what I mean. *Nice*."

"You sure do take to people, don't you?" said Julius.

"I've learned to," said Wanda.

"What?"

"If you don't take to people," said Wanda, "you sit alone . . . and there's not much to be said for *that*, believe you *me*."

"You ought to get married again," said Julius.

"Not hardly likely," said Wanda. "Twice burned is twice warned, or however it goes."

"That's a shame," said Julius.

"Well," said Wanda, "I expect the world will survive."

"I expect so," said Julius.

"This voice of mine is *nothing*. I mean, compared to other things."

"True enough."

"I'll get along," said Wanda.

"Wouldn't surprise me a bit," said Julius.

Wanda did get along, and later—when she and Inez Ridpath went to war with one another—she did more than get along; she became *necessary*. Her life sorted itself out, and she never again was lonely. As for her absurd voice, well, it remained with her until the end of her days, but she did manage to modulate it most of the time, and she always carried two handkerchiefs for the blowing of her nose. Her physician was a man named Button, and he told her she had developed something called an allergy, but he was unable to discover the allergy's source. (Perhaps it was fruit pies. Perhaps it was limburger. Perhaps it was daffs or creosote or frankfurters or green beer or pincurlers or linoleum or grass. Who knew? Only the Lord, and He was—as usual—keeping His own counsel.) But the fact is this: Like a wen or a wart or some sort of immense purplish birthmark, an absurd voice subsides in absurdity the more familiar it becomes. And so nothing really changed in the life of Wanda Gwendolyn Carper Harper Ripple. In her middle thirties she began to gray rapidly, and a great deal of tone went out of her flesh, but her bones sharpened (despite all the cake and pie and limburger and beer that she took to assaulting with more and more zeal), and she told her sister: "By rights I ought to weigh about three hundred pounds, but it just doesn't work out that way for everyone. Maybe my allergy is an allergy to *fat* . . . what do you think of *that* notion, huh?"

Muriel and her husband, old Fritz Hesketh, were sitting with Wanda in her kitchen. It was another Saturday night, and the colossal odor of the limburger was an inspiration. Fritz was leaning back in his chair, and he appeared to be about half asleep, and a bottle of Joe Masonbrink's green beer was pressed against his shirtfront. Muriel sliced him a fine hunk of the limburger, nudged his belly and told him: "Here. Take some of this. It'll wake you up. Put hair on your chest."

"Who?" said Fritz, blinking open his eyes.

"Not *who*," said Muriel, laughing. "I'm . . . I'm talking about *what*, you ninny. I'm talking about this here cheese. I want to cut down some of the effect of that there beer. In a little bit, I got to walk home a whole seven squares with you, and I'll be *switched* if I'll *carry* you, not with that old tummytum *you* got.''

Fritz frowned a little. "I was just resting my eyes," he said.

Muriel grinned at Wanda.

"Resting my eyes," said Fritz, shaking his head.

"From what?" said Muriel. "Looking at beer bottles?"

Wanda laughed. So did Fritz . . . a little. He took the cheese from his wife. He ate the cheese while still pressing the bottle of beer against his shirtfront. He washed down the cheese with beer. Gently he belched. "Hey," he said, "I feel like I just got my old crankshaft reamed out." He smiled at Muriel. "I thank you kindly," he said.

"Think nothing of it," said Muriel to her husband.

Wanda was working on her fourth beer, and she felt warm and benevolent. "You're good people," she said. "You're the . . . best . . ."

"You're not so bad yourself," said Muriel.

"I am much . . . obliged," said Wanda.

Muriel leaned forward. "Can I speak to my baby sister straight from the shoulder?"

"Ah . . . surely," said Wanda.

"You got to start giving yourself more credit. You—"

"What?"

"Now hear me out," said Muriel. "*Hear. Me. Out.* Don't break in. What I'm trying to say is that you're absolutely right, Wanda—you *don't* weigh three hundred pounds, and you got no growth on your neck, and you speak up to people just as nice as anybody, so how come you got to just *sit* here all the time? I mean, it's been a good spell now since Tom died and then Vance, and I expect . . . if you *wanted* to, and never mind that your voice don't exactly make the world forget Miss Gladys Swarthout . . . I expect you could *do* more. Woman like you, keeps a neat house, washes her floors and irons her curtains all the time, keeps her hair just so, fixes the best cakes and pies in Paradise County—why, a woman like *that* has got a lot of *value* to the world, and she shouldn't just *sit* here and wait for *Julius Purdue* and old *Lloyd Box* and maybe some *insurance drummer* to come along and talk to her and eat her cake and make it so her days don't clap together like loose boards in a high wind. Seems to me a woman like *that* has got a whole lot more to *give,* if you follow me."

"No," said Wanda.

"Pardon me?" said Muriel.

"I don't think I got more to give," said Wanda to her sister. "I mean, if you're trying to tell me I should go out looking for a new husband, that's *one* thing that's *never* going to happen. I already have put *two* good men in the ground, and two are two too many."

"*You* didn't put them in the ground," said Muriel. "It was acts of God."

Wanda sighed. She drank more of the green beer, and bubbles moved around in her chest. "All I know is," she said, "they were married to *me*. They weren't married to *you*, and they weren't married to *Aimee Semple McPherson*. And in fifteen months they both were gone. And I really loved them. *Loved* them. And so what happened? They just didn't last hardly at all, did they? And especially Vance. Poor Vance. We hardly got a chance to shake hands and say howdo, and it was goodbye, Vance, sleep tight and try to keep the devil away . . ."

Old Fritz Hesketh slumped back. "Hooray for my . . . good old . . . crankshaft . . ." he said, closing his eyes.

Muriel glared at him. "My hero," she said.

Wanda smiled. She was a little sleepy. "It's all right," she said.

"I *know* you loved your husbands," said Muriel to Wanda, "but what's *that* got to do with the terrible . . . with, well, *you* know . . . with them dying so quick?"

"Maybe if I was to have *hated* them," said Wanda, pressing her beer bottle against a cheek, "they'd be alive today."

"Oh dear God," said Muriel.

"Think on it," said Wanda.

"I'll think on no such a thing," said Muriel. "I've never heard such foolishness in all my life."

"*Me*," said Wanda, "*I* think on it a whole lot."

Which was true. Even though Wanda had at least partially disentangled herself from the silence she now despised (thanks mostly to her baking and the reasonably frequent visitors her baking attracted), she still saw herself as somehow having inflicted some sort of brainless malediction on her two late husbands—and perhaps her *love* had been the instrument of their destruction. Again—her *love*. She looked around, and she saw dozens of women who had loveless marriages (Muriel surely was one of them), and she knew that some of those women (not Muriel, though) actively *hated* their husbands . . . but most of *those* marriages, the loveless marriages and the hating marriages, were uneventful and even serene, at least to an outsider. *Those* women's husbands went swimming safely; *those* women's husbands did not keel over while throwing a switch. *Those* women bred children and paraded their families to church every Sunday morning, with birds all atwitter and everywhere a murmur of polite conversation, and the hapless unloved husbands of *those* women were most attentive, and the poor fellows grinned; they tipped their skimmers; they bowed a little and they spoke of farm prices and mortgage rates and railroad wrecks and automobile cylinders, and you just *knew* that they and their wives never *once* had played King of the Mountain over a commode, and you just *knew* that they would be *scandalized* by the very *notion* of such a vulgar and preposterous bit of silliness. And yet the only thing was—*those* marriages went on and on, without incident. Longevity records were established. Silver wedding anniversaries were celebrated. *Golden* wedding anniversaries were celebrated. So what was the logical conclusion to be reached from all this? That lovelessness and even downright hate were more *healthy* and *proper* and *natural* and kept a body alive longer? It surely was something for Wanda to muse over while digging in her garden, or stabbing and fussing with her curling iron, or mixing pie filling, or chatting with the men who stopped by to gobble up her goodies. It surely was something to muse over while sitting at her muslin curtains and waiting for Julius Purdue . . . or old Lloyd Box . . . or anyone . . . *anyone at all* . . . to stop by and acknowledge her existence. She sat there primly hour after hour, day after day, and her knees were drawn tightly together, and no man would be so unfortunate as to spread them ever again, and she listened to her hair soften and droop and turn gray, and she felt her bones sharpen, and she felt her flesh resolve itself into strings and knots, and sometimes she wondered what her hollow and tattered voice sounded like to the rest of the world (a person never heard his own voice the way the rest of the world heard it, she had been told), and every now and then she asked herself: If God sits all holy and proud in all of us the way Scripture says, and if Tim and Vance died because of *acts* of God the way *Muriel* says, then *I'm* just as responsible as *the Lord* is. I mean, as long as *He's* in *me,* then it all keeps going around and around, and there's no getting away from any of it. Which means, I suppose, I'm just straight flatout crazy.

Crazy or not, that was how Wanda Gwendolyn Carper Harper Ripple saw the situation . . . even after she was visited by a young woman named Miss Margaret Ridpath one day in May of 1938. To Wanda Gwendolyn Carper Harper Ripple, if you were standing at a blackboard in a classroom, you could take a piece of chalk and firmly write LOVE = DEATH and the teacher would mark down a large bold 100% next to your name, and then you could take that same piece of chalk and just as firmly write HATE = LIFE, and wouldn't the teacher have to mark down *another* large bold 100% next to your name? And didn't it follow that you would be acclaimed far and wide for the extent of your wisdom? Wanda firmly believed all this, and anyone who tried to play King of the Mountain over a commode was doomed, and she invited disbelievers to consult a book entitled *The Majesty of Grief*, by F. F. Geer, of Ottumwa, Iowa. In that book it was written: *The glory of acceptance fair shreds the soul with its beauty! If we accept Him, then all contradictions and ironies cease to exist! Dust to water! Stones to feathers! Birds to reptiles! Nothing is impossible! There are no mysteries within the Mind of the great governing Intelligence!*

So why not then LOVE = DEATH and HATE = LIFE?

If Mr F. F. Geer's words were true, then Wanda's theory was true.

And so Mr F. F. Geer's book became enormously valuable to her.

It all simply meant: God surely did have sneaky and peculiar ways of going about his business.

Then came the day Wanda was visited by this Miss Margaret Ridpath. It was a Sunday afternoon, heavy and gray and a little muggy, but Wanda was not sitting at her curtains when Miss Ridpath came along. As luck would have it, Wanda was out back in the privy, and so she did not hear Miss Ridpath's knock. It wasn't until Miss Ridpath began hollering yoohoo that Wanda hastily dabbed at herself, rose from the Throne, pulled up her bloomers and came arunning. (This was a new voice. It was not Muriel's voice. It was not the voice of any of the neighborhood women. It was a voice Wanda never before had heard, and she said to herself: I am surely glad I baked that chocolate cake last night.) It turned out that this Miss Ridpath was quite a pretty young woman, even though sometimes she displayed too many teeth when she smiled and even though she *was* a little large in the bust, at least in comparison with Wanda. But Wanda did recognize Miss Ridpath from Steinfelder's, even though she (Wanda) seldom bought anything there, not being all that rich. And Wanda seemed to recall that Miss Ridpath's father had been a pet doctor who had killed himself or had drunk himself to death or some such thing. Ah, but it was not fair to visit the weaknesses of the father on the daughter, and anyway, what on *earth* could such a person as *Miss Margaret Ridpath* want with *Wanda*? And so, for all Wanda cared, Miss Ridpath's father could have been responsible for the Sack of Rome and the Rape of the Sabine Maidens. The thing of it was—*Miss Ridpath* was *here,* and Wanda didn't know whether to whoop or poop. It turned out Miss Ridpath had a shy voice, and she sort of held back when Wanda insisted she come into the kitchen for a piece of fresh homemade chocolate cake and maybe a nice glass of milk, good sweet *thick* milk from the Omar Peterson farm, milk that was generally acknowledged to be the best in Paradise County. (There was something about Omar Peterson's cows, or the way he took care of them, or his grazing acreage . . .) And Wanda kept talking and talking as she ushered the reluctant Miss Ridpath into the kitchen, and naturally Wanda was about to *burst* out of curiosity as to why such a person as *Miss Ridpath* would come calling on *Wanda Ripple* on a Sunday afternoon down here on tacky old *Roundhouse Street,* with the damp air pressing down a stink of coalgas that was enough to make a hog burp. Perhaps Miss Ridpath's errand really was important—and didn't it almost *have* to be? Otherwise, she surely would not have been *here* on a *Sunday afternoon.* (Sundays always were Wanda's worst days as far as the silences went, and she hated Sundays, and that was the unfortunate fact of the matter. There was no bread delivery on Sundays. Nor was there ice delivery. Nor did survey takers or salesmen come to call. And yet *now* . . . *here* . . . *right now* . . . *all of a sudden* . . . a young woman of some standing in the community was sitting in Wanda's kitchen, and it all was a happy miracle, and so Wanda silently rejoiced as she cut an enormous slice of the cake and poured a large glass of milk for her guest . . . *Omar Peterson's* milk, an *apotheosis* of milk, so thick you could just about spread it on a piece of bread.) Miss Ridpath smiled shyly as she ate her cake and drank her milk, and she told Wanda my, such a delicious snack. She and Wanda then spoke briefly of the weather, and it wasn't until she was done with her cake and her milk that she came to the point. "I know it's rude to come calling unannounced this way," said Miss Ridpath, "especially on a Sunday afternoon, but you see, Mrs Ripple, you have no telephone, and so I just had to take the bull by the horns, so to speak, and, ah, come calling unannounced." Miss Ridpath hesitated. Now *she* was talking too much, explaining too much, and she knew it.

Helping her, speaking quickly, Wanda said: "Oh, no. That's . . . ah, there's nothing to concern yourself about. I live alone, and most of the time I just poke around the house, you know what I mean?"

"Yes," said Miss Ridpath.

"Oh?" said Wanda.

"Ah, that's what Julius Purdue told me," said Miss Ridpath.

"Oh?" said Wanda. She was a little miffed. She would have to speak with Julius. She didn't want him to be making her out to be an object of pity. He was no friend of hers if he was doing such a thing.

"It's why he said you might be interested," said Miss Ridpath. "He is very fond of you, do you know that?"

"Well," said Wanda, "that's nice to hear." She frowned. What was it she was supposed to be interested in? What had Julius been discussing with Miss Ridpath?

"That was really very good cake," said Miss Ridpath.

"I thank you kindly," said Wanda. "Would you care for another piece?"

"Oh, no," said Miss Ridpath. "No, thank you."

"There's plenty. And plenty more milk, too."

"No," said Miss Ridpath. "Thank you very much, but I have no more room."

"Was it my baked goods you and Julius were talking about?" Wanda wanted to know. "I mean, did you come over here to sample a little? You want to know something? There have been *some* people who've suggested that I go into the bakery business, but of course I got no money for that sort of foolishness. And with these times and all."

Miss Ridpath smiled a little. "No," she said, "the cake was a bonus." She carefully wiped at her mouth with a napkin. "I'm here because, well, because it hasn't only been Julius Purdue who's spoken so well of you. There's been Lloyd Box, for instance. And Fritz Hesketh, for another instance. Fritz Hesketh, your brotherinlaw. Well, anyway, Fritz was working on our roof and downspouts last week, and we got to talking a little, and he told me yes, his wife's sister might be interested. He told me yes, Mrs Ripple might just be interested in making a little bit of change."

"Interested in *what*?" said Wanda. Impatience scratched at the edge of her voice like bright little shreds of glass. She was able to feel the action of her heart, and she supposed she was being a dumb ninny, and maybe she was going through some premonition of The Change. Any second now perhaps a hot flash would come up.

"Yes," said Miss Ridpath. "I should stop tiptoeing all around Robin Hood's Barn, shouldn't I?" She nodded. "Ah, my sister Sarah and I live with our mother, but Sarah is getting married next month and moving out, and, ah . . . well, you see . . . I am away all day at Steinfelder's . . . and, ah, I was wondering if perhaps you would be . . . um, interested . . . well, you see, Mother isn't *dangerous* or anything like *that*, but she *does* need someone to look after her, and . . . what with all the good things I've been hearing about you . . . I was wondering whether perhaps you'd give, ah, some thought to coming and living with us. Now, ah, please don't misunderstand. It's not as though Mother is some sort of, ah, doddering *invalid* . . . but she *does* need someone to be on hand in case . . . well, just in case she might . . . oh, I don't know . . . fall down maybe . . . or forget to button up her dress . . . I . . . well, what I'm trying to say is . . . some people get that way sometimes . . . little parts of them come loose . . . or whatever . . . if you know what I mean . . ."

"Oh," said Wanda. Really, if she were altogether honest, she already would have said yes to this Miss Ridpath. Because she *would* accept; *that* she *knew*. In a real way that had nothing to do with pies or limburger, she was about to become *necessary*. But for some reason Wanda decided that for once in her life she would give the impression that she could take a proposition or leave it alone. She would not appear too eager. She would imitate a cucumber (for however long as she could, which probably wouldn't be very long at all).

"I would be able to pay you fifteen dollars a week, plus room and board of course," said Miss Ridpath. She spoke quickly, a little breathlessly. "And your Sundays would be free. And I'd cook most of the breakfasts and suppers. All you'd be responsible for would be the noon meal . . . and keeping an eye on her. And, oh yes, now and then I go away to Columbus or Cleveland or Cincinnati for a bridge tournament, and I'm gone perhaps two or three nights, which means of course that you would have to—"

"Can I ask you a straight question?" said Wanda.

"Certainly," said Miss Ridpath.

"Is she crazy?"

"A little," said Miss Ridpath.

Wanda nodded. "Thank you for the straight answer," she said. "I appreciate that."

"Well, it's nothing you wouldn't find out for yourself right away," said Miss Ridpath.

"Yes, but some people would hem and haw."

"Um, but she's not *dangerous*," said Miss Ridpath. "She won't come after you with a butcher knife. There's no such a thing as *dangerous* in this."

"You've come down hard on that," said Wanda.

"I want it to be clear," said Miss Ridpath.

"There's something else I need to know," said Wanda.

"I'll tell you if I can," said Miss Ridpath.

"Is she lovable?" said Wanda.

"What?"

"I want to *know*," said Wanda. "Is she *lovable*?"

Miss Ridpath shrugged. Her palms pressed the surface of the table. "Ah, she is *my* mother, and so *I* love her."

Wanda nodded. "All right," she said. "Fine. She is *your* mother, and *you* love her. But what about the rest of the world? How does the rest of the world feel about her? How do you think *I* would feel about her? Are you sure you wouldn't like another piece of cake? I could make it a little one."

"No thank you," said Miss Ridpath. "*Really*. But it *was* delicious, though. Don't think it wasn't."

"Lovability is very important to me," said Wanda. "I had two husbands, and I loved them both very much."

Miss Ridpath's bewilderment showed mostly in the corners of her eyes, which were gray and quite large. She said: "Lovability?"

"Yes," said Wanda. "Now, please, I'm sorry, Miss Ridpath, but I need to have my question answered—how does the rest of the world feel about your mother?"

Miss Ridpath looked at her hands. "I have a brother and two sisters," she said, "and I expect *they* love her too. But as for the *rest* of the world . . . I don't suppose the rest of the world cares much one way or the other . . ."

"Oh," said Wanda.

"Why does it matter?" Miss Ridpath wanted to know.

Wanda briefly shook her head. She made a deprecating movement with a hand. "It doesn't really matter," she said. "It's just that sometimes I get silly notions in my old noggin about lovability."

"Oh," said Miss Ridpath, and it was clear she didn't have the slightest idea what Wanda was trying to say.

"Lovability hurts when the lovable person is taken away," said Wanda.

"Oh yes," said Miss Ridpath.

Wanda's eyes were warm. She said nothing. She blinked at Miss Ridpath, and she wanted to stuff Miss Ridpath with cake so that Miss Ridpath would know how much—

"My father used to say something to that effect," said Miss Ridpath. 'He was a veterinarian, but we never had pets in our home. According to Father, the pets would become too . . . ah, *cherished* . . . and we'd eel too badly when they died. Or at least that's the way Father saw the situation."

Wanda nodded.

Miss Ridpath smiled vaguely. "Distance perhaps is better," she said.

"Oh, lovability is fine *in its place*," said Wanda.

"A nice way to put it," said Miss Ridpath. "*In its place.* Yes. Fine."

"Thank you," said Wanda.

"Ah," said Miss Ridpath, "perhaps I *would* like another piece of that fine cake of yours . . . "

"Very *good*," said Wanda. "And another glass of milk?"

"Yes, please," said Miss Ridpath.

There was no question about accepting Miss Ridpath's offer. After sixteen years of living alone, Wanda surely knew that even the company of a crazy woman was better than the aloneness, and all the silence, and the curlers, and the foolish curtained vigils, and all those delicious and pathetic pies and cakes, baked with agonizing care for the *bread man* or the *ice man* or whatever stray visitor happened to wander into the kitchen. So Wanda sold the Roundhouse Street house for three thousand seven hundred dollars, realizing a profit of two hundred dollars over the original purchase price. This remarkable sum, when averaged over the eighteen years since Tim Harper had bought the place in 1920, came to eleven dollars and eleven cents a year . . . not exactly a killing, but then it *was* Roundhouse Street, and your Vanderbilts and your Rockefellers weren't exactly trampling one another in their anxiety to buy property there. So Wanda took her three thousand seven hundred dollars and was grateful to have it. The purchaser was a bachelor schoolteacher named John Dietz, and he told her she should not fret herself; he would not let the house fall into rack and ruin, and he certainly would work very diligently on the grounds. He allowed as how he was especially fond of flower gardening, and he said he looked forward to using the old elbow grease on the soil in the front yard. "When I came here to look at the place," said John Dietz, "I could tell first thing off the bat that you'd done a lot of gardening yourself—and it showed me the sort of person I wanted to do business with. A person who has respect for grounds is a person of substance . . . a person worth cultivating, if you'll excuse my little joke . . ." (John Dietz always called the tiny front yard the *grounds*, and Wanda had trouble not laughing in his face. But he was too serious a man this John Dietz, despite his talk of persons worth cultivating, and he would not have understood the laughter. In addition to his teaching duties, he coached the football team at Paradise Falls High School, and he was said to be a severe taskmaster. Wanda wondered whether he would give pep talks to the roses and the begonias. Exhortations: *Grow straight and tall and brilliant, damn your eyes!* Florid urgings: *You there, third begonia from the left! You're getting just as much sunlight as the rest of them, and there's no excuse for you to droop and wither that way, and I won't have it, so pull yourself together!*) The sale of Wanda's house was completed a week before Sarah Ridpath married the handsome Pete Saddler, and Wanda also sold off most of her household possessions, netting herself another two hundred dollars. And so, when she moved into the Ridpath home and began overseeing Inez Ridpath, she was worth close to four thousand dollars, and the money was a comfort. Which was just as well. After all, this crazy Inez Ridpath might drop dead or something, and *then* where would Wanda be? Miss Ridpath would have no further use for her, and so she would be dismissed, and where would she go? To live with Muriel and Fritz? *Never!* The county home? *Worse yet!* And anyway, she had three thousand nine hundred dollars, and so she would not even *qualify* for the county home. No indeedy bob and *sir,* that money, in addition to the two small C&O pensions, in addition to the two small insurance policies, would shield her from the cold nights just very well indeed, thank you very much. And yet . . . well, and *yet* . . . whenever Wanda thought about her money and the protection it afforded, she was not all that comforted. It was the sort of thinking that implied some day she would have to return to her curtained vigils and her pathetic pies. And it was the sort of thinking she could not abide. What is more despicable than silence . . . really, what *is?* Wanda knew all there was to know about silence, and it was the largest enemy she ever had encountered. Now and then, instead of thinking of her husbands' deaths, she thought of her own death, and she hooked her fingers and palms into claws, and she tightened, and she heard the forever *silence* of death, and it angered her as much as it frightened her . . . that endless cottony *void,* without even the occasional sound of a horse or a locomotive or a faroff radio, let alone a kind voice or a laugh or an expression of love. And so, even before Wanda met Miss Ridpath's mother, she determined that she would project and preserve the woman until hell was turned into a skating rink, world without end, bless the Lord. And of course Wanda summoned to mind her special formula, and she saw the special blackboard, and the special words were LOVE = DEATH and HATE = LIFE, and therefore she determined that she would under no circumstances ever love the crazy woman, this Inez Ridpath. That way, Inez Ridpath would survive. That way, Wanda would be necessary. And this was before Wanda even had set eyes on Inez Ridpath.

Her experiences with Tim and Vance had taught Wanda nothing if they had not taught her the hazards and the outright fatal futility of *love,* and she would not make that mistake with the crazy woman. She would *hate* the crazy woman with energy and unswerving concentration, and therefore the crazy woman would live forever, and therefore Wanda would have a job forever, and never again would Wanda have to go someplace and rattle around all alone. And she praised God. (*If we accept Him, then all contradictions and ironies cease to exist! Dust to water! Stones to feathers! Birds to reptiles! Nothing is impossible!*) And so Wanda oiled all her gears and greased all her spokes and cranked herself into an immediate war with an uncomprehending Inez Ridpath, and the war lasted twentytwo years, and Inez Ridpath remained more or less healthy as a brood mare. She and Wanda sat in the Ridpath parlor for hour upon merciless hour of those twentytwo years, Inez Ridpath in her antimacassared chair and Wanda on the sofa and sometimes the windowseat, and they exchanged insults that now and then were heated but more often were fleshless and desultory, and Margaret's bridge trophies proliferated all around them, looming heavily on the mantel, squatting on tables, sitting all atumble in a bookcase. And Wanda glared at Inez Ridpath. And Wanda watched Inez Ridpath's nose run, and the sight was enough to make Wanda sick—but Wanda never offered to wipe the harpy's leaking nostrils; to have done so would perhaps have revealed concern, which would have been dangerous. Concern sat too closely to love, and love simply could not be allowed to be possible. So Wanda told Inez Ridpath that she (Wanda) was there only because of the worst luck, what with two husbands dying on her. And Inez Ridpath told Wanda that she (Wanda) was there because nobody else wanted her, and why not face facts instead of telling stories that would make a jubjub bird blush? And Inez Ridpath writhed comfortably in her antimacassared chair after getting off *that* one, and so Wanda said to her: "I came here because your daughter is a decent girl and I don't want to see you ruining her by strapping her down with your peculiar ways so she won't have any sort of life of her own. If you think anything *else,* you're not only *crazy*; you're *stupider* than Adam's off ox."

Inez Ridpath's comfortable writhing stopped. "I've never done anything to you," she said. "I didn't even *know* you before you came here. So how come we got to *do* all this . . . I mean, how come we got to *talk* the way we do?"

"You ought to be grateful you got somebody to talk to *at all,*" said

Wanda. "Never mind whether or not I *like* you. I wasn't *hired* to *like* you. The important thing is—I'm here. I change you when you wet yourself. You disgust me, but I do for your daughter what I promised her I would do, and by jumbo you're not going to make me go back on my promise . . . and I don't care *how* disgusting you get."

"Promise?" said Inez Ridpath. "What sort of promise? To sit here all day and treat me like a cockroach?"

"I treat you the way you deserve to be treated," said Wanda. "A woman who won't even bother to wash her private parts. What am I supposed to do? Write to your friend Roosevelt and get him to give you a medal?"

Fluttering a hand, Inez Ridpath said: "I'm hungry. Did you make me a lime pie today? I used to make a fine lime pie myself, but *he* never liked my lime pies, said they were too tart for his taste . . . and this despite the fact that Paul and the girls all liked my lime pies; they said the lime made their teeth feel good."

"I was talking about your private parts," said Wanda.

Inez Ridpath's voice was thoughtful and remote, like quiet old friends dimly heard in the next room. "A nice tasty lime pie," she said.

Wanda sighed. "Lord have mercy," she said.

"A lime pie with homemade whipped cream on top," said Inez Ridpath, "and oh, weren't we talking about cockroaches just now? Well, you can forget the cockroach for *my* piece of lime pie. Never liked cockroach on lime pie. Never liked the flavor. It's like basting a porterhouse steak with prune juice, ah hah, if you can imagine such a thing. Say, do you know that His Nibs worried all the time about the Russians and what he called the criminal syndicalists? He said nobody was safe. He said they'd as leave blow up the post office as blow their own noses. I'd eat my lime pie, and he'd swill away at his beer, and he'd say to me: 'Inez, there's more to this life than meets the eye, what with people running around behind your back and meeting in cellars and plotting things you just can't imagine. So you got to watch yourself at all times, and that is a fact.'" Inez Ridpath hesitated. She snuffled. She shook her head. She smiled. It was only a brief smile, though, and then it went away, and she said: "Well, that's where that late husband of mine really *was* right, even though dumb old *me* didn't know *how* right at the *time*, if you get what I mean. That is to say, he was telling me things like that at the same time as *he* was running around behind *my* back, and maybe *they* were meeting in cellars too. Or sewers. Or I don't know where all. But it was Dorothy Hall, if you can *imagine* such a thing. *Dorothy Hall.* Not somebody *pretty* and *vivacious* and *young*, somebody I could at least *understand* where the *attraction* was, but *Dorothy Hall*, who was about as *pretty* as your aver-

age *horse trough* or *fireplug* or *pile of sand,* if you follow what I mean.
And great God, *I* was prettier than *her*; you can just ask anybody. Maybe
you remember her. Do you remember her? What? How's that? Cat got
your tongue? Oh . . . *well* . . . all right, *don't* talk. Just *sit* there. Fine.
Let the old lunatic get it all out of her system. Hey, you ever stop to realize how much pain there's got to be when a person just ups and steps in
front of an *interurban car*? The top part of him came out all right, so we
were able to keep the coffin open for the viewing. But the *bottom* part of
him . . . well, talk about your *mess.* Well, Zimmerman's sewed him
together best as they could, sewed him together at the waist, and he
wound up looking pretty decent, all things considered. There were flowers, and people came, but there weren't as many flowers as I thought
there should have been, and there weren't as many people either. There
should have been *more,* and I don't *care* about the Dorothy Hall thing. I
mean, I expect a lot of people saw it as some terrible *scandal,* and that's
why they didn't show up. Which is, though, come to think of it, sort of
contrary to human nature, right? I mean, you'd have thought the scandal
would have, ah, *attracted* them. But it didn't. It's surely a funny life, I
must say. Can you imagine a man speaking right up, bold as you please,
and telling you your lime pies are too *tart* while at the same time *he's* got
himself a *tart* of his *own* that's walking around town on two fat legs and
spreading those fat legs for him like maybe she's a *tunnel* in a *mountain*
and he's some sort of big old *express train* roaring along with maybe port-
ers and Pullmans and a dining car that's got white table linen and those
there big heavy water carafes? All the hair and all, and choo choo choo
choo, here it comes, the Midnight Express, apumping and asnorting,
stand back, world, and clear the track. I . . . I mean to tell you . . .
some people just . . . well, *you* know . . . they don't seem to care
how some *other* people *feel* . . . maybe, well, maybe suppose he'd have
come to me and told me about her . . . *before* she died, I mean
. . . maybe then we could have sat down and worked out something. But
he didn't do *that*; instead he did *the other.* He got up from supper and told
me he was going for a little walk, and he kissed me on the mouth, and he
walked out the front door, and that was the last time I saw him alive. The
interurban car hit him out by the Lancaster road. The motorman was a
man named Schoenling, and he told me, he said: 'I swear to God, ma'am,
your husband just came out of the dark and he *dove* in front of the car like
maybe a man in a swimming pool, you know? With his arms forward and
his hands together, you know? Like maybe he was diving and praying at
the same time, you know?' And this Schoenling went on and on, and he
was crying, and I told him it was all right; I told him I knew it wasn't his

fault, and then some woman or other . . . his wife, I expect . . . came and led him away. And I was left so I could be alone with my thoughts, which are always real nice things to be left alone with, as I'm sure you must know, right, Wanda you angel you? Ha. And so I thought: He was diving and praying. And dying and praying. And diving and dying and praying. *Whoosh,* out of the dark he comes, and it surely must have done a job of work on Mister Schoenling. I mean, people who knew Mister Schoenling said he never was the same again. I hear he developed some sort of twitch or tic. And it made him wink. It surely must be an aggravation to wink when you don't *want* to wink. Could get you into a lot of trouble. Get your face slapped, ha ha, that sort of thing . . . but anyway, *my husband* . . . never mind *Schoenling* . . . I don't want to talk about *Schoenling* . . . I want to talk about *John* . . . I want to talk about what's important . . . we, ah, we had him buried out of Zimmerman's because Zimmerman's is the best undertaking place Paradise Falls has *got* . . . and certainly, *of course* I knew her husband worked there . . . but it didn't matter all that much. I went to Alf Zimmerman and I said: 'Alf, I don't want a man named Clarence Hall to lay a hand on my husband. I don't care if he's the best embalmer you *got*; he's not to *touch* my husband. Under no circumstances, and I want your word on it.' Well, Alf Zimmerman looked at me in a peculiar fashion and asked me why, and I told him none of your beeswax, Alf; you just do as I tell you. And he shrugged and told me all right. He and a man named Clemens put John back together again, sewing the bottom of him to the top of him, or whatever it was they did, and of course I wasn't *there* when they did it, but Alf Zimmerman swore up and down Clarence Hall had nothing to do with anything, and I believed Alf Zimmerman, and I still do. The Zimmermans have a good reputation in the community, which you may or may not know, depending on how ignorant or not ignorant you are, which of course is difficult for *me* to know, seeing as how all you ever do is insult me and make fun of me and in general behave toward me and treat me like I'm something hanging from a chicken's rear end. But anyway, Paul and the girls never did know their father had been cut in half, or at least not until after the funeral. People *do* like to blab, you know. Word *does* get out, you know. I mean, even Wanda, *even Wanda,* dear *Wanda,* Wanda who loves Inez Ridpath so much, even dear sweet little *Wanda* likes to blab, doesn't she? Hot air keeps out cold winds, right?''

*

There are passages in *The Majesty of Grief* where the author, F. F. Geer, of Ottumwa, Iowa, becomes a trifle carried away:

Stones to feathers! Ashes to wine! Principalities of crumbs and thread and torn cardboard! Princesses sucking locomotives! Books of water! Thimbles full of zoos and skyscrapers and the entire population of North Platte, Nebraska! Under the Lord, nothing is impossible! Iron lemons! Palaces of hair!

One day Inez Ridpath said to Wanda: "Better anything than the silence, eh, Wanda my pet? Better the twisted slanting flabby blabber of a lunatic, eh, Wanda you irresistible glamor girl you? We sit forever locked in words, but better words than silence. Better a breakfast of horse manure than silence. Better the devil. Better bad dreams and dead dogs and fallen trees. If there is sound, that means we are *hearing* sound, which means we are alive. Defeat is one thing. Destruction is another. Anger is one thing. Silence is worse. I had prospects such as you cannot comprehend. Inez McClory, a girl with slender ankles, breasts perky and firm as the season's newest apples. Now my belly is gray, and you holler at me because of my private parts, and I am ruined, but *I am still here*, and I am still able to turn back silence with my flabby blabber. The trouble with Ozymandias was he should have *kept talking* . . . night and day . . . no matter *what* . . ."

"Shut up," said Wanda.

"Fat chance," said Inez Ridpath.

From 1938 until her death in 1960, Wanda Gwendolyn Carper Harper Ripple never relented in her hatred of Inez Ridpath. And once cranked and spinning, with all its moving parts functioning properly, the hatred was like a perpetual motion machine; it sustained itself, and it required no maintenance whatever. Existing absolutely on its own, it had a logic born of fear and loneliness, and by the end of Wanda's life both she and Inez Ridpath had come to take it for granted. One time, thumbing through the *Reader's Digest*, Wanda had come across the phrase *shared experience*. Well, she and Inez Ridpath had a shared experience, all right. For Wanda, it was glorious; it sustained her; she wouldn't have known what to do without it. For Inez Ridpath, it was something to occupy her attention, which was enough. Which was perhaps more than enough. And Inez Ridpath thrived; she belched; she wet herself; she uttered occasional obscenities; she scratched her private parts; she prowled nude; she plucked at her precious antimacassars; she summoned 1904 and her late husband's immaculate fingernails; she smiled; she farted; she became enormously fat—and, most importantly, she gave promise of surviving the universe. Which of course delighted Wanda. Which of course was the purpose of the war. To *cherish* with *hatred* . . . to *preserve* with *contempt* . . . ah, it was such a pity Wanda could not have applied these principles to her marriages. Had she done so, she probably never would have known widowhood and all that crushing muslin limburger loneliness in the little place on Roundhouse Street. The green beer never would have been consumed. The switch never would have been thrown.

Occasionally, when she was alone in her room, Wanda studied *The Majesty of Grief.* It had been sold to her for a dollar by a young man who had said he was working his way through Ohio University. The young man had had red hair and freckles, and it had been back in the Roundhouse Street days, and so she had treated him to two slices of apple crumb cake and two glasses of buttermilk, and he had been most appreciative. His name was Bob Fischer, Fischer with a C, and he told her she would not regret purchasing the book. According to him, F. F. Geer, of Ottumwa, Iowa, was one of the great undiscovered thinkers of the age, but it wouldn't always be that way, not as long as the Bob Fischers of this life kept knocking at doors and spreading the word. "I run into a lot of people who won't even give me a puny thirty seconds of their time," said Bob Fischer, "and yes, I'll admit it; there are times when I become mighty discouraged. But then it always comes to me that new things never are assimilated quickly—and secondly, every so often I encounter someone such as *yourself*, someone who has the *capacity* to *explore.* And then it all suddenly becomes worthwhile, and I'm again able to withstand the doors being slammed in my face." A grin, and Bob Fischer said: "I thank you for that . . . I really do." And later, after reading the book, Wanda believed she had an idea why the young fellow was so devoted to the ideas so movingly expressed by the eloquent Mr Geer. Reading slowly, following many of the words with a finger and now and then working her lips, Wanda nonetheless was able to capture the thrust of Mr Geer's words: *If we accept Him, then all contradictions and ironies cease to exist*! Which caused her to march to her invisible blackboard and write LOVE = DEATH and HATE = LIFE, for which she was graded 100% and 100%, and she kept Inez Ridpath alive and alive and alive and healthy and healthy and healthy, and Wanda's mornings were endless, and Wanda was (until her death, of course) forever necessary.

The F. F. Geer hyperbole more often than not just about squirmed off the page:

Accept! Accept! Frogs to aeroplanes! Legless tap dancers! Bearded newborn babes! Fish with thumbs! Stuttering tombstones! Cookie bullets! Stuffed toothpicks! Singing concrete! Woolen watermelon!

No doubt about it. Wanda's last twentytwo years were good ones. She ate well, even though she never gained any weight, and Margaret Ridpath treated her like a member of the family. She even was invited to the holiday family gettogethers in the homes of Miss Ridpath's sisters, and it wasn't long before she was on a firstname basis with both of them, calling them Ruth and Sarah just as casually as you please. She exchanged Christmas presents with Ruth and Sarah and their husbands (and occasionally she even had mildly sexual dreams about the handsome Pete Saddler), and of course she also exchanged Christmas presents with Miss Ridpath (whom she came to call Margaret, but not immediately, and certainly a good deal later than she had come to address Margaret's sisters by *their* first names), and at that time of the year she even baked a lime pie for the old crazy woman. With the price of limes what it was, this was no doubt an extravagant gesture that perhaps revealed too much, that came dangerously close to being an act of *kindness* and thus ran the risk of damaging the splendid lifegiving hatred that had given Wanda's days definition. But she took the chance anyway, even at the very real risk of killing the old loony with the kindness. Ah, such a household it was, and Wanda came to be an absolute necessity to both Margaret and the old loony. And say what you will, Wanda did exercise control over Inez Ridpath, whether out of fear or whatever. In other words, when push came to shove, Wanda was the boss as far as Inez Ridpath was concerned, bathing her every day and more or less breaking her of the habit of the nude wanderings, making her presentable enough so that from time to time she was permitted to sit on the front porch glider and wave vaguely at passersby. And of course Wanda soon learned of the slapless slaps that the daughter sometimes inflicted on the mother, and she came to understand the daughter's sense of accomplishment and the mother's jubilant pain, and for the first time since girlhood Wanda was part of a *family situation*, which was almost the same as a *shared experience*, and so she rejoiced in the slapless slaps; they meant she was in on something *hidden* and *bizarre*; they meant she *belonged*. As, oh, she surely did. The Ridpath home was a fine place, and Wanda enjoyed touching the banisters and the door frames and the mantel. They all were dark and heavy, and they caused her to tell herself: I am like a little boat attached to a big anchor. As a matter of fact, the anchor is bigger than the boat. I bet you an earthquake could come along and it wouldn't faze this place the littlest *bit*. Yes sir, some people live the way everybody ought to live, and that is the Gospel According to St Wanda, and Lord strike me dead if I am not telling the truth. Ah, my God, *feel* this place. Ah, my God, there is no way in Creation I'm going to allow that old rip to die.

But the risk of unconscious, inadvertent kindness always existed. So Wanda devised a table of rules, and she seldom deviated from it. The things she did for Inez Ridpath were things she told Inez Ridpath she *had* to do because of her job. In other words, *bathing* Inez Ridpath was a *duty*, and so she bathed Inez Ridpath. On the other hand, *wiping* Inez Ridpath's *nose* was a *favor*, and so she did not wipe Inez Ridpath's nose. The distinction was perhaps too delicate for the world to understand, but *Wanda* understood it, and no one else really mattered.

In addition, Wanda just about completely put an end to her baking. And she never did do much housework. It was more important that she always be near the old loony, that she make sure the old loony continued to breathe. And she was successful. The old loony breathed and breathed and breathed, and she remained alive and alive and alive and healthy and healthy and healthy, and Wanda was necessary and necessary and necessary. And so yes, when the real push came to the real shove, those twentytwo years were better than simply *good* . . . they were absolutely the *best* years Wanda ever had known. And she clasped her hatred to her gray and bony bosom with hoops of the proverbial steel, and she and the old rip sat glaring and cussing by the hour and the day and the month and the year. She fed the old rip a great deal of candy and pastry (storebought), since food kept a body alive, and sugar was good for you (everybody knew *that*), and of course the old rip became fatter and fatter (Wanda's knowledge of cholesterol was about as extensive as her knowledge of classical Greek). The old rip spoke of tea dances and hair and betrayals, and sometimes she removed her teeth and clacked them impishly at Wanda, and the bridge trophies and medals and plaques closed in on her, and on Wanda, and on the sofa and on the antimacassared chair, and one day she said: "Your average person wouldn't understand very much of this."

"Very much of what?" said Wanda.

"All these *things*," said Inez Ridpath, indicating the trophies and medals and plaques.

"You should be proud of your daughter," said Wanda.

"Because of a silly *game*?"

"Yes. To millions of people, it's not a silly game at all, and they wish they could play it half as good as your daughter does."

"But they don't know how she *hits* me," said Inez Ridpath.

"Oh, *sure*," said Wanda. "She surely does *hit* you *hard*, doesn't she?"

"Well, how would *you* know? She doesn't hit *you*."

"Well, *I'm* not a *bad girl*," said Wanda.

"I want to ask you something," said Inez Ridpath.

"Ask it," said Wanda. "Stop wasting my time with your coyness."

"Margaret's skill at the game . . . you think maybe she inherited any of it?"

Wanda laughed. She took care to make the laugh harsh, which was not all that difficult, considering the absurdity of her voice. Ah, but the absurdity of her voice was not the point. What *was* the point was the fact that she could not afford to make the laugh appreciative—that would have diminished the necessary hatred that was sustaining the old rip's life. So Wanda twisted the laugh, and it came out nasal and slatted, and finally she said: "You got turkey buzzards circling around in your brain, you know that?"

"Thank you," said Inez Ridpath.

"What?" said Wanda.

"That's the nicest thing you've said to me since Christmas," said Inez Ridpath.

Never then, by word or deed (with the single exception of the annual Christmas lime pie), did Wanda reveal how deeply she cherished the old rip—this stupid, dotty, fat, unclean, dentureclacking woman who had rescued Wanda from the Roundhouse Street curtains and cakes and curlers and sorry limburger Saturday nights.

As a matter of fact, from time to time Wanda even went out of her way to expose and proclaim what she wanted everyone to believe was her contempt for Inez Ridpath. In about 1949 or so, the old rip developed a genuinely ripe and juicy cluster of reasonably severe hemorrhoids, and it became impossible for her to sit on hard chairs. So Margaret bought her a folding chair, and it was light enough that the old rip could carry it from room to room when she went wandering through the house. Now then, Wanda had seen such canvas chairs in movies about Hollywood, and so she bought a small can of Glidden's best red paint and smeared the word *STAR* in wavery capitals on the back of the chair. But there was only one catch—the old rip was delighted. She said to Wanda: "That's the nicest thing you've done for me in years. You must be falling apart. Maybe some of those turkey buzzards are flapping around in *your* brain, too, do you think?" And Inez Ridpath sometimes carried the chair out into the front yard and seated herself with her back to the street and the sidewalk (so the world could see the word), and from time to time she would laugh and swivel around and raise a loose liverspotted fist at some motorist or pedestrian and proclaim: *"Look at ME! I am a STAR!"* Which meant of course that Inez Ridpath was Wanda's active *adversary*, not her *victim*. Which meant of course that matters were seldom dull during Wanda's final terrific and *necessary* twentytwo years.

Margaret didn't really see where *she* could do anything about the situation. And anyway, the slapless slaps were enough. Anything *further* was beyond her. And so she came to a point where she was able to defend the situation. When discussing it with her sisters, she would say: "Mother and Wanda *enjoy* it. They really do. They bicker all the time, and Wanda gets to rolling her eyes like the last of the Christian martyrs whenever Mother sets off on one of those *monologues*, but I'll *tell* you something . . . Wanda almost never lets Mother out of her sight, and she really does take good care of her. She may not *like* Mother, but she is *devoted* to her, and I think that's all anybody has a right to expect. After all, Mother isn't exactly the most *lovable* person in the world, now *is* she?"

"But Wanda ought to do more of the housework," said Ruth.

"Well, she *is* busy with Mother," said Margaret.

"It's going to wear you out," said Sarah. "The housework, *plus* your job, *plus* the bridge tournaments."

"I'll be all right," said Margaret.

"But the bickering must get on your nerves, doesn't it?" said Ruth.

"It's not all that terrible," said Margaret. "I know some married couples that get along a great deal worse."

"Such as who?" said Sarah.

"Oh, present company excepted," said Margaret, speaking quickly.

"I should *hope* so," said Ruth.

And the sisters smiled, and they drank lemonade or hot chocolate, and the subject drifted away from their mother and the implacably devoted Wanda. Yet Margaret was softly aware of some sort of distant wind coming up, like the voice of a fat and terrible ghost, but she swallowed the sound (it threatened to be an *iron* sound, and she did not want to hear it, let alone look to see what had caused it, what menace it perhaps carried), and she spoke of some bridge tournament or other (why that awful wind? what sort of disorder did it imply?), and Ruth spoke of how well George was doing at the drugstore, and Sarah (flibbertygibbety as ever) spoke of Pete and the bank and tricycles and her children. And then, grinning, she told of an indiscretion her little Olive had committed the other evening after a supper of wieners and baked beans. "Jane Underwood and Frieda Rolfe stopped by," said Sarah, "and Frieda talked Olive into playing *Country Gardens* on the piano . . . and, well, you know Olive, the biggest showoff in the world. So she sits herself down at the piano and tears off *Country Gardens* nice as you please, and Jane and Frieda clap for her, so she gets off the bench and gives them a little curtsy . . . and, ah, you can *imagine* what happened *next* . . . it was like a *frog* had *died* in her little *bottom* . . . and she, ah, she didn't know whether to *faint* or *die* or *what* . . . and as for *Yours Truly* . . . well, Yours Truly thought *she* was going to have a *heart attack* . . . but I was lucky . . . it turned out all right . . . I mean, what with Frieda being a little, ah, hard of hearing, and Jane having all the sense of humor of a rock in the middle of the desert . . . they neither of them reacted *at all*, and nothing was said, and they just sat there and clapped and clapped like maybe Olive had given them a little teeny *encore* . . ." And here Sarah fell apart in giggles, and Ruth laughed outright, and Margaret managed a smile. But Margaret was thinking of that threatening wind. She was thinking of her mother. She was thinking of Wanda. She was thinking of disorder. She rubbed one of her wrists, and it felt like tinfoil. She could not even enjoy a little story about a poor child's unfortunate semipublic flatulence. Dark iron things nudged at her, and she was too frightened even to speculate on what they were. But she did smile. She did do that. And her bust was splendid. And she kept her upper lip pressed firmly over her teeth. And she managed not to embrace herself.

Wanda Gwendolyn Carper Harper Ripple died of a stroke in November of 1960 two days after John F. Kennedy had been elected President of the United States. (She and Margaret had voted against Kennedy, Wanda because she had felt an obligation to honor the extent of her father's and Tim Harper's urgent Masonic dislike of Catholics, and Margaret because *she* simply would not have voted for *any* Democrat under *any* circumstances, and certainly not a *Catholic*.)

By the time Wanda died, it was almost as though she were a fourth Ridpath sister, and the three real Ridpath sisters mourned her deeply and with generous hearts (even though Margaret still felt the fat threatening wind, and even though she still had no idea of its source). Wanda's real sister, Muriel Hesketh, had died years earlier, as had Muriel's husband, old Fritz. There were no close relatives, and so Wanda's will was not contested in court. Margaret had no idea Wanda even had *made* a will, and its provisions came as something of a shock, to say the least. But it did exist, and it was all properly lawyered and witnessed and notarized, and it provided that all Wanda's money and worldly goods be left to the detested Inez Ridpath, with Margaret serving as executrix.

When Margaret first read the will, she immediately said to herself: It is a mistake. Some sort of typing error has been made. She looked at the lawyer and said: "I can hardly believe this."

The lawyer was a former Congressman named Underwood. "Well," he said, "it *is* a little peculiar. I mean, at her age, what is your mother going to do with the money or the property? Certainly by rights it all should have been left to *you* if Wanda wanted to leave it to someone in the Ridpath family . . ."

"No, I didn't mean *that*," said Margaret. "I don't care about *that*. What I *mean* is—Wanda and Mother never got along all that well . . ."

"I remember that I asked her at the time. 'Wanda,' I said, 'you really mean *Inez* and not *Margaret*?' And she said: 'Yes sir. That I do.' And I seem to recall that her voice was clear and firm."

"Goodness," said Margaret.

"Well," said Underwood, "it's all really moot anyway."

"I beg your pardon?"

"I don't mean to sound crass, but the chances are you'll outlive your mother, in which case the money will be yours anyway. Your sisters' husbands are well off, and your brother is dead, and you know as well as I do that back in, oh, '32 or '33, your mother made out a will leaving her money and the house to whichever of her children still was single at her death . . . or, if all were single, the estate was to be divided equally . . . or, if all were *married*, the estate also was to be divided

equally . . . and of course there was nothing . . . ah, *wrong* with your
mother in those days . . . so what I'm *saying* is—Wanda's estate will be
yours soon enough anyway, and pardon me if I sound too . . . ah, as I
said, *crass* . . . but there's no real sense pussyfooting through the buttercups, is there?''

Margaret said nothing.

"It is six of one and half a dozen of the other," said Underwood.

Margaret embraced herself.

Wanda never had touched the original three thousand nine hundred
dollars she had deposited in the bank after the sale of her Roundhouse Street home and possessions. In fact, she had added to the money,
since she had had few expenses while living at the Ridpath place. This ad-
ditional money, plus interest, brought Wanda's estate to more than eleven
thousand dollars—after taxes and probate fees. Included with the will
was a brief note to Margaret. It read:

DEAR MARGARET:

I always tried to do my best. What you saw as one thing was really altogether something else. Use the money to buy her whatever little things she
wants—soaps maybe, or sweets, or maybe a new chair with STAR on the
back. I kept her alive, and so the two of you gave me a home. It was a fair
exchange, and I am grateful for it, and I hope my sour old Picklepuss didn't
put you off too much. I love all of you, and I love your mother. Yes, your
mother, I can tell you that now. In God's realm, nothing is impossible.
Please try to remember that, and be of good faith. I am sorry I had such a
funny voice, but maybe there was some reason for it that we just can't understand.

Your friend who always loved you and your dear mother,

WANDA

Margaret saved Wanda Ripple's note and read it many times, but
she never did quite figure out all of of it. Wanda was only sixtytwo
when she died, so it wasn't that she had been *senile;* it was just that the
note clearly had private meanings only Wanda could unravel. But Wanda
was gone, and the entire tone of the thing was vaguely ominous, and per-

haps it had something to do with the fat frightening wind Margaret never quite was able to get out of her mind.

It is perhaps unfortunate that Margaret did not read and understand more of *The Majesty of Grief.* Then she might not have been quite so frightened, and the wisdom and rhetoric of F. F. Geer would have led her to see the logic and transcendent rightness of:

Riveted hummingbirds! Blathering corncobs! Blind chick sexers! Rubber boilers! Candied skulls! Cellophane midgets! Chocolate onions!

Oil is sand, and sand is wine, and green beer and too much sulphur water will seduce the unwary. Blessed be the Name of the Lord.

Margaret did go back again and again to Wanda's valedictory note, and its elusiveness really was most vexing to her. And sometimes she almost was ready to believe she could hear Wanda's ridiculous voice laughing at her. But there were other times when Margaret actually felt a sort of love. Something fierce and perhaps beautiful was inside Wanda's words, and surely it had a quality of iron.

Inez Ridpath never really was able to accept Wanda's death. She missed Wanda a great deal, and it was possible that she saw Wanda's death as a betrayal. And one time she did say to Margaret: "You just never know who your friends are."

"Are you talking about *Wanda?*" Margaret wanted to know.

"Of course," said Inez Ridpath.

"*She* was your *friend?*"

"Well," said Inez Ridpath, "we *did* talk. Which is better than nothing. Which is better than counting the roses in the wallpaper."

"Oh," said Margaret.

"But she had to go and *go*," said Inez Ridpath.

"Yes," said Margaret.

"You just can't count on a *soul* any more," said Inez Ridpath.

When Margaret remembered Wanda, it was with a sort of love, yes, but it was an intimidated love. She was afraid not to love Wanda. In a sense, this was related to Margaret's skill as a bridgeplayer. She was afraid not to play well. Iron things—spikes and shields and tongues and walls and hammers and plates and blades—forever surrounded her and nudged her flesh, and of course her flesh was made of tinfoil. *Actually*, if the truth were known, the twentytwo years Wanda had lived in the Ridpath home had intimidated Margaret *right from the start*, and all Margaret's brave words to Ruth and Sarah had been so much bushwah. First crack, as soon as it became apparent that Wanda was bound and determined to despise Margaret's mother no matter what, Margaret felt her bones curdle. Why would the woman hate Margaret's mother *first crack*? Did anyone, acting on no facts or experience whatever, have a right to behave that way? Was there anything that could be done to change the situation? Well, it turned out there wasn't, and the result was that Margaret did most of the housework. She would stand over the supper stove and fry chicken and roast corn on the cob while Mother and Wanda were quietly and earnestly insulting one another out front in the parlor. And she would beat rugs and wash dishes and water the plants and dust the bridge trophies while Mother spoke to Wanda of suicide and crocheting and silly women who sent obscene mash notes. But it was clear . . . and never mind Wanda's lack of attention to her household duties that had nothing to do with Inez Ridpath . . . that Inez Ridpath *needed* Wanda. She became mercilessly cranky when Wanda was out of the house, and there was little Margaret could do with her except—in cases of extreme emergency—deliver the slapless slaps. So Wanda stayed on . . . and on . . . and on . . . for twentytwo years. And really, once her hatred of Inez Ridpath was conceded, Wanda was not a bad person, and her presence *did* make it possible for Margaret to journey to countless bridge tournaments—and to take a trip to London in 1959, London, lovely London, where Irv Berkowitz was able to reveal to Margaret (however briefly) that romance and manners and lack of iron were neither sinful nor degrading. "We shall take tea at the Ritz," said Irv, "and we shall stroll in Green Park, and you have my permission to hang onto my arm as tightly as you like, and you'll not be threatened . . . that I guarantee." So all right yes, getting back to Wanda, she was not perfect for Margaret, but she probably was perfect for Mother, and Mother probably was perfect for her, and surely those twentytwo years must have had value, despite Margaret's curdled bones and all the rest of it. And she genuinely mourned Wanda, and all three of the Ridpath sisters—Margaret, Ruth and Sarah—wept at the cemetery. They uttered high splintered cries when the moment came to pray over Wanda for the last time and lower her coffin into the earth.

Inez Ridpath was unable to attend either the funeral or the burial. She was home sitting in her antimacassared chair, talking to a vacant sofa and being watched by a woman named Pauline Jones, who worked with Margaret at Steinfelder's. Pauline was staying with Margaret . . . on a temporary basis *only*, mind you . . . until a replacement for Wanda could be found.

In his book, *The Majesty of Grief,* F. F. Geer wrote:
To love God is to succumb to Him. To love God is to equate inconsistency with the clear logic of Pythagoras. To love God is to accept. Tomorrow, should the sun rise in the west, the true servant of God will fall down and murmur thanks. If the universe slants and crackles, it is all in His name. To believe this is to survive.

Part Four

PAULINE JONES

Consider a world that is made of iron. Then consider a Margaret Ridpath who is made of tinfoil. Then consider a Pauline Jones. If Margaret Ridpath is (was) to the world what tinfoil is to iron, then Pauline Jones is (was) to Margaret Ridpath what sawdust is to tinfoil. The rabbit may not be much, but surely the carrot and the lettuce leaf live in terror of him. So it was not as though Margaret existed in the deepest final circle of fear. There was always Pauline Jones, and Pauline Jones was ridiculous, and the sawdust forever leaked from her in loose foolish trickles. Oh, there were *some* people in Paradise Falls who felt sorry for her, but there were a great deal more who were amused by her—not pleasantly, though. She had loved a man who had not been a man, and she had destroyed her beauty and her spirit because of him, and the people who laughed at her considered her to be the most stupid woman in town . . . or at least the most recklessly romantic and unrealistic. Which made them uncomfortable. Which angered them. Somehow her stupidity, or her refusal to keep her feet on God's abiding ground, or even her stubbornness, call it what you prefer, made all the laughter nasty . . . and perhaps even guilty. But who knew for certain? Intricacy of this sort was not all that often encountered in Paradise Falls; it itched the brain; it confounded.

The man had been reasonably young, and his name had been Lloyd Sherman, and he had possessed a sopping salivary lisp. He vanished, lisp and all, in 1956, and Pauline Jones had *adored* him (and there never would be anyone else for her), and he'd not even left a note behind. Not even a *scrap* of *paper*. For all she and the world knew, he had been abducted, or murdered, or he had drowned in his saliva, or he was sitting somewhere in a bra and panties and hose and heels and a sleeveless frock, with a blond wig perched perkily on his head, with his makeup *careful* and certainly *always* and a *day* most *tasteful*.

In Columbus, the doctor said to Pauline: "There is such a thing as working too hard to solve a problem. I suspect that you and he and I worked too hard, and finally, he was able to accept no more, even though I am convinced he did love you . . . after his fashion, that is to say. Please try to remember. Perhaps it will provide a sort of comfort."

153

In a sense, Pauline was like Inez Ridpath or even Wanda Ripple—she had begun well. And perhaps she had begun better than
well. Surely she had been beautiful, and no one had disputed her beauty.
If you had seen her in 1943 or 1944, say, or 1945, and had you been male,
and had your blood and other liquids and your gonads been functioning
properly, you unquestionably would have been swept away by her looks
. . . plus a gentle ambience that she possessed, a secret quality that was
like something sweet and flowering, unaffected by seasons or hatreds or
catastrophes. She was the youngest of seven children of a benevolent and
loving couple named James N. and Elizabeth B. Jones, and she was
reared in an unrelentingly clamorous atmosphere of raffish and polyphon-
ic goodwill, with doors forever slamming, with hollerings, with tears and
grapplings and teeth and sweat and laughter. She and her brothers and sisters jostled and grunted and got in one another's way, fighting over bowls
of oatmeal, disputing whose turn it was in the bathroom, running, tum-
bling, tasting earth and stones, tonguing the blood from an occasional
mashed nose, blinking at sunlight and the days' unending whirl of leaves
and birds and treetops, pressing flesh, squeezing, twisting, yelping (and at
night sleeping like axed cattle), and now and then they drew broomstraws
for an occasional odd porkchop or chicken wing, and Mama always was
there to adjudicate—and many times Papa, too, even though he was a
dress salesman and was away a lot. (He liked to say he traveled in wom-
en's readytowear, and everyone always giggled from imagining the picture of *Papa* in *women's clothes;* it was really just too too *dumb* for
words.)

In Paradise Falls, keeping up with the Jim Joneses was not all that difficult. Papa's commissions fluctuated from season to season and year to
year and good times to bad, but Pauline for one never thought of herself
as being poor . . . not as long as there was a library in Paradise Falls.
She had become a reader early on, and she had some kindly and understanding teachers who spoke well of Scott and Tennyson, and then there
was her mother, who would wink at her and say: "There are worlds and
there are worlds, and I do believe you have found yourself a nice world.
Don't let anybody take it away from you or laugh you out of it."

"Yes, Mama," said Pauline.

"The laughers could be the worst," said Elizabeth Jones. "They could
hurt you the most. Laughter can be very painful."

"I'll be all right," said Pauline.

"Good for you," said her mother.

Pauline's love of books made it so she was able to taste beautiful words
on her tongue. She was especially fond of *palindrome* and *lilypad* and *cor-*

uscate and *dreamer* and *jonquil* and *lapidary* and *benevolence*, and her favorite name in the whole wide world was *Olivia DeHavilland . . .* which was a song in itself, anachronistic and discreet, like a Frenchman's serenade, mannered and elegant, accompanied by mandolins and recorders.

And her frenzied crowded home did not distract Pauline. Not really. She somehow developed patience and gentleness. Her mind did not wander; rather, it walked away—and all noise and all proddings and all laughter vanished, locked in some neat closet and reclaimed when the proper time arrived. And her mother said: "Of all my children, you are the most *in hand."* And Pauline smiled. And sometimes she and her mother embraced, and her mother always had an odor of starch and milk. And then, as Pauline's older brothers and sisters (or at least most of them) got married, she came to suffer numerous nieces and nephews; she laughed with them; she kissed them; she played endless silent games with them, everything from Pit and Touring and Monopoly to Pin the Tail on the Donkey and Run Sheepy Run. But the games *were* for the most part silent. The nieces and the nephews came to understand that those who played games well were those who concentrated, those who did not distract themselves with useless talk, those who were *serious* and did not *fool around.* And the nieces and nephews (most of them) loved their Aunt Pauline. She was beautiful, and they did not want to annoy her. If they did, perhaps somehow they would damage her beauty. Actually, several of her nieces and nephews were not all that younger than she was. She had two sisters and four brothers, and the oldest of them . . . a sister, Alice . . . was *seventeen years* older than Pauline, which meant Pauline had been born when Alice had been a junior in high school (the year had been 1925), and sometimes it almost seemed to Pauline that her nieces and nephews were her sisters and brothers, which made her sisters and brothers her aunts and uncles, which made her mother and father her grandmother and grandfather, and it all was a little like the words to some silly song she once had heard, a song she believed was entitled *I'm My Own Grandpaw,* and sometimes she even became a trifle confused, but only a trifle. A lesser person might really have been troubled by the ambiguity (or whatever it was, if it was anything at all, which it probably was not, since quite often Pauline's lockedcloset, walkaway ruminations were little more than cerebral . . . ah, *palindromes).* But Pauline Jones was not a lesser person (not at the beginning), and so she was able to accept her loud and confused family situation with humor and balance. She had her books, and she had her beauty, and her days were golden and splendid. And that certainly was the way she was in 1943 or 1944, say, or 1945, when she was generally acknowledged to be the most beautiful girl in Paradise Falls, when she had prospects, when she honored the mornings with her eyes and her smile, when she had the status of a slender and glamorous legend. And she did suffer her nieces and nephews; that was her nature. She suffered them, and so they clustered around her. And never mind the silly Grandpaw song; she really was able to keep an accurate count of which was a niece, which was a nephew, which was a brother, which was a sister, which was a mother, which was a father—and she really never was perplexed; she really never had to draw back and ask: "Now let's see . . . are you Kitty or are you Kristine?" But she did ask such questions from time to time. A little joke never hurt anyone—and besides, it kept her from perhaps edging around the bend. By any definition, she *was* engulfed by multitudes, and she did require some sort of defense. Anyone would have. The first sister, Alice, was married to a man named Morris Bird II, and they had two children who were named Morris III and Sandra. Next was a brother named Jim, who eventually became the Paradise Falls chief of police, and Jim was married to a woman whose maiden name had been Emily Hockstader, and they had a son named Peter. Then came a bachelor brother named Alan, who was a telegrapher for the Chesapeake & Ohio. Then came a sister named Phyllis, who was married to a man named Harry Dana, and they had five children whose names were (honestly!) Kenny, Kitty, Kristine, Karen and Karl. Then came a brother named Howard, and Howard was married to a woman whose maiden name had been Edythe Breitenbach (she played the harp), and they had four children whose names were Tom, Larry, Jane and Howard Junior. Finally came a brother named Walter, who was married to a woman whose maiden name had been Iris Schmidlapp, and they were childless, glory be (Iris was one of three Paradise Falls young women who had joined the WACs in World War II). The older sister, Alice, lived with her husband and children in Cleveland, but all the others had remained in Paradise Falls. Every so often everyone would get together for a picnic or Thanksgiving dinner or whatever, and everyone would talk at once, and Papa would laugh and joke, and Mama would shake her head with a sort of happy besieged bewilderment, and the children would giggle and dart, and likely as not Phyllis's husband, Harry Dana, would get to complaining because *he* had the *title* of secretary and treasurer of the Paradise Falls Clay Products Co at the same time as a man named Erwin F. Truscott, who was older than God and should have retired a decade ago, was at least *theoretically* holding the same positions, which made no sense *at all*, which vexed Harry Dana *no end*, which caused him forever to harangue the family because of the *injustice*. The official explanation was that old Truscott was staying on the job—*with the same title*—until a man named

Elmer Carmichael, who was president of the Paradise Falls Clay Products Co was absolutely certain that Harry Dana would be able to handle the responsibilities. And therefore, in point of fact, the Paradise Falls Clay Products Co had *two* secretaries and *two* treasurers, and it all was too much for Harry Dana, and he would say: "Who ever heard of such a thing? If I was any kind of man, I'd tell Elmer Carmichael to stuff his job up his old bung hole. Next week I'll go to him . . . that's what I'll do. I'll tell him it's either Truscott or me. I'll tell him there isn't a business in the country that's run with two men holding the positions of secretary and treasurer. I talked with him about it once, and he said to me: 'Hell, Harry, I thought the position would *please* you.' And I said: 'Sure, Elmer, if I held it *all by myself.*' And he said: 'In good time, Harry. In good time. And just try to keep in mind that I wouldn't of named you to the same job if I hadn't of had faith in you.' Which is all like making chocolate cake out of horse cock, right? I mean, who does he think he *is?*"

And Harry Dana's words rolled out, and on, and forever—or so it seemed, since in 1962, when old Truscott finally upped and made a die of it, Carmichael did in fact name Harry full secretary and treasurer. But by that time Harry's outrage was such a part of him that he barely was aware he had prevailed. After all, a cherished enemy is not someone to be lightly abandoned. And the same of course can be said for a cherished injustice. And so, haranguing his way up and down the corridors of all those years that preceded 1962, he would say: "I do about ninety percent of the work, and that's a fact. And the old bastard, old Erwin F. just sashays in late every morning and drinks buttermilk and lounges with his goddamned feet on the desk. I swear to God, it's almost like he *knows* something about Elmer Carmichael, and it's almost like they're playing some sort of sneaky *game.* Myself, I don't go in for sneaky games, but I think I can recognize one when I see one. And I think the old bastard is forcing Elmer Carmichael to keep him on the payroll. Which maybe explains why I got the same title, right? I mean, Elmer Carmichael's got to have *somebody* do the work, right? So he names me to the job, and all old Truscott does is drink buttermilk and read the papers . . ." And knowing Carmichael, knowing Carmichael to be a loudmouthed limping bear of a man who was as devious as he was rich (and no one in Paradise Falls was richer, not even Hugo G. Underwood, the lawyer and former member of Congress), Harry Dana figured there really had to be something interesting going on between Carmichael and Truscott, but he did not have the remotest idea what it was. He speculated on it for years, and nobody in the family really cared all that much (except his wife, plump Phyllis), but he did not even mind talking to himself if no one would listen. And he did not even mind talking to the walls. Or trees. Or blades of grass. And he would say: "Buttermilk. The old fart has it delivered to his office every morning. *Delivered*. And you know something—his complexion is pinker than a goddamned rosebud, and I wouldn't be surprised if he just went on and on and lived forever, like a rock maybe, or God." And Harry Dana would shake his head, and plump Phyllis would tell him there, there, he would just have to be patient, and he would say to her: "Yes ma'am . . . until maybe the year 2000." And plump Phyllis would pat her husband's hand, or his cheeks, and sometimes Pauline would watch all this—and sometimes, when her resistance was low, she even would *listen*. And she would say to herself: Is that all there is for Harry? Is that all that keeps him alive and taking nourishment? And she wanted to tell Harry there was more *to* him than all his obsessive martyrdom, but she never quite got around to it. After all, if obsessive martyrdom was what kept him going, who was she to interfere? And anyway, since Pauline was human and never claimed to be anything more (despite the kind things people forever said about her looks), sometimes her brotherinlaw's incessant talk about the situation at the Paradise Falls Clay Products Co was almost enough to make her want to do something stupid but at the same time enjoyably and hammily melodramatic—such as throwing herself into the furnace, or slashing her wrists, or sticking her head in a cement mixer. And of course she smiled when these thoughts occurred to her. That was the thing about existing in a situation where so many people came and went—one tended to think in excessive terms. Otherwise, attention never was paid. But Pauline Jones never did an excessive thing in her life—except fall in love with a young man named Lloyd Sherman. Unfortunately, it was one excessive thing too many, and it did destroy her, and she became the only person on God's earth who ever feared Margaret Ridpath. She was the lettuce leaf, and Margaret Ridpath was the rabbit. But that all came later. It all came after Pauline's girlhood, which she carried well, which interested her, which abounded with clear eyes and sweet ambience. She did enjoy the family gatherings, and even Harry Dana's talk. After all, he was a human being, and perhaps something could be learned from his behavior. Pauline always sought to learn from the behavior of others . . . or at least as a girl she did. (Later, after Lloyd Sherman vanished, she sought nothing—except perhaps to hide from the laughter that pursued her.) As a girl, for instance, she listened to her brother Walter discuss the enormous hazards of driving a bus for the Paradise Valley Traction Co, or she shepherded her nieces and nephews off for their quiet games, or she listened to her brother Howard talk about the problems he was encountering as basketball coach at Paradise Falls High School, or she helped Mama wrap sandwiches and slabs of cake and pie, and she dipped her fingers in Mama's thick chocolate batter, or she listened to the hearty and urgent rasp and chuckle of Papa's voice as he told a joke or pulled someone's leg or went chomping through a slab of Mama's cake like (in his words) "the human garbage truck," to which Mama always would object, telling him: "My *cake* is not *garbage, you oaf.*" And so it was that Pauline forever heard feet and smelled breath and held out warm hands, to her nieces, to her nephews, to her sisters, to her brothers, to her loud rasping father and her serene and humorous mother. And in good times and ugly. The picnics, yes, and the Thanksgiving dinners—but also the times when her brother Alan, the bachelor telegrapher, would for no real reason simply sit and blink at his hands and speak to no one, or the times when her brother Walter would take her aside and tell her look, Iris is a fine woman and all that, and as a veteran of World War II myself, I certainly am proud of her for having served in the WACs, but isn't there some way somebody could get her to fix herself up a little better? Or the times, the worst times of them all, when Pauline's brother Jim (who drank heavily and really was not all that much of a police chief) was led by her to the porch railing, where he would lean over and vomit into Mama's cheery red impatience plants. Ah, but children were forever running to Pauline, and she always kept an extra handkerchief for the wiping of eyes and the blowing of noses. And her brothers and sisters liked to *touch* her. And they all told her she was beautiful. Yet somehow this all made her feel removed from them, loving them but not quite *of* them, and the feeling disturbed her. Harry Dana and the silly dispute over his title. Alan and his bachelor silences. Plump Phyllis and the way her flesh gathered itself around Harry, attempting to protect him. Howard and his concern over how many games the Paradise Falls High School basketball team won and lost. Walter and his mannish wife. Jim and the whisky. Papa and his jokes, his unyielding optimism. The clatter and skip of the nieces and nephews. Oh, how Pauline thanked the Lord for the gift of books, for the capacity her mind had to walk away. And one day her mother said to her: "You really do understand the secret of all this, don't you?"

"What do you mean?" Pauline wanted to know.

"How to stay sane. By keeping quiet, I mean."

"Well," said Pauline, "listening is fun too."

"Only if you can hear yourself think," said Elizabeth Jones. "And *you* can hear yourself think, can't you?"

"I believe so," said Pauline.

"But please don't misunderstand," said Elizabeth Jones.

"Misunderstand what?"

"I love them all. Those that can hear themselves think. Those that can't."

"Oh," said Pauline. "And so can I."

"*Both,*" said Elizabeth Jones.

"Yes," said Pauline.

"There's a lot of love here," said Elizabeth Jones.

"Yes," said Pauline.

"There has been right from the start," said Elizabeth Jones. "Right from when I was fifteen but I told your father I was eighteen."

"My Mama the Child Bride," said Pauline.

"Yes indeedy," said Elizabeth Jones. "I fibbed to him, and it was in a hotel lobby, and I was in that hotel to take part in a dance in the grand ballroom, and he was in that hotel on one of his selling trips, and the thing he did was, he went out and rented a suit of tails and a top hat and a cane, and he barged in on that dance big as you please, as though he were the leader of the band or the majordomo or whatever. And he literally swept me off my feet. Came to me . . . I was sitting by the punchbowl . . . and *picked me up* without so much as a By Your Leave or a Pardon Me Miss or an anything . . . and we danced, oh I don't remember what it was . . . maybe the maxixe . . . and he told me, he said: 'God has had a hand in all this, and He has presented me with you this fine evening, and I thank Him very much.' "

"It's a nice story, Mama. I know."

"It's not a *story*," said Elizabeth Jones. "It's the *truth*."

"I'm sorry," said Pauline. "I didn't mean *story* in the sense of a *lie*. I meant it in the sense of something *nice* . . . something *romantic* . . . like a *poem*."

"Do you want me to go on with it?"

"Yes."

"Even though you've heard it all before?"

"Doesn't *matter*," said Pauline. "I *enjoy* it."

Elizabeth Jones nodded. "Thank you," she said. She smiled. "All right then. So, anyhow, after a dance or two, we sort of wandered into the lobby, and it was then that I fibbed and told him I was eighteen, and he said to me: 'Good. You are old enough so we can get married right away. We'll find somebody to do it, get somebody out of bed or whatever. Five dollars should wake somebody real quick.' *Well*, as you can *imagine*, you could have knocked me over with a baby's breath . . . but . . . well . . . we did go ahead and . . ."

"What was the man's name? Ingraham?"

"Ingerman," said Elizabeth Jones. "A strange name. Never heard of it before or since. That was 1907, mind you, and we had to sit up in a train all night from Richmond to Hagerstown, and it was nine in the morning when this Mister Ingerman performed the ceremony. There was egg on his vest, and his moustache was frayed. His wife sang something. She had a terrible voice. It came out all thick and confused, as though she had bumps on her tongue.''

"And it was the next day you told Papa you were only fifteen?''

"Yes," said Elizabeth Jones.

"And he turned pale?''

Elizabeth Jones laughed. "Next to what *he* was, *pale* was like a *sunrise.* And who could blame him? There he was, a *salesman* and *worldly* and all *that*, with a *derby* and a *watchchain,* and he practically *abducts* a girl from a hotel in Richmond, Virginia, where she'd gone to attend one of the really whoopdedo dances given by the girls of Miss Farrington's School for the young gentlemen of the Tidewater Military Academy, and so he discovers that his bride is *fifteen years of age* . . . and *pale* isn't even the word for what he turned. It was as though something had sucked out his blood with a pump. And you should have heard the uproar that came from my mother and my father and my Aunt Leora!''

"I can imagine," said Pauline.

Elizabeth Jones hesitated. She patted one of her daughter's hands. "I *know* I've told you all this before—and told it and told it and *told* it. But, well, I still like to tell it . . .''

"It's all right," said Pauline.

"If it gets too much for you, please don't hesitate to let me know," said Elizabeth Jones. "I mean, if necessary I would not be averse to telling the story to *the walls* . . .''

"I am not *the walls*," said Pauline, "and I enjoy hearing it.''

"Well, I thank you for that.''

"No need to," said Pauline. "I like romantic stories. Why do you think I read so much? It'd be like thanking a little child for giving it candy.''

"You really do enjoy words, don't you?''

"Very much," said Pauline.

Nodding, Elizabeth Jones resumed her story. *"Well,"* she said, "getting back to that astonished husband of mind. His first thought was—the marriage should be annulled. But *I* wouldn't *hear* of it. I told him I didn't *care what* my mother and my father and my Aunt Leora said or did . . . I was now *in every way* Mrs James N. Jones, if you follow my meaning, and I was not *about* to let him abandon me to all that clucking and scolding . . . fingers being waggled in my face . . . all that sort of thing . . .''

"And so the two of you stood up to them," said Pauline.

"Yes," said Elizabeth Jones. "My father was the worst. He threatened your father with everything including the gallows and the electric chair, as I recall, but all your father did was grin that big salesman's grin of his and say to *my* father: 'I'm sorry, sir, but done is done, and I really *do* love Elizabeth, you know. If you give it a chance, we'll get along just fine, and you'll learn that I'm not a bad sort of fellow. I work hard, and people back home most of them like me a whole lot, and Elizabeth here'll never want, and I'll never come begging to you for money or anything else. That's my solemn oath.'"

"And?" said Pauline. She knew the rest of it, and of course she had known the rest of it for years, but she did not want to disappoint her mother by not asking the question—and anyway, the story always was fun to hear. It was never quite the same two times running. Details came and went. Memory leapfrogged happily, and Pauline always was delighted. And she liked to watch the expression on her mother's face. It was crinkly, quick, and sometimes there was moisture in the eyes.

"And, well," said Elizabeth Jones, "my father began to give way. My mother and Aunt Leora weren't all that convinced, but there was a sort of softness that pulled at the corners of my father's mouth, and that was when I knew we had him. And finally he said to your father: 'Mister Jones, you are a swine and a bounder, but why am I having so much trouble maintaining my anger?' And your father said: 'Mister Bagley, I may be a swine and a bounder about a lot of things, but your daughter is excluded. Nothing of this was planned, believe me. I walked into that hotel, and I was hot, and I was tired, but there Elizabeth was, all in white, dressed so prim and proper, mingling and giggling with all those other girls who were all in white, but *she* was the only one I saw, and it was as though Teddy Roosevelt had hit me on the head with one of his Panama Canal steam shovels.'"

"And so?" said Pauline.

"And so the annulment never came to pass," said Elizabeth Jones. "And less than a year later your sister Alice was born. I was only sixteen, but she came easy as pie. *And*, as a matter of fact, your brother Jim *also* was born that year, which was 1908, and a busy one, believe me. And he came easy as pie. And *they all* came easy as pie, yourself included. And my Aunt Leora journeyed here and bought herself a house so she could sort of watch over me, which was sort of funny, but I didn't really mind all that much. You can't remember a whole lot about her, seeing as how you were so young when she died, but she was a good woman, and she never had anything but my best interests at heart."

"Papa didn't mind?"

"Not a bit. She opened a rooming house, and it was the best rooming house in town, and it certainly had the best *food*, and your father was forever wangling us invitations for Sunday dinner. He was shameless that way . . . especially seeing as how there were so many of us . . ."

"I only remember her a little bit," said Pauline.

"That's too bad," said Elizabeth Jones. She shook her head. "So now you've heard it again—the courtship story. I expect I'm like everybody else in this family, everybody except you, that is."

Pauline frowned.

"I expect I talk too much," said Elizabeth Jones, grinning.

"But I *enjoy* listening," said Pauline.

"You really do?"

"*Yes,*" said Pauline. "It's a *sweet* story. And nobody was *hurt.*"

"And very romantic."

"Yes," said Pauline. "What's wrong with that?"

"Elizabeth Bagley Jones, the Child Bride."

"But she married the right man," said Pauline, "so what difference did her age make?"

"Well," said Elizabeth Jones, "I do thank you for hearing me out so many times. You are a kindly and generous person, and never mind your *looks* for a moment. I only wish there was a little more quiet in your life, instead of all the time this *commotion*, this *zoo.*"

"Do you hear me complaining?"

"No. But then I don't expect I've ever heard you complain about anything."

"Now don't make me out to be a *saint*," said Pauline. "You know better than *that.*"

"Pauline . . . oh, Pauline . . ."

"Yes, Mama? Please, why are you crying?"

Elizabeth Jones blinked, coughed, cleared her throat. "I just . . . well, with *you* I can *talk* . . . which means . . . well, it means you're the only real listener in this whole crazy blabbermouth family . . . and I just hope . . . well, I just hope everything goes well with you. I mean, as long as you keep on being yourself, with your reading . . . and the way you look . . . and all of it . . . I mean, you really just might have a *future* . . ."

"I don't know about my future," said Pauline, "but I do know that I'll always try to keep on being myself."

Elizabeth Jones took a handkerchief from an apron pocket and blew her nose. She wiped at her eyes with her fingers, and then she said: "Can you imagine my behaving this way in front of *Alice* or *Jim* or *Phyllis*? They'd put me in the Athens State Hospital . . . or worse. And with all the love in the world, too, as though they were doing me a great big favor . . ."

"That won't happen," said Pauline.

"And I do love them," said Elizabeth Jones. "I love them all. It is nice to work for people for year after year and not come out hating them. I mean, whether they're your children or *whoever* they are . . ."

"Yes, Mama," said Pauline. "That is absolutely right."

"There is no such a thing as a dull day or a dull person—not if you look at them in the proper light."

"Yes, Mama. Every day is a miracle, and every person has a story."

"I hope you'll always believe that," said Elizabeth Jones.

"I will," said Pauline.

"And try not to be afraid of what the world might think of you. Always do what you believe to be the right thing."

"Yes," said Pauline.

"Your father, when he brought me here, and the town found out I was only *fifteen years of age* and he'd *plucked* me, so to speak, from a *girls' school*, well, you can *imagine* what was *said*. This was before Aunt Leora came to Paradise Falls, and so there was no one I really could turn to. Your father and I were living out on Wells Street in those days, 1907 it was, and every morning and afternoon I swear every nibbynose in Paradise Falls would walk by our little house and crane her . . . or *his* . . . neck trying to get a peek into the front room . . . as though maybe we were doing Lord knows *what* in there . . . dancing naked around the sofa . . . I don't know . . . *now* it's funny, but *then* it wasn't. The first two years, I couldn't even go outside to keep a *vegetable garden* for fear all the nibbynoses with their nibby eyes would maybe burn holes in me. I mean, I couldn't even hardly go outside to the *privy*. I kept feeling as though the nibbies were watching me with great big nibby *spyglasses*. And of course the fact that I was pregnant most of the time didn't exactly help matters."

"It must have really been terrible," said Pauline.

"In a way," said Elizabeth Jones. "And especially when your father was off selling. But then, when he'd come home, we'd sit in that little front room and he'd say to me: 'Lizzie, you're a famous personage, you know that?' And then he'd laugh, and he'd make me laugh, and—seeing as how in those days I really *was* most of the time in the family way—he'd press his head against my middle and try to listen to the baby. And myself, I'd sort of rumple up his hair, and I'd tell him: 'Mister Jones, I would greatly appreciate it if you did not call me *Lizzie*. It keeps reminding me of the stories I've read about that oldmaid in Massachusetts. The one with the ax. *My* name is *Elizabeth*, and I got no interest in axes . . .' "

Pauline smiled. Her hair was long and dark. She pushed it back. "You and Papa never have regretted a thing, have you?"

"Not really," said Elizabeth Jones. "Not even all the commotion. I didn't really bargain for *seven* of you, but then things don't always work out . . . ah, *neatly*."

"And I was the seventh," said Pauline. "The straw that broke the camel's back."

"I am *your mother*," said Elizabeth Jones. "I am not a *camel*. Do I look like a camel? Do I look as though my back has been broken?"

"Nothing really shows," said Pauline.

"Thank you for that small favor," said Elizabeth Jones.

"I am really one of the world's outstanding humorists," said Pauline.

"You could have fooled me," said Elizabeth Jones.

Pauline smiled at her mother. One of her favored precious words came to mind, and it was of course *benevolence*.

"There are a great many special things about you," said Elizabeth Jones.

"That's not true," said Pauline.

"Don't talk that way," said Elizabeth Jones. "The road to You Know Where is paved with false modesty."

"All right. Then name something special."

"Your looks."

"My *looks*," said Pauline. "I have no control over that. I—"

"Your quietness then," said Elizabeth Jones. "You were the quietest of all my babies. Perhaps you couldn't get a word in sideways . . . I don't know. But you never were any bother. And you never *have been* any bother. Except as far as *boys* are concerned, and you seem to bother *them* a great deal."

"I don't mean to," said Pauline.

"I know that," said Elizabeth Jones.

"I don't *push* anything," said Pauline. "The things they say to me, I don't *ask* them to say those things."

"I believe you," said Elizabeth Jones.

"I'd just as soon read a book," said Pauline.

"Which is one of the reasons you drive them mad," said Elizabeth Jones.

"Now, *Mama*, I don't drive anybody *mad*," said Pauline.
"That's what you think," said Elizabeth Jones, winking.
Blushing a little, Pauline looked away from her mother.

But Pauline's demurrers and blushes were simply an appropriate expression of what she saw as a necessary maidenly modesty—at least
in 1943 or 1944, say, or 1945. She was graduated from Paradise Falls High
School in 1943 as valedictorian, and the previous autumn she had been
overwhelmingly elected Homecoming Queen for the annual big football
game with Logan, a traditional rival. Bookish and quiet, she nonetheless
was unable to suppress her ambience, or whatever it was, so she received
notes, some poetic . . .

> You are majestic as a sunrise
> And limpid as the dew
> On the vernal morn's
> Sweet meadows and rills.

some more direct . . .

> I LOVE YOU, PAULINE. I LOVE YOU I LOVE YOU I LOVE YOU I
> LOVE YOU I DO! I DO!! I DO!!!

and some downright indecent . . .

> whenever Im aloan and I get to thinking of too hard on you I get a hard on of
> my own and so I jak off and I see your tits and your pussie and your begging
> me for my cock and I say to you Yes Pauline beg for it and beg for it some
> more THATS WHAT I FEEL AND I THOT YOUD LIKE TO KNOW

and usually these notes (always anonymous, of course) were slipped into
one of Pauline's schoolbooks, or occasionally they were shoved through
the tiny ventilation slot in her hall locker, and once she even found one
folded neatly inside her clothes in the girls' gym locker room. It was written in a fragile backhand, and the *i*'s were dotted with circles, and it was
fascinating . . .

> There is more to life, Dear Heart, than the OBVIOUS and the CONVEN-
> TIONAL. I shall go to the grave loving you with all the frenzy I possess. I

shall reveal myself to you in due course, and you will know true happiness. You see me every day, but I am more than you ever imagined, yet there is no reason to fear me. I adore you. YOUR (TEMPORARILY) INVISIBLE LOVER. (An Urgent Postscript—Beware all boys who have sweaty hands and long filthy tongues!)

and surely it was the most puzzling but at the same time intriguing of all the unsigned notes Pauline received. She was intelligent enough to realize that it unquestionably came from a girl or woman, and she was not particularly shocked, but she just wished everyone, male and female, would leave her alone for a little while longer. Oh yes, in due course she no doubt would fall in love, but due course was soon enough. In the meantime, she wanted to be alone with her books, to enjoy apartness, to take long walks and suck sassafras and put the various parts of herself together in a way that would make sense, a way that she could endure. And so she said to herself: My goodness, why can't they all just please *pretty* please leave me *alone*? Why does there always have to be such a *fuss*? I mean, isn't there enough fuss in this crazy family of mine, with Harry Dana forever complaining about old Mr Truscott, with Kenny and Kristine and Morris and Sandra and all the rest of them and all those games of Pit and Touring (and yes, they do play quietly, but I have to keep *working* at them to play quietly), and all the time doors are slamming, and everybody is trying to be heard over everybody else, and I pity any little bunnyrabbit or pussycat that would come wandering around *our* place by mistake . . . the poor thing would keel over from heart failure. Oh my goodness, to be where it's quiet . . . oh my, oh *my* . . . quiet, with maybe one person who'd say to me: *Pauline, you are a Deep Person, and it wouldn't matter to me if you had fifteen warts on the end of your nose and nine harelips and three wooden legs* . . . quiet, with maybe that person saying: *We can read aloud to one another. Would you like that? Would it please you, dear Pauline?*

Pauline eventually found that one person.

And they read aloud to one another.

They read aloud to one another for many years.

They read aloud to one another and they read aloud to one another and they read aloud to one another.

And finally they decided they perhaps needed to visit a doctor.

And they told the doctor how often they read aloud to one another.

And the doctor smiled and said: "My God, it's a wonder the two of you don't have permanent laryngitis."

"I don't think that's very funny," said Pauline.

"Neither do I," said Lloyd Sherman.

The doctor looked at Pauline and said: "But tranquil days were your goal, weren't they?"

"Yes," said Pauline, "but now I want more."

"From *him*?" said the doctor, indicating Lloyd Sherman.

"Yes," said Pauline.

"I see," said the doctor.

"And I want more, too," said Lloyd Sherman.

"Really?" said the doctor.

"Yes," said Lloyd Sherman.

"I wish I could believe you," said the doctor.

Lloyd Sherman sucked on his knuckles.

Pauline looked narrowly at the doctor and said: "Are you supposed to be trying to help us, or do all you care about is getting Lloyd upset?"

Lloyd Sherman removed his knuckles from his mouth. "Thank you, darling," he said to Pauline.

"And the cow jumped over the moon," said the doctor.

"What?" said Pauline.

"Perhaps it might be useful to recite nursery rhymes," said the doctor. "God knows, we're not accomplishing anything else."

Pauline burst into tears.

Lloyd Sherman went to her and embraced her. He murmured something salivary and indistinct.

"Right," said the doctor. "Typical. I really shouldn't have expected anything else."

At this point, Lloyd Sherman also burst into tears. He sucked spit.

"Terrific," said the doctor.

The doctor's name was Karl Weinshank, and he had spent his boyhood in Chicago, and for years people had asked him whether he was related to a man named Al Weinshank, who had been one of the victims of the St Valentine's Day Massacre. But now a great deal of water had gone over the dam, and hardly anyone remembered the names of the victims of the St Valentine's Day Massacre, and anyway, Karl Weinshank happened to be no relation to the late Al. He had never moved in the same circles; he had no use for violence; it seldom was creative. Now, though, talking with this pathetic couple, Dr Weinshank felt it had become necessary to pull their dignity out from under them . . . a form of violence, to be sure, but at least one that perhaps was aimed toward truth. This did not mean, though, that Dr Weinshank was insensitive. Far from it. After about twenty seconds of watching Pauline Jones and Lloyd Sherman embrace and weep and snuffle, Dr Weinshank turned away from them. He glanced out a window and saw a brown autumn lawn and gray autumn trees, and he saw a white cat licking its private parts. The year was 1954, and the lawn and the trees were part of the grounds of the Ohio State University, in Columbus, Ohio, and Dr Weinshank had been a staff psychiatrist at the university hospital since the end of World War II. Miss Jones and this poor androgynous Sherman had been referred to him by a general practitioner named Groh, from Paradise Falls. In the letter of referral, this man Groh had written: *I do not want to color your judgment, but in my view the situation is hopeless, almost farcical and not a little sad.* And Dr Weinshank agreed. This was his third session with these two, and he had no real idea why he was allowing them to waste their time this way. Was it curiosity? Amusement? God, no, certainly not *amusement*! No . . . the thought was intolerable. Abruptly Dr Weinshank turned from the window. He stood up. He went to the weeping huddled Miss Jones and Sherman. He did not know what to say, but he knew he had to say something, and so he said: "We can never be what we can never be."

There was a break in their sobbing. They blinked up at Dr Weinshank.

The doctor shrugged. *"We can never be what we can never be,"* he said. "Ah, such profundity. The college atmosphere, you see. The groves of Academe. Perhaps I am in the wrong profession. Perhaps I should write inspirational articles for *Christian Century*."

"What?" said Miss Jones, frowning.

Dr Weinshank could think of nothing further to say.

Sherman was wearing a herringbone jacket, and it was quite smart. He took a handkerchief from its breast pocket and dabbed at Miss Jones's eyes. "A nice clean hanky for my Pauline," he murmured. Then he dabbed at his own eyes, wiped his wet mouth, snuffled a little and said to Dr Weinshank: "I want to marry her, and she wants to marry me, and you're supposed to be able to help us."

The doctor snorted. He returned to his desk and sat down. He felt terribly tired; his neck ached; there was pain in his shoulders. "You've got to be kidding," he said.

"No," said Sherman.

"No," said Miss Jones.
Grimacing, Dr Weinshank rubbed the back of his neck.

Lloyd Sherman and Pauline were not kidding. Their love had been ordained in the stars and nourished on Ross Lockridge and Claude Debussy and *Our Town,* and it would overcome Lloyd's agony, and he and Pauline would read to one another for the rest of their lives . . . quietly . . . with dignity . . . with compassion and understanding and respect. (And no one would laugh.) And from time to time, if the reading proved too moving, he would give her his hanky. (And no one would laugh.) Or perhaps she would give him hers. And they would stroke one another. (And no one would laugh.) And perhaps then he would show her he was a real man. He would become stiff, and he would throb. (And no one would laugh.) And she would not have to manipulate him, or get on top of him, or give him her gloves to wear, or anything like *that.* (And no one would laugh.)

It is no easy or quick journey from ambience to sawdust, from demurrers and pretty blushes to first love, then to sentimental words, then to grotesque desperation, then to astonishment, then to loss, then to defeat, then to fear and tears and curdled emptiness. Certainly the Pauline Jones of 1943 or 1944, say, or 1945 gave no hint of that sort of decline. Not *that* Pauline Jones. Not on your *life.* She was tall and longlegged, with square shoulders that were ideal for the boxy blouses and suits and dresses of those years, and her dark hair, her moist mouth, her enormous hazel eyes . . . all combined to make the young men of Paradise Falls (those who weren't off to the war) just about want to fall down and suck their tongues and make weak jerking movements with their knees and elbows. Strangely enough, though, the young *women* of Paradise Falls really did not resent Pauline. They sensed that she refused to use her good looks to take advantage of them, and they sensed that she did not *seek* all the ardent declarations of the young men who pursued her, and they sensed that she would rather read a book than entangle herself with one of the young men in the back seat of somebody's Studebaker. A severe shortage of young men surely did exist in 1943 and 1944 and much of

1945, but the young women (perhaps out of wisdom, perhaps out of generosity, perhaps out of both) did not take out their frustrations on Pauline. And what clearer proof of this had there been than the Homecoming Queen election of 1942? After all, both boys *and* girls had participated, and Pauline had received close to seventy percent of the vote. And she was just as surprised as she was pleased. The thing was—she did not *mind* the ardent declarations. There was nothing *wrong* with her. Quite a few times, depending on the fellow, she actually out and out *enjoyed* the sessions in the back seats of the Studebakers or whatever. But it wasn't as though she *lived* for the sessions. It wasn't as though she counted the hours. But she certainly was not *cold*—and a number of the young men, wracked with shooting pains and intense postfacto nausea, surely could attest to *that*. Oh, she found it all pleasant and just as gosh and golly diverting as the dickens, but really now, weren't there *other* things in life that were at least equally important? And she would say to her mother: "It's all of it very nice in its place, Mama, but that doesn't mean twenty-four hours a day, does it? I mean, I like to feed birds, too. And water the plants. And listen to music on the radio. And Jack Benny. And drink the water from the spring out back of the old Soeder place. I mean, fine . . . I like it, the kissing I mean, the kissing and the hugging . . . but there's got to be something sweet and gentle to go along with it, something besides all the *sweat* and the *groaning* and all. Oh, Mama, am I some sort of nitwit, or isn't it important that *feeling* be there, that all the *breathing* and all the *talk* and all the *moving around* have got to be more than just some sort of . . . ah, *ceremony*?" And Pauline's mother always assured her that yes, she was on the right track; she had a good grasp of what was important and what wasn't. And then came that astonishing Homecoming Queen election of 1942, and Pauline tried to figure out exactly what it meant. That she was the most beautiful senior girl at Paradise Falls High School that particular autumn? Well, maybe so, even though it made her uncomfortable to admit that so many others believed it. But was there anything *beyond* that? Did she project some sort of magical quality that was beyond beauty? Unfortunately, she did not think so. She had no close girlfriend . . . and this distressed her. Granted, she had no serious enemies either, but sometimes she so fervently wanted a *chum* to *talk* with, someone besides Mama, someone who simply *liked* her without being *in love* with her or sending her unsigned notes or stuff like *that*. So Pauline supposed that her seventy percent of the vote was simply an acknowledgment of how she looked, and nothing more could be read into it. In October of 1942, at Paradise Falls High school in Paradise Falls, Ohio, great store apparently was placed in acknowledgement—yet Pauline had no choice but to admit that there was no real *liking* involved, or *popularity,* or *effervescence,* or any of the conventional factors that usually won a Homecoming Queen election. (There was a gold and crimson float, and Pauline sat on an enormous throne that had been flocked in more gold and crimson, and her two attendants—Frannie Loomis, who had received fifteen percent of the vote, and Jane Masonbrink, who had received seven percent—stood behind the enormous flocked throne and waved and smiled at the crowd, and of course Pauline's dress was gold and crimson, and her crown was a great glistening oval of rhinestones, and she waved and smiled at the crowd, and there was a strong wind that afternoon, and it came from the north, and it put goosebumps on her arms and the exposed part of her bosom, her *upper* bosom of course, and she kept sweeping her hair back from her eyes, and the float was propelled by a dozen boys who pushed it from inside its gold and crimson skirt, and now and again she was able to hear the boys grunt and curse, and Frannie Loomis and Jane Masonbrink giggled, and Pauline *wanted* to giggle, but *she* was the *queen,* and it would not have been *proper,* and so she simply continued to wave and smile at the crowd, and many were the boys who whistled and made hubbahubba noises, and the PFHS marching band tootled and bleated and thumped, and Pauline was introduced at halftime over the public address system, but Logan won the game, 34–13, and Mr Dietz, the Paradise Falls coach, became so wrought up he was just about carried off the field in a bucket. Pauline's date for the Homecoming Dance that night was a boy named Lew Amberson, whose father was an English teacher at the school. Lew was the best player on the Paradise Falls team, and he was upset that the game had turned out so badly. So later that night, when Pauline and Lew were necking in the back seat of his father's car, she allowed Lew to stroke her breasts . . . which apparently made him feel a bit better, at least for the moment. Years later—many years later—Lew Amberson was elected mayor of Paradise Falls, and Pauline voted for him, but of course by that time he had nothing to do with her and would not have been seen with her if one had placed a revolver to his temple—and he probably would sooner have swooned and perished than admitted that he'd once sought and found succor in her bosom. But *she* knew *differently,* and sometimes the thought almost made her smile. But she never did quite smile. There was too much sawdust within her by then, and a smile might have caused her to rupture something and spring a leak and blow away like an old croker sack. Who knew?)

*

In 1967 or so, Inez Ridpath said to Pauline: "Once a person lets go a little, then an *army* of Katies cannot bar the door, and the house will fall down, and chipmunks will feast on the roofbeams, and the light of an abiding sun will never be obliterated. The person to pity is the person who had potential. The person not to pity is the person who was a pile of horse poopie right from the start. You boil a chicken too long, its bones will fall out. *You,* you are like a boiled chicken. A chicken is stupid. *John* didn't even like chickens, and *that* is saying a *mouthful,* since there was hardly a single tiny beastie that *he* didn't like, him being so good with animals and all. But *chickens* . . . well, one time he said to me: 'Any creature that eats gravel is not a creature to be admired.' Which seems to make a whole lot of sense to *me.* What ever became of Wanda Ripple? Has anyone ever found out? I mean, compared to *you,* she was a picnic at Paradise Lake. And you surely never would catch her eating gravel."

In 1943 or 1944, say, or 1945, when Pauline was eighteen and nineteen and twenty, it was clear to everyone that she had numerous happy options open to her. As beautiful as she was, she could have made a good marriage with just about anyone she chose. As valedictorian of her class, she could have gone on to college (on a scholarship, since her family had never been well off), and there was a good chance college would have led to some sort of rarefied and glamorous career. But she neither married nor went to college. Hard family times got in the way, and so she went to work at Steinfelder's, in the sportswear department, immediately upon her graduation from high school in June of 1943. (In point of fact, she *was* the sportswear department.) Marriage and/or college was not *canceled,* though, not in Pauline's view. They were only *postponed* until the family problems resolved themselves. She clung to this view for the better part of a decade, until the thought finally became too painful. And anyway, by that time she was so wretchedly involved in the Lloyd Sherman nightmare that she could not afford to divert her attention with a simple and conventional unfulfilled pipedream. But in the summer of 1943, when she went to work at Steinfelder's, the pipedream was very large indeed, and very real, and she just *knew* that she had what she thought of as absolute *oodles* of happy options. For the time being, though, the family problems would have to come first, and she permitted herself to be drafted to help out, so to speak. Her father succumbed in the late summer of 1943 to cancer of the pancreas, and the hospital bills had been enormous.

And Pauline's oldest brother, Jim, had an alcoholic condition that required frequent absences in a Lancaster sanitorium, and—since he was
only a sergeant of police in those days—Pauline was called upon to help
Jim's wife, Emily, take care of part of *their* household expenses. And
then, in late 1943, Pauline's mother moved to Cleveland to take care of
Alice's two children (Alice had found some sort of lucrative War Job, and
the Extra Money was too much to turn down), which meant that suddenly
Pauline was thrust willynilly in charge of the Jones home on Mulberry
Street, seeing as how she (Pauline) was the only member of the family still
living there—which meant that she was thrust willynilly in charge of (a)
herself, (b) the furniture and (c) keeping the place clean and picked up.
That way, when Mama returned after the war, she (Pauline) would not be
chided for letting everything go to pot. Naturally then, she (Pauline), so
recently honored and courted and throned and hubbahubbaed, had little
time to pursue any interests beyond her job and the house, and she felt a
tightening in her chest, almost as though someone had drawn a chain
around it. But that was *dumb,* and she tried to ignore it. Still, she somehow began to suspect that her beauty had started to chip and curl at the
edges. She did not consider herself vain about her looks, and yet for the
first time in her life she examined her face every night with a hand mirror,
squinting at her reflection, seeking wrinkles or dry spots or who knew
what.

But no one else in Paradise Falls believed Pauline Jones was losing
her looks. For instance, any night back in 1943 or 1944, say, or 1945,
all a man had to do was walk into the Sportsman's Bar & Grill and mention the name of Pauline Jones, and the response would be sort of rever-
ential licking of lips, and the customers and the bartender would become
solemn and warmly restless and almost silent.

With only here and there someone saying: "God *damn.*"

Or: "Anybody who'd *fuck* that before *eating* it is nothing better than a
lousy *pervert.*"

The place had sawdust on the floor, and the sawdust was anachronistic,
but for some reason it pleased the owner, Sam Goettling. It gave him the
notion that he was a *thinker,* that his place was *different,* or *quaint,* or
whatever the hell. There were few tables, and almost everyone stood at
the bar, and almost everyone was 4F, but 4F did not necessarily mean
lack of balls, and someone likely as not would say: "I hear she lives all

alone in that place on Mulberry Street now that her mama's gone off to Cleveland or wherever."

And someone else likely as not would say: "All alone . . . what a waste . . ."

And someone else: "She's probably laying in bed right now . . ."

"Me, if she let me at it, I'd brush my teeth and wear a bib."

"Let *you* at it? She'd have to be some kind of loopy."

"I can taste it . . ."

"Shut up. Don't you know there's a war on? Don't you know about the meat shortage?"

And sometimes, laughing, Sam Goettling would buy a round of beers for the house, and lips would be licked for another reason, and heads would shake, and shoes would scuff the sawdust into arcs and mounds.

Pauline wept when her mother left for Cleveland to care for Alice's children, but Elizabeth Jones hugged her and patted her and said: "You'll get along just fine."

"All *alone*?" said Pauline.

"But think of the nice silence," said Elizabeth Jones.

"I want quiet, not silence. Maybe quiet is different than silence."

"That's splitting hairs."

"I hope so," said Pauline.

"You'll do very well," said Elizabeth Jones.

"Maybe I'll rattle around like a pebble in a big bass drum," said Pauline.

"Maybe so . . . but at least if you want to say something, you won't be interrupted. And doors won't slam. You're not *afraid,* are you?"

"I don't think so," said Pauline.

"I don't think you are either."

"Thank you," said Pauline.

"And remember . . . if I didn't *trust* you, I wouldn't go traipsing off to Cleveland or anyplace else. You know that. And anyway, it's only for the duration of the war, and then I'll be back quick as you can say Matthew, Mark, Luke and John."

"*Trust* me?" said Pauline. "You mean with boys?"

"I mean *young men.* You're beyond *boys.*"

"I'll be good," said Pauline.

"I *know* that," said Elizabeth Jones. "You don't have to *tell* me."

"I just hope the war doesn't last forever."

"It won't. Nothing ever does."

"And then who knows what will happen," said Pauline.

"Only the Lord, and He's not giving out much information," said Elizabeth Jones.

Pauline was indeed a good girl . . . but if the truth were known, she had little choice. Except for underage boys and the liplicking 4Fs, there were hardly any available young men in Paradise Falls. And beyond all that, Pauline's beauty was too much of an intimidation. There were those who seriously believed she should posthaste chuck her job at Steinfelder's and catch the next train for Hollywood. One was a woman named Alma Miller, who was about thirty and kept her long blond hair in a Veronica Lake peekaboo. She was in charge of the shoe department at Steinfelder's and she had been married and divorced twice, and it was rumored that she was indulging in some sort of hankypanky with the store's owner, a man named George Wolf. She would shake her head and sigh whenever she saw Pauline, and she would say: "If I were your age and had *half* what you have, I'd be shut of this town so fast it would make your old beezer spin like a top. I'd hike me down to the C & O depot and buy me a ticket for anyplace . . . Timbuctoo or *anyplace* . . . and I'd lean out the train window and I'd holler: '*Excuse my dust, Paradise Falls! I'll see you in the funnypapers!*' In other words, my girl, I would *use* what I *had* until it *fell off,* if you follow me, and I'm not necessarily meaning that in any dirty way. I'm only saying to you: Pauline, you're only going to have what you got for a short time, so don't let it dribble out of you without there at least being some *fun* involved. Now you take *me,* for instance . . . married at seventeen, divorced at nineteen; married at twentytwo, divorced at twentyseven . . . whatever it was *I* had (and it was nowhere near what *you* got) has mostly dribbled out of me, and I got two kids who are very much present, and two husbands who are very much absent, and all day long my fingers smell of *shoe polish,* and at night . . . well, never mind *that* . . . all I'm trying to say is that you're living very precious days, but they're only the *right now* kind of days, and you don't want to waste them." And Pauline smiled. But didn't understand. Not really. When love finally did arrive, it was ridiculous, and she and her lover became laughable, and she clearly would have been better off without both it and him. Back in 1943 and 1944, say, and 1945 (for the most part), she had no way of anticipating her absurdity, though, and all she really knew was those were poor years for young women who sought romance . . . especially young women of beauty, young women who intimidated. She lived all alone in the house on Mulberry Street, and at first she did indeed rattle like a pebble in a bass drum. But then she began receiving visitors. And visitors. And visitors. Her brothers. Her sister Phyllis. Their spouses. Their children. Everyone forever *dropped in* on her, apparently to make certain she had not been raped, or she had not gone mad from silence and loneliness, and the upshot of it all was that in no time whatever the house was just as clamorous as it ever had been, and the poor pebble no longer was audible, what with all the comings and goings, the slamming of doors, the greetings and the farewells and the tears and the giggles, the yap and squeak of the children (until finally Pauline would have to gather them together for one of her quiet games . . . Pit and Touring and whatever), but there were few young men who came calling to see *her,* to pay attention to *her,* and *of course* she understood about the war, and *of course* she understood that her looks intimidated, *of course* she understood those things, but if Alma Miller was telling the truth about precious days (and why should she lie?), then perhaps something already had begun to splinter. But Pauline tried to dismiss whatever it was. She tried to be amusing about it. One Saturday night in February of 1945 she sat up late and wrote a lengthy letter to her mother. It read in part:

This would have been a nice Saturday night maybe to have gone dancing, or off to a movie—there's a new Greer Garson at the Ritz. But oh, no, your dear Pauline sat at home like a lump, and she did her nails and put up her hair, and the telephone rang three times, once from Phyllis just to see how I was doing and was the furnace working okay, once from Emily to tell me that Jim was into what she said was his ninth day on the wagon, and once from some man who wouldn't give his name and said the most *awful* things you could imagine. My mind keeps going back to something I said to you when you went away—something having to do with how I would rattle around like a pebble in a base (bass? I'm too lazy to look it up) drum. Well, as you know, I was wrong as wrong could be. Jim and Emily and Phyllis and Harry and the children and all the rest of them keep rushing in and out, making blessed sure I am "safe" and "all right" and "warm enough" and not "sad" or "lonely" or whatever, and of course the more things change, the more they *don't* change—which means that Harry still is beside himself over the Old Man Truscott situation, which means that if Jim has been on the wagon nine straight days, then Yours Truly is none other than the Queen of Siam, which means that poor Howard's basketball team (poor Howard's poor basketball team) has won only two of thirteen games so far this season, with no relief in sight, which means that Phyllis is of course still taking her singing lessons, but she has changed teachers from Miss Brenner to Miss Kleinsinger because (according to Phyllis) Miss Brenner's breath has in the past year turned so awful and stinky that it's enough to knock over a horse, three mules, five cows, a pig and a frame house—and on and on it goes, you know? The voices, you know? The telephone. The gossip. And so nothing really changes. Or is that all the way true? Sometimes I'm almost ready to believe I can hear the pebble in the base (bass?) drum after all. But how can this be? You'd think there'd be enough to occupy my time, what with all the whooping and hollering. But there isn't, Mama. Not really. I mean, how many times can I listen to Harry complain about Old Man Truscott's butter-milk? I swear, one of these days I am going to buy a *quart of* buttermilk *and pour it right over Harry's head and laugh like the very dickens!!!* I suppose that would mean I am an awful person, but at least it maybe also would be some sort of hint that I am alive. The fact is: I could have a thousand broth-ers and sisters and nieces and nephews, and I could see them every day of my life, and I could receive telephone calls from them every hour on the hour, twentyfour hours day, and yet—*right now, the way I feel these days and nights, with my hair in curlers, with my nails sharp and clean, sitting here like something that's maybe preserved in a jar*—I just too often still think of myself in terms of that dumb pebble in that dumb drum, base or bass or whatever it is. If I seem cranky, I'm sorry, but it's all as though I'm hanging suspended in a burlap bag that has *eyeholes* so I can *see* out but no *opening* so I can *get* out. The war can't last much longer, can it? I mean, what do I care about Miss Brenner's breath? I mean, Phyllis and her dumb singing lessons *anyway.* Who does she think she is—Lily Pons? (I looked up the difference between base and bass, and in this case the right word is bass, which came as a surprise to me, but then who am I to argue with the English language? I got enough on my mind without that.)

It turned out that the letter was not all that amusing, but at least an at-tempt had been made.

As a child, Pauline had had a small gift for painting, and in 1945 . . . probably because she had so little else to do with her spare time . . . she took it up more or less seriously. It was also in 1945 (late in the year, after the Japanese had surrendered) that she fell in love. The man's name was Lloyd Sherman, and he was neat and doublebreast-ed, and he had a shiny Ruptured Duck poking from a lapel. He came to work at Steinfelder's, and her love for him was immediate. He *under-*

stood so much; he was so *kind;* he did not *press* or *rush* or *become impatient.* And he told her her paintings were utterly splendid.

Pauline had taken several art courses in high school, and the teacher, a Mrs Schiller, had told her she had a feel for watercolors and pastels (a *delicate* and *fragile* feeling, to be sure, according to Mrs Schiller . . . but nonetheless rather moving . . . and intelligently so), and so Pauline purchased paints and brushes and an easel, but mostly she worked with the watercolors, and she did cows and trees and hills and barns and such. She trudged. She muddied her shoes. She sought perspective. She tied her hair in a bandanna, and she did not wear lipstick. She breathed with her mouth open, and she smiled. The hills jumbled down on her, and she smelled animals and grasses, earth, vegetables, torn bark. And it came that Old Man Truscott's buttermilk did not really matter. If Walter wanted to blow off about what a hero he had been in the war, and if Phyllis insisted on tearing apart the sky with her godawful singing, and if Jim drank the bats out of the trees and the vultures out of the belfries and if the children forever pestered Pauline to lead them in their silent games of Pit and Touring . . . *all right* . . . *fine* . . . there was a way now Pauline could move out from under the fuss and the hooraw; there were places she could go; there were silences and odors she could cherish. So did she ever trudge, and did she ever paint, and then Lloyd Sherman came along, and he loved her as deeply as she loved him, and so the year 1945 became just about glorious.

Pauline's mother returned home in October of that just about glorious 1945 (Alice had been discharged from her War Job once the Japanese had caved in), and Mama simply could not get *over* how well Pauline had kept the Mulberry Street house clean and picked up, and she told Pauline she really had appreciated the letters, and Pauline said: "They helped me as much as they helped you. Maybe more."

"How so?" said Elizabeth Jones.

"Well," said Pauline, "the telephone just about rang off the hook, but it was almost always the *wrong people* calling, if you get what I mean."

"Oh," said Elizabeth Jones.

"Like if I wanted it to be some young man . . . or even *boy* . . . I got so I wasn't all that fussy . . . to take me to the picture show, it'd be *Phyllis,* and she'd be talking about her singing lessons—or she'd invite me over to her place to sit with her and look at the movies of Papa's funeral . . . the color stuff she paid that man to take. What was his name?"

"Slooper," said Elizabeth Jones.

"Yes," said Pauline. *"Earl Slooper.* How could I forget a name like that? Earl Slooper. Rhymes with pooper."

"He is a friend of Harry's," said Elizabeth Jones.

"Why did she have those movies taken?"

"I don't really know."

"You've never looked at them, have you?"

"No," said Elizabeth Jones.

"Neither have I," said Pauline. "I always tell her no when she calls."

"Good," said Elizabeth Jones.

"But *anyway,*" said Pauline, "it's calls like *that* that I mean. *Dumb* calls."

Elizabeth Jones nodded.

"But . . . well, I still read a lot," said Pauline, "and the painting is a whole lot of fun . . . "

"But there's no young man in your life—that's what you're trying to say, isn't it?"

"Yes," said Pauline.

"Don't worry about it."

"Pardon?"

"Right now your looks scare them off," said Elizabeth Jones, "but one of these days someone'll come along who *won't* be scared. You have to remember, though—*most* of them are telling themselves: Why, that glamorous Pauline Jones, I bet she's so popular she's booked up six months in advance. A young fellow doesn't like to be said no to, even if he's only asking to take you to the picture show or whatever."

"I miss a lot of movies that way," said Pauline.

"But it *will* change," said Elizabeth Jones. "Trust me."

"Promise?"

"Yes," said Elizabeth Jones. "Absolutely. Someone will come along and sweep you off your feet. And he won't be frightened by your looks. He'll just come up to you bold as you please . . . the way your father did with me in that hotel. And all I had to do was *take one look,* and I *knew.* I was only fifteen, but I expect I was an *old* fifteen, if there is such a thing, and I believe there is."

"I miss Papa," said Pauline.

"Yes," said Elizabeth Jones. "I know you do. And it ought to go without saying that I do too. I really loved him, and in every way there was, or at least every way *I* knew about. He used to laugh and joke and call himself nothing but a loudmouthed old *salesman* who *traveled* in *ladies' readytowear*—but there was more to him than just a lot of silliness. He cried for dead things, you know that?"

"Yes," said Pauline.

"You remember when Skippy died?"

"Yes," said Pauline.

"He scooped up Skippy from the street and he ran with Skippy all the way to Dr Westenheimer's office."

"Yes," said Pauline. "And old Ara Cassidy was driving the car that hit Skippy, and he jumped out of the car, and *he* was crying."

"Yes," said Elizabeth Jones. "And Skippy was dead by the time your father got him to Dr Westenheimer's office. He was fourteen years of age, was Skippy, and he was every breed known to man, and to him your father was God."

"Yes," said Pauline.

"When your father came home, it always was an occasion," said Elizabeth Jones.

"Yes," said Pauline.

"Full of noise," said Elizabeth Jones.

"But there is noise and there is *noise*," said Pauline. "With him, it was always happy noise."

"Even Alice loved him," said Elizabeth Jones.

"Yes," said Pauline.

"She hasn't changed any," said Elizabeth Jones. "In her entire life she has loved her father and no one else."

Pauline nodded. Her sister Alice was skinny, close with money. Alice's husband, whose parents once had been welltodo, had lost a foot in an automobile accident, and his parents had lost their money in the Depression. Now he worked as an announcer for a radio station in Cleveland, and Alice nagged at him about everything under the sun, and Pauline had no idea how he stood it. If marriage meant what Alice had with that man Morris Bird II, then Pauline would be very, very careful before taking such a step, and no fooling.

"She resented me all the time I was up there," said Elizabeth Jones.

"Oh?" said Pauline.

"Morris and Sandra are the best little children you'd ever want to meet, and we got along just fine. But one night Alice came barging into my bedroom and told me I was poisoning their minds against her. I was sitting up in bed, and I was reading *Forever Amber,* and I just about swallowed my back teeth.''

"You read *Forever Amber*?''

"We're not talking about *Forever Amber.* We're talking about Alice.''

"But is it all everybody says it is? The Paradise Falls library didn't stock it. Some women from St Thomas Aquinas Church put on a petition drive, and , well . . .''

"Catholics.''

"Yes.''

"Well,'' said Elizabeth Jones, "to answer the *Forever Amber* question, it is no.''

"You mean you weren't . . . *you* know . . .''

"No,'' said Elizabeth. "I was *not* you knowed. Not a *bit.* Now will you let me get back to Alice?''

"I'm sorry,'' said Pauline.

"And sometimes I *still can* you know, even at *my* advanced age,'' said Elizabeth Jones. "I mean, if a person is in a proper frame of mind and has the proper attitude, he can just continue to you know and you know and you know until who knows.''

Pauline smiled. She held up a hand. "I give,'' she said. "Tell me about Alice. You say she accused you of poisoning her children's minds?''

"Yes,'' said Elizabeth Jones. "It seems we had been talking that day, Morris and Sandra and I, something about money, and all I said to them was that there were certain things and feelings that were a sight more important. Which was a very *big deal,* as they say—right? A *deep observation,* as they say—right? But, anyway, little Sandra said something to her mother about it, and so Alice came chugging into my room like the Midnight Express, and it was: '*How dare you belittle my War Job and the Extra Money? If you and Papa had had any respect for money, and if you hadn't gone around having babies every six weeks or so, we would have been a whole lot better off.*' And so I received a lesson in both thrift and birth control, all in one swell foop. With a lot of ets and a lot of ceteras.''

"And what did *you* say to *her*?''

"I told her to go drink some prune juice,'' said Elizabeth Jones. "I told her I was sure it would help make her feel a whole lot better in the morning.''

Pauline laughed.

*

Ah, but it was good to have Mama home again! It would be the best autumn ever, and any day now the right fellow would come along for Pauline. She just *knew* she would find someone (and she was right). But there was one sour thing that smeared Pauline's days, and so what should have been a *completely* glorious season was only a *just about* glorious season. The sour thing was revealed the evening of the day Pauline and Mama had discussed romance and Papa and *Forever Amber* and Alice. A full group had gathered in the kitchen of the Mulberry Street place. It included Mama, Pauline, Jim, Emily, Alan, Phyllis, Harry, Howard, Edythe, Walter and Iris. And Mama said: "I have a little bit of a surprise for you folks."

"My God, she's pregnant," said Jim.

"Hush," said Emily.

"Don't even *joke* about that," said Elizabeth Jones, laughing. "With *my* record, who knows?"

"Looks like Mama's been having a good time up there in the big city," said Jim. His uniform shirt was open at the neck, and he was drinking beer.

Mama laughed again, and so did some of the others. And some of the others didn't. Pauline didn't.

Except for Jim, everyone was drinking coffee and eating slices of an enormous apple strudel Edythe had baked. "Now let's be *serious,"* said Phyllis, wiping away crumbs. She looked at her mother. "Now please tell us . . . what's the surprise?"

"I've sold this place," said Elizabeth Jones.

"What?" said Phyllis.

Everyone else sort of leaned forward.

"I . . . ah, I don't believe it," said Walter to his mother. "You only got here this afternoon."

"Oh, it didn't happen today," said Elizabeth Jones. "It happened two years ago. I sold this house to the Paradise Falls State Bank for six thousand dollars. What do you think of that?"

"I can't believe it," said Harry.

"Myself, I don't know what to think," said Howard, adjusting his hearing aid. (He had had to buy one last year. It had a microphone that was attached to a pocket of his shirt. His doctor had told him he had been involved in too many basketball games and had been exposed to too many screaming crowds.)

Elizabeth Jones looked at Pauline. "You and I have technically been tenants here the past two years."

"Tenants?" said Pauline. "But that means rent. Who has been paying it?"

"It was part of the sale agreement that I pay thirty dollars a month until I came back from Cleveland and found another place," said Elizabeth Jones. "A smaller place . . . either for you and me . . . or for myself alone, depending on whether you were married yet . . ."

"I've been taking care of a house you don't even own?" said Pauline.

"Yes," said Elizabeth Jones.

"I'll be goddamned," said Jim, sipping at his beer.

"*Hush*," said Emily.

"Mama," said Pauline, "are you telling me that every month you mailed *thirty dollars* to the bank from *Cleveland?*"

"Yes," said Elizabeth Jones.

"But why? Why pay rent for *me?* I could have moved out and found a *room* or something."

"It didn't seem fair," said Elizabeth Jones.

"Fair?" said Pauline.

"Yes," said Elizabeth Jones. "You're the youngest, and you've lived in this place all your life, and I didn't think it was right that you be . . . well, uprooted . . . just because Alice wanted someone to come take care of her children."

"But why?" said Pauline.

"Why what?" said Elizabeth Jones.

"Why sell the house at all? Or why didn't you at least wait until you came back?"

"I just didn't want to own this place any more," said Elizabeth Jones.

"Pardon?" said Pauline.

Elizabeth Jones had been munching on a piece of strudel. She set it down. She looked directly at Pauline and she said: "I have had *enough* of this place. I have seen enough of it. Your father has been dead for more than two years now, and there's nothing here that doesn't carry his mark. Can you understand that?"

"I think so," said Pauline.

The others were silent.

Elizabeth Jones resumed: "If Alice hadn't asked me to come up to Cleveland, I don't know what I'd have done. Actually, I'd already started talking with that young Mister Saddler at the bank when the letter came from Alice. I mean, enough is enough. Don't you know how much I loved your father? Don't you realize that sometimes all I have to do is look at a *wall* or a *table* or a *doorknob* and I want to fall down on my *knees?*"

Pauline shook her head. "Yes, Mama, *yes*," she said, "I *understand* all that. I *understand* how you feel—even though you're not really being all that logical."

"Logical?" said Elizabeth Jones.

"Yes," said Pauline. "Papa dies, and so you want to sell the place. Fine. But at the same time you don't want to uproot me. What would have happened if you hadn't heard from Alice?"

"This is getting pretty murky to *me*," said Jim.

"*Hush*," said Emily.

Elizabeth Jones tried to smile at Pauline. "Well," she said, "if I hadn't heard from Alice, I suppose I would have uprooted you. But she solved the problem for me, didn't she?"

"Is all this really germane to anything?" Walter wanted to know.

"Let them get it out," said Iris.

"Yes," said Alan, the bachelor telegrapher.

"Mama," said Pauline, "whatever the total comes to, thirty dollars times however many months it was, I want to pay it back."

"Balderdash," said Elizabeth Jones.

"I'm *serious*," said Pauline. "This is *important*. What am I supposed to be—some sort of *orphan* on *charity?*"

"No," said Elizabeth Jones. "Of course not. But look at it this way—if *I* had been your landlord, would you have paid *me* thirty dollars a month?"

"Yes," said Pauline.

"On what?" said Elizabeth Jones.

"Then I would have moved out," said Pauline.

Elizabeth Jones shook her head. "You *earned* your keep," she said. "You don't owe anybody anything. I called the bank today. Mister Saddler was out, but I did talk with Mister Pflug. You know Mister Pflug, I'm sure. His father, Charley Pflug, used to own Cameo Taxi. Anyway, Mister Pflug said to me: 'Your daughter has cared for the place very well, and you ought to be proud of her.'"

"How does *he* know?" said Pauline.

"This is *Paradise Falls*," said Elizabeth Jones. "It is a *small town*. The nibbies are everywhere. *You* ought to know *that*. But anyway, all I'm trying to get through to you is that you earned your keep by taking care of this place."

"But doesn't the bank want to sell the house? Do banks just buy houses and *rent* them? Don't they *sell* them, too?"

"Yes," said Elizabeth Jones.

"Which means we could be evicted at any time."

"Yes," said Elizabeth Jones.

"So what we really have to do is start looking for a new place right away," said Pauline.

"Maybe yes, maybe no," said Elizabeth Jones, "depending on how quickly the bank can find a buyer."

"But I thought you couldn't *stand* this place," said Pauline.

"All right," said Elizabeth Jones. "All *right*." Her voice was weary. "Yes. I'd like to get out as soon as I can."

"With me?" said Pauline.

"If you want," said Elizabeth Jones.

Pauline glanced around the kitchen. Jim was sipping beer, and most of the others were drinking coffee and munching on Edythe's strudel. Alan, the bachelor telegrapher, was leaning back with his eyes half closed, and he was gnawing on a toothpick. He looked at Pauline, and he half smiled, and he said: "You're the youngest, which means this place is more important to you than it is to the rest of us, seeing as how we've been gone from it for awhile. And we can all understand how you feel. But the world does go on, you know? And we get to a point where we have to face changes, where we have to tear ourselves away from . . . ah, familiar surroundings."

"Happens to all of us," said Jim over his beer.

"Yes indeed," said Phyllis.

"Yes," said Elizabeth Jones. "Yes. Exactly." Then to Pauline: "It goes for me as well as it goes for you. I've lived here thirty years, ever since your father and I came from the place on Wells Street. Which is why I say enough is enough. Things do have a way of coming to an—"

"Don't any of you *understand?*" said Pauline.

They looked at her.

"I'm not saying there's anything *wrong* with selling the house," said Pauline. "I'm only saying that I am not some sort of *baby*. It would have been *all right* to have *told* me so I could have paid my share of the rent."

"Is it all that important?" said Elizabeth Jones to Pauline.

"Yes," said Pauline.

"Well, in that case I'm very sorry."

"I can't ride on a flocked throne all my life," said Pauline.

"What?" said Elizabeth Jones.

"If everybody in this room can face the world, so can I," said Pauline.

"I'm serious," said Walter. "I'm serious about my question. I want to know—is all this really *germane* to anything?"

"Yes," said Elizabeth Jones to Walter. "I do believe Pauline's words gave gotten through, and I do believe they're germane."

Walter shrugged, scratched his head.

"Mama?" said Pauline.

"Yes?"

"I do want to stay with you."

"Really?" said Elizabeth Jones.

"Yes," said Pauline.

"Ah," said Jim, "a happy ending."

"*Hush,*" said Emily.

"I'll try not to cramp your style," said Elizabeth Jones to Pauline.

"What?" said Pauline.

"What?" said Howard, adjusting his hearing aid.

Harry laughed. So did Jim and Walter. Their wives shushed them. Phyllis helped herself to another slice of the strudel. Harry blew on his coffee and said: "Pauline, I'm only an inlaw, which means a person couldn't exactly call me prejudiced. But I can certainly sympathize with how you feel. In a sense, it's like my trouble with my old friend Truscott. Carmichael gives me the same *jobs* and the same *titles,* but they're really only *half* the jobs and *half* the titles, which means he might be thinking I'm not quite *all* a man. Ah, but I won't bore you with all *that* again. I *will* say, though, that you are a beautiful and intelligent girl, and I'm not just whistling down Aunt Hannah's wishing well. And you'll probably make your way very successfully. So just because your mother tried to make things a little easier for you for awhile, don't hold it against her. And remember, you *were* working, and you *did* contribute to your father's medical bills, and . . . " Here Harry hesitated for a moment and glanced at Jim. "Well, there have been other expenses. And you helped with some of *them,* too. Now, though, *now* is the time when your life is about to open up. And so when your mother says she doesn't want to cramp your style, what she's *really* saying is: Pauline, you now are free to pursue your prospects, and I will not push myself between what you are and what you want."

Elizabeth Jones looked at Harry with an expression that was wide, astonished and perhaps even admiring. "Why, *Harry Dana,*" she said, "you have it *exactly.*"

"Well, hooray for me," said Harry.

"Hooray for you," said Phyllis, munching.

Harry looked at Phyllis and gave her the old raspberry. Everyone laughed except Phyllis, Alan and Pauline. Alan was sitting next to Phyllis, and some of the spittle from Harry's raspberry had smeared one of Alan's lapels. Alan carefully got out his handkerchief and wiped the spittle away.

"Thank you very much," he said to Harry.

"My pleasure," said Harry.
Pauline looked away from all of them.

Pauline supposed it all really *was* trivial. She supposed she had made too much out of nothing. Who really *cared* that her mother hadn't told her about selling the house? What *difference* did it make? Ah, but if it made no difference, why had Pauline been shielded from it? The question spat and dug at Pauline, and it probably produced the first scrapings and curls of the sawdust that would build within her, what with one thing and another. And she squinted at herself in the hand mirror. And she told herself: You'd better hurry and find someone, my girl. She told herself: I think I'm beginning to melt a little, or maybe more than a little, like that teeny babydoll I had when I was maybe seven and I left it out in the sun one summer afternoon and all its features ran together, all sort of squishy and blobby. I left it out on the front walk and when I went to pick it up the back of its teeny head was stuck to the cement, and so I wrenched it and I twisted it, and the back of the poor teeny head came loose like old chewing gum, and I ran bawling to Mama, and she told me: *I expect it was just little Tootsie's time. Poor little Tootsie. She was a good dollbaby, but when your time comes, there's nothing you can do about it, and after all, you have to remember—it was God's own sun that did her in. At least she didn't* freeze *to death.* And now I wonder maybe I'm about to be a Tootsie. (And so Pauline squinted. And she was willing to swear she could see the beginnings of lines at the corners of her eyes, and there seemed to be some sort of ominous *wrinkle* in her *left knee*, for heaven's sake, and her right nipple had unquestionably become larger than her left nipple, and surely a decline was setting in, right? And Pauline thought of the things Alma Miller had said. And she decided she would have to get a wiggle on. The lines and the wrinkled knee and the swollen nipple were *signs.* Next thing you knew, Pauline would develop a *double chin,* or maybe *her hair would fall out,* or maybe who knew *what* would happen?)

Pauline and her mother never again did live together. They spent a week or so looking for a nice little place to rent, but then Elizabeth Jones collapsed with severe pains in her stomach. She had a cancer, and all her life savings went for hospital bills. At the end, when she was terminal, she lay in a big brass bed at Jim's home on South High Street. She died in 1948.

From the autumn of 1945 until she went to work for Margaret Ridpath in the autumn of 1960, Pauline lived in two rooms over Hoffmeyer's Restaurant on Main Street. She decorated the rooms with books, posters, dolls, antimacassars and her own watercolors. She and Lloyd Sherman often drank tea there, and they played with one another. She masturbated frequently (she was no Margaret Ridpath), and Lloyd often helped her, and she often tried to help him. Tried.

Pauline occasionally discussed her mother's sale of the house with Lloyd, and one day . . . probably in 1949 or 1950, certainly no longer than that after the death of Elizabeth Jones . . . Pauline said to Lloyd: "Can you understand why I was so upset? Can *you* understand?"

"Of course I can," said Lloyd, "but I still think it's a lot of nonsense."

"It's *not*," said Pauline.

"Oh, come *on*," said Lloyd. "You were just barely *eighteen years old* when she went up to Cleveland. What was she supposed to do? Throw you out onto the street? Stuff you into a trash can?"

"She could have told me the truth," said Pauline.

"Oh," said Lloyd, "it doesn't *matter.*"

"Maybe to *you* it *doesn't*," said Pauline. "But to *me* it *does*. I want to be a *person.*"

"Don't you think you're a person?"

"Not if all the time I'm spared things."

Lloyd shook his head. He and Pauline were sitting on a bench in the Elysian Park. The bench faced the river, and the water was brown and heavy. He was holding both of Pauline's hands in both of his. It was a little late to be still wearing a Ruptured Duck, but Lloyd was wearing one. It winked from a lapel of his jacket, which was a light blue, freshly sponged and pressed. He said: "*I* don't spare you anything."

"I know that," said Pauline, "and we'll work it out."

"You may come to wish that I *had* spared you," said Lloyd.

"Not true," said Pauline.

"One of these days we're going to have to set a deadline and settle the thing for once and for all."

"All right," said Pauline.

"I don't want to hurt you," said Lloyd.

"I know that," said Pauline.

Lloyd looked away from her. "But if I don't spare you anything," he said, "then it'll follow that I'll hurt you."

"Well, that goes with what I want. It goes with being a person."

"I love you," said Lloyd.

"Yes," said Pauline. "And *I* love *you.*"

He looked at her. "It's an easy word to throw around," he said. His voice was white and pinched.

"Lloyd, I *love* you. I am not *throwing* the word *around.*"

"Even when I . . . when I . . . when all your work . . . oh, you know . . . when it just doesn't—"

"Yes," said Pauline. "I know. And even then."

Lloyd grunted. He released her hands. He embraced her, and he kissed her cheeks and her ears and her hair, and she told herself it all would work out; it all *had to* work out. If it did not, then Lloyd was ridiculous, and she was ridiculous, and they did not deserve ridicule. Lloyd was gentle and dear . . . and as for Pauline, why, she had been *Homecoming Queen,* and she had sat in a flocked throne, and the legendary Lew Amberson had stroked her breasts, and the hubbahubbas had been enough to make deaf the heavens. (How many girls got to sit in flocked thrones? Surely those who *did* were *worth* something, correct?)

One Saturday night in the autumn of 1945, about a week or so after Pauline's mother returned from Cleveland, Pauline's friend Alma Miller, the thirtyish blonde with the peekaboo Veronica Lake hair, went on a blind date with a girlfriend's first cousin. The man was a glassblower from Corning, New York, and the next day he and Alma (and Alma's two children) eloped, leaving an abrupt vacancy in the shoe department at Steinfelder's. Pauline did not know *for sure* whether any hankypanky had been going on between Alma and the boss, Mr Wolf, but she *did* know he was quite upset when he learned of Alma's abrupt departure. "And with the *Christmas season* coming on, *too,*" said Mr Wolf peevishly. "And with nobody else knowing the stock or beans from right field." Shaking his head, he placed a Help Wanted ad in the Paradise Falls *Journal-Democrat* and several other newspapers in that part of the state, and about ten days later he hired a replacement, a young man from Wooster. The young man's name was Lloyd Sherman, and he was a little sissified, but he seemed to enjoy meeting people, and Mr Wolf saw him as something of a gogetter. And later Lloyd said to Pauline: "It was the finest thing that's ever happened to me. I came to Paradise Falls, and I found my true love, and by Jimminy Cricket the autumn of 1945 has become immortal. A golden time. A heroic time. I found my darling Pauline, and she says she loves me, and she says she wants to help me, and do you want to *know* something? I *believe* her."

Lloyd Sherman was born and raised in Wooster, where his father had been a judge in the Wayne County Court of Common Pleas and his mother had been active in various garden clubs and temperance organizations. Lloyd was the youngest of three sons, and the other two became lawyers. Lloyd, though, entertained notions of being a college English instructor and then maybe even a professor. He entered the College of Wooster, and he chose the Nineteenth Century as his field, especially Nineteenth Century American Literature. His instructors were impressed with his abilities, his willingness to work, his open enthusiasm for such as Hawthorne, Thoreau, Poe and Whitman. But then sometime late in 1941, just after the attack on Pearl Harbor, Lloyd abruptly resigned from the College of Wooster and joined the Army. He never explained to Pauline what had happened, but later she was able to make an educated guess . . . or two or three or six. At any rate, he somehow got through infantry basic training, but then he was transferred to Special Services, where he attained what he called the *absolutely stratospheric* grade of T/5. Eventually he was sent to North Africa, then Sicily, then Italy. His principal activity was the showing of movies to the GIs. "Actually I sometimes showed them 'mid shot and shell," he told Pauline. "And one time even in a cave in Sicily. There she was, Paulette Goddard, and the Germans were zeroing in on us with those dreadful 88s of theirs, but there was dear Paulette, flickering away, bitchy and glittering, flirting with Ray Milland, and the men were sitting crosslegged on the earth, and they were whistling at her lovely heaving décolletage, and some of them were even sort of rocking back and forth (if you follow my meaning), and the Germans and those infernal 88s might as well have been on *Mars;* they cer-

tainly didn't distract *anyone's* concentration. Oh, ha ha, I tell you—it was some war. Best war I ever saw. On a graduated plane of A down to Z, it *had* to be a B Plus, and that is the absolute *Gospel,* my dear, according to St Lloyd of Wooster. And then, in the fullness of time, your hero here was shipped home, and naturally he was in charge of the movies that were shown on the ship, and one of them was *The Ox-Bow Incident,* and poor Dana Andrews, when they hanged him, someone actually threw a tomato at the screen, and, *kasplat,* a protest was registered. And I for one shared the thrower's outrage. Ah, injustice is a terrible thing, isn't it? The crucifixion of the innocent. Terrible. Just terrible. People don't have all the facts, but they go off halfcocked anyway, so to speak, and they can ruin someone's life *forever.* Well, *anyway,* I was discharged at Camp Kilmer in New Jersey, and I went straight home all right, but I didn't want to go back to the college. It's a long story, but I just wanted to get away from all the *fuss* of academic life. At the same time, though, I didn't want to sit around the house and listen to Dad and Mother. They're both pretty far along, and sometimes Dad still thinks he's on the bench, and sometimes poor Mother still thinks there's *Prohibition,* for goodness' sake. And so most of the time the house makes me feel *sticky* and *antsy,* which may not be a very nice way to *put* it, but it *is* the truth. So, at any rate, I answered the ad, and I lo and behold *got the job,* and so here I am in Paradise Falls, where I perhaps shall be able to find some serenity . . . or, as the fellow says, peace and quiet. And what I didn't know about shoes you could have filled a Webster's Unabridged with, but now I seem to know a lot about shoes, and isn't it all almost amusing though? *Arch supports* . . . *clogs* . . . *bunny slippers* . . . *white ducks* . . . ah, such a tangled web, eh? And to think that I am *really* here because a lady decided to elope to *Corning, New York,* with a *glassblower* . . . can you *imagine?* The Great Chain of Life, eh? Action. Reaction. We are constantly being deflected and bounced about. Ah, like basketballs. Like beans in a bag. And so now here I am, in a place that has such a ponderous and silly and mock profound name as *Paradise Falls* . . . but I am with the purest and most beautiful angel on earth . . . and she says she loves me . . . and our devotion is sweet . . . and oh dear, oh *dear* . . . there's no business like shoe business, wouldn't you say?''

One day in late 1955 Dr Weinshank met alone with Lloyd Sherman and said to him: "I know we have gone over it, but I want to go over it again. Tell me, with as much detail as you can summon, precisely how you feel about her."

"And what I feel I've done to her?" said Lloyd Sherman.

"Yes," said Dr Weinshank.

Lloyd Sherman nodded. He pooched his lips. He said: "I have no idea how other people feel when they love. I only know how *I* feel when *I* love. And the thing *I* feel is a *pain* . . . a *longing*. Oh, how do we prevent ourselves from talking in clichés?"

"Just be straightforward," said Dr Weinshank. "Don't concern yourself with the clichés."

"All right," said Lloyd Sherman, "then if ever a man loved a woman, I love Pauline. And at the same time I am drawing her and quartering her."

"Isn't that a little extreme?"

"No," said Lloyd Sherman. "You should have seen her ten years ago. She was twenty, and she was slender and leggy and unmarked, and she had to be one of the great beauties of the Western World. Now she is thirty, and she is no longer a beauty, great or otherwise, but I still do . . . I still do . . . I mean, ah, pardon me, I mean, what I should *do* is *go away* . . ."

"Have you discussed that with her?"

"No," said Lloyd Sherman.

"Why not?"

"Because it's out of the question. I don't mean to sound pretentious, but I am the world to her. I am everything she values. Her family doesn't understand, and I'm sure a great deal of the town laughs at her, but *those things don't matter*. We have picnics, you see . . . and she does watercolors . . . and I read to her while she works at her watercolors . . . and then, when the light isn't right and she can't work with her watercolors, *she* reads to *me* . . . and we *hug* . . . and we *kiss* . . . and we go to her place, and we listen to the Debussy *Images* on her phonograph . . . and I . . . and I feel everything except *that one thing* . . . I mean, no matter *what* she does, nothing happens . . . unless I . . . I mean, if I go to the closet and—"

"Do you consider yourself a homosexual?"

"No."

"Have you ever had sexual relations with a man?"

"No," said Lloyd Sherman.

"So you don't consider yourself a homosexual?"

"I do not," said Lloyd Sherman. "I am a transvestite. I am not a homosexual. You know that as well as I do. And anyway, aren't we getting off the topic of Pauline?"

"Yes," said Dr Weinshank. "And that's my fault. I apologize."

Lloyd Sherman nodded. "She is considerate," he said. "She will do anything I want whenever I want to do it. We have been engaged for nine years, but she never has become angry. Oh, she *has* indicated *impatience,* but not *anger.* Which of course was why we came to you. She was and is impatient. And so was I. And so I still am."

"You know, you could go ahead and get married," said Dr Weinshank.

"No," said Lloyd Sherman. "That is *absolutely out of the question* until it is *right.* Proper. The on the top on the top, and the on the bottom on the bottom, and everybody wearing the conventional clothing, with me not staggering to that closet. And Pauline feels the way I do. You know that."

"Yes," said Dr Weinshank.

"Nothing in this is hateful," said Lloyd Sherman. "No deliberate hurt ever has been intended."

"Yes," said Dr Weinshank. "The possibility exists that I never have known a more devoted couple. I really mean that."

"Thank you," said Lloyd Sherman.

"But I have helped you not at all."

"But you haven't given up, have you?"

"I have not," said Dr Weinshank.

"Good," said Lloyd Sherman.

"*Not* so good," said Dr Weinshank.

"Why do you say that?"

"Because I *should* give up," said Dr Weinshank. "I should simply tell the two of you that whatever charade is necessary, follow through on it and don't concern yourselves with the top on the top and all that. That is not terrible, and it should not produce guilt, and you should be able to understand that."

Lloyd Sherman shook his head no. He shook it abruptly, like a child rejecting medicine. "No," he said. "No. Never."

Dr Weinshank did some headshaking of his own. He said: "If anything ever comes of this, if anything ever is improved or made *normal* the way *you* persist in thinking of normal, then my name will be in all the psychiatric journals, and I shall be considered a worker of miracles, and I shall be something of a celebrity."

Lloyd Sherman smiled. "We have come to love you," he said.

Dr Weinshank nodded.

"It's not all that unusual, is it?" said Lloyd Sherman.

"Depends," said Dr Weinshank.

"Well, we *do,*" said Lloyd Sherman.

Dr Weinshank had a wretched lunch that day, and late in the afternoon he suffered an attack of gas and heartburn. He drove home and vomited, and he could not get the sad hopeful faces of Pauline Jones and Lloyd Sherman out of his mind's eye. His wife later fixed him some tea and toast, and he had a mild argument with her over the Israel Question. The next morning he had his secretary cancel all his appointments. He lay on the sofa in his office and slept with his arms wrapped over his eyes and his ears. His mouth was full of straw and mice and little balls of lint.

The rhetoric of *purity*, the rhetoric of *angels* . . . for years Pauline and her Lloyd Sherman were able to use words optimistically, and one time he said to her: "If we *love* hard enough, and if we *want* hard enough, we shall by the force of our *will* knock down the Great Wall of China, or cause rivers to reverse themselves, or cause the planet to be pressed flat." And they read to one another from *Raintree County*, from *The Web and the Rock*, from *A Farewell to Arms* and *Spoon River Anthology* and *By Love Possessed*. God dealt the seasons gently, and the great Paradise County sky, endless and profound, seeking its John Wickliff Shawnessey, caused tears to sprout from the eyes of Pauline Jones and Lloyd Sherman, and she told him: "If we die today, if we die with no more than *this*, we shall die with more than most people have." They held hands, and they suckled, and Lloyd Sherman wept, and he said: "I did not *ask* for any of this. I did not *seek* it." And he said: "Sentimentality is bad, and Dr Weinshank says it is one of the things that has prevented him from doing much about our trouble—but don't you think he's just maybe a little bit jealous?" And Lloyd Sherman said: "There is no way this can be understood by anyone beyond the two of us." And Pauline embraced him. And her flesh gave way. And one day she knew she was beyond worrying over Alma Miller's warning. And she rubbed her face, and she acknowledged the wrinkles, and the next time she was with Lloyd she said to him: "I have decided that the only vanity that really matters is the pride I take in my ability to please you." They lay on dry grass at the edge of the river, and he reached under her skirt, and he tugged at her panties, and he masturbated her, and his face was remote and benevolent, and later he thoughtfully sucked on his fingers, and she moaned, and he said to her: "I . . . I need to pleasure you . . . I need that . . . you are my true love . . ." And Pauline, drenched and immense, kissed him. And writhed. And sucked his fingers. And he said something to the effect that the circle was complete, so to say. And he spoke of purity, of angels, of the golden light of hope. He recited passages from Lockridge and Wolfe, passages having to do with trees and passion and the cries of goats, and he said: "We are of course ridiculous. We are a *departure,* and of course we *must* be ridiculous. Otherwise, we would pose too much of a threat. The rest of the world might get to believing *we* knew something *it* didn't." And he and Pauline sometimes sat crosslegged like tailors on the floor of the bedroom in her apartment over Hoffmeyer's Restaurant. They sat naked, and they touched one another, and Pauline responded, but Lloyd Sherman did not. He smiled. He told her the warmth of her hands was a comfort. But never was there anything more than the comfort. "It is a *benevolence* I feel," he said, "and it is *so* sweet, *so* dear, *so* precious . . . but it is not the conventional response, is it? Oh, God." And he would squeeze his eyes tightly shut. And Pauline would nuzzle his belly. And idly he would stroke her hair, and it was as though her hair were an abstraction, and his agony came in dry murmurs, and sometimes it was *she* who was the first to yield to that agony; sometimes it was *she* who went to the closet and found him an appropriate ensemble.

Pauline's first date with Lloyd Sherman was sometime in November of 1945. They went to the Ritz, and they saw a silly Fred MacMurray comedy called *Murder, He Said,* which was all about a lot of people being chopped up in a hay baler. Later they sat at the counter of Burmeister's Drug Store, and they ate tinroof sundaes, and Pauline said: "I wish my father would have seen that movie."

"Oh? " said Lloyd. "And why is that?"

"Well, he was a salesman, and the Fred MacMurray character was *sort* of a salesman. And, well, my father used to tell us all sorts of stories about people who treated him with about as much hospitality as Marjorie Main and that bunch showed poor old Fred."

"Well, they *were* a bit *rude.*"

"Marjorie Main is really something."

"She's *something,* all right," said Lloyd, "although I'm not quite sure *what.*"

"I think Papa ran into a lot of Marjorie Mains—as dress buyers for all the little department stores he visited."

"Oh?" said Lloyd.

"But he took them in stride," said Pauline.

"Good," said Lloyd.

"He did not let them get him down."

"Glad to hear it."

"He had a sense of humor about his work."

"Oh?"

"Yes," said Pauline. "For instance, he liked to say that he *traveled in ladies' readytowear,* which makes for sort of a nice funny image, don't you think?"

Lloyd Sherman dug at his ice cream. He spooned it up. He said nothing.

In 1956, after Lloyd Sherman disappeared from Paradise Falls and never was seen again, Pauline and Dr Weinshank decided that they had worked too hard. And she said: "I would have settled for what we had."

"Yes," said Dr Weinshank. "If it gave him pleasure."

"It *did*," said Pauline.

"Private activities are never grotesque as long as no harm is done," said Dr Weinshank.

"I believe that," said Pauline. "Oh, I do indeed."

"Is there anything I can do?" said Dr Weinshank.

"Show me how not to fall apart," said Pauline.

"I know of no way."

"It didn't matter how he looked," said Pauline.

"To him it did," said Dr Weinshank.

"If he'd wanted to do it hanging from the ceiling, where would the harm have been?"

"Only in his mind," said Dr Weinshank.

Pauline began to weep.

Dr Weinshank nodded. There was nothing he could say. He studied the walls of his office. They were painted a light green, and they were decorated with framed diplomas, certificates and photographs.

Pauline rocked and moaned.

Dr Weinshank took his wife out to dinner that night. They smiled and joked. Later, in bed, he told her he had watched a patient come apart forever. "The woman is about to make herself invisible," she said. He embraced Mrs Weinshank. He said: "My mother was right. I should have been an optometrist." And Mrs Weinshank, who had put away three Manhattans at dinner, snickered a little. Dr Weinshank turned his face to the wall. Pauline's face had been theatrical and loud, but it probably never would be threatrical and loud again. There is a final shriek before most final silences, and he was convinced he had witnessed one. He never saw Pauline again. There was no reason he should have.

Perhaps the wind grieved them. Surely they would have liked to have thought so. They did, oh sweet Jesus, hold hands a great deal. Her watercolors proliferated. They read to one another. They read to one another. They read to one another. They kissed and fumbled, and their days diminished, and sometimes Lloyd would speak of their lives and their terror and their shame, and he would say: "I answered an ad, and it turned out to be a blessing. I answered an ad, and it turned out to be a curse. I've never been what I've seemed to be, but who's to *know* that? How can I *convince* anyone? And why should you have to share whatever this dreadful thing is? Oh, my darling . . . my dearest . . . here yet we have the abiding hills, and the green of them, and the odors of the earth . . . yet words and attitudcs keep shouldering at us, *poking* us, telling us top is top and bottom is bottom and therein lies the only true path to fulfillment . . . but what of the *good* times? What of our *reading?* What of your *watercolors?* What of our *music?* If we are silly and pretentious and floundering in cheap romance, does that mean we are *evil?* Does that mean we should be *punished?* After all, whom do we *harm?* Is it a capital offense to be moved by *Der Rosenkavalier?* When I show you my collection of Aubrey Beardsley sketches, does that mean that the pillars have been pulled out from under the sky? We are laughed at, which of course you know. I am thought to be a homosexual, which of course you know. Your family despises me, which of course you know. What is there *for* us really? Where can it all *go?*" And then sometimes, if they were sitting naked on the floor of Pauline's bedroom, Lloyd would reach for her and stroke her cunt, and Pauline would erupt, and she would nod, and she would tell him yes, yes, do it; go to the closet, and hurry, please, hurry Sighing, Lloyd would get to his feet and walk to her closet and open it and find himself panties, bra, slippers and a robe. And he would fit himself in the blond wig he had bought in Columbus. And he would use Pauline's lip stick and blusher. And by then his erection would be immense. And she would stand. And she would await him. And she would tug down his pan ties. And he would kiss her swollen nipples. And they would fall to the floor. And they would thresh and giggle. And it would end with Pauline on top, with Lloyd's legs spread, with Pauline riding Lloyd, and she came in bursts and spurts and pops, and he flooded her, and he called her LOVER, and he called her MY SALVATION, and he called her PRECIOUS DARLING DEAREST HEART OF MY LIFE, and she kissed her lipstick off his mouth and onto her own, and she licked her blusher, and she stroked his adorable wig, and to fuck him was to fuck herself, but better herself than no one.

Her brother Jim absolutely would not have that goddamned fairy in his home, and on several occasions Mr Wolf took Pauline aside and told her she and Mr Sherman of course were *adults,* but perhaps for their own good (and certainly the good of Steinfelder's) they should not be seen in public quite so often. Still, Mr Wolf in no way threatened Pauline or Lloyd. It just so happened they were too good at what they did. And *separately* they really were liked. Lloyd, for example, was an absolute *demon* in the shoe department, and dollar volume was doubled in the decade 1945-1955. He fussed and smiled and made little jokes; he always was neat, and he always knew sizes and preferences, and he never failed to compliment the ladies. Oh, *everyone* knew what he *was,* but that didn't mean he wasn't a *nice person*—within *limits,* of course. (He never would be allowed to be a scoutmaster or a YMCA swimming instructor, but once his *peculiarity* was noted, he was really a rather gentle and generous little fellow, in the town's view.) But the *courtship* of Lloyd and Pauline was altogether another cup of beeswax. To see them together was to see a hint of some sort of offense against nature, and Pauline received any number of unsigned letters (nothing like her old high school crush letters, though), and they said: *Juliet was in love with Romeo; Juliet was not in love with Juliet.* And they said: *He'd rather fuck one of your brothers than fuck you, you dippy cunt.* And they said: *Under God, degeneracy cannot be tolerated or forgiven. So fall down. Crawl naked on the cobblestones. Plead for absolution before the degeneracy is completely in POSSESSION of your body and the torn remnants of your spirit.* And they said: *One of these days you will be KILLED, you and your pervert BOTH, and the REVELS and ORGIES will forever be ENDED.* And Pauline never mentioned the unsigned letters to Lloyd, although she supposed it didn't really matter, since he had to be receiving similar ones, and probably worse. But somehow she and Lloyd survived for nearly eleven years. Her beauty fell away, and people would have nothing to do with her and Lloyd when they were together (not acknowledging them on Main Street with even the tiniest smile or nod), and these people were the same people who treated them decently and respectfully as long as they were *apart,* and Lloyd said: "Together, my love, you and I seem to them to be the possessors of some enormous secret that just might be worth learning. Because we *are* happy together, and I believe we give that impression. Or at least as much as we can, considering the dilemma out of which we are trying to work ourselves, if you'll pardon my professorial tone." And Pauline said: "You answered the ad. You came here. What happened, happened. I love you. Whatever is necessary, is necessary. They don't know what they're seeing. They don't understand what they're seeing. If they did, I think they would envy us." And Lloyd said: "Oh, my God . . . my angel . . ." And he wept. And Pauline stroked his shoulders and his chest and his bra and his wig. And she closed her eyes and remembered the sweet things her mother had said about her father, about *their* courtship, the jolly salesman and the adoring bride of fifteen. And Pauline shook her head, and her fingers played with Lloyd's wigged curls. Her veins had emerged, and she no longer would be eligible for a flocked throne. *What became of precise little faces? What became of girls who swam palely naked in rural waters?* There were times when, reading to her from Lockridge (or Wolfe, or whomever), Lloyd would stroke her hair and pull her head down until it rested on his lap, and simply the music of his voice and the opaque and endearingly pretentious words carried her dreamily into a sort of gushing and maidenly discovery of who she was and where she was: *In some oriental garden, the seed of it was sown, but it had had its nurture in a womb of fair and fecund ideas on the rim of an inland ocean, and it had ridden west in wingèd vessels, and it had rebuilt itself through more than four levels from its earliest antiquities. Now, impending in the still night was the world of mystery, the world that hovered forever beyond the borders of the County. What was Raintree County except a Columbian exploration, a few acres of discovery in a jungle of darkness, a few light-years of investigated space in nebular vastness! That which lay beyond its borders was simply—everything potential.* And Lloyd's voice rolled richly through this massively earnest curl and stumble of words, and its boyish poetry caught at Pauline's belly like forks and chains, and he said to her, "Perhaps we have passed the borders. Perhaps we are casting about within the potential. Are a few acres of discovery enough?" And Pauline said: "Then marry me. Then forget your . . . . well, your . . ." And Lloyd said: "*No. Absolutely not.* We can free our spirits, my love, but we never can free our bodies, and this is because we never can free ourselves from finite reality and finite attitudes and finite procedures. If, in the final analysis, we are unable to fit the finite roles assigned to us, then we shall go mad. I do not want madness, and neither do you. So we shall continue to *work* at this thing. Wolfe speaks of distant soaring ranges. We shall seek them. Failing to find them, failing to overcome our burden, then we must . . . well, we must perhaps move in opposite directions . . ." And Pauline said: "I'll die." And Lloyd said: "No. You are my Pauline, and you will not die, and you must promise me that you will not die." And so Pauline said: "I promise." And she kept her promise.

One night in the summer of 1956 Lloyd Sherman used his key to enter Steinfelder's. He made off with a number of dresses, women's suits, lingerie, hose, hats and shoes. The total value was more than five hundred dollars, and he left the cash on Mr Wolf's desk. He drove out of town, and no one saw him leave. Pauline had been with him earlier that evening, and they had read to one another from Wolfe, and Lloyd had not indicated that anything was wrong. And he did not leave a note. Not a *scrap* of paper. Not a *word*. All he left was the cash on Mr Wolf's desk. He simply drove away. He simply vanished. Pauline got in touch with his brothers in Wooster, but they had no idea where he had gone, and they gave no particular indication of caring. As for Lloyd's mother and father, *they* were in a nursing home, and they barely knew what their names were. Pauline rode a Paradise Valley Traction bus to Columbus and hired a private detective agency. Six weeks later, after running up a bill of nearly a thousand dollars, the private detective agency reported to her that there was no sense throwing good money after bad: Lloyd Lewis Sherman would resurface only if he *wanted* to resurface—which was not likely. And anyway, the chances were he was living somewhere as a woman. Which meant he really did not want ever to resurface. Which meant he was as good as dead. Which was a fact that had to be faced. And Paradise Falls knew of all this. And Paradise Falls sniggered. And the sawdust came from Pauline Jones in smears and streams. And she embraced those clothes of hers Lloyd had worn. And she masturbated. And she read Lockridge. And she read Wolfe. And she listened to Debussy, Chabrier, Offenbach. She kept Lloyd's wig in a dresser drawer. She examined the past. Apparently endings were not always logical. Apparently they sometimes were nothing more than permanent interruptions. Pauline ached. And she did indeed masturbate. Her family was no help. Her sister Alice was dead, and her brother Alan (the bachelor telegrapher) was dead, and her mother of course had long been dead, and that silly Harry Dana still was worrying about Old Man Truscott, and Phyllis was too fat, and Howard was just about as deaf as a stone, and Walter was too frightened of the manly Iris, his former WAC of a wife, and Jim never was quite sober enough, and all the children were scattered now, and they had forgotten their quiet games of Pit and Touring with their beautiful Aunt Pauline, and

Paradise Falls sniggered; every stone sniggered; every leaf sniggered, every unfound door sniggered, and Pauline's days passed with tearful astonishment, fearful astonishment; they were the days of the leaf of lettuce. Nothing had prepared her for any of this. She had been beautiful, and so she had been spared. Now she was no longer beautiful, and so she was no longer spared. She continued to work in the sportswear department at Steinfelder's, and she continued to follow fashion reasonably closely, which meant her performance as an employee of Steinfelder's did not suffer all that greatly. But it was as though she were performing her job from inside an enormous bowl of soup. She had to *grope* through her eight hours, and she smiled timidly at her customers, and some of them shook their heads. And they whispered to one another, using such words as *ridiculous* and *outrageous* and *unclean*.

In 1943 or 1944, say, or 1945, the planet had rolled within the reach of this Pauline Jones like a bright marble on a mirrored tabletop. It is not everyone who is overwhelmingly elected to sit on an enormous flocked throne and receive the acclaim of one and all. But then it is also not everyone who is so shortsighted and romantic as to believe that 1943 and 1944, say, and 1945 are forever. Alma Miller had spoken the truth. But Lloyd had interposed himself between Pauline and those words. His rhetoric had interposed itself. His gentleness. His absolute love. And never mind the absurdity. Consider only the love. So why then had he suddenly decided to vanish? What specific event had brought it about? Pauline knew she never would know. She knew now of endings that had no note of grace. She deteriorated. She cringed. She masturbated. She abandoned her watercolors. She hid them in the closet that once had held Lloyd's robes and lingerie and slippers. She sat at her front window and looked down on Main Street. Perhaps she expected it to move. It did not move. She listened to the sounds made by the diners downstairs in Hoffmeyer's. She breathed grease. Strange, but all the time she had known Lloyd she never had been aware of the grease. She breathed grease and oils and soups, and her appetite fell away to just about nothing. She grieved. She masturbated. Sometimes she forgot to comb her hair. She read Lockridge. She read Wolfe. She read Whitman. Cadenced phrases pulled at her, but she was unable to rise; she was unable to overcome. If a certain decade is destroyed, then a life is destroyed, and it does not matter if that life embraces seventy years. If certain juices are drained away, they never are recovered. Romantic rhetoric is like insects poking at a concrete floor. So Pauline sat. Pauline decided she was dead but didn't know it. She sat, and she read, and she sucked the cadences, but they did nothing to diminish the sawdust. Yet she continued to see his dear face and hear his dear words. She was flattened, and she clutched; she plucked, but she did see and hear. And she shook her head. And the Hoffmeyer stinks embraced her. And she wept. And she masturbated. And she saw. And she heard. And she read: *O lost, and by the wind grieved, ghost, come back again.* (He never did.)

Margaret Ridpath of course knew all about the absurd Pauline and Lloyd all those years at Steinfelder's—and, in point of fact, she'd been rather fond of both of them. She suspected that perhaps there was not all that much iron in them . . . and then, after Lloyd disappeared and Pauline more or less withdrew from everything except her job, Margaret sensed that perhaps *Pauline* had no iron in her *at all,* and of course Margaret was astonished.

Occasionally they ate lunch together in one of the rear storerooms, and one day Margaret said to Pauline: "What is that you're eating?"
Pauline held up a slice of unbuttered white sandwich bread.
"Is that *all?*" said Margaret.
"Yes," said Pauline.
Wanda Ripple had packed Margaret's lunch, and it consisted of a chicken drumstick, a jelly sandwich, a chocolate cupcake and a Thermos of coffee. Margaret shook her head. "I wish I had your willpower," she said.
Pauline munched on her bread. It had been in a small paper sack. She wadded the sack. "I don't have all that much of an appetite anymore," she said.
"You should not go on and on feeling sorry for yourself," said Margaret.
Pauline said nothing.
"You're still a young woman," said Margaret.
Pauline munched, said nothing. Her jaws moved slowly, and the soft bread made gummy sounds against the roof of her mouth.
Margaret glared at Pauline. It was becoming increasingly clear to Margaret that Pauline was . . . well, not a person to fear. And so Margaret said: "It was all foolish, you know. Nothing could have come of it but

what *did* come of it. So why are you so down in the mouth all the time? You should face what *was*, and you should face what *is*." Margaret wiped her mouth with a paper napkin. She was done with the drumstick, and so she started in on the jelly sandwich. She said: "Oh, I'll be the first to admit that life isn't easy, but that doesn't mean that a person has to—"

"You are a great lady," said Pauline.

"What?"

"The way you play bridge and all . . . you play it well . . . people know who you are . . ."

"That doesn't make me great," said Margaret.

"You are the greatest person I know," said Pauline.

"Balderdash," said Margaret.

"Now that Lloyd is gone," said Pauline.

Margaret swallowed. The jelly went down in a lump. Anger rose sourly. She decided to change the subject. She spoke of sportswear and balances and Mr Wolf's heart condition.

Pauline listened and nibbled.

Finally Margaret left off speaking of Mr Wolf's heart condition. She leaned forward, and she licked jelly off her upper lip, and she said: "You really believe *Lloyd Sherman* was a great person?"

Pauline nodded.

Margaret wanted to belch. She said: "But *you* know what he *was*. You know better than any of us."

"Yes," said Pauline.

"Why?" said Margaret.

"Because I love him."

"Loved him?"

"*Love* him," said Pauline.

"Even though . . . well, the town . . . the things people say . . ."

"I can't help the things people say," said Pauline, weeping. She twisted the wadded paper bag, and it tore.

Margaret wanted to reach out and stroke Pauline, but she did not. Instead, she opened her Thermos of coffee, poured herself a cup, added powdered milk, stirred it, sipped, cleared her throat, then said: "Tears won't help. I'm sure you must know that."

Pauline nodded.

"So stop your crying," said Margaret.

Pauline nodded.

"*Now*," said Margaret.

Pauline nodded, dropped the torn paper bag, rubbed her eyes.

"Tears never solved anything," said Margaret.

Pauline nodded.

"We have to go on," said Margaret.

Pauline nodded.

"He was not a great person. He took advantage of you."

Pauline blinked at Margaret, blinked again, started to shake her head no.

Margaret held up a hand. "*It* was ridiculous, and *you* were ridiculous, and *he* was ridiculous, and the sooner you not blink at the truth, the better off you'll be."

Pauline bent double and wailed.

Margaret wanted to hug herself, but she did not. She'd never experienced anything like this. She said: "He was nothing. Say it."

"No," said Pauline, whimpering.

"*Say* it," said Margaret.

"No," said Pauline. She was bent so far forward her forehead was just about touching her lap.

"If you can't say it, then get out of my sight," said Margaret.

Pauline tried to stand up. Her knees spread. She dropped back.

"Do you respect me?" said Margaret.

Numbly Pauline nodded.

"Then believe me when I tell you it's all for the best."

"The wind . . . the wind grieves . . ."

"What?" said Margaret.

"I . . . the words . . . *his* words . . . all the soft wind . . . and now it grieves . . . the times we had . . . the afternoons . . . him and his books . . . he was *so* able to take me away from principalities of despair . . . *his* phrase . . . and project me into some sort of—"

"*Stop this!*" said Margaret.

Pauline cringed.

"*It's nothing but blah and blah and blah!*" said Margaret. "*He was a ridiculous man, and he was a fraud, and you and he lived a ridiculous life, and you are well shut of him!*"

Pauline drew up her knees.

"*He was ridiculous,*" said Margaret, "*and I want you to admit it!*"

". . . no."

"*Get out of my sight!*"

Pauline began to shake.

"*Go away from me!*" said Margaret.

". . . yes."

"*What was that?*"

". . . yes," said Pauline, choking.

"*Yes what?*"

". . . yes . . . he . . . all right, yes . . . he was ridi . . ridiculous . . ."

"All right," said Margaret.

Pauline nodded.

"All *right*," said Margaret, gasping.

Gagging, Pauline spat up the pasty bread.

Margaret gave her some Kleenex and told her there, there, everything was just fine now. There was nothing to fear. Life went on. Truth was truth. Those who faced facts were cleansed.

What had it been? Vanity? Probably so. If Pauline had not placed Margaret one step behind the scandalous and preposterous Lloyd Sherman, Margaret probably never would have experienced any sort of power to dominate. But Pauline's sentimental judgment had so offended Margaret's sense of rightness and accomplishment (or call it by its rightful name, call it vanity) that for once in her life Margaret had jeopardized herself by coming into conflict with another human being, by actually *hollering* at another human being, by actually *forcing* that human being to *give in*. And all right, so that human being was only the sawdust Pauline Jones, but at least Margaret now knew that her tinfoil spirit had encountered one even less substantial. The discovery had come because she had behaved cruelly, at least for a few minutes, but it had been a glorious discovery, and she really didn't feel all that badly about it. After all, had she *lied* to Pauline Jones? Had she forced Pauline Jones into an *improper* or *untruthful* confession? Of course not. She had simply *exerted* her *will* on the woman . . . and in the cause of truth. It was all very exhilarating. The next time Margaret saw her friend Irv Berkowitz, she would have to tell him all about it. He had been after and *after* her to be more assertive, and he no doubt would be quite pleased with the way she had behaved.

But Margaret never did tell Irv Berkowitz how she had treated Pauline that day. It came to her rather quickly that domination of the likes of a Pauline Jones really didn't represent much of a step. And so she remained silent. But she *did* dominate Pauline Jones, from then until the end of her life. And so, in 1960, after Wanda Ripple died, Margaret chose the line of least resistance (or the person of least resistance). She insisted that Pauline come be her housekeeper. And Pauline obeyed. Pauline packed her belongings, and she packed her watercolors, and she sold her furniture, and she quit her job at Steinfelder's, and she moved into the Ridpath home, and Inez Ridpath never really knew why the situation had changed. Inez Ridpath kept wondering what had happened to Wanda Ripple, who somehow had betrayed her. Inez Ridpath sat and plucked, and the afternoons had broken legs. Pauline wept frequently, and she continued to masturbate, but she was better at the housework than Wanda had been. She made more of a contribution. She cooked more of the meals. Her surviving borthers and sisters all were delighted with her new job. The Ridpath family was a good family, and it had good connections (George Prout was a good connection, and Pete Saddler *certainly* was a good connection, and Harry Dana for one simply could not get over Pauline's good luck), and one day Inez Ridpath said to Pauline: "At one time, I expect there were thousands who courted favor from Ozymandias, wouldn't you say?" And Pauline, who had *heard* of Ozymandias but couldn't *place* him, nodded absently.

The first time Pauline sat with Inez Ridpath was the day of Wanda Ripple's funeral. At that time, Pauline believed she was there only on a *temporary* basis, mind you, until a replacement for Wanda could be found. (She had met Wanda two or three times, and she remembered the woman as having been thin, narrow and not all that friendly.)

It was a bright November morning, cloudless, full of crunchy whirling leaves. Pauline sat with Inez Ridpath in the front room, and she glanced out a window, and she just *knew* that Lloyd would have had something poetic to say about the morning. But all Pauline did was squint, and so finally she drew the curtains, and Inez Ridpath did not seem to notice. Then Pauline perched on the windowseat. Inez Ridpath plucked at the antimacassars on her chair. Pauline scratched her elbows. She pressed down her skirt.

"I know about her pies," said Inez Ridpath.

"Pies? Whose pies?" said Pauline.

"One lime pie a year and she thinks she's doing me a favor," said Inez Ridpath.

"Who?" said Pauline.

"Wanda," said Inez Ridpath. "Who'd you *think* I meant? Queen Marie of Roumania?"

"Oh," said Pauline. "I'm sorry."

"Everybody's sorry," said Inez Ridpath. "The whole world's sorry. But that didn't get me any more lime pie. And I *know* about her. Before she came *here,* she baked pies and cakes until they came out of her *ears.* But now it's one lime pie a year, and if Inez doesn't *fall down on her knees* in *abject gratitude,* there won't even be *that* one."

"But she is dead," said Pauline.

"Who is dead?" said Inez Ridpath.

"Mrs . . . ah, Mrs Ripple," said Pauline.

"Oh," said Inez Ridpath. *"Well."* She turned down the corners of her mouth.

Pauline rubbed her knuckles together and looked away.

"We all are dead," said Inez Ridpath.

"No," said Pauline.

"Wanda has been dead since the day I met her," said Inez Ridpath, "but that doesn't mean she couldn't have baked me more than one lime pie a year. I never have done anything to offend her. I don't know why she has to treat me this way—especially since she is dead and all. Oh, I tell you, what with one thing and another, what with your Mussolinis and your Al Smiths and the poor Lindbergh baby, it's so hard just to *get up* in the morning, isn't it? And never mind whether you're alive or dead. Just to get up is enough. Maybe of a summer morning to smell the flowers in the garden. I like to go out back and sit in my STAR chair. It puts me in mind of a throne."

"I had a throne once," said Pauline.

"And were you . . . ah, coronated?"

"Yes," said Pauline.

"But I expect you don't know where Wanda is. *I* expect she's off hiding with my lime pie."

"I don't want to hear any more about your lime pie," said Pauline.

"What?" said Inez Ridpath.

Pauline stood up. "What are you trying to do? Tear me apart? Well, I won't hear of it."

Inez Ridpath plucked. "Talk more slowly," she said.

"If I have to be struck down, then somebody else will have to be struck down," said Pauline.

"Say again?"

"I do not want to have to hurt you," said Pauline.

"What?"

"Listen to me carefully," said Pauline. "*You* are ridiculous, and *your life* is ridiculous, and I will not *tolerate* any *backtalk* or *whimpering* from you on either of those subjects."

"You sound like Wanda," said Inez Ridpath.

"I am *Pauline*," said Pauline.

"Good for you," said Inez Ridpath.

Pauline went to Inez Ridpath's chair. She knelt in front of the old woman. She pulled up Inez Ridpath's skirt, reached between Inez Ridpath's legs, seized a section of loose thigh and squeezed it.

Inez Ridpath yelped.

"You will do as I say," said Pauline, squeezing.

Inez Ridpath yelped more loudly.

"*Stop* that," said Pauline, squeezing.

Inez Ridpath bit a wrist, and the yelping ended.

"We are at the end of the line here, and we are starting back up on the other side," said Pauline. "Your daughter fears you, doesn't she? And I fear your daughter. So why then shouldn't you fear me? That way, the circle is perfect. I know what she wants. She wants me to come live here on a permanent basis. All right. If she asks me, I will. And when those times come that I have to hurt you, I *will* hurt you but she'll never know, because you'll never tell her, because *you* fear *me* the way *she* fears *you* the way *I* fear *her*. The wind grieves ghosts, and God works in mysterious ways His miracles to perform, and I always will be the quiet and fearful Pauline, but you and I always will know better, won't we?"

Tears drained from Inez Ridpath's eyes. She nodded.

"A secret," said Pauline.

Inez Ridpath nodded.

"And don't talk to me of lime pie," said Pauline. "And don't talk to me of thrones." She released Inez Ridpath's flesh. She pulled down Inez Ridpath's skirt. She said: "And the rivers flow to the sea, and the magical Raintree forever abounds, and the maidens with their precise faces pout and laugh, and we cannot go home again, any of us, not you, John Wickliff Shawnessey; not you, Eugene Gant; not you, Monk Webber; not you, Lloyd Sherman . . . so then all that remains is the words and their thunderous flatulence . . . and they will have to do, won't they?" And so, kneeling in front of a bewildered Inez Ridpath, Pauline lifted her own skirt and reached inside herself and earnestly masturbated. So she did in fact accept Margaret's order to come live in the Ridpath home. Iron is to tinfoil as tinfoil is to sawdust as sawdust is to iron. And Pauline was genuinely appalled by the slapless slaps. And sometimes, when she squeezed one of Inez Ridpath's thighs and busily kneaded the flesh, she would say:

"I am so frightened." And, weeping, Inez Ridpath would try to explain the pleasure the slapless slaps brought, the happy acknowledgment of guilt. And Pauline would shake her head no. She did not want to *hear* of guilt. And she said: "O lost. O dear. O my." She tried to weep in Margaret's presence as often as was believable . . . and her tears were timid . . . and Margaret told her she needed to get hold of herself . . . and sometimes Pauline even embraced Margaret . . . and most of the time Margaret pushed her away as though she were a smelly incontinent child. But Pauline was the first one to understand the circle. Which was her private triumph. Which was larger than any old *flocked throne,* for goodness' sake.

 Pauline did not attend Margaret's funeral and burial in 1974. After all, someone had to stay in the house and take care of the old woman.

Part Five

MISS RIDPATH...

BRIDGE AND TEETH,

LOVE AND GRIEF,

DAYS

It takes no particular display of bouldered tablets to know that a human life is simply an accumulation of evidence. Nor does one need to be some sort of intellectual colossus to understand intersections, collisions, sequences, attitudes, accidents, reactions and coincidences. Everywhere are histories, and either they mesh or they clash, but it is never enough simply to examine *one* history. *Other* histories forever intrude; they are part of the accumulated evidence that defines the human life originally being investigated. In other words, no Margaret Ridpath really exists without a knowledge of Wanda Ripple. And Pauline Jones. And Inez Ridpath. If they had not been what they were, she would not have been what she was. And of course the opposite also is true. If she had not been what she was, they would not have been what they were. After all, she did not live inside a paper sack. She did have a certain impact, and others did have a certain impact on her. (It is 1917, and she is six, and she encounters for one day a beautiful tall lady who wears a white hat, and Margaret and the beautiful tall lady intersect warmly and lovingly that day, and no one can do away with that day. It cannot be erased from Margaret's history. No matter that nothing came of it. No matter that Margaret eventually was saddened because of its failed promise. It *did* exist, and it *did* affect her, and she carried it with her until the day she and those three children had their confrontation, and therefore it was significant, and its existence had to be acknowledged.) Margaret never kept a journal or diary, but in her later years she wished she had. Perhaps a journal or a diary would have given her some understanding of why she had yielded so quickly to George Prout. Oh, granted he was made of the finest iron. Still, he *had* been her sister's husband, and what had drained the decency so readily from her? Geriatric lust? Absolute fear of the sort common to such a sawdust person as poor Pauline? In the last two or three years of her life, often while sitting in the front room with her mother and Pauline and half listening to her mother's imprecise summoning of times past, Margaret would tell herself: One of these days I must take *off* some days and go someplace and sit quietly and sort *out* my days. Someplace with wicker porch furniture, where courteous waiters serve tea and little cakes. (There is no *structure* to *events*. There is no *pattern* to *destruction*. What is it that seeks to dismantle the universe? And why? How do we identify those forces? How do we point out those people?)

Irv Berkowitz smoked cigars in bed, and Margaret told him he was a *terrible* man. She told him the practice offended her maidenly sense of the proprieties. And he smiled at her and said: "Hey, that's the closest I think you've ever come to showing what just might pass for a sense of humor."

"Which means I am *really* being corrupted," said Margaret.

"How so?" said Irv, puffing, rolling the smoke around his tongue.

"In Paradise Falls, there is no future in the possession of a sense of humor," said Margaret.

"Maybe you're selling Paradise Falls short," said Irv.

"Rubber bladders," said Margaret.

"What?"

"Oh, I was just thinking aloud. I was thinking about rubber bladders. The sort that make rude noises when you sit on them. Well, anyway, a rubber bladder is what passes for humor in Paradise Falls."

"Whoopee cushions," said Irv.

"Yes," said Margaret. "That *is* what they're called, isn't it?"

"Yes . . . but still, I think you might be selling Paradise Falls at least a *little* short."

"How?" said Margaret.

"Well, perhaps *women* aren't allowed to have much of a sense of humor, but it seems to me that *male* humor is pretty universal."

"That sounds like a very condescending remark," said Margaret.

"I guess it is," said Irv. "But all I'm really trying to say is . . . oh, hell, I don't even *know* what I'm really trying to say."

"You have talked yourself into a corner," said Margaret.

"Yes," said Irv.

"Would you like me to help you out of it?"

"I'd be much obliged, ma'am."

"Well, I will—*if* you promise to discontinue your Gary Cooper imitation."

Irv's voice rose to a falsetto. "Yesm, Miz Scarlett," he said.

"*And* your Butterfly McQueen imitation," said Margaret.

Grinning, Irv nodded. He rolled more smoke with his tongue.

Margaret was lying flat. She smoothed the bedcovers. She folded her hands on her belly. She said: "In such a place as Paradise Falls, humor is neither *condoned* nor *tolerated* in women. It is enough for a woman to have children, to teach school, to . . . ah, keep the books at a store. These are solemn activities, and it is not *seemly* of her to say something funny. She becomes known as a flibbertygibbet. She is thought of as being a little . . . ah, irresponsible."

"Has it bothered you all that much?" Irv wanted to know. "Have you felt confined?"

"No," said Margaret. "Of course I have not felt confined. It is impossible to miss something you've never known."

"Now aren't you selling *yourself* a little short?"

"No," said Margaret. "Why do you think I am such a good bridgeplayer?"

"What?"

"Oh, come *on* now, Irv—how many funny bridgeplayers do you know?"

"Well, I think I'm not exactly all that dull and humorless a—"

"You are an exception," said Margaret. "Name another."

"Charlie Goren can be amusing."

"Well, he's a *celebrity*. He *writes*. Name me a funny bridgeplayer who *isn't* a celebrity, who *doesn't* write."

"Truman Clapsaddle," said Irv.

"Who?"

"Truman Clapsaddle, of, ah, Saddle Brook, New Jersey, winner of the 1941 Pan-American Whist League Cup. Bid and made six straight grand slams, and his partner was a drunk from Cape Girardeau, Missouri, a man named Eldred Hogsett, and poor Eldred Hogsett didn't have the vaguest idea what was going on."

"You are . . . ah, spoofing me."

"I am?" said Irv.

"You are," said Margaret.

"I suppose I am," said Irv.

"And so you are proving my point, aren't you?"

"Which is?"

"That bridge is not exactly a game for your Laurels and your Hardys," said Margaret.

"Okay," said Irv.

"Which is one of the large reasons I am such a good player," said Margaret.

"And such a modest one," said Irv.

"Be quiet, or I'll . . ." said Margaret, hesitating.

"Or you'll what?" said Irv.

"I'll think of something," said Margaret.

"Good," said Irv.

*

Margaret was a junior at Paradise Falls High School when she began to play bridge. Her brother Paul had come home on furlough from Fort Benning (he was twenty that year and already a staff sergeant), and he and three friends were playing auction in the Ridpath front room. One of the friends, a young man named Herb Pfister, was a member of the Paradise Falls Volunteer Fire Department, and he was called away by a blaze in an old shed out at the fairgrounds. Margaret had been watching the game and from time to time fetching beer and pretzels for the players, and so she was drafted to replace Herb Pfister. Later, whenever she told this story, she would smile and say: "Oh, it'd be nice to report that I sat down and immediately pulled off three triple finesses, a double squeeze and the Albanian Coup, but it didn't quite work out that way. Oh, I *did* know a heart from a club from a diamond from a spade, and I *did* know the deck consisted of fiftytwo cards, which meant there were thirteen in each suit . . . and I think I knew one had to follow suit until one was void . . . but that was about the extent of it. I'll never know how they put up with me that night. I believe I was Paul's partner, and I believe he spent a lot of time cursing whatever it was that had caused the little fire out at the fairgrounds. The other two players were named Tom Cowens and David Lanier, and I do seem to recall that they laughed a great deal. Oh well, it may have been the beer. It was strong stuff, enough to scald your scalp, I'm told." And then, likely as not, Margaret would say: "I decided to study the game a little. I figured I *had* to. Lord knows, another shed might have burned down, and I didn't want to be torn limb from limb by someone perhaps a little less understanding than my brother." And study the game Margaret did. She became infected by its rhythms and its progressions. Sometimes she spoke to her chum Lexie Musser about it, and Lexie was of course both baffled and angered. "Great day in the holy *morning*," said Lexie, "you have a *boyfriend,* and you have your *looks,* and you have the one and only *me* as your best friend, and so why do you waste your time with your whatchamacallums, your trumps or whatever?" And Margaret said: "If you took up the game, maybe you'd understand." And Lexie said: "You want to bet?"

In the year 1930, playing with a girl named Doreen Pauley as her partner, Margaret won sixteen of the fortysix weekly duplicate games held in the Acterhof House under the auspices of the Paradise Falls Bridge & Whist Association.

The following year, Doreen eloped to Pikeville, Kentucky, with a boy named Junior Mayes, and Margaret was forced to play with a number of partners. Nonetheless, she gained tops in fourteen of fortyfour games.

In 1932, with a young man named Otto York as her partner, Margaret won an unheardof twentytwo of fortysix games, and most of the other members of the Paradise Falls Bridge & Whist Association were convinced that Otto and Margaret were of state tournament caliber.

In 1933, therefore, Otto York and Margaret Ridpath entered the Ohio State Contract Bridge League open division tournament, held that year in Toledo. For the sake of the proprieties, Margaret's mother traveled with them, but it was a short stay. Otto and Margaret became quite nervous, and they underbid, and they were knocked out in the first qualifying round. On the train returning to Paradise Falls, Inez Ridpath shook her head and said: "It surely does seem like an awful lot of riding back and forth for an awful lot of nothing." (In the meantime, though, Otto and Margaret *did* win twenty of the fortyseven weekly duplicate games at the Acterhof House.)

In 1934, Otto York fell in love with and married a girl named Norma Soeder, and she told him in no uncertain terms that she refused to be what she called a Bridge Widow. And so Otto apologetically brought his tournament playing to an end. Which meant Margaret once again had to make do with whatever partners she could find. But by that time she was such a splendid player that her partners' abilities—or lack of abilities—really didn't matter all that much, at least in Paradise Falls. So she ended the year as winner of seventeen of fortytwo of the Paradise Falls Bridge & Whist Association duplicate games.

In 1935, she again participated in the Ohio State Contract Bridge League open division tournament, and this time her partner was none other than Mr Elmer Carmichael *himself,* president of the Paradise Falls Clay Products Co and reputedly the richest man in town. He was a reasonably good player, even though he did have a tendency to overbid, and he and Margaret came out of the tournament with one section top, which was not bad for relative beginners. He made a sort of lackluster pass at Margaret in the cocktail lounge of the Neil House. She was of course petrified, but she had little trouble pushing him away, and in point of fact he even got to laughing a little about it, and after a time he told her: "Well, a man does have to do what's expected of him. I mean, I wouldn't want you to think I'm too old. Not *Elmer Carmichael.* Not on your *tintype.*" He grinned. "The only thing is," he said, "don't let it wither away." His grin was not unkind. He patted her knee. He told her he was sorry if he had embarrassed her. Margaret nodded. She could not speak. Her mother had not accompanied her this time. It was 1935, and of course by that year Inez Ridpath had wandered too deeply inside her forest of grief and guilt. The day after the tournament, Elmer Carmichael drove Margaret back to Paradise Falls, and he said to her: "You are so good at the damned game that it's almost *spooky,* do you know that?"

"I wasn't aware of it, no," said Margaret.

"Well, be aware of it," said Elmer Carmichael. "This is Elmer Carmichael talking, and he knows whereof he speaks. That woman from Galion . . . I don't know what her name was . . . the woman who wore the pink dress and had the sevencard spade suit to the ace, queen . . . and the way you went and doubled her on your void . . ."

"But it was only logical that you had five. And if *you* had doubled, her partner might have rescued at five hearts, which he could have made with all the proper finesses. But with *my* doubling the spades, and since he *did* have *one,* and since *I* was the one who was finessable, and since from the way she was bidding he couldn't have been blamed for believing she had *eight* or *nine* . . . well, the double just seemed like a good bid."

"True," said Elmer Carmichael, "but you made it as though you were asking the butler to please fetch you another lump of sugar and maybe a watercress sandwich."

"Well," said Margaret, "after all, it's only *bridge.* It's not *grand opera.*"

"How old are you?"

"That is not a proper question to be asking," said Margaret, smiling.

"And I am the proper person to be asking improper questions," said Elmer Carmichael. "They have been my trademark."

"I *bet,*" said Margaret.

"So answer it."

"Well, for your nosy information, I am twentyfour years of age."

"*Twentyfour*? Is that *all*?"

Margaret glared at Elmer Carmichael. "Are you trying to suggest that I look older?"

An amused sound came from deep in Elmer Carmichael's throat. "No," he said, "I am not. I am, though, suggesting that you *act* a hell of a lot older."

"Is that some sort of sin?"

"Not at all," said Elmer Carmichael. "The only thing is, try not to become old before your time."

"I'll try," said Margaret.

"I certainly didn't mean any offense," said Elmer Carmichael.

"None taken," said Margaret.

"Thank you," said Elmer Carmichael. He was silent for a moment or two. He grimaced out at the highway, which was Ohio US 33-A. He said: "You hear the sound the tires are making on those bricks?"

"Yes," said Margaret.

"Those are Paradise Falls Clay Products bricks," said Elmer Carmichael. "Those are *Elmer Carmichael* bricks." He hesitated, shook his head. "A very important piece of information, right? I have good friends in the Ohio Department of Highways, and . . . well, Democrat or Republican . . . makes no nevermind . . . I work hard at what I do . . . and, ah, I had a brother once. He was much older than I was, and *he* worked harder than *I've* ever thought of working, and *he* had strength like it was coming out of him like *iron ore* . . . but I don't know . . . it seems to me he missed an awful lot . . . and as for Yours Truly here, well, I got all wrapped up in all the fussing *too* . . . in all the backing and filling *too* . . . and I suppose that's the way a man is supposed to behave . . . and I'm not saying I *mind* it . . . because I *don't* mind it, and I wouldn't know what to do without it . . . and if you think I'm sentimental or falling apart, you got another guess coming . . . but the thing is, young lady . . . the thing *is* . . . there got to be times when a person can sit back and *relax,* you know? What I mean, times when maybe a person even can be a little *silly,* you know? And a person such as yourself, how often in your life have you been silly?"

Margaret did not reply.

"That's what I figured," said Elmer Carmichael.

Margaret hugged herself. "I don't see why it's so important to be silly," she said. "*My mother* is silly just about *every day,* and there's nothing much *to* it, believe me."

"I'm only saying that there's more to life than counting trump," said Elmer Carmichael.

"*I* never said there *wasn't,*" said Margaret.

"But sometimes you sort of give the impression," said Elmer Carmichael. "I mean, now and then I talk with George Wolf, and he tells me you are a *miracle*; he tells me he doesn't know how you *do* it."

"Do what?"

"Work the way you do," said Elmer Carmichael. "Concentrate the way you do. Oh, I suppose it's what makes you such a hell of a bridge-player—but, well, I think it probably scares off a lot of people."

"I'm sorry if it does," said Margaret.

"A goodlooking girl such as yourself, it shouldn't be allowed to happen," said Elmer Carmichael.

"What do you think I do . . . *push people away?*"

"Well, *do* you?"

"No," said Margaret.

"How many close friends do you have?"

"I have lots of close friends," said Margaret.

"How many close friends do you have?"

"I just *told* you," said Margaret.

"*Close* friends?"

Margaret embraced herself more tightly.

"You got a world ahead of you that's beyond belief," said Elmer Carmichael.

"Pardon?"

"*If* you want to take advantage of it," said Elmer Carmichael. "*If* you don't shove it away by not giving in a little now and then."

"*Giving in*—to *this* world?"

"Absolutely," said Elmer Carmichael.

"Never," said Margaret.

"Why not?" Elmer Carmichael asked her, and he glanced quickly at her.

Margaret spoke quickly. "Because I don't want to be eaten up and spat out," she said. "And anyway, I'm not all I seem." She wanted to weep, but her eyes were dry, and she knew she would not weep. She was not much for weeping. Tears were too disorderly. Tears revealed too much. They gave the iron world and its iron people reason to close in and destroy her.

Elmer Carmichael shook his head. He told her she was remarkable. She told him she didn't think so. The two of them participated in several more Paradise Falls Bridge & Whist Association duplicate games that year, and they never finished lower than third. She told him he would really be an outstanding player if he took the necessary time to play the game, and play it, and play it. But all Elmer Carmichael ever did was smile a little sadly and tell Margaret there really were better things a person could do with spare time. And he spoke vaguely of trees and warm hands, and he was no Elmer Carmichael anyone else *knew*; he was no Elmer Carmichael anyone else even would have *believed*. But Margaret liked him a great deal. She was unable to listen to his words, however. They did not take her fear into account, her tinfoiled innards, her certainty that she was a match for no one, her knowledge that the only reasons she played bridge so well had to do with first, her talent for arithmetic, and second, the *dread* she had of *not* playing well. So her game forever improved. She almost never had lapses. She almost never had spells where the cards fell badly for her. She felt herself tyrannized by her success, by the necessity that it be perpetuated. To *relax* . . . to be *sentimental* . . . perhaps to *fall in love* and attend to *normal* days . . . no, there was too much danger involved, and Margaret could afford to take no chances. Which was why she permitted Rosemary Hall to seduce Eugene Pearson and make off with him. *Actually,* Margaret was a little relieved. *Actually,* when it came to confrontations, when it came to taking some sort of severe and honest stand, Margaret leaked and quavered (except later, much later, in her dealings with the even more leaky and quavering Pauline Jones), but barely a hint of the leaking and the quavering ever came through, and certainly never at the bridge table, where Margaret was utterly superb, and she knew it, and so did everyone else. Comely, combed, hatted, suited and brassiered, with her knees pressed tightly together and her voice always flat, matteroffact and precise, her virgin loins dry and invulnerable, Margaret moved through the tight and tense world of serious tournament bridge, that place of boards and tops and bottoms and voids and squeezes and counts and trumps and revokes (inadvertent, of course), with a serenity that some believed was cold, and others believed was simply a rigid control of nerves. And of course both interpretations were incorrect. Margaret Ridpath was never what she seemed, not even at the end, when she and those children and poor Otto York were rendered raw and forever silent.

Margaret saw her brother Paul for the last time early in 1939 when he came home on leave shortly before his assignment to the Philippines. He was past thirty, and he was a first lieutenant of infantry, and he reminded her a great deal of Richard Arlen. It was possible to see one's face reflected off his boots, and there was a cleft in his chin that was so deep it appeared to have been scooped out with a trowel. He and Margaret sat in the kitchen late one evening while Wanda was bathing Inez Ridpath and putting her to bed, and Paul looked at Margaret and said: "You have a lot of courage, do you know that?"

"No," said Margaret. She bit off the word.

"Well, take my word for it," said Paul. "Putting up with what you have to put up with. And the way those two go *at* it . . . my God . . . where did you dig up that Ripple woman anyway? I've been home four days, and she hasn't fixed a single meal *yet.* And the way she and Mother go at it . . . the way they sit there in the front room and . . . ah, *dig* . . . and *dig* . . . the hatred is so strong I could suck it up with a straw . . ."

"Well," said Margaret, "it's not as though people were beating down the doors in their anxiety to take care of Mother. And besides . . . in some strange way, those two have found a certain meeting of the minds . . ."

"It would *have* to be strange," said Paul.

"That's supposed to be funny, isn't it?" said Margaret.

"Very good," said Paul.

Margaret nodded. "I suppose it is," she said. "One oldmaid, plus one old crazy woman, plus one skinny shrew . . . the mixture is enough to make a person roll in the proverbial aisle . . ."

"Look, I didn't mean to insult you," said Paul. "If I did, I'm sorry. But the thing I *started out* to say is that you have a lot of intestinal fortitude— not only because of *this* situation, but also because of the name you're making for yourself as a bridgeplayer. And don't be modest about it. You have strength."

"No," said Margaret. She bit off the word.

Paul sighed. There was no need to smooth back his hair, but he went ahead and smoothed back his hair anyway. He glanced at his fingernails, picked at a piece of loose skin. He said: "I am an Army officer, and I am a damned *good* Army officer, and so when I speak of strength, well, I know what I'm talking about. You *have* to be strong, or you don't command an infantry company in a peacetime army, I'll tell *you*. It's like trying to make bank robbers into policemen . . . it's the real *dregs*, Margaret . . . *scum* . . . and so don't you sass *me* when I tell you you have strength. You put up with Mother. You put up with that Ripple woman. You're here with all the memories that *have* to keep you thinking of Father and the thing he did to himself, the thing he did to *all of us*. Myself, I ran. I joined the Army. I got away. And Ruth and Sarah ran, too. They got married—which I'm told is like joining the Army, only sometimes worse. But *you* did *not* run. You stayed. You know as well as I do that Mother could be placed in some sort of home, but—"

"People in *our* family don't get *placed* in *homes*," said Margaret.

"I suppose not," said Paul.

"So don't talk a lot of bushwah," said Margaret.

Paul shrugged. "Fine," he said. "And don't *you* talk a lot of bushwah either. If I tell you you deserve credit, then you deserve credit."

"Yes *sir*," said Margaret. "Should I salute?"

"If you'd like," said Paul, smiling.

Margaret brought up her right arm in a brisk salute.

Paul returned it. "Very *good*," he said.

"Thank you," said Margaret. "But just let me ask you one favor."

"What's that?"

"Don't talk to me about strength. I don't know a thing about strength. The song tells it: *I'm here because I'm here because I'm here because I'm here.* It's no more complicated than that. Remember when we were children? Remember who always was forced to be the Filthy Hun?"

"Well," said Paul, "that was a long time ago . . ."

"Ah, but the girl is mother of the woman," said Margaret.

"Now you're sounding pompous," said Paul.

"Ah, but the way you pushed me around. And the way Babs Hamilton pushed me around. And the way you used to call me Sister Sis the sissy."

"I did?" said Paul.

"You certainly did," said Margaret, pressing her upper lip against her overbite.

"I don't remember that at all," said Paul.

"Take my word for it," said Margaret.

"That was all more than twenty years ago. How do you remember it?"

"Because I was hurt. Because I was afraid."

"I'm sorry," said Paul. "I really am."

"All right," said Margaret.

"Ah, whatever happened to Babs Hamilton anyway?"

"She married a man named John Bricknell, and she has six fine little children. He works at the Paradise Valley Ice & Fuel."

"Did you say *Babs Hamilton* has *six children?*"

"Yes. Babs Bricknell now. And she is quite lovely and feminine."

"I'll be dipped," said Paul. "When I knew her, she was about as lovely and feminine as Lou Gehrig. Did I ever tell you that once she showed me everything she *had*—warts and all, so to speak?"

"Paul!"

"It's an absolute fact," said Paul. "We'd been at some sort of picnic over across the river at the Elysian Park, and we were down in the weeds or the willows or the cattails or I don't know what. We were about eleven, and she said to me: 'Paul Ridpath, I'm *stronger* than you. I got nothing *hanging* on me to hold me back.' And then, whippo presto, she pulled her dress over her head, and she tugged down her bloomers, and there she was—the essential and very real Babs Hamilton, standing there with her bloomers all fussed and wrinkled at her feet . . ."

"So what did you do?"

"What do you *think* I did? I did *nothing.* My God, I couldn't have been more than *eleven years old.* I think I said something like: 'You'd better watch out before the cattails scratch you.' And then I turned around and climbed the riverbank and went on my merry way."

"That's all very hard to believe," said Margaret.

"Why would I lie to you?" said Paul.

"No reason, I guess."

"I only wish you'd believe me when I tell you there's more to you than you're willing to—"

"Hush," said Margaret. "I *mean* it."

Paul nodded.

"I'm here because I'm here because I'm here because I'm here," said Margaret.

"Now I have heard insights in my time, and I have heard insights," said Paul.

"Hush," said Margaret.

That was the last time Margaret saw her brother. He went away, and about three years later he died on Corregidor. He had never married, and so he had no children, and to Margaret it was almost as though he never had existed. The telegram arrived one morning in early May of 1942, and the next night Margaret drove to Zanesville, where she and a woman named Naomi Pierce gained an easy top in one of the state's better regional tournaments.

Paul had taken their father's death very badly. He had screamed, and he had writhed. He was seventeen that year, and he had spent much of his spare time in Dr Ridpath's office, helping Dr Ridpath with the little animals. Margaret remembered that at one point, while screaming and writhing, Paul had expressed concern for the animals. *"Who'll take care of them now?"* he had asked, sobbing. *"They won't starve to death, will they?"* And Inez Ridpath had embraced Paul, and she had assured him that the puppydogs and the kittycats would be fine, just fine. But he would not believe her, and finally she had to take him to the office, and they inspected the cages, and the puppydogs and the kittycats were just fine, and another veterinarian—a young fellow named Westenheimer—was on hand to care for them. It was this Westenheimer who bought the practice from Inez Ridpath, and he gave her what everyone acknowledged to be a fair price.

Bees and canoes always were with Margaret Ridpath. Other people had trolls and Hitler. Margaret Ridpath had bees and canoes.

The year 1936 was the first one in which Margaret traveled extensively from bridge tournament to bridge tournament, although she did not leave the state of Ohio. She only participated in fourteen Paradise Falls Bridge & Whist duplicate games, but she did manage to win nine of them—and with an assortment of partners. She knew (and so did just about everyone else) that she had passed beyond the competition offered in those quiet little Acterhof House games, and late in that year of 1936 it became increasingly apparent to her that she no longer was particularly welcome. The president of Paradise Falls Bridge & Whist was a man named Frederick T. Boyd, a retired chemistry teacher at the high school. He was a genial and somewhat randy old fellow, but one night he took Margaret aside and had a serious talk with her. He told her: "You are a genuine *darling* . . . you really *are*. And there isn't a person in this club who dislikes you. But you are wiping us out. Whenever you show up (and after you find a partner, whoever that lucky person might be), it's as though all the rest of us are playing for second. Which isn't much fun. Especially when there's snow on the ground and a person has to come mushing out into the cold. We take no *offense*, mind you, but, well, some of us were wondering if perhaps you couldn't find . . . ah, what I mean is . . . if perhaps someplace there isn't *sterner* competition for you." And Margaret nodded, but she felt stunned and hurt. Everything old Mr Boyd had said was true, but nonetheless Margaret felt stunned and hurt. Her iron world's iron people (and never mind their lack of ability at bridge) again were punishing her. She sat in an easy chair in a corner of the Acterhof House lobby, and Mr Boyd was perched on an arm of the chair, and he patted one of her hands and said: "Don't look so down in the dumps. My Lord, we're all of us such a gang of duffers compared with *you*. It seems to me you'd be glad to be shut of us." Then, nodding, Mr Boyd said: "The barrel has run out of fish. Not a one is left to be shot." He smiled. He said: "The world will go on, I'm sure." Again Margaret nodded. She and a man named Frank Bannerman, a very poor player indeed, had registered a sixtyseven percent score that evening, and in twenyeight boards Margaret had bid and made nine games where no games had existed. She nodded for a third time. Then she said: "All right. I think understand." And Mr Boyd said: "But no offense intended. Please be-

lieve that." And Margaret said: "All right." Mr Boyd squeezed her hand.
"Well then, I expect I'll get on home before Martha gets to believing I've
been abducted by Saracen pirates," he said. He went to the lobby door.
Margaret watched him. The rest of the bridgeplayers (including an ecstat-
ic Frank Bannerman) had already left, and the only other person in the
lobby was the night clerk, Bill Akers. Mr Boyd pushed open one of the
twin lobby doors, and he gave a sort of squeak. At first, Margaret thought
it was the door that had given the squeak. But then Mr Boyd wrapped his
arms across his chest and toppled backward, striking his head on the
floor. Bill Akers, a skinny middleaged man with wens and bifocals,
rushed out from behind the desk, but Mr Boyd was dead and gone, and
Margaret knew it as surely as she knew her own name. Bill Akers pressed
an ear against Mr Boyd's chest, then fumbled at Mr Boyd's wrist, evidently searching for a pulse. Finally Bill Akers looked up at Margaret and
said: "Would you believe it?" Margaret did not hear him. Her ears were
blocked by a sound of iron. That was the first time she'd ever seen a human being die. It would happen one more time before she herself died,
and Otto York died, and the children died.

"You were with him," said Martha Boyd to Margaret. "Do you remember what his last words were?"

"Yes," said Margaret. "They had something to do with Saracen pirates."

Martha Boyd was sitting with Margaret in a side room at an undertaking
establishment called the Charles Palmer Light House of Rest. She and the
late Frederick T. Boyd has been married for nearly fifty years. She looked
at Margaret and said: "Ah, did you say Saracen pirates?"

"Yes. He didn't want you to worry about him. He, ah, I believe his
words were he didn't want you to worry that he'd been, ah, abducted by
Saracen pirates."

"And then he went to the door?"

"Yes," said Margaret.

"Did he seem to be in pain?"

"I don't believe so."

Martha Boyd was a tiny old woman. She wore a long black dress, and a
cameo was at its throat. The cameo showed a woman's face in profile, and
the face was vaguely reminiscent of Martha Washington. "It's too bad
you don't know anything about comfort," said Martha Boyd.

Margaret looked at her.

"You could have told me something different," said Martha Boyd.

"How's that?" said Margaret.

"You could have said he *asked* about *me*," said Martha Boyd.

"But that wouldn't have been the truth," said Margaret.

"Do you think I *care* about the *truth*?" said Martha Boyd. "I always hated bridge—do you know that? It's been years since I've played. But Fred loved the game, and every Tuesday night, as sure as God makes green apples and cuckoobirds and the rising of the moon, my husband was off to the good old Paradise Falls Bridge & Whist, and then . . . after he got home, while the two of us sat in the kitchen and I gave him a glass or two of warm milk so his nerves would slow down . . . he replayed all the hands, who *had* what and who *did* what and how dumb Soandso was in comparison with Soandso, and to me it was all about as interesting as a pile of old chicken claws, but I put up with it, and I fed him the warm milk . . . and the reason was I cared for him, do you follow me? All those years, and I really *cared* for him. And now you tell me his dying words were about *pirates*. You could have said he had asked about *me*, but oh no, *that* wouldn't have been the *truth*. And oh *my*, is the truth *important*. Without the *truth*, we are *nothing*, correct? We then become simply a Notion in the Mind of the Lord. All right. Good enough. But the thing I ask you is this, Margaret Ridpath—what about the feelings of this old woman you see here before you? Couldn't you have told some sort of kindly fib, something maybe like *my name* had been on his dying lips? But of *no*, not *you*. Instead, you tell the truth, and it's some silly thing having to do with Saracen pirates . . . and I . . . well, ah hah, the point is . . . I think I got more coming to me than *that* . . . even if it would have had to have been a lie . . . I mean, all that warm milk . . . O dear Jesus, spare me this . . . see me away from all this . . . I love You, and I need to be comforted, and where are the words?" And now Martha Boyd was weeping.

Margaret did not touch Martha Boyd. Instead, she embraced herself.

Then, from 1937 until the summer of 1951, came the years when the game of bridge dominated Margaret's life, punctuating it, dictating what days she took off from her job, sometimes even forcing her to work overtime in order that Steinfelder's books were absolutely uptodate while she was off participating in some tournament in Chicago or Wheeling or

Birmingham or Kansas City or wherever, and each year brought her more recognition, and by 1940 most of the best players in the nation were only too eager to have her as a partner, and the game enveloped her; it made her eyes hot; it brought lines to her forehead; it pursued her sleep, dragging its odds and strategies through her brain, and of course it became reflexive, but at the same time it never failed to terrify her (or at least her fear of failure never failed to terrify her), and oh dear, such a world this tournament world was, of hotel ballrooms and great glass chandeliers, of the slide of the cards in and out of the duplicate boards, of the inferences and hints and threats that came from the bidding, when two touching suits were bid and the lower was bid first, then the bidder had a stronger hand than if he had bid the suits the other way around, and a queen never could be finessed through an ace for a missing king unless one also had the jack, and it is not always wise to play the doubler for the missing trump, and the Rule of Eleven will aid the no-trump declarer far more often than it will hinder him, and there were of course players who drank (some, but not all that many), and there were of course players who smoked (many, but not all), and there were of course players who munched and nibbled on peanuts and potato chips and the like (Margaret was one of those), and there was no real humor attached to any of this, with voices low so the people at the next table could not overhear the bidding, with occasionally a disgruntled player burdening his or her partner with all sorts of pejoratives, including Nitwit (*how could you reach so deep just to pick up a crumby ninespot?*) and Fool (*you ought to know Shapiro half the time leads from a king, even if it means making the king bare*) and Ass (*my sevenspot had to be a singleton the way the bidding had gone, so why in God's name did you lead back a diamond when you knew I had diamonds coming out my nose?*) and Gutless Wonder (*everybody in the room had to be going for the overtrick, and you knew it, and so what do YOU do? you play for the lousy DROP; you DON'T take the obvious finesse, and so we end up with an absolute bottom, and by God if I weren't married to you, I'd take that so-called brain of yours and fry it in bacon grease and feed it to the cat*) and Nincompoop (*if you know a contract is unbeatable by any means this side of assassination, then go out and buy yourself a revolver and take target-shooting lessons, but for Christ's sake don't take some wild defensive chance that likely as not will turn an average into a bottom quicker than you can say Dumbbells Are Losers*), with perhaps forty or fifty nights a year consumed by smoke and bids and blather and tenseness, and none of it was designed to appeal to the likes of a Margaret Ridpath, she of the tinfoil bones, but still she was fascinated, and her trophies and plaques multiplied, and her sense of order, of structure, of neatness and reason and logic rejoiced in the purity of the game when it was played by people who knew what they were doing (and yet she never was arrogant, no matter how cold she might have seemed . . . fear, after all, had no room for arrogance . . . your oil and your water never commingled, correct?), and so she played the game with enormous zeal, and there were those who said she was just about flawless; she never sorted her cards, yet in perhaps two seconds she was able to sequester them in her mind; she never sorted her cards because she absolutely knew that some sharp-eyed opponent would be able to draw dangerous inferences; still, now and then there were occasions when she *did* sort her cards, but in no particular order and never by suit, which was a little misleading and perhaps even unfair, but then so were the sharp-eyed opponents, those who sought to read her too closely, and so around and around it all went, murmuring, with now and then a frail feather of laughter but usually little more than the murmur, a life of hotel rooms and rehashings and hot eyes and the tumblered click of the lubricated mathematical mind calculating odds and possibilities, and a war passed; Mussolini and Claretta Petacci were hung by their heels; Sinatra caused riots; the Fred Allen radio show sponsored the Henry Morgan radio show; Snuffy Stirnweiss won the American League batting championship; Hitler shot himself; Dresden was leveled; Veronica Lake's peekaboo hair came and went; Veronica Lake came and went; Franklin Delano Roosevelt went; Inez Ridpath blabbered to Wanda Ripple, and their mutual hatred curled around Margaret's trophies and plaques like gas or fog or whatever; the ink at Steinfelder's was mainly black; Miss Margaret Ridpath remained girdled and majestic, revealing not even a shred of tinfoil; a great many Japanese were incinerated in two cities, one of which sounded like a leaky tire, the other of which sounded like a collapsing pile of sticks; Jean Sibelius died; *Citizen Kane* came and went; United States Senator Joseph R. McCarthy (Republican, Wisconsin) waved a list of subversives in front of a crowd in Wheeling, West Virginia; Glenn Davis and Doc Blanchard conquered the nation for the brave old Army football team; Margaret O'Brien captured your heart; Monty Woolley was nasty to Grant Mitchell in *The Man Who Came to Dinner*; Raymond Massey was nasty to Cary Grant (*and* Peter Lorre, *and* Rosemary Lane) in *Arsenic and Old Lace*; Harry S Truman gave the Republicans hell and then whipped them (to the surprise of one and all); colored men began to play professional baseball; Stalin ordered the slaughter of thousands of Polish officers; the Japanese probed the Aleutians; Charlie McCarthy prospered; W. C. Fields died; George Kaftan and Bob Cousy were the stars of a splendid Holy Cross College basketball team; Henry Agard Wallace told the nation it needed to be more understanding of the Soviet Union; Rita Hayworth drove George Macready and Glenn Ford up the wall in *Gilda;* Gable came back, and Garson got him; Coventry was bombed; Rotterdam was bombed; Tokyo was bombed; Ploesti was bombed; Stalingrad was bombed; Jack Benny accused Phil Harris of excessve drunkenness; Phil Harris accused Jack Benny of excessive cheapness; Dagmar breasted her way into the hearts of America's burgeoning numbers of television viewers; Jews were shot, gassed, boiled and burned at Dachau, Treblinka, Auschwitz; Hemingway published *For Whom the Bell Tolls,* which later became a film starring his friend Gary Cooper; Manila was bombed; London was bombed; Moscow was bombed; Normandy was breached; Lidice was wiped out; Count Folke Bernadotte was murdered; Eben Emael fell; King Zog of Albania was toppled; the prisoners were massacred at Malmédy; Goering took poison; Lupe Velez took pills; Carole Landis took pills; the patriots of France shaved the heads of those women who had slept with the occupying Germans; Warsaw was raped; the Warsaw ghetto was betrayed; Bud Abbott and Lou Costello never did quite get it straight Who was on first and What was on second; Gabriel Heatter usually had more baaad news tonight than gooood news; Adolf Eichmann vanished; Latvia vanished; white men fought colored men on the streets and in the parks of Detroit, Michigan; Inez Ridpath spoke of animals and youth and lime pie and her late husband's good manners; babies suckled, and rapists labored, and Otto York was told his wife, his beloved Norma, had multiple sclerosis; Okinawa fell; Saipan fell; Laval and Pétain fell; Faith Domergue came and lingered, and the people at RKO worked long and hard to make her a star; Greeks fought Greeks in Greece; Koreans fought Koreans in Korea; then Koreans fought Koreans plus Americans in Korea; MacArthur lost, fled, returned, won; a bomber crashed into the Empire State Building; Randy Heflin was for a time the best pitcher on the staff of the Boston Red Sox; Gloria Vanderbilt was beautiful, and Rita Hayworth was the World's Great Pneumatic Jackoff Queen, and a girl named Elizabeth Taylor was enough to melt a pile of boulders; the monastery at Monte Cassino was destroyed; Franco thrived; the state of Ohio elected one Frank J. Lausche governor, then threw him out, then elected him again; cards were dealt; trumps were established; the screams of the dying were heard to the farthest shadows of the universe; a revoke cost the revoker the revoked trick plus a penalty trick; fourcard majors were forever being bid and made; cards came down carefully; eyes moved quickly; Miss Margaret Ridpath thrived; each new trophy and/or plaque made her eyes hot; she was tinfoil, but now the tinfoil had been wrapped in cellophane, and the screams of the dying were heard only vaguely, and she seldom was aware of the flags, the rhetoric, the falling rubble, the casualty statistics, the rhetors, the warriors, the tribunals, the blood, the awful monuments; she was more aware of the new refinements in bidding and play, the various styles of the great masters, the irrefutable fact that an opponent was weaker when playing the twentyfourth board than when playing the first (and therefore the alert and fatiguefree Margaret Ridpaths of that tight little cellophane world could make hay while the smoke swirled and the cards came down, so to speak), and by 1942 or so she could not have imagined herself *not* a part of that taut and isolated patch of the planet occupied by those for whom the game's lovely and virginal perfection had become something that was part a religion, part a physical need that had a capacity to affect even the brain (one did not count sheep in one's sleep; one did not count Chevrolets or asparagus stalks or former Vice Presidents of the United States; one counted trumps; one squeezed; one pulled off impossible coups), and Margaret Ridpath could no more have turned her back on that game than she could have grown a great curved horn in the middle of her forehead and rooted up tree stumps. She was all fear. She was all mind. She dared not relax or relent . . . and finally, after 1942 or so, she did not even want to.

Now and then Wanda Ripple would discuss bridge with Margaret, and it all was a great mystery to Wanda, and she had no idea how Margaret could stand the *strain*. "It's almost like you *welcome* it," said Wanda.

"I believe perhaps I do," said Margaret.

"But why?"

"Because look at me."

"I'm looking at you," said Wanda. "What is it I'm supposed to be seeing?"

"Everyone has to have . . . ah, no, that's putting it wrong . . . I mean to say, the game makes it possible for me to *exist* . . . "

"I'm not so sure I get what you mean," said Wanda.

"Well," said Margaret, "without the game of bridge, I'd curl up and blow away."

"Baloney," said Wanda. "The world is full of people who aren't good at bridge. It's full of people who aren't good at *anything*. And I'm one of them—except maybe for when I was living over on Roundhouse Street and I baked, which I wasn't bad at, which you may recall. But anyway, my old baking days aside, I'm nothing to write to the King of England about. And most people are like me. But they don't *curl up* and *blow away.*"

"Well, *I* would," said Margaret.

Wanda shook her head. "All those stuffy rooms," she said. "And the people, what do they do, hunch over their cards like Charles Laughton in that movie about the French cathedral? Do they ever say it's a nice evening, or how were the pork chops, or who's President these days?"

"Well," said Margaret, "either a person loves the game or a person doesn't. If not, there's no way it can be explained."

"I *guess,*" said Wanda.

Margaret felt safer within her iron world if she could divide it into compartments, using something like the columns and thin fastidiously straight lines in a ledger. When she thought of her mother, when she thought of Wanda, when she thought of her sisters and her late brother and her late father and the other forever lost people such as Hazel Muehlbach and Eugene Pearson and Lexie Musser and even poor old Frederick T. Boyd, Margaret would sit quietly and *concentrate* on them, bringing them into focus as fully as she knew how, even though sometimes the thinking made her uneasy. And she kept trying to keep her days *summed,* with a running tally, so to speak. And she included bees and canoes. She included horseradish. She included the longago fragmented sound of Mme Bird's voice, memories of enormous legendary locomotives, of hail and windstorms and band concerts, even of the obscene gesture made by Lexie's husband Eddie Spangler, the Eddie Spangler of the home brew and the cupped hand. And Margaret blinked at the blazing sheetmetal roofs of the terrific Paradise Falls summer afternoons, with the heat rubbing the sky in fat undulant waves, and she smelled dogs and sweat and grasses and brick and hollyhocks and the eternal fume of grape arbor, and sometimes she even made a point of listening to her mother, and Inez Ridpath would blink fatly up from the immortal and famous *STAR* chair and say: "It only means something if blood is involved. The heart's blood, eh, Horace my darling? Oh my, a Coke of *any* sort would do right now. But the blood. Hear me on the subject of the blood, Harvey. I beg leave that you try to follow me when I tell you that it profits us nothing if we never are engaged below our necks, which is not to say we should be *indecent* but *is* to say that we should be willing to expose our heart's blood for the sake of *humanity,* for the sake of *goodness,* for the sake of *grief* and *remorse* and all the misaligned *clutter* that never leaves us unless of course we want to be dead while still breathing, which really doesn't sound like an awful lot of fun to *me.* And I said to John: 'Dorothy Hall?' And he said to me: 'I loved both of you. I *love* both of you.' Perhaps he was, ah, incorrect. Perhaps he even was indecent. But did that make him something on a par with pus leaking from the devil's bowels? I have sat here and I have sat here, and I have discussed grief for years and years, and I surely do know my lines, and so Wanda Ripple has decreed that I am a *STAR,* but the thing I would like to know from *you* is . . . Margaret or Ruth or Sarah or *Phoebe* or *Ermentrude* or whatever your name is . . . do you have any idea yet of the *commitment* one must make to one's *blood*? And all right. I have turned out to be a bad girl, and there are times when you must strike me to remind me of my badness, and to remind me of how your father died, and to remind me that I cannot make weewee or poopy at the table, which is all *fine* and *dandy* and *right* and *justified* and I wouldn't have it any other way if you were to place the world's biggest twelvegauge shotgun to my poor fat old head . . . but, Lucinda, the thing is—bad girl or no, I do have some idea what I'm talking about, and all I ask you is that *for your own sake* you begin an investigation of *something beyond* cards and trophies and Steinfelder's and whatever else it is you do when I don't know where you are . . . because you can't hide behind the mulberry bush all your life, Reginald . . . you can't crawl into the old gopher hole . . . eventually Old Mister Gopher comes home, and he wants his hole back, which means you got to get out into the cold mean world . . . and so you'd better prepare yourself . . . is there a Coke somewhere? Could I have a Coke? Could an old woman have a Coke before she melts? What did that nasty Wanda Ripple do with my Zimmerman Funeral Home fan anyway? The one with the color retouch of Jesus? You know the one I mean? A Zimmerman palmleaf fan is the best palmleaf fan in the county, bar none. I used to hear the Lutherans had a pretty fair palmleaf fan, but I don't really know whether that was a fact, not having ever set foot in a Lutheran church and not ever intending to, even if I should live to the year Nine Thousand, which maybe isn't so out of the question, isn't that right, Leo?'' And Inez Ridpath smiled at Margaret, and Inez Ridpath's dentures waggled, and sometimes Margaret even nodded. And sometimes Margaret even came close to understanding the sense in her mother's words. But at the same time she was *Margaret Ridpath,* and she was too *sensible* to spend *all* her time blundering through the rocks and underbrush of her interior landscape. And so she compartmentalized it. Her fears . . . and her virginity . . . and her mother's words . . . and the encroachments of Wanda, Ruth, Sarah and the rest of them . . . all were carefully hidden in the underbrush and compartmentalized there—but neatly, of course, with the rocks no doubt piled in precise pyramids. And so, once establishing that territory (bleak as it might have been) as the repository of what her mother perhaps would have called her blood, or perhaps passion, Margaret was able to create another compartment, this one for the daytoday Margaret Ridpath whose activities were cluttered with no rocks or underbrush whatever. This was the Margaret Ridpath of statistics, of routine, of Christmas cards always promptly mailed, of bills always promptly met, a Margaret Ridpath whose life had a rhythm and a structure. She always gave Steinfelder's a solid and honest eight hours, and Mr George Wolf came more and more to rely on her. He developed some sort of mild heart condition in 1946, and he called Margaret into his office and told her: "I don't know what the rumors around here are, and I don't know whether the people who work here expect me to drop dead at any moment, but that's not going to happen. What *is* going to happen is that Evelyn and I will have to take an extra vacation or two every year. Is your doctor Hendrickson? No, it's Groh, right? Well, anyway, *my* doctor is Hendrickson, and he says I'm just going to have to find more free time." A nod. Mr Wolf was astigmatic and pale. His wife, Evelyn, also was astigmatic and pale. They looked a little like brother and sister. He said: "Which means more or less you' re going to have more responsibilities—at least *part* of the time . . . the times when I'm away, I mean. Ah Hah. I almost said when I'm *gone,* but I didn't like the way that sounded, you know? So, anyway, you have been a jewel, Margaret, and of course your success as our reigning bridge celebrity has brought pride to all of us, and so—in a sense—I'm trying somehow to *acknowledge* how successful you have been. At any rate, you know more about the Steinfelder's operation than anyone in the world with the possible exception of myself (and I'm not even too sure about *that*), and so all I'm trying to *say* is that I am raising your salary fifteen dollars a week, and from now on you will be expected to step in whenever you are needed—and in whatever capacity you are needed. As you know, *Evelyn* is technically the vicepresident and secretary of the corporation, and her sister Ernestine Westfall is as you know the treasurer, but in actuality it will be none other than *Margaret Ridpath* who from now on will sit at the right hand of George Wolf. Ah. Hah." So Margaret's responsibilities increased, but she was equal to them. She simply placed them all in the proper compartments, and they all were easily available, and she lost nothing. Her pen was precise; her adding machine never lacked for oil. Her brassiere always was full, and her knees always were locked together. She was polite. She nearly always attended church. She did most of the housework (these were the Wanda Ripple years). She ate well, but she did not become fat. She read bridge magazines. She traveled to tournaments. Most of her male partners attempted to seduce her, but of course she was terrified, and she pushed them all away. Herman Soeder took her for a ride in his rented automobile and told her she was one of the nation's great untapped natural resources. And he pointed out to her that she embraced herself too often. She always kept herself bathed and combed, and her hose never had runners. She crossed streets in crosswalks, and she never was arrested for speeding. She never smoked. She never drank. She never masturbated. She preferred fresh fruits and vegetables over what she called The Canned. She knew all there was to know about taxes, local, state and federal. She knew all there was to know about uncollectible balances due. She seldom laughed when she was alone. She did laugh, though, when others laughed. In church, she sang when others sang. She bowed her head when others bowed their heads. She enjoyed listening to the radio in her hotel room when she was off playing bridge in some strange city. She indulged herself in splendid room service breakfasts, and she always insisted that her cereal be brought to her with real cream—and warm real cream, at that. She visited her doctor twice a year. She visited her dentist twice a year. He was a sour old fellow named Millerspaugh, and his father had been editor of the old Paradise Falls *Journal,* and he told her: "Margaret, if you don't stop eating so much sweet stuff, you're not going to have a tooth in your head." And Margaret said: "But I *brush.*" And Dr Millerspaugh said: "Of course you do—but the only thing is, all you're brushing *these* days is *fillings.*" And he clucked over Margaret's mouth, and his breath was warm and minty. There always was a radio playing, and it usually was tuned to WWVA, Wheeling, and Margaret became rather familiar with the music of Ernest Tubb and other artists of the country persuasion. She came to associate sawing fiddles with Dr Millerspaugh's drill, and sometimes she had to bite her tongue to keep from crying. Dr Millerspaugh gave her enough Novocain to put a Percheron in a coma for six weeks, but still she had to bite her tongue to keep from crying—even though most of the time she couldn't even *feel* her tongue what with the Novocain. And sometimes, while working over her, Dr Millerspaugh would absently mutter little phrases. Such as: "Ah, hah, Sani-Flush: Cleans your teeth without a brush." Or: "If bad teeth were whisky and I were a duck, I'd dive into your mouth and never come up." Or: "Don't you worry about pain, dear lady. Tom Millerspaugh can be trusted. As the undertaker said to the dying man: 'Have no fear—I'll be the last to let you down.' " And Margaret gripped the arms of the chair so tightly it was a wonder she didn't splinter her hands. And Dr Millerspaugh dug and scraped and tugged. And he sometimes said: "Who knows? We might strike oil, and then maybe we can rent out your mouth and call it a second Oklahoma." And Margaret, her mouth full of cotton and Novocain and blood and fragments, sometimes nodded and made trapped gargling noises, and Dr Millerspaugh smiled in his preoccupied way, and Margaret felt heat, then cold, then heat, then cold, and it all pounded at her in waves, but she did not cry. Even when she could have, she did not. Ever. Clearly Dr Millerspaugh was full of iron, and she could not let him know what she was. And so he invariably said to her: "Margaret, I only wish all my patients were as good as you. I've had some of them *run screaming out of here* like your absolute *banshees,* and without even bothering to take off the *sheet,* which surely made a *sight,* I'll tell you. But my friend Margaret Ridpath is an altogether different proposition, and I give her creidt." Then, likely as not, Dr Millerspaugh would pat one of Margaret's shoulders, and occasionally he even would pat one of her cheeks (the one opposite the one where he had done his work), and he would lead her gently into his waiting room, and she always managed to walk erectly, and the waiting patients (nearly all of them anxious and full of dread) looked at her with what she supposed was admiration, and oh dear *goodness,* if they'd only known the truth, wouldn't they just about have *swallowed* their *toes* and *then* some! It almost was amusing—and perhaps, to anyone except Margaret Ridpath, it *was* amusing. But *she* never really thought so. She was too concerned with giving tinfoil the illusion of iron. She was too concerned with keeping her personal categories neat, with not permitting herself to become disorganized. Obviously, if that ever happened, the tinfoil would shred and disintegrate. So then her life was her mother; her life was taking care of the house (the Wanda Ripple days never relaxed that demand on her time); her life was her sisters; her life was the memory of her father; her life was first Paul and then the memory of Paul (such as it was); her life was the various nieces and ncphews that came along; her life was her job at Steinfelder's; her life was the trust of Mr Wolf; her life was her virginity; her life was the nights of hot eyes and intricate calculations over the bridge table; its periphery was skirted by dotted lines, and every so often someone would stray through the openings between the dotted lines and vanish forever, and there were nights . . . nights and nights *and* nights . . . when Margaret lay implacable and comely (and alone, always alone), and her bed was soft and feathery, and she thought of slapless slaps; she thought of the inexplicable antagonism between her mother and Wanda Ripple; she thought of wars and explosions and love and ejaculations and tight flesh;

she thought of defensive strategy, the lead of a singleton trump against a slam contract; she listened to dogs and the wind; she decided she would rather pass a weak opening club than mislead her partner, especially when she was the first bidder; she thought of all the times she had pruned grape arbor and rhubarb; she thought of Dorothy Hall, who had betrayed her mother; she thought of *Rosemary* Hall, who had stolen Eugene Pearson; she lay quite still, and it never occurred to her to take liberties with herself, and the bed was full of softly anachronistic homemade blankets and comforters, and sometimes her jaw gave her pain, and sometimes she took aspirin, but every one of those nights she knew exactly what her schedule should be for the next day; her mind was a timetable, a précis, a Calendar of Events. If it had not been, she would have been mad. The wounds would have revealed themselves; the compartments would have been ransacked; the iron world would have sliced her open quicker than a razor at work on a rotten peach.

In the late summer of 1951 Margaret and a woman named Katherine Kleist (who was a widow three times, lived in Kansas City and was worth in excess of twenty million dollars) were partners in an invitational Life Masters' tournament sponsored by the Rillington Club in New York City. The club's rooms were in an old mansion on upper Fifth Avenue, and the tournament was limited to thirtytwo teams. Four sessions were held in two afternoons and two evenings, and at the end of the first three sessions Margaret and the Kleist woman were in third place, but only nine points from the top. Katherine Kleist was one of Margaret's favorite partners; she was also a conservative player, but she always could be counted on—and, like Margaret, she never bluffed. Occasionally she and Margaret missed games and slams because of their conservatism, but they both had stamina, which in large measure evened matters out, since the more mercurial pairs usually ran out of energy in the last halfdozen boards or so, enabling the likes of Katherine Kleist and Margaret Ridpath to pick up a great deal of the ground their earlier conservatism might have cost them. The thing one had to do was play each hand as though it were the only hand, to forget the last hand and the next hand and simply *concentrate* on the *specific issue* of the hand being played. Katherine Kleist, a fat woman with a wrinkled neck and rings on all ten of her fingers, was at least sixtyfive, but she still was able to focus her mind with a quickness and energy that Margaret admired enormously. And of course Margaret, who was just forty that year, was considered to be entering the peak of her career, and some experts already had publicly predicted that within a decade or so she just might be the best woman player in the country, and *a few* even believed there was a possibility she would be the best *player,* period. As for Margaret herself, all that sort of thinking was beyond belief—but then *those people* didn't know what *Margaret* knew . . . the tinfoil business and all that. And so she sat stolidly, and she was aware that a lot of money had been wagered in side bets (herself, she'd never played bridge for money in her *life,* and she never would), and the rooms of the Rillington Club were tall, heavy, dark, full of smoke and the relentless and forever murmur of bids and questions and quiet comments. Waiters came with drinks and snacks. Katherine Kleist drank white wine and ate nothing. Margaret drank ginger ale and munched on peanuts. She and Katherine sat North and South that session, and so they did not have to move.

Their last two boards of the session were played against two men with New York Jewish accents. One was tall and curlyhaired, and his name was Rosenberg. He was about fifty. Margaret had competed against him in a great many tournaments, and he was a solid player, thoughtful and quiet. He sat to Margaret's right. His partner was a bald man with a short moustache. He had introduced himself, but she had not caught the name. He was overweight, and he smoked a cigar. Margaret had seen him in a few tournaments, but she could not remember much about him. He and Rosenberg had played against Katherine and Margaret on only two other boards in the first three sessions, which meant both teams had sat the same way the other two sessions. Margaret looked briefly at Katherine when the two men seated themselves, and Katherine simply shrugged a little and let it go at that. She knew as well as Margaret did that the team of Kleist and Ridpath had had a brilliant session, and two good final boards could bring Katherine and Margaret a top for the session and quite possibly the tournament. The bald man smiled at Katherine and Margaret, indicated his cigar and said: "Does either of you ladies find this objectionable?"

"Not I," said Margaret, speaking quietly.

"Nor I," said Katherine. "That's a Trocadero from Havana, isn't it?"

"Yes indeed," said the bald man. "I am *impressed.*"

"My second husband smoked them," said Katherine. "I've always had a very sensitive . . . ah, smeller . . ."

Rosenberg shook his head. "In that case," he said, "you will find our game tonight quite offensive."

"It seems that every time poor Aaron zigs, I zag," said the bald man.

"One of those nights," said Rosenberg, shrugging. "And now we have to go up against a couple of celebrities."

"Horse feathers," said Katherine.

"Horses don't have feathers," said the bald man, "except perhaps in Kansas City, where I suppose anything is possible . . ."

"Spoken like a man who has never been west of Scranton, Pennsylvania," said Rosenberg.

"Let's play cards," said the bald man.

"A good idea," said Rosenberg.

Katherine and Margaret smiled. For the first board neither side was vulnerable, and Margaret was the designated dealer. She and Katherine and the two men exchanged information on their bidding systems, and it turned out both pairs played straight Goren with no frills. Margaret's hand was four, three, three, three, and she had four points—the king of diamonds and the jack of clubs. "I pass," she said.

"One heart," said the bald man.

"I shall pass," said Katherine.

"Two hearts," said Rosenberg.

"Pass," said Margaret.

"Four hearts," said the bald man.

"I shall pass," said Katherine.

Rosenberg studied his hand for a moment, then shrugged and said: "I'm going to leave well enough alone. I pass."

"I pass," said Margaret.

The hand played itself like a piano. The bald man pulled three rounds of trumps, ruffed two clubs in his hand, then ran a stiff club suit from the dummy. He conceded two diamond tricks at the end. "Four and an overtrick," he said, "and brilliantly done, if I do say so myself."

Katherine and Margaret smiled.

"Charlie Goren would fall down dead of envy," said Rosenberg.

"Look," said the bald man, "that will be an average, right?"

"It doesn't make six, does it?" said Rosenberg.

The bald man looked at Katherine, and then he looked at Margaret. "Oh, my God, *does* it?" he asked them.

"Provided you revoke," said Katherine.

The bald man puffed on his cigar. "Stop giving me heart failure," he said to Rosenberg.

"The way you and I have been playing," said Rosenberg, "heart failure would be a gift from God."

Katherine was scorekeeper. The board was an average, and everyone knew it. She jotted down the total; the cards were returned to the board, and the players then went on to the final board of the session and the tournament. Katherine and Margaret were vulnerable, and the bald man was the dealer. He glanced at his cards and said: "The Phantom strikes again. I bid one spade."

"Double," said Katherine.

"Pass," said Rosenberg.

Margaret's hand had no spades. She held the ace, king, queen bare of hearts. She had five diamonds to the jack. She had five clubs to the jack. She reached for some peanuts and began chewing on them. She decided she would respond with a reversal. "Three clubs," she said.

"Terrific," said the bald man, grinning sourly. "I'll bid three spades."

"Five clubs," said Katherine.

"Five spades," said Rosenberg.

Margaret did not hesitate. "Six clubs," she said.

"This little ribbon clerk bails out," said the bald man. "I pass."

"I shall pass," said Katherine.

"Double," said Rosenberg.

Margaret sipped at her ginger ale. She took another handful of peanuts. She popped the peanuts into her mouth. She began to chew, and then one of her molars broke in half. The pain immediately spread throughout her mouth. She carefully set down her cards and rubbed her jaw.

Katherine and the two men looked at her.

Briefly Margaret closed her eyes. The pain was white. She opened her eyes. She barely was able to see. She swallowed the peanuts without attempting to chew them any further. She sipped ginger ale, but her tongue blocked the cold liquid from the broken tooth. She blinked. She said: "I redouble."

The bald man frowned. "Is something the matter?"

Margaret waved a hand. "Nuh . . . nothing . . . "

"Okay," said the bald man. "I pass."

"I shall pass," said Katherine. Then, to Margaret: "Are you sure you're all right?"

Margaret nodded. She looked at Rosenberg.

He studied his cards. He studied them and he studied them. Margaret knew he was wondering whether to take out with a sacrifice at six spades. Clearly, he and the bald man held about eleven or twelve spades between them. He scratched his head, looked at his fingernails. Margaret placed her tongue over the broken tooth. The warmth was something of a comfort, but not much.

"*Margaret,*" said Katherine.

"I'm . . . fine . . . " said Margaret.

"Are you in some sort of pain?" said the bald man. "You ought to *see* yourself."

Margaret briefly touched her forehead. It was sticky. Her head moved from side to side. "I'm . . . all . . . *right*," she said.

Rosenberg sighed. "I pass," he said.

Margaret nodded. Again she briefly closed her eyes. When she opened them, Katherine was spreading the dummy. It had five clubs to the queen, a singleton small spade, four hearts to the jack, and the bare ace, king, queen of diamonds. It was a splendid dummy—except for the fact that neither it nor Margaret had the ace and king of clubs, which happened to be trump.

"A beauty," said the bald man. He had led the king of spades.

"We aim to please," said Katherine.

"No wonder she redoubled," said Rosenberg.

Margaret said nothing. She pointed to the singleton spade on the board, and Katherine played it for her. Rosenberg played small. Margaret trumped with the deuce of clubs. Only three clubs were out against her—the ace, the king and the sevenspot. She was faint with pain. She tongued the broken tooth. She led the four of clubs from her hand toward the queen in the dummy. It was the only play. If the bald man had ace doubleton, he would hold off, and Rosenberg would win the trick with a bare king. If the bald man had ace singleton, he would win the trick, and Rosenberg would gain the setting trick with the king. If the bald man had king singleton, he also would win the trick, and Rosenberg would gain the setting trick with the ace. *If,* however, the bald man had *king doubleton,* then he had a bit of a problem. If he did not go up with the king, and Margaret had the ace, then she would pull the king the next lead. But why would she make that sort of lead? The question *had* to be moving through the bald man's mind, and in the meantime Margaret was in agony, and tears were pressing behind her eyes. She supposed there was a good chance he would come to the proper conclusion—namely, if she had the ace, why not go to the board and finesse *toward* it? *This* way, she appeared to be giving up. The conclusion was reasonably elementary, and Margaret knew this, but she also knew that the lead toward the queen was the only prayer she had of making the hand. In the meantime, the bald man was frowning and grunting. Across from him, Rosenberg was leaning back and looking at the ceiling. Finally, shaking his head, the bald man played the king of clubs. And that did it. He caught Rosenberg with the singleton ace. Margaret then hurriedly ran off all the rest of the tricks, and at the end tears were streaking her face, and she was rubbing her jaw, and the bald man said to her: "Young lady, you are *in pain,* and don't deny it."

Margaret nodded.

"Something's wrong with a tooth, right? Did you break something on one of those peanuts?"

Margaret nodded.

The bald man stood up. "Let me have a look," he said. "I'm a dentist."

Margaret nodded. She opened her mouth.

"Cock back your head," said the bald man.

She cocked back her head.

"Beautiful," said the bald man. "Just beautiful."

Margaret's mouth was about to explode.

"Come on," said the bald man. He seized her by an elbow.

She looked at him.

"I am a *dentist,*" he said. "I have an office about six blocks from here. I'll take you there, and we'll get rid of the tooth."

Margaret nodded. Katherine said something sympathetic. Rosenberg ran outside onto Fifth Avenue and hailed a cab. Katherine found Margaret's hat and coat for her. A number of players clustered around Margaret, but the bald man told them everything was going to be all right. He led her outside, and now she was just about whimpering. Rosenberg was waiting with the cab. Margaret and the bald man piled inside, and the bald man gave the driver an address in the East Sixties. The driver said something to the effect that maybe it looked like rain, and the bald man told the driver this was an emergency and never mind the filibuster. Margaret groaned. The bald man put an arm around her. The driver asked the bald man how sick the lady was. The bald man told the driver the lady was plenty sick. The driver was thin and wore a cloth cap. Margaret blinked at the identification card, and it said SAUL GARTENBERG. The bald man stroked Margaret's shoulder. He told her to hold on, just *hold on,* and it'll all be taken care of, kid, before you know it; you just trust me; a lot of things I am, but a liar is not one of them. The night was muggy, and Margaret blinked at the lights and pressed her jaw against the bald man's chest. He told her yeah, fine, you do whatever's necessary. The cab pulled up to the address in the East Sixties. The bald man paid the driver and helped Margaret out onto the sidewalk. He steered her to a tall concrete building that had a canopied entrance. The building was dark. He unlocked the front door and ushered Margaret inside. A man came running up to them, and this man was wearing some sort of uniform. The bald man grinned at the uniformed man. Greetings were exchanged. The uniformed man helped the bald man escort Margaret to an elevator. The uniformed man operated the elevator, and the elevator swayed a little, and the swaying hurt Margaret's jaw. She had locked her fingers together in front of her belly. The bald man told her it wouldn't be long now *at all.* They stepped out of the elevator, and the uniformed man followed along. They moved down a hall. They came to a door, and there was lettering on the door, but Margaret could not quite make out what it said. The uniformed man held Margaret while the bald man opened the door. Then they were in some sort of outer office, and it smelled antiseptic. The bald man and the uniformed man helped Margaret through a low swinging gate and down another hall, this one much narrower and shorter. They took Margaret inside a room and seated her in a large leather chair. Her head moved from side to side, and her fingers would not unlock. The bald man thanked the uniformed man, and the uniformed man went away. The room came full of light. Margaret blinked, tucked her jaw against an arm. The bald man stripped off his coat, then ran water and washed his hands. "Doctor Kildare to the rescue," he said. He leaned over Margaret. "Open wide for nice Doctor Kildare," he said. His breath had an odor of cigar. He used a small flashlight and a mirror. "My God," he said, "I never thought I'd get to see Pompeii in my lifetime. One of these days you'll have to show me the dirty pictures." Margaret didn't have the vaguest idea what the bald man was talking about, but perhaps it all would be clearer when the pain went away. The bald man made a sort of chirruping noise that came perhaps from his nose. He said: "First the Novocain, then we get rid of whatever's left of that tooth. What did you do? Try to eat somebody's sidewalk?" He busied himself with a needle. He said: "Now, looking back on it, there was no reason in the world I should have gone up with my king. If you'd had the ace, you'd either have played it and hoped for the drop, or you'd have finessed through Aaron, who after all *was* the doubler. But *at the time* I had some idiotic notion you were trying for an overtrick. *Now,* though, in good old retrospect, I see I was thinking craziness. The contract already had been doubled and redoubled, and you didn't *need* an overtrick. It was either a top or a bottom without any little old overtrick, and you *knew* that, didn't you, you devil you?" He injected the Novocain in Margaret's mouth. She felt nothing. "Fear not, fair maiden," he said, "before you know it, your jaw will feel nice and fat, as though it's full of warm and heavy air, and the pain will be gone. Won't that be terrific?" The bald man grinned. He poured Lavoris into a cup and swished out his mouth. "I don't imagine my cigar breath is very inspiring, is it?'' he said. He spat into a bowl, then rinsed again with water. He winked at Margaret. "Hi, Good Looking," he said. "You feeling any better?" Margaret, whose jaw had begun to numb a little, nodded. "Good," said the bald man. "Then it *was* Novocain I gave you and not Sal Hepatica. I am a little nearsighted, and sometimes I get the bottles confused." He began fussing with instruments. "Ah *hah* ant oh *ho*, now I haf you in my *powww*er," he said, doing a passable imitation of Bela Lugosi. Then: "I am sure, what with that mouth of yours, you perhaps know more dentistry than I do, and I wouldn't be surprised if some dentist in your home town hasn't become a rich man because of you, but I'm still going to have to tell you something you probably already know—namely and to wit, *there is a difference between pressure and pain.* I am about to *tug*, but I will not *hurt*. May God turn my vital organs to ashes if I am lying. Now open as wide as you can so we can get *at* that treasonous little bugger." Now Margaret's jaw was puffed enormously, but she opened her mouth as widely as she could. "Goot," said the bald man, "now you shall be my obediendt slave *forever* . . . " And he laughed maniacally, but under his breath, in a sort of preoccupied whisper. "Ant ve shall run nakedt through fieldts of sgunk cabbadge ant ze poison ivy . . . " He tugged. "Oh, vhat a *sweedheardt*," he said. Margaret's eyes were jammed tightly shut, and she still had not unlocked her fingers, but she was able to feel only the gentlest movement. "I should have held off on that king," said the bald man. "There was no excuse for what I did—top to bottom in one swell foop. Aaron'll never forgive me." A grunt. "I wonder what you'd be feeling right now if I'd given you a shot of Sal Hepatica?" A tug. "Funny name, Sal Hepatica. Sounds like the madam of a railroad brothel. Madam is the same forwards as backwards. A palindrome. Otto is a palindrome. Bob is a palindrome. Good old Bob, never would have believed it. And then of course there is the famous Genesis Palindrome. Eve is sitting alone in the forest, and she is plaiting her hair or doing some such silliness, and along comes this naked fellow and he smiles at her and says: *Madam, I'm Adam.* Which is the same from west to east as from east to west. Or the Napoleonic Palindrome. Poor guy, sitting off in exile, and a friend comes along, and Napoleon smiles sadly at the friend and says: *Able was I ere I saw Elba.* The world's shortest tragic story, if you ask me." Then there was a suppressed liquid noise, a sort of squirt. "I believe we have met with some success," said the bald man. But Margaret did not open her eyes, nor did she unlock her fingers. Her armpits were sopping, and her legs itched, but she did not move. She heard a clink, and then the bald man said: "So much for our evil culprit

The sound you just heard was his consignment to his final resting place—the wastebasket. But please keep your mouth open for just a little longer. I want to do some packing with cotton. Also, if you concentrate hard enough, perhaps you'll realize that it's all over, and you can open your eyes any time you'd like. The mad doctor has completed his vile deed." Then the bald man gave Margaret a paper cup of warm water and told her to rinse out her mouth. He assured her she would feel nothing. He had to wrench her fingers apart before he was able to hand her the cup. He said: "Open your eyes." She opened her eyes. He said: "Look to your left, and then look down." She looked to her left, and then she looked down. She saw a small drain. "That's the Spit Place," said the bald man. "I want you to rinse out your mouth, and then I want you to spit in the Spit Place, okay?" Margaret nodded. She rinsed. She swished. She spat in the Spit Place. The bald man told her she was doing great. He handed her another cup of warm water and had her repeat the process. Then, smiling, he packed cotton into the place where he had extracted the tooth. He told her she could close her eyes again. He told her to lean back and relax. She closed her eyes. She leaned back. She did not particularly relax. He told her he had to make a telephone call, and he would be right back. He went out of the room and down the hall, and then Margaret heard him dialing a telephone. The conversation was brief. He returned to the room where Margaret sat. "Please open your eyes," he said. She opened her eyes. He took her right hand and kissed it. His moustache tickled. He said: "I was just talking with the people at the Rillington Club. I assured them you would survive, and they put Mrs Kleist on the line, and I told her the same thing. Then she had some information for me to give you. You and she had a top for the session, and it gave you a top for the tournament. So congratulations, dear lady. For someone who doesn't know any better than to try to eat sidewalks, you are one hell of a player of the game of bridge . . . with *my* help, of course . . . and I do insist on part of the credit . . . "

The bald man's name was Dr Irving M. Berkowitz, and he was fifty in that year of 1951. And Margaret fell in love with him in less time than she really wanted to admit. It all put her vaguely in mind of those sappy magazine stories she sometimes read while sitting under the dryer in the beauty shop back home, and naturally she was frightened just about

out of her senses, but she found there was very little she could do about the situation. And then, after perhaps six months, she found there was very little she *wanted* to do about the situation.

Later, in discussing those first six months with Margaret, Irv said: "I never knew a woman to be so skittish. In a way, that made you a pain in the tush. In another way, though, there was a sort of joy in it for me."

"And you did not believe me when I told you I was a virgin," said Margaret.

"I absolutely did not," said Irv.

"You thought I had round heels," said Margaret.

"You know better than that," said Irv.

"Then why didn't you believe me when I told you I was a virgin?"

"What's a virgin?" said Irv.

"Very funny," said Margaret.

"I should have put you to the lion test," said Irv.

"The what test?"

"The lion test," said Irv. "There are two stone lions facing the sidewalk on the Fifth Avenue side of the New York Public Library. It is my understanding that they roar whenever a virgin walks past."

"You are a rascal," said Margaret.

"I hope so," said Irv.

"Now, though, it's too late," said Margaret. "They would ignore me They wouldn't make a sound."

"Thank God," said Irv.

The bald man introduced himself, and they shook hands, and then he sat quietly with Margaret, and they waited for the swelling to subside. He said something to the effect that she had a remarkably high tolerance for pain. She tried to smile, but her face was too stiff. He waved hand and told her to take it easy. They sat together perhaps an hour, an then he escorted her back outside, where he hailed another cab. Her hotel was the Plaza, where she was sharing a suite with Katherine Kleist. D Berkowitz was impressed. He rode with her to the hotel and insisted o seeing her upstairs to the suite. Katherine was waiting there, and she embraced Margaret. Dr Berkowitz gave Margaret more cotton and told her to change the swabbing whenever she liked. "By morning," he said, "the bleeding should be finished."

"I certainly am . . . grateful . . . " said Margaret, speaking hollowly.

"No bother," said Dr Berkowitz. "It's what makes my job so much absolutely gingerpeachy fun."

"*You*," said Margaret.

Dr Berkowitz grinned. He shook hands with Margaret, and he shook hands with Katherine, and he congratulated them on their victory in the tournament. "I don't suppose Aaron'll ever forgive me," he said.

"Oh, *now*," said Katherine. "It's only a *game*."

"Sure," said Dr Berkowitz. "Try telling *him* that." Still grinning, Dr Berkowitz went out.

Margaret waved at him.

Katherine frowned at her for a moment, then drew her a warm tub and helped her out of her clothes. Margaret was aware of no pain at all. The tub was enormous, and the water steamed, and Katherine had laced it with bathsalts, and Margaret lay very still. She tried to keep her tongue from playing with the swabbing. She spread her fingers. They still hurt from having been locked so tightly. She spread her fingers, closed them, spread them. Then she plunged them deep into the water. She shuddered. Her belly was knotted. She soaped her breasts. She tried to remember what Dr Berkowitz had looked like—no hair, a moustache, a paunch. And of course the voice of the New York Jew. She had been playing bridge against New York Jews for years, and they usually were excellent players, and most of them never would have fallen for the maneuver she had pulled on Dr Berkowitz. And he was a Life Master. One had to be, or one was not invited to play in the Rillington Club tournament. It was a little puzzling—a *Life Master* being taken in by such an elementary stratagem. Oh well, one did not look gift horses, blah, blah.

The next morning the swelling was gone, but Margaret was tired, and she decided to remain in New York a day or so longer. She telephoned Wanda in Paradise Falls, and everything was fine with Mother. She told Wanda she would be home perhaps two days later than she had expected. She told Wanda she and Katherine had won the tournament. "Congratulations," said Wanda. Nodding, Margaret hung up. She ordered breakfast and a *New York Times* from room service. She and Katherine were mentioned in a brief item headed MIDWEST WOMEN WIN BRIDGE TOURNAMENT; it was on page 33 next to the meteorological report. Katherine, who had gone downstairs to the Edwardian Room for breakfast, returned to the suite and began to pack. She offered to stay over and care for Margaret, but Margaret told her no, it was only a matter of rest. "Just give me a day or so to lounge around," she said, "and I'll be fine. I've called home already, and everything seems to be under control, so I think I'll just loll here in the lap of luxury."

"And you have no pain?" said Katherine.

"Not a bit," said Margaret. "That man is a good dentist."

"Not much of a bridgeplayer, though."

"Well, no one is perfect—and anyway, who are *we* to complain?"

Katherine smiled. She bustled around the room. She told Margaret it had been a *fine* tournament, and she hoped they would be able to get together again very soon. Margaret nodded. She glanced at the telephone. She was propped up in bed, and she didn't really *want* to glance at the telephone, but she *did* glance at the telephone, and she was being an absolute ninny, and she needed no committee of wise elders to deliver that particular news. She smiled. She tongued the cotton. She pressed down on her belly, and all the knottiness was gone. I am no longer knotty, she said to herself. I am only nutty.

 There were a great many hugs and kisses when Katherine left at about eleven that morning. Her hands fluttered, and her rings glittered, and the bellman grunted mightily with her suitcases. Then, abruptly, there was silence, and Miss Margaret Ridpath, the prize ninny of the North American continent, kept glancing at the telephone.

A dozen longstemmed yellow roses were delivered to the suite shortly before noon. Included was a note: *If you aren't careful, you just may receive a telephone call this afternoon. So be warned.*

The note was signed: *The King of Clubs.*

Margaret fussed with the roses, arranging them just so in their vase. She did her nails. She took another bath—but she kept the bathroom door open so she would be able to hear the telephone if it rang. She lay in the tub and puckered. The maid came to clean the room, and so Margaret put on a robe, sat in an easy chair and listened to the radio . . . WQXR, a Vieuxtemps violin concerto and several Mozart cassations. The maid worked silently, and Margaret thanked God for small favors. The telephone rang shortly before three o'clock. "I was hoping you still would be there," said Dr Berkowitz.

"Yes," said Margaret. She had deliberately held back, answering the telephone on its fourth ring. The maid, who had been working with the bedspread, had frowned at her a little.

"How do you feel?" said Dr Berkowitz.

"Ah . . . . oh . . . *fine*," said Margaret. "A little weak, and a little tired, but not bad at all, everything considered. And thank you for the roses. They are lovely."

"I enjoy gestures," said Dr Berkowitz. "At my age, they're about all I have left."

"Now *stop* that," said Margaret.

"Well, obviously my brain has begun to rot. Otherwise, you never would have faked me out with that lead to the queen of clubs."

"Am I going to be hearing that for the rest of my life from you?"

"That would be nice," said Dr Berkowitz.

"I beg your pardon?" said Margaret.

"You just implied that we'll be . . . ah, *knowing* one another for the rest of your life. And I'm saying that would be nice."

"Oh," said Margaret. "Well, all I meant was—"

"I don't want to hear what you *meant*," said Dr Berkowitz. "The words are enough. Meanings I can do without. The thing I. Well. That is. Ah. The thing I want to say is I believe it would be best if we had dinner tonight in your hotel, what with your condition."

"Oh," said Margaret.

"I'll make a reservation for the Oak Room, and I'll come pick you up at eight. Are you in good enough shape to go downstairs to the Oak Room?"

"Yes," said Margaret, speaking quickly.

"You're sure now?"

"Yes," said Margaret, speaking quickly.

Margaret took *another* bath, and it occurred to her that she was in imminent danger of puckering herself to death. She devoted thirty minutes to the combing of her hair, and she felt girlish and absurd. She

powdered her face, and she powdered her bosom, and she even powdered
her belly and thighs. The cotton in her mouth was no longer bloody, and
so she did not bother with it. Carefully she brushed her teeth, and pain
was absent. She spat the cotton into the toilet bowl, and she was pleased
with how white the cotton was. She had a knowledge that tonight would
be enormous. Not a feeling but a knowledge. She turned on the radio and
listened to the war news from Korea. The WQXR announcer had a bland
voice, and he could have been talking about horticulture or the principles
of banking. Margaret carefully wriggled herself into her garterbelt. She
attached her hose to it. She turned in front of a mirror to make certain the
seams were straight. She looked at her palms, and they were pink. She
felt her cheeks, and they were warm. She snapped on her brassiere, then
flopped down on the sofa in the sitting room. She drew several large
breaths. She shuddered. A window was open, and she listened to the
sounds of New York City. Now the news was done on WQXR, and a
woman was singing something from one of the Mahler song cycles. Margaret decided she would wear her plain black dress, and she would adorn
it with no jewelry. She tugged it on over her head, and she zipped it up the
back, and then of course she had to comb her hair again. She seated herself in the bathroom, and the bathroom was fragrant, and she combed and
fussed and clucked and hummed. She felt like a bride . . . and a virgin
bride, at that. She told herself she was being stupid, but she also told herself she did not care. She told herself it was about time, and she also told
herself this man probably did not have much of a capacity for being cruel.
She glanced down at her right hand, and she remembered how his moustache had tickled it. She combed. She tapped her tongue against the roof
of her mouth. She probed the open place where the tooth had been, and
she felt nothing. She closed her eyes. Briefly she embraced herself. She
thought of her mother, and she thought of her sisters, and she thought of
Wanda Ripple. She opened her eyes. She smiled into the mirror. She was
fastidious with her lipstick. She stroked her neck, and it was without
wrinkles. She powdered it. She dabbed perfume behind her ears. She decided she was behaving like little more than a common prostitute, and she
also decided she did not *care* how she was behaving. Perhaps tonight she
would not be aware of bees or canoes or horseradish or the awful sound
of iron.

Dr Berkowitz ordered himself a dark Löwenbräu and he ordered
Margaret a ginger ale. The Oak Room was crowded, but they had

nice side table, and he said: "I really have good taste, if I do say so my-self." He wore a dark blue suit and a flowered bow tie that did not go with the dark blue suit. He said: "This is my favorite place in New York City." He made an expansive gesture with an arm. Margaret looked around. She was aware of jewelry, bow ties, breadsticks, soups, a casual and relaxed atmosphere of people who were in this room because they *be-longed* in this room, of crystal and linen and polite accented waiters. She had dined here before, but always with women, and the place had not been the same. She wished she could explain all this to Dr Berkowitz, but she could not. Or not *yet*, at any rate. Grinning, he concluded his expansive gesture. He folded his hands on the table. "All right," he said. "So much for the Stokowski imitation." A hesitation. "Hey, did you see your name in the *Times*?"

"Yes," said Margaret.

"I'm going to make a star out of you," said Dr Berkowitz.

"That would be very nice," said Margaret.

"You look beautiful this evening. But then I've told you that, haven't I?"

"Yes," said Margaret.

"Upstairs," said Dr Berkowitz. "In the room."

"Yes," said Margaret. "But that's all right. If you want to repeat your-self, you have my permission."

"Thank you," said Dr Berkowitz. He fussed with a corner of his mous-tache.

The waiter came with the beer and the ginger ale. He made a ceremony of pouring the ginger ale, then the beer. Margaret and Dr Berkowitz thanked him, and he went away.

Dr Berkowitz and Margaret touched glasses. "To whatever," he said.

"All right," said Margaret.

"Do you understand what I mean?"

"I believe so," said Margaret.

"Thank you," said Dr Berkowitz. He drank.

Margaret drank.

Dr Berkowitz set down his glass. He said: "I suppose you have it figured out that I'm married."

Margaret looked away. She wanted to hug herself, but she did not hug herself. Instead, she simply looked away. She was aware of more jewel-ry, more bow ties, the sheen of the splendid oak paneling.

"She is not a bad person," said Dr Berkowitz. "I wish I could say she misunderstands me, but she doesn't misunderstand me. And I wish I could say she is ugly, or deformed, or crippled, or dying of cancer, or any of the other conventional and convenient things. But there's nothing at all the matter with her. She's actually kind of nicelooking for a woman her age, and she's as healthy as . . . well, as an ox. The only thing is—she and I just do not get along. Do you mind hearing all this?"

Margaret shrugged. She sipped at her ginger ale. She tried to concentrate on the bow ties and whatever.

Dr Berkowitz smiled. "I feel a little as though we're in a movie."

Margaret looked at him.

"The setting," said Dr Berkowitz. "The toast. The unspoken implications. You and the way you look. And now my sad story. In a movie, you would be Ingrid Bergman, and I would be God Knows Who, and Harriet would be oh I don't know, someone on the order of Ruth Hussey. Do you remember Ruth Hussey?"

"Yes," said Margaret. "And is Harriet your wife?"

"Correct," said Dr Berkowitz. He drank more of his beer, and a trace of foam collected at a corner of his moustache. "Her maiden name was Harriet Stern, and we have a fine apartment on Riverside Drive, and we have been married twentyfour years, and we have no children, and she occasionally sleeps with a writer named Harold Gore, and she occasionally sleeps with another writer named John Behrman, and for all I know perhaps she occasionally sleeps with both of them at the same time. She is what is known as a senior editor at a place called Universal Publishing, which I think is a pretty ambitious title . . . after all, it just isn't your average rinkydink little *printer* who seeks to *publish* the *universe* . . . "

"No," said Margaret. "I suppose not." Her palms were warm. She pressed them around her glass of ginger ale.

Dr Berkowitz finished off his beer. "Would you like to order?"

"Whatever you say," said Margaret.

Dr Berkowitz nodded. "Well then," he said, "I think we should go ahead and order. There's still a lot of talking we have to get behind us, and we might as well not be interrupted."

"All right," said Margaret.

Dr Berkowitz suggested an omelet for Margaret because of her tender mouth. She agreed that it was a good idea. She also ordered bouillon. Dr Berkowitz ordered cold borscht and the London broil for himself. The waiter nodded and went away, and then Dr Berkowitz said: "Harriet and I have divided the apartment the way the Russians and the Allies have divided Germany, but we have stipulated that we have equal access to the kitchen and the bathroom. We are so *reasonable* about everything it is enough to make a great sperm whale grow wings. We nod. We smile. We go our separate ways; we sleep in our separate rooms; we have our separate dreams . . . "

"If everything is so separate, why don't you *separate*?" said Margaret.

"It isn't done," said Dr Berkowitz.

"What?" said Margaret.

"Harriet won't hear of it," said Dr Berkowitz. "She is *Mrs Irving Berkowitz*, and her husband is the distinguished dentist, and he makes a great deal of money, and she is exactly where she wants to be for the rest of her life."

"What about you?" said Margaret. "Are *you* where *you* want to be for the rest of your life?"

"I wish I knew."

"Could you explain that?"

"All right," said Dr Berkowitz. "There are a number of things to be considered. First, Harriet and I have been married for a very long time. A certain routine has set in. Or inertia. Call it whatever you like. But the thing is, Harriet and I have come to depend on our arrangement."

"That doesn't make any sense," said Margaret.

"Ah, but it does," said Dr Berkowitz. "If you *think* about it, it really *does*. It has to do with *familiar misery* as opposed to the *possibility* of unfamiliar danger. It is so much easier and less hazardous simply to let things slide . . . can't you understand that?"

Margaret nodded.

"Most people fear plunges," said Dr Berkowitz.

"Yes," said Margaret.

"You know *exactly* what I'm talking about, don't you?"

"Yes," said Margaret.

"And it does make sense, doesn't it?"

"Yes," said Margaret.

"I am fifty years old," said Dr Berkowitz. "I am overweight, and I am a little preposterous, but I *am* good at what I do. I am your proverbial dentist's dentist, if you'll pardon the expression, and I make an indecently large income every year, and I even keep some of my money from the clutches of Mister Truman and good old General Dugout Doug, the gentleman with the corncob pipe whose photo you may see in the paper now and again."

"I believe I do," said Margaret.

The waiter came with the bouillon and the borscht. Margaret sipped carefully at the bouillon, but Dr Berkowitz spooned up the borscht with almost a sort of zeal. "God, this is good," he said. "I really appreciate fine things . . . food, hotels, women, whatever. I figure I've earned them, and never again in my life am I going to travel second ticket. I come from a place called Newark, New Jersey, and you don't want to hear about it. And I won't bore you with ancient history, except to say that I wasn't exactly brought up in Mrs Rockefeller's lap. My father blocked hats, and my mother had something wrong with her bones, and she died when she was seventeen, which was a year after I was born. Pop said three words to me maybe once every two weeks, and he was thirtyseven when *he* died. He collapsed on the job, and I'm told he fell against a case and knocked down about a dozen shelves of hats. Which meant he died in a blizzard of hats. I think there's some sort of symbolism in that, but I'm not quite sure what it is. Anyhow, I was twenty that year, and I went to live with my Aunt Esther in Riverdale, and somehow I got through dental school, and I married Harriet, and I prospered like you wouldn't believe. *And* I became interested in the game of bridge, thanks to Harriet. She told me it was *sociable* to play the game. So I got involved. And I mean *really* involved. Which I think you know what I mean?''

"Yes," said Margaret, smiling.

Dr Berkowitz was done with his borscht. He pushed away the bowl. He said: "So within a year I was playing in duplicate games, and Harriet—who'd only wanted me to be a *sociable* player—was sort of left behind, if you follow me. And the better I became as a player, the more she came to hate the game, and it was almost as though the game was another woman . . . which I suppose in a sense it was . . . and so finally we began to have scenes . . . tears . . . blah, blah, blah, you love *that game* more than you love *me* . . . the usual blah, blah, blah . . . "

Margaret nodded.

"So about two years ago," said Dr Berkowitz, "I gave up playing in tournaments. I said to her, I said: 'Okay, Harriet my pet, so much for bridge. From now on I am yours whenever you want me, and we shall live happily ever after, and we shall trip over buttercups and bunnyrabbits, tra la.' But there was only one catch. By that time she'd begun to entertain the troops, not to mention the fleet, not to mention those two writers whose names I flung at you a little while ago. And so she said to me: 'Irving my pet, I thank you very much, but no thanks.' And so there I was still kneeling in the ondeck circle, and I really hadn't even gone to bat, let alone reached first base. But I *was* sort of chopped down, you know. There it was, my Grand Gesture, but she'd not allowed me to make it . . . and I ask you, is there anything worse than a *spurned* Grand Gesture? The very thought is . . . well, I mean, honest to God, you'd have thought she'd have had *some* decency . . . " He looked around. "I wish the food would get here," he said. "One thing about your friend Irv Berkowitz—disasters may come, and disasters may go, but Irv Berkowitz' appetite goes on forever . . . like the, ah, Montauk Tidal Basin, if there is such a thing. I mean, what do I know from tidal basins? Sounds like a place where maybe Neptune would wash his tootsies, right?''

"Oh yes indeed," said Margaret.

"I love you," said Dr Berkowitz.

"What?" said Margaret.

Dr Berkowitz opened his mouth to say something, but then the waiter came with the omelet and the London broil. He spooned the omelet onto Margaret's plate, and he spooned the London broil onto Dr Berkowitz's plate, together with parslied potatoes and some boiled onions. He asked Dr Berkowitz was everything all right, and Dr Berkowitz assured him yes, yes, everything was absolute perfection. Smiling, the waiter moved away. Then Dr Berkowitz went to work with his knife and fork, slicing the meat, spearing the potatoes. And he said (without looking up): "Miss Ridpath, so help me *God* I love you. And there's no sense walking around the edges of it."

Margaret looked at her omelet. She did not even try to taste it, let alone eat it. Instead, she embraced herself.

Dr Berkowitz spoke as he ate. He did not quite look Margaret squarely in the eye. Either he looked down at his food or he looked at a point somewhere beyond her right shoulder. He said: "At fifty, I got no time for crap. Neither do I have time to say boyish things I don't believe. I've been seeing you in tournaments now for the past seven, eight years, but *you* never saw *me* for Sour Owl Squat, did you? I was just some faceless opponent to be punished or steamrollered or whatever it is you do. I mean, my dear lady, you are *some* bridgeplayer. But it's not because of bridge that I'm in love with you. God forbid. The reason I'm in love with you, Miss Ridpath, has to do with what I sense is something very . . . ah, vulnerable . . . and, ah, delicate . . . that you've never really allowed to emerge. I see it in your eyes now and then. Something very human. A sort of reluctant willingness to admit that warm winds just might count for more than a nine-card suit to a hundred honors. Miss Ridpath, I want to *know* you. I mean that in any way you would like to take it . . . ."

Margaret attacked her omelet.

Dr Berkowitz hesitated. Now he looked at her directly. He set down his knife and fork. He wiped his moustache with a corner of his napkin. He said: "Please don't be insulted."

Margaret swallowed. The omelet was enormous with mushrooms, but she tasted nothing. "No," she said. She swallowed again. "I am not . . . insulted . . . ."

"Something has happened, right?"

Margaret nodded.

"Are you enjoying it?"

"I think so," she said.

"You are some lady," said Dr Berkowitz.

"Thank you," said Margaret.

"I was away from the game for quite a while. I am rusty—which is why you were able to fake me out with that lead toward the queen of clubs."

"I accept your excuse," said Margaret.

"It is no *excuse*," said Dr Berkowitz. "It is a *fact*."

"Oh," said Margaret. "I'm very sorry."

"I have not had sex in nearly two years," said Dr Berkowitz.

Margaret set down her knife and fork. There was no sense eating. She might as well have been eating the napkin.

"I told you there would be no crap," said Dr Berkowitz.

Margaret nodded.

"I want you very much."

Margaret nodded.

"Does that mean all right?"

Margaret nodded.

"Then please tell me," said Dr Berkowitz.

"You want me, and it's all right," said Margaret.

"That sounded difficult for you to say."

"Of course it was," said Margaret.

Dr Berkowitz resumed eating. He said: "A stranger could walk into this room and look at me and what would he see? An overweight middleaged man cutting a slice of London broil. Nothing very thrilling to write home to Cousin Silas about. But what that stranger doesn't see is the state I'm in. And I mean *right now*." A nod. A smile. "At my age, well, a man gets to wondering . . . "

Margaret embraced herself.

"But now I don't have to wonder, and I thank you. From the bottom of my whatever."

Margaret nodded. She supposed they would go upstairs. *Supposed*, nothing. She *knew* they would go upstairs. And then Dr Berkowitz would learn that she was a virgin, and a frightened *tinfoil* virgin at that. And perhaps he would laugh. Surely he would shake his head, and surely he would make some sort of *crack*. Margaret embraced herself more tightly. She wished she were in the beauty shop. She wished she were sitting under the dryer. Perhaps one of the women in one of those magazines could have suggested what to do.

Dr Berkowitz finished his London broil. He pushed away his plate. He smiled at Margaret. He said: "Rusty."

"What?" said Margaret.

"I . . . hah . . . I was talking about how rusty I am. Which is why I brought up bridge. I want you to be my partner. Maybe you'll help me chip away the rust. And *now,* when I think about *that,* I *also* think about rusty in *another* sense, and maybe you'll be able to help me *that* way, too."

"You are in for a surprise," said Margaret.

"Really?" said Dr Berkowitz.

"Really," said Margaret.

Why Irv Berkowitz? Why *him* . . . *there* . . . at *that* time, after more than forty years? It was an interesting question, of course, but it was not all that difficult to answer. One factor was curiosity. Another was lust. A third was Margaret's final realization that she could bear frustration no longer. If she didn't hurry and do *something,* the question would become moot. There was nothing *wrong* with her, for heaven's sake. She *had* responded to Eugene Pearson and the other boys and men who had been interested in her. But she had been too frightened. She had always been aware of bees and canoes. With Irv Berkowitz, though, she did not feel that particular sort of fear. With Irv Berkowitz, she did not feel that she would be chopped or sliced. She did not believe he would assault her with his iron. And then, beyond all that, beyond all considerations of lust and fear, there was the fact that she loved him. Why? She did not really know . . . at least with any finite certainty, the sort that could be totted up in the books at Steinfelder's. Perhaps the answer sat somewhere within those magazines in the beauty shop. But none of this meant that she was not afraid. She *was* afraid; it was simply that she heard no bees, and she sat in no canoe. Which perhaps meant that her love was genuine. Which perhaps was as good a yardstick as any. Which perhaps was better than any. At any rate, Irv Berkowitz was the first of her two men—and the second, George Prout, was the same but altogether different. The difference was clear in Margaret's mind. Irv never had used iron against her, and George always did. (One afternoon shortly before her death, Margaret lay down for a nap on the front room sofa. Just as she was dozing off, it occurred to her that her grand total of two lovers had both been bald, and she said to herself: Never once in my life have I run my fingers though the hair of a man with whom I have had The Physical. Dear me, such a strange life this is. Bald heads on the pillow. Sounds like the title of a song. *Three Coins in the Fountain.* Bald heads on the pillow. Be still, my heart.)

It was perhaps an hour after their dinner in the Oak Room, and Margaret and Irv lay naked in her bed, and she was embracing him, and she was trembling, and he said: "I can't get over it."

"I expect not," said Margaret.

"We are a couple of real dillies."

"If you say so," said Margaret.

"A *virgin*," said Irv. "My *God*."

"The last one in the world," said Margaret.

"Probably," said Irv.

"I told you you were in for a surprise," said Margaret.

"I should have believed you," said Irv.

"I'm sorry that I'm shaking like this," said Margaret.

"Nothing to be sorry for," said Irv. "How do you . . . how do you feel? Did I hurt you?"

"I feel all right," said Margaret.

"Did I *hurt* you?" said Irv.

"A little," said Margaret.

"I sound like a dentist," said Irv.

"You look like one, too," said Margaret.

"You mean to say I don't look like Charles Atlas?" said Irv.

"I'm very sorry," said Margaret.

"I ought to take a bite out of your ass for that," said Irv.

"You don't have to be vulgar," said Margaret.

"No, but it's fun," said Irv.

"I guess New York people just *enjoy* being vulgar," said Margaret.

"Yes," said Irv. "Especially since right now what I'm really trying to do is divert you."

"From what?" said Margaret.

"Well," said Irv, "when a *virgin* goes to bed with a man who is *rusty* the results aren't all that sensational. I apologize. I feel like the Tin Woodman."

"Who?" said Margaret.

"The Tin Woodman," said Irv, "from *The Wizard of Oz.* Judy Garland

and the rainbow and the yellow brick road."

"Oh," said Margaret. "Yes."

Irv was silent.

"You did *too* do very well," said Margaret.

"How would you know?" said Irv.

"Now don't get me angry," said Margaret. "Don't belittle me." ·

"All I'm saying is you have no way of judging," said Irv.

"I enjoyed it very much," said Margaret.

"I love you," said Irv.

"And *I* love *you*," said Margaret.

"You said that when I was entering you," said Irv.

"I know," said Margaret.

"The proverbial heat of passion," said Irv.

"I never say things I don't mean," said Margaret, "heat of passion or no heat of passion."

"It'll be better," said Irv, "once the rust gets scraped away."

"And once your partner gets the hang of it," said Margaret.

"Don't use the word *partner*," said Irv.

"It make you think of bridge?" said Margaret.

"Yes," said Irv.

"What word would you like me to use?" said Margaret.

"Girl," said Irv.

"I'm too old," said Margaret.

"How about mistress?" said Irv.

"I'm too proper," said Margaret.

"Not any more," said Irv.

"You be *nice*," said Margaret.

"Too late," said Irv.

"The question still is—what do I want to be known as?" said Margaret.

"Love," said Irv.

"Pardon?" said Margaret.

"You are my *love*," said Irv, "and *that* is what you'll be known as."

"That's very nice," said Margaret.

"And it'll get better and better," said Irv.

"Promise?" said Margaret.

"May I be struck by lightning," said Irv.

"I was very frightened," said Margaret.

"But the shaking is beginning to go away," said Irv.

"Yes," said Margaret.

"Fright is understandable," said Irv.

"Almost everything frightens me," said Margaret.

"I don't believe that," said Irv.

"Well, it's *true*," said Margaret. "I keep having a feeling that the world will walk all over me if I give it half a chance. You wouldn't know it to *look* at me, but . . . well . . . "

"But well what?" said Irv.

"But well if I find myself in a strange situation, I am liable to go to pieces," said Margaret.

"But does anyone ever really know it?" said Irv.

"Occasionally, but not often," said Margaret.

"You hide just about everything, don't you?" said Irv.

"Yes," said Margaret.

"Tears?" said Irv.

"Yes," said Margaret.

"A good laugh?" said Irv.

"Most of the time," said Margaret.

"Perhaps those things have to do with why you play bridge so well," said Irv.

"Maybe so," said Margaret.

"You need educating," said Irv.

"Yes," said Margaret.

"Tears," said Irv.

"Yes," said Margaret.

"Belly laughs," said Irv.

"Yes," said Margaret.

"Would you marry me if I didn't have Harriet hanging around my neck?" said Irv.

"Probably," said Margaret.

"It would mean bringing a Jew into your family," said Irv.

"My sisters would have simultaneous strokes," said Margaret. "Their names are Ruth and Sarah."

"*Ruth* and *Sarah*?" said Irv.

"Yes," said Margaret. "And even *I* see the humor in *that*."

"I want to be serious for a second," said Irv.

"All right," said Margaret.

"I know myself," said Irv. "And I think I understand inertia. Would it make any sense to you if I told you I don't believe I want to divorce Harriet and go through all the *tsimmis*?"

"The what?" said Margaret.

"*Tsimmis*," said Irv, "which loosely translated means a big deal."

"Oh," said Margaret.

"Well?" said Irv.

"I think I can understand," said Margaret.

"Will you work at it?" said Irv.

"Yes," said Margaret.

"At my age," said Irv, "it's just about impossible to do without the routine, even if it's an unpleasant routine. Harriet and I have lived together a lot of years, and experiences build up . . . *times* . . . you know?"

"I believe so," said Margaret.

"It would be too much of a disruption," said Irv. "Too much of a *tsimmis.*"

"Thank you for being honest," said Margaret.

"I love you," said Irv.

"The feeling is mutual," said Margaret.

"And it'll get better," said Irv. "You'll be surprised how fast the rust will go away."

"That's very nice to know," said Margaret.

"Yes," said Irv.

"I feel very comfortable," said Margaret.

"You aren't shaking," said Irv.

"I know," said Margaret.

"You'll be skittish, though, at least for a time," said Irv.

"I'll try not to be," said Margaret.

"Don't worry yourself about it," said Irv.

"All right," said Margaret.

"You're funny," said Irv.

"How so?" said Margaret.

"When I pulled your dress over your head," said Irv, "you very clearly and emphatically stated: 'Thank you, Doctor Berkowitz.' "

"I called you *Doctor Berkowitz*?" said Margaret.

"Clear as a bell," said Irv. "And so now I want you to call me Irv."

"Now?" said Margaret.

"Now," said Irv.

"Irv," said Margaret.

"Very good," said Irv. "Now there's something else I'd like to ask you."

"What's that?" said Margaret.

"Have you ever given any thought to playing a forcing club?" said Irv.

*

Exactly a year later Margaret received a registered airmail special
delivery package from New York City. It contained a can of peanuts, a jar of rust remover and a deck of cards, all of which were the king
of clubs.

Irv was right. It did get better. He explained to Margaret about the
female orgasm, and he did various things to bring it about, and she
told him she would love him forever. She also told him she knew she was
talking like a schoolgirl, but she couldn't *help* it. And anyway, after all her
years of virginity, perhaps she had a *right* to talk like a schoolgirl. Laughing, Irv told her she could talk like a Bessarabian vampire bat for all he
cared; he was as much a schoolboy as she was a schoolgirl, and it all was
ridiculous, and God bless it.

They saw one another every month or so for nearly eight years, and
they did in fact become bridge partners. Even though he was a Life Master, he was not a particularly good player, and his special problem was
stamina. He was really quite dangerous and unreliable over the crucial
last halfdozen boards, and Margaret had to take special precautions to
overcome his tiredness. And she was successful. And she and Irv won
perhaps more than their share of prestige tournaments. It was no particular secret among their bridgeplaying peers that they were fond of one
another and probably lovers. But the bridgeplayers were not affected by
this—it would have diverted them from bridge, and *that* of course was not
tolerated.

Margaret and Irv participated in tournaments in New York City, Chicago, Denver, New Orleans, Boston, San Francisco, Miami, Mexico City,
Detroit, Honolulu, Cleveland. Irv put on weight (*more* weight), and he
came down with some sort of mild cardiac condition that he never fully
explained to Margaret. All he did was joke about it, telling her: "Yes
ma'am, I have a mild cardiac condition all right, and it goes by the generic
name of Margaret Ridpath, and I suppose one of these days a proper medical term will be dreamed up—perhaps on the order of myocardial
ridpathicus. And won't that make you proud? You'll feel the way Hale
did when the comet was named after him."

"You're not being all that funny," said Margaret. "You ought to take
better care of yourself. You ought to watch what you eat."

"Oh, I do watch what I eat," said Irv, "while I'm eating it—so nobody
steals it."

"What am I going to do about you?" said Margaret.

"Not much," said Irv.

"Perhaps I should stop going to bed with you," said Margaret. "Perhaps it is too much of a strain on your heart."

"Perhaps," said Irv, "but if I'm going to go, at least it'll be with a smile on my lips."

"Very funny," said Margaret.

"You'll think I'm coming," said Irv, "but I'll be going."

"You're impossible," said Margaret, laughing.

"At my age, I should certainly hope so," said Irv.

She told Irv nearly everything of any importance about herself. She told him of her father's death. She told him of the time she had spat on Dorothy Hall's grave. She told him of the loss of Eugene Pearson. She told him of her late brother Paul. She spoke of Ruth and Sarah and their husbands, and she spoke of her mother's garrulous madness, the famous *STAR* chair, her mother's war with Wanda Ripple, the annual lime pie, the afternoon with the tall lady at the depot, Mr George Wolf and *his* heart condition (plus, shyly, quietly, an admission that yes, Mr Wolf did trust her with just about the entire operation of Steinfelder's). And Margaret even tried to explain to Irv her feelings about tinfoil and iron. But she never told him of the slapless slaps she occasionally had to inflict . . . or perhaps bestow . . . on her mother. And she never told him of her mother's occasional ambulatory nakedness. She loved Irv as deeply as she suspected she was capable of loving anyone, but there were a few private things she would not relinquish to him. She ransacked most of her compartments for him, but she never ransacked all of them. And she never really did make him understand her fears, nor did she really make him understand the importance of order, of structure, of standards that did not deviate, of anchors that could not be wrenched loose. She said to him: "Whatever it is that's inside me and recognizes love, then *now* it has finally sent me a message, and it tells me I shall love you for however long as we have."

"Thank you," said Irv.

"There's more," said Margaret, "more I want to explain."

"All right," said Irv.

"I also need to be in a situation where truth is respected," said Margaret. "When my mother told me about my father's suicide, I prodded her and I *prodded* her. You see, I wanted *all* the truth, not just *her version* of it. And I believe she thought I was trying to harm her. But I wasn't. I was only trying to find the *essence* of the thing that happened. *She,* though . . . she thought I was trying to . . . oh, I don't know . . . *punish* her. But I wasn't. No. I am not that sort of person. And then, a few years later, when old Fred Boyd died in my presence . . . I've told you about him . . . I know I have . . . well, anyway, his widow asked me what his final words had been . . . and they had been, ah, trivial . . . but I told her the *truth* . . . I told her *exactly what he had said* . . . and you know what she *did?* She *became angry.* She told me she did not want the *truth.* She told me she wanted something *romantic* and *sentimental.* She said to me: 'Couldn't you have told me my name had been on his lips?' And, Irv, I'm sorry, but all I did was *sit* there. I didn't know what to *do.* When a question is asked, isn't the responder under an obligation to be truthful?''

"I'm a dentist," said Irv.

"What?" said Margaret.

"I'm not a psychiatrist," said Irv. "I don't even know what psychiatrists *do.* If you want to talk to somebody about psychiatrists, talk to Harriet. She's had two, maybe three. I don't remember. I pay the bills, and the hell with it."

"*I'm* not talking about psychiatrists *either,*" said Margaret. "I'm only trying to arrive at something that is necessary so you understand me. And I'm asking your help."

"But you've lost me," said Irv.

"All right," said Margaret. "Here it is . . . and as simply as I know how to say it. *Number One:* I love you. *Number Two:* I also love truth and order, and I cannot understand those who do not see what I see in truth and order. *Number Three:* In the interest of truth and order, *and* because I love you, I just want you to know that I still retain part of my privacy. There are certain secret things about me that you'll never learn . . . "

"Is that it?" said Irv.

"Yes," said Margaret.

"Do you think *you'll* ever know all there is to know about *me*?" said Irv.

"I suppose not," said Margaret.

"You can bet your left whatchamacallit on it," said Irv. "My God, what a terrible thing it would be if we knew everything there is to know about each other. I mean, suppose you were to learn of the time I was caught in sexual dalliance with those nine male members of the Lower Slobbovian Olympic gymnastics team? We told the police we were rehearsing a new kind of pyramid, but for some reason we were not believed. Or, I . . . ah, really now . . . if you think *for one minute* that I'm going to give you the lowdown on what happened during the nine years I was married to Zasu Pitts, you have another think coming, young lady. Or if you are hoping that I shall relive every moment of that glorious afternoon when I outlasted six of my peers and won the finals of the 1914 Greater North New Jersey Circle Jerk Tournament (with a lastminute spurt, so to speak), I must tell you that I shall go to the grave with my lips sealed as far as that particular episode is concerned. If you'd like, I shall raise a hairy palm and take my oath on it . . . ''

"Irv, for heaven's *sake*, I am trying to be *serious*," said Margaret.

"All right," said Irv. "Good for you. You are trying to be serious. Then I'll try to be serious, too. No more Circle Jerk talk, I promise. *Now*, if what you're saying to me is that you'll forever have locked places, *and* if you're trying to *defend yourself* for having them, let me be the first to tell you you don't *need* to defend yourself—any more than *I* need to defend *my*self because *I* have locked places. And I do. All kidding aside, all nonsense aside, I really *do*. What do you think Harriet and I have been going through? Something we want to have published in six juicy installments in *Confidential* along with the prison record of Rory Calhoun? Look, Margaret my girl, *everyone in the world* has a secret place. It all *goes without saying.* And maybe it can't always be faced, but it does have to be lived with. Take it from your Uncle Irv—you are no different than anyone else."

"But why?" said Margaret.

"Why what?" said Irv.

"Why must I have a section roped off?" said Margaret.

"What?" said Irv.

"The section no one can enter," said Margaret. "The section that fills me with shame. I try to face truth, so why can't I face shame?"

"Oh, for God's sake, stop plucking," said Irv.

"Plucking?" said Margaret, and she frowned. "Plucking what?"

"Navel lint," said Irv.

"Naval what?" said Margaret. "What's the Navy got to do with this?"

"Not *naval*," said Irv. "What I *said* was *navel*. N-A-V-E-L, as in bellybutton. And what I said to you was: Stop plucking lint from your navel. You are *alone* too much. Therefore, you *pluck* too much. You sit there in that store with your statistics and your balances, and your mind scurries around like a mouse in a pile of toothpicks. You ought to have *my* job for a day or so. You ought to look in all those mouths. It does a lot to cut down on the hours you have for plucking the lint. You're in touch with reality and *then* some, and you just don't have *time* for *secrets* and *guilt* and *fear*. I mean, your average *mouth* is truth, if truth is what you *want*, what you *really* want . . . which, frankly, sometimes I kind of doubt . . . "

"Doubt?" said Margaret.

"Yes," said Irv. "I think what you *really* want is *facts*, not *truth*. Which is why bridge appeals to you and you play it so well. Which is why bookkeeping appeals to you and you are so good at it. Also, you talk to me so much about fear. Don't facts. . . or at least *abstract* facts . . . shield you from fear? What's to be afraid of from the Rule of Eleven or Eight Ever Nine Never? You have told me you play well because you are afraid not to play well. Okay, maybe that's true. Correction. Maybe that's *a fact*. But are your guts any less tight because of facts? Do you sleep more easily? Do facts help you come faster? Do they make you laugh? Do they make you love sunshine and balloons and puppydogs and a bacon and tomato sandwich with lettuce hold the mayo? You seem to think that being afraid is some sort of sin. Well, it's *not*. We're *all* afraid. In other words, welcome to the human race; pull up a chair and we'll talk about it, and we'll get your passport validated. But forget all this abstract theorizing about truth. Take whatever comes along. Face up to it or run away from it, but try to accept it as being a part of the imperfect *world* . . . or *life* . . . or whatever the goddamned hell you would like to call it . . . that we all share. I have spoken to you about Presbyterian guilt. Well, the Presbyterians haven't cornered the market, no indeed. But the thing is—*it's all part of the experience of being alive*. So just . . . well, just let it *happen* . . . and if the people down the block don't like it, tell them to go make cockie in their soup tureens . . ."

". . . ah, I wish I could," said Margaret.

"Work at it," said Irv.

"All right," said Margaret.

"Trust me," said Irv.

"Yes sir," said Margaret.

"That's what I appreciate," said Irv. "Respect."

And perhaps, in those eight years Margaret and Irv were lovers, she did work at what he called joining the human race. Still, she never was certain. She kept trying to take deep breaths, but she was afraid that too many deep breaths would get the tinfoil to come loose and reveal itself. So she was careful, and she supposed her carefulness was not what

Irv had meant. *Supposed,* nothing. She *knew* it was not what he had meant. But how was one to teach her new tricks? It turned out to be impossible. The illusion of courage and coolness persisted, but the *facts* of Margaret Ridpath . . . the *facts* . . . the *facts* . . . the *facts* consisted of *facts* . . . the *facts* consisted of *logic* . . . the *facts* consisted of *order* . . . which was why the children died . . . and not courage . . . never that . . . and surely not even Otto York would have understood . . . he perhaps least of all . . .

So the evidence accumulated; Margaret was crowded by her days, by routine, by housework, by statistics, by her trips to the bridge tournaments, her nights with Irv and his love and his humor and his cigars. She doubled all settable contracts. She listened for bees. She combed her hair. She thought of her father, and she remembered her father's beer breath, and yes, she *had* turned out to be comely. Downspouts came and went. Underthings were discarded, contributed to the Goodwill people. Meatloaves were plumped into shape. The grape arbor constantly pleaded to be pruned. She never nagged Irv about his wife. She had plenty of money, and so she was able always to pay for her hotel rooms and transportation. (George Prout and Pete Saddler never relented in their generosity, and nearly every year Mr Wolf increased Margaret's salary.) And Wanda Ripple said: "Margaret, you do not have to worry about your mother as long as she is with *me.* It may not *sound* that way, to hear us fuss and aggravate one another, but I got what is called a *vested interest* in her, and she couldn't be more safe and protected if she was inside a *bell jar.* She means a lot to me. She means more than you ever could guess, so don't even *try* to bother working at it in your mind; you wouldn't come anywhere near the answer." And Inez Ridpath said: "At the fair in that year of 1904, was I ever something. *Heigh ho, come to the fair*—the world beckoned your Inez McClory, late of the great city of St Louis, Missouri, and whoopsydaisy, almost before you could say Jack Robinson along came a young man named John Ridpath and he *kissed* her *hand* and he stole her heart forever, and there aren't enough interurban cars in the *world* to slice away the memory of him. So yes. Hit me. Yes, I say. Whenever you like. If *I* had been the one to die, would he have had his little rendezvous with the interurban car *then?* That is my puzzle, you see. That is my *forever* puzzle." And Margaret's sister Ruth said: "We're both very lucky, do you know that? I mean, here we are, no longer what anybody would exactly call *pullets,* but we have moved inside what we want. More or less, I mean. Me and my kids, and George, and the house. You and your job, and the way you play bridge so well, and travel so much. I feel like an old stickinthemud next to *you,* and that is a certifiable *fact.* And to think you do all you do with Mother sort of . . . ah, on your back. Oh, I *love* Wanda Ripple. I absolutely *do.* But the fact is, when it comes down to where the skin gets tight, *you* are the one who is in charge of Mother, *really* in charge of her, and an *army* of Wanda Ripples won't change that little fact, right? Ah, but don't get the wrong idea. I'm not lording it over you. I'm *not* saying to you: 'Nya, nya, *nya,* she's *your* burden and not *mine.*' I *am* saying to you: 'Margaret, don't think for a second that Sarah and I don't know how much we owe you.' " And Margaret's sister Sarah said: "Sometime before I die I want to go to Beverly Hills, California, and look at the homes of the stars that I'm always seeing on my TV. And you know, I'd like to *steal* a *clump* of Burt Lancaster's *grass.* The kids are fine. I love them. Pete is fine. I love him, and he's still cute. But old Sarah here, for one day in whatever life's left in her she'd like to tuck in her belly and put on a tight yellow dress and big old spiked heels and go *sashaying* through Beverly Hills, California . . . with her hair just so, and her, this glamorous Sarah Saddler, wearing a pair of *mysterious* and *provocative* . . . ah, *sunglasses* . . . and I swear to you, I wouldn't ask for another thing as long as I lived except for maybe Burt Lancaster to run out onto his front lawn and yell: *'Hey, you! Stop plucking my grass!'* But I would just keep on plucking, and he would come forward, and he would *see* my *beauty* and my *hair* and my *glamor* and maybe *smell* my *perfume* . . . and, well, ah, then he would *forget all about* his dumb old *grass* . . . and next thing you knew . . . well, next thing you knew it would be like I was *Deborah Kerr* . . . and it would be *From Here to Eternity* . . . with the surf and all . . . and Burt would be saying to me: 'My God, a *banker's wife* . . . from *Paradise Falls, Ohio* . . .' "

In late 1958 Margaret asked Irv a serious question, and she insisted he give her a serious answer. It was morning, and they were eating breakfast in the Edwardian Room of the Plaza, and she said: "Irv, is the entire world the way I think it is?"

"You coming on with that iron stuff again?" said Irv.

"I suppose I am," said Margaret.

"To you, the world's the Mesabi Range, isn't it?" said Irv.

"Please don't make fun of me," said Margaret.

Irv looked up from his eggs Benedict. He and Margaret and a couple from Indianapolis had finished third in a team of four game the night before, and they would have won except that he went down on two straight four-spade contracts, both of which he should have made (they were the last two boards of the evening). He said: "Margaret, I know you're ticked off at me because of the way I butchered those two hands, but I—"

"It has nothing to do with *bridge*," said Margaret. "I swear it doesn't."

"Then what are you trying to ask me?" said Irv.

Margaret looked around the room. The morning was bright, December bright, and the sun was brilliant on the Fifth Avenue side. The room was white; waiters moved crisply. Odors of toast and fresh coffee caught high in Margaret's nostrils. She said: "I'm asking you is there any place in the world where such a lunatic as myself can go to *get away* from the iron? Here . . . this restaurant . . . the Oak Room . . . the Palm Court . . . the musicians . . . this entire hotel . . . all right, *here* I get a *hint* that there maybe *is* someplace I can go . . . or we can go . . ."

"Someplace without iron *people*," said Irv, "without iron *sounds*, without iron *tension*, right?"

"Right," said Margaret. She was eating oatmeal, and she had drenched it in warm cream.

"In other words," said Irv, "whatever your fears are, you can't overcome them, so you want to run away from them."

"I suppose so," said Margaret.

"How long have you been thinking this way?" said Irv.

"I don't really know," said Margaret. "All I'd like to do is just go somewhere and *sit*."

"Is it because of the Change?" said Irv.

Margaret shrugged. She had gone through the Change a year earlier. She was fortyseven now, and it had not been an easy Change, but at least she no longer had to contend with her copious menstruations. She said: "I suppose at least partially. But it's more than that. It's just that one time before I die I'd like to be somewhere that made me not feel . . . *threatened*. Do you know such a place?"

"The grave," said Irv.

"Be *serious*," said Margaret.

"I *am* being serious," said Irv. "If you want tranquilizers, I can write you a prescription, and I can personally guarantee that your body chemistry will be altered to such an extent that you will never suffer even the slightest *hint* of anxiety for the rest of your life. But that's just *a substitute* for *the grave,* Margaret. We have to *pay dues* in this life. We have to *expect* anxiety.''

"But all I'm talking about is maybe two weeks," said Margaret.

"Two weeks of what?" said Irv.

"Two weeks free of the iron," said Margaret.

"Has this been working at you?" said Irv.

"Yes," said Margaret.

"How long?" said Irv.

"A year or so," said Margaret. "But only *coincidentally* with the Change. You see . . . well . . . in the years since I've known you, I've been schoolgirlish enough to come to hope that the . . . *possibility* . . . exists . . . that I can for a *little while* anyway . . . get rid of the . . . the . . ."

"Fear?" said Irv.

"All right," said Margaret. "All right. Fear. And it's been in the past year or so . . . what with my age and all . . . what with knowing that perhaps . . . ah, *probably* . . . I've reached the limits of whatever I am . . . that *now* it doesn't *matter* any longer . . ."

"What the hell are you trying to tell me?" said Irv.

Margaret swallowed her oatmeal, her warm cream. She moistened her lips with her tongue. She said: "Irv, please please *please* . . . please help me . . ."

"Help you what?" said Irv.

"I don't *know* what," said Margaret. "Only just . . . well, where can I find a little *silence?*"

"Could I share it?" said Irv.

"Yes . . ." said Margaret.

"By silence," said Irv, "do you mean good manners? Do you mean being in the presence of people who aren't made of what you call iron?"

Margaret nodded.

"White tablecloths?" said Irv. "Politeness?"

"Yes," said Margaret.

"A hole you can pull over your head?" said Irv.

". . . yes," said Margaret.

"What will happen if you don't find such a place?" said Irv.

"I think I might go crazy," said Margaret.

"But all you say you want is two weeks," said Irv.

"Two weeks would be enough," said Margaret. "Two weeks of peace and quiet and you. Two weeks when I don't have to hold my breath or look over my shoulder. Two weeks of *no bridge*. Two weeks of *nothing to prove*. Of no one to fool into thinking I *am* what I am *not*."

"You said *no bridge*?" said Irv.

"*Absolutely* no bridge," said Margaret. "Just Margaret and Irv, period."

"My God, the sky is falling," said Irv.

"I believe," said Margaret, "the expression is: '*Dear me*, the sky is falling.'"

"England," said Irv.

"England?" said Margaret.

"Yes," said Irv. "I was there in '37, and I was there in '48. I think the English have bought the course, but they *do* have *style*; they *do* have *manners*. And maybe you wouldn't be afraid."

"Perhaps a village," said Margaret.

"Yes," said Irv, "but London, too. It's a city, but it's not like *this* city. People seldom blow their horns, and there are places I can take you where waiters wear white gloves. And Fortnum & Mason's, where a man in a morning coat will measure out fresh tea that you can take home with you. And we can walk in Green Park and stroll down Piccadilly past Lord Palmerston's home. And with an independent air."

"A village, though?" said Margaret. "At least for a few days? Somewhere maybe where we can see . . . oh, I don't know . . . the English Channel maybe?"

"That could be arranged," said Irv.

"I am not *fooling*," said Margaret. "I don't want this to be a *pipedream*."

"I didn't think you were fooling," said Irv.

"Could we go in the spring?" said Margaret.

"By ship?" said Irv.

"Yes!" said Margaret.

"I believe it could be arranged," said Irv.

"But I have to pay my own share," said Margaret.

"After all these years, I still can't officially make you my mistress?" said Irv.

"That is correct," said Margaret.

"That's too bad," said Irv. "If you were my mistress, I think I could get some sort of income tax deal on you. I mean, maybe I could declare you."

"Hush," said Margaret.

Irv swallowed the last of his eggs Benedict. He drank coffee. "And no bridge?" he said. "Not even on the ship?"

"I promise," said Margaret.

"May this day forever be preserved in the corridors of time," said Irv.

"May my . . . *head* . . . ah, *shrivel up* and . . . *fall off*," said Margaret.

"Now don't get carried away," said Irv.

"Hush," said Margaret.

"You may be disappointed," said Irv.

"Not if I'm with you," said Margaret.

"But there are some points that have to be made—not about *England* so much as about *hiding*," said Irv.

"I don't want to hear them," said Margaret.

Irv looked at her.

"I know all about your *points*," said Margaret.

"Well, maybe you do," said Irv.

"And they don't *matter*," said Margaret. "I don't *care*."

"All right," said Irv.

"I love you," said Margaret.

"Finish your oatmeal before it gets cold," said Irv.

"I love you anyway," said Margaret.

Irv Berkowitz smiled.

Margaret and Irv sailed to England aboard the *Queen Elizabeth* in the late spring of 1959. They had separate first class cabins, and the expense was horrendous—especially since Irv spent every night crowded with Margaret in her berth. They were neither of them exactly scrawny, and it made for an interesting fit. Margaret won four hundred dollars in a bingo game, and she did not become seasick. The food was extraordinary, and she saved a number of menus. It was a quiet passage, and she and Irv did not even once become involved in a bridge game, even though several tournament acquaintances of theirs also were making the crossing and made ardent representations to them. The weather was warm enough that Margaret and Irv were able to spend two afternoons on deck, where they bundled in light blankets and held hands and blinked at the white North Atlantic sun. And now and then they sipped on bouillon and munched on crackers. And Paradise Falls was elsewhere. Paradise Falls was gone. Paradise Falls did not exist. This ship was Xanadu; it was Atlantis; it was mythic and benevolent, and there was absolutely no way it could have occupied the same niche of the universe as Paradise Falls. And Irv said: "I guess I told you a long time ago that I appreciate good things . . . food, travel, companionship, whatever. Now, here, look at us, two people well along what the TV folks like to call the Road of Life, and yet by any definition you would care to name we are *lovers* . . . ah, all right, so I am just the way you are . . . I want the hole pulled over *me,* too . . . I am sometimes very tired, Margaret . . . I think back on my father buried in all those hats, and I wonder whether I'm any different than he was, and I get to thinking no, no, don't let *that* dig at you, Irv old boy . . . the thing to do is find the hole . . . the thing to do is relax and sip bouillon . . . after all, what do I think I am going to be? An immortal and epic and earthshattering *dentist*? I am well off, and I have my heart condition to warm me when the nights are cold, and Harriet still now and then humps one or another of her writers, or a busboy, or a National Guard regiment, and okay . . . let her . . . after all, what am *I* doing here with *you*? Oh, if we *allow* ourselves, we really can be tortured, can't we? But who needs to *allow* himself? The thing to do is make your pile, hold your breath and tighten your eyes and look inside who knows how many thousands of mouths that *bleed* and *stink* and *rot,* and okay, okay, *okay,* I know, I *know* . . . it's not, ah, *worthy* of me to talk that way . . . but I cannot acknowledge my comfort without acknowledging where the money to buy the comfort has come from . . . but all right, once having stipulated *that,* is there anything wrong with enjoying what is *here,* the way you grin when you look at the menus, the look of you *right now* with the sunlight streaking your face . . . my God, you are a beautiful woman, and a fine figure of a woman, and a gentle woman, and a brilliant woman . . . my God, Margaret, whatever it is we have, and however long we have it, you are *absolutely correct* when you say we deserve a little peace . . . and if this trip can take you away from your *iron* or whatever you call it, then I will be the luckiest man on the face of the earth. Lou Gehrig said that when he retired in '39. I was there. Yankee Stadium. He said he was the luckiest man on the face of the earth. He was dying, but he went ahead and said that anyway. I cried. Everybody around me cried. And I almost want to cry *now,* do you know that? I want this to be so very right for you. That way, I'll be the luckiest man on the face of the earth. Which'll mean I'll be the *happiest* man on the face of the earth. I . . . you . . . please . . . please believe that . . ." And then, snuffling, Irv groped inside his blanket and came up with a handkerchief. He dabbed at his eyes and blew his nose. He said something about the salt air. Margaret nodded. She did not speak. There was nothing she knew to say. There was nothing she really *had* to say. She knew what he knew, and she supposed he also was trying to tell her he was dying. She patted his knee. The sunlight made her squint. It was such *white* sunlight. Here he was, probably dying, and yet he was able to say he was the luckiest man on the face of the earth. She vaguely remembered Lou Gehrig. Hadn't he been a baseball player? And wasn't he dead now? And hadn't he been dead for a long time? Margaret breathed deeply. She breathed with her mouth open. The salt air *was* there. It rubbed her tongue. She told Irv she loved him. She told him there never could be anyone else. He grinned. He blinked. He said: "Be quiet. Look at the sky. Think of God." She nodded. She felt melodramatic and foolish, but she was not afraid. She smiled. That night she wore a red dress, and it exposed a good deal of her bosom. The next night she and Irv were invited to dine at the captain's table. Margaret wore a black dress, and it exposed a good deal of her bosom, and she danced with three junior deck officers, plus Irv, plus a junior engineer officer, plus a man named Robertshaw, from Edinburgh, plus a man named Max Clyde, from Aurora, Illinois. She ate oatmeal, and she ate finnan haddock, and she ate muffins and croissants and toast and jam and great slabs of melon. She sipped bouillon; she nibbled on cold meats. She ate Dover sole; she ate salmon; she ate roast beef; she ate trifle; she ate torte awash in *schlag*; she told Irv she was *shameless*; she told him she *might as well* wear those dresses that exposed a good deal of her bosom— after *this* trip, it was obvious she never again would be able to squeeze herself into them. Irv laughed. He told her he did not mean to be ungal-lant, but she might as well admit the fact that she had the sort of appetite normally found in a drayhorse or perhaps a pack of wolves. And Margaret laughed. And she and Irv even held hands when they sat reading in the sa-loon. He sipped at dark beer, and she sipped at ginger ale, and she even now and then carefully chewed on some peanuts. The great ship was everywhere polished, everywhere fragrant with waxes and soaps, and the room steward (a tall man whose name was Forster) assured Miss Ridpath that there was not a lovelier woman aboard this ship. He had curly red-dish hair, this Forster, and his voice was tenorish, and he said: "I do not mean to be what you would call fresh, mum, but you are a *smasher,* you are. Go ahead and report me to the chief steward if you like, but I am quite *smitten* with you, and I very much envy the gentleman who appears to be your constant companion. He must be quite a gentleman. Quite a gentleman indeed." And Margaret said: "He *is* quite a gentleman, and I love him very much." And she was astonished by the quickness of her words, a quickness that meant lack of fear. She smiled at Forster and said: "You don't care all that much about iron, do you?" And Forster said: *"Iron?"* And Margaret said: "Never mind that. Sometimes I talk aloud to myself, and it sounds as though I am talking to someone else."

And Forster smiled and said: "Mum, we are all of us entitled to our own peculiarities. Myself, I never have learned how to keep my *place,* as it is called. I have what some consider to be a deplorable habit of speaking up . . . and sometimes it has earned me quite a severe scolding from my superiors . . . but, well, at least I know I'm alive, wouldn't you say so?" And Margaret said: "I would." And Forster made a little bow and said: "Thank you very much indeed." And he moved off down the corridor. And Margaret smiled after him. And he received a generous gratuity the morning the ship docked at Southampton.

The itinerary did not immediately include London. Something special would come first.

Irv had told his travel agent of Margaret's wish for a few days in a village on the English Channel, and so the agent had arranged for Irv and Margaret to stay at a place called The Midshipman, in Cornwall, the village of Mousehole—a little west of Penzance and only a few miles from Land's End. (*Mousehole,* the man warned Irv, was pronounced *Mouzel,* and God help the unwary tourist who tried to say something witty about rodents or proctology.) The train connections from Southampton to the end of the rail line at Penzance were wretched, and it was not until nearly nine o'clock in the evening that Irv and Margaret arrived in Penzance. Then they rode by taxi to The Midshipman, which was operated by a couple named Buttermore. Mousehole was on hills overlooking a small curved harbor, and The Midshipman was a low white stone building only a few yards from the water. A pub was in the cellar, and Mr Buttermore also was the barman. He and his wife were in their late fifties, and they were small and silent, and they had identical pink spots on their cheeks. It was almost as though the spots had been applied with rouge and a brush. Irv and Margaret had an enormous room, and the bed sagged with quilts and comforters. The room was chilly, though, and Mrs Buttermore brought them tea and biscuits. Her vocabulary seemed to have four words—"yes" and "no" and "sir" and "mum." Downstairs, the sounds of the pub were a steady roar, but Irv and Margaret were too tired to investigate the place that night, *and* they were too cold to take baths, so they simply removed their clothes, slid under the blankets and comforters, sipped tea, ate biscuits, chatted awhile and went to sleep. They slept all night with the ceiling light burning, since the room was so cold neither of them wanted to hop out of bed, skitter across the floor and flick the wall switch. The next morning, though, was an enormous improvement. There was an excellent little dining room, and Margaret ate kippers and her beloved oatmeal, and then she and Irv went for a walk. They walked slowly, and Irv gasped a little. They saw hillsides covered with what Margaret believed was called gorse. They listened to gulls, and they were amused by those gulls that walked the streets like pedestrians. They sat for a time on a bench at the edge of the small curved harbor. They watched the tide go out, and they watched children scamper in the mud. It was a Saturday, and the enormous Channel sky was high and cloudless, and Irv pointed in the direction of the Scilly Isles. "The English call this part of their country the Cornish Riviera," he said, "and they insist there is no warmer location in the British Isles. So never mind how cold we were last night. It was an illusion, a jest of nature." He drew his coat collar around his neck. "Thank God for the Cornish Riviera," he said. "I certainly would hate to be someplace where it's *cold.*" He grinned, and so did Margaret, and after a time they got up and went browsing in the little shops lining the narrow streets that snaked away from the harbor. Margaret's sister Sarah was fond of cats, and so Margaret bought her a small brass doorknocker in the shape of a cat's face. Then Margaret and Irv climbed a long steep hill to the west of the village, and Irv began to make trapped noises in his throat. "Are you all right?" said Margaret. "No—I'm *old,*" said Irv. But he managed to smile at Margaret. Then, at the top of the hill, he and Margaret stood at the edge of the road and looked out over the Channel, and he said: "You know, this is something like the coast of Maine. I've been told that the people of Cornwall are to the people of England what the people of *New* England are to the rest of *us,* and I think I can understand why. I mean, thank God for fishing . . . otherwise, what the hell would these people *do?*" He shook his head. "Listen to me," he said. "We didn't come all this distance so I could deliver a lecture on economics." He looked around. "Ah," he said, pointing to a hillside, "consider gorse . . . consider the rocks and the earth and this blasted martyred landscape . . . oh Jesus, I think I feel an attack of poetry coming on . . . but the thing is, Margaret my love . . . the, ah, *whoo,* a little *winded* there is the kid . . . the thing *is* . . . many of the people who live here have owned this blasted martyred landscape—or, rather, *their families* have owned it—since the time of William the Conqueror or maybe before. So they hang on, and they apparently don't give a damn about economics, and you have to give them credit . . . you really do . . ." Irv turned back in the direction of the Channel. "Godalmighty," he said, "those gulls. I'm sorry, my love, but I am a *city boy,* and all this *moves* me . . ." He went to Margaret and embraced her. She lifted his hand and kissed it, and his pulse was galloping, and she said: "Would you like to sit down for a little while?" And Irv said: "No thank you. When I told you I was old, I *was* old. But now I've rested a little. I have flung out whatever it is that passes for my barbaric yawp, and I have refreshed myself. Which means I am no longer old, okay?'' And Margaret, nodding dubiously, said: "Okay." And they moved back down the hill, and she steered him a little, and he said: "Well, here we are, headed downhill . . ." And Margaret said: "Thanks a lot for reminding me." And they laughed. And she looked around. And the wind pushed against her chest. And it was not all that warm a wind. But she was not afraid. Children screamed, and the gulls screamed, but she was not afraid.

That night, after a good dinner of steak and kidney pie, she and Irv went downstairs to the pub. She drank lemonade, and Irv became a little tiddly on three pints of Guinness. The place was crowded, and it was more than an hour before anyone besides Mr Buttermore spoke to them. The ceiling was low, and a pinball machine was in a corner, and everyone was dressed in wool, and the wool had a rank odor, and finally a little whitehaired man—spectacles, wens, knobbed hands—came to Margaret and said to her: "You and the gentleman here must think we are stand-offish." Margaret and Irv were sitting at a corner table, and they were sharing it with two girls in their early twenties (both of them stocky and pink, they had chatted and giggled for more than hour without once glancing in the direction of Margaret and Irv), and Irv said: "Well, perhaps we make a strange appearance. Myself, I don't mind all that much. We're sort of *soaking up* the *atmosphere,* so to . . . well, so to speak." He held up his pint of Guinness. "Yes," he said, "so to *speak*." And the little whitehaired man nodded and said: "Myself, sir, in my day, I have soaked up atmosphere as though it were water." He seated himself and continued, and the two pink girls paid him no mind. He said: "You should consider yourselves fortunate." Frowning, Irv said: "How so?" And the little whitehaired man said: "There've been those who have come here and *lived* here *twenty years* and never had a soul speak to them- . . . beyond the civilities." And Irv said: "But you have marched up to us after only an hour." And the little whitehaired man said: "Ah, sir, I am considered peculiar, and there are those who would have me put in a room with soft walls. In Cornwall, the *rocks* are often more talkative than those who are called *persons* and stand around and draw breath. But Tom Stevens is your round peg in your square aperture, myself being Tom Stevens, and my, isn't the Guinness splendid this evening?" Laughing, Irv summoned Mr Buttermore and ordered a pint for Tom Stevens and a pint for himself. Tom Stevens then nudged the pink girls and said to Irv: "Would you be believing these are my *granddaughters?* Well, they *are*. The one on the left is Brenda Esterbrook, and the one on the right is Berenice Esterbrook, or perhaps it is the other way around, and my daughter

Frances has *five* girls all told, and all their names begin with B—first Barbara, then Beryl, then Brenda and Berenice here, and finally little Belinda. And I defy anyone to say those names at any considerable rate of speed . . . Barbaraberylbrendaberenicebelinda . . . a dextrous tongue is required, and in Cornwall such a thing as a dextrous tongue is considered useless and probably dangerous . . . Barbaraberylbrenda-berenicebelinda . . . or perhaps backwards: Belindaberenice-brendaberylbarbara . . . ah, *relief* is approaching . . . relief from this fruitless blather . . ." And Mr Buttermore arrived with the pints of stout. And now the two girls were smiling at Margaret and Irv as though they all had been friends forever, and later, over his fourth pint, the little whitehaired Tom Stevens had gathered most of the pub's patrons around him, and Irv had bought a round for everyone, and the press of bodies had produced an enormous woolly gag of an odor that made Margaret turn her face away from time to time. And yet she was not annoyed. In fact, she was smiling. And Tom Stevens was speaking thickly now, but he still was speaking, and he said: "Aye, there is more to Cornwall than gulls and gorse and Druids and clotted cream . . . there is a *feeling* here, you see, my dear Yank mister and missus, a feeling that the Lord has created a special cut of dauntless fellow . . . the Cornishman . . . up the Cornishman . . . who is no Englishman . . . no Irishman . . . no Scot . . . but only, you see, a *Cornishman* . . . who faces into the winds, who pushes aside boulders . . . who . . . ah, you see, with all we have to do simply to survive, simply to pass with reasonable safety through our days . . . ah yes, the days the Lord has granted us, thank You very much indeed, Lord . . . so that then . . . *then* . . . we cannot but wonder who on this earth would come here of his own *violation* . . . no, that is to say, vo . . . vo . . . *volition*. The pamphlets say Cornish Riviera, and the pamphlets make this place out to be as though . . . as though . . . one comes here to be a *lizard* and . . . *laze* . . . in the *sun* . . . but none of that is true. We are *honest* here. We do not *laze*. We drink stout and lager and bitter and whisky, yes. We *soak up atmosphere*, yes. But we do not *laze*. If you expect *lizards*, my very mister and missus, you have come to the wrong place, eh?" And Tom Stevens looked around. And everyone laughed. And everyone nodded. And hands clapped his back. And Brenda squealed. And Berenice squealed. And now Margaret, having consumed her fourth lemonade, having earlier even been persuaded to participate in a game of darts with two thin and silent fellows who wore caps, heavy sweaters and old suit trousers, lifted her fifth lemonade and said: "To Cornwall. To Mousehole. To survival." And everyone nodded. And even Mr Buttermore smiled a little. And all drank. And Irv bought a final round for the house. And he said to Margaret: "I don't know if this is what you mean, but perhaps it is a start." And Margaret said: "Yes . . . it is a start . . . and I love you . . ." And she kissed him. And Brenda squealed. And Berenice squealed. And just about everyone else whooped and applauded. Tom Stevens, though, was sinking fast, and he was unable to finish his valedictory pint. Giggling, Brenda and Berenice helped him to his feet, and they told Irv and Margaret it had been a super evening, thank you very much indeed. They needed no help with the old man. A path was cleared for them, and they escorted him out of the pub and up the stairs to the street. A young man sat down with Irv and Margaret. He wore dungarees and a sweatshirt, and on the sweatshirt were written the words ELVIS FOREVER. His eyes were small and reddish, and his hair was cut short, and his hands were hairy. He was holding a pint in both his hands, and he banged it on the table. He said: "Everything . . . ah, everything old Tom said was true . . . and I wouldn't want you to be believing otherwise . . . but there was a hint . . . there was, ah, a *hint,* you see . . . that perhaps we believe our land and our life to be *ugly* . . . and *that* would be an *untruth* . . ." The young man lifted his pint, drank from it with a sort of sloshing belligerence. Then he again banged it on the table. "I . . . I mean no disrespect," he said, "but it would not do for you to look down on us. Many tourists do—English as well as American (and we're even getting some of those bloody damned Germans here now). So if you look down on us, do so at your own hazard. We are the descendants of *smugglers,* my friends. We are the descendants of *those who flashed false lights so ships would founder and be plundered.* We are not to be taken lightly. If you seek to share our life for a few days, fine, and be welcome to you, but understand it for what it *is* . . . and do not employ such adjectives as *quaint* or *charming.* I have been to university. I can spell words that have five letters. I can spell words that have ten letters. I can read without moving my lips, and I can add two plus two, and I have seen perhaps more of Shaw's plays than you have. If I am indeed a savage, I am a savage with *definition,* with a *home,* with a *tradition.* Do you have some idea of what I am saying?" Another series of sloshing gulps, and again down came the pint, and it was then that *Margaret*—not Irv—spoke to the young man, telling him: "*One,* we mean you no harm. *Two,* we respect you. *Three,* we envy what you call your definition. You see, in our country definition hardly exists. It has given way to what we call progress, and its absence means that most of us are forever governed by fear." She smiled at Irv. "This gentleman is not governed by fear . . . or at least he carries nothing hurtful or hurting within him that affects me. Myself, though, I fear just about everything. Which is why I am here. Which is why *we* are here. It has been my desire to find a place where perhaps I am not afraid, where perhaps I can permit whatever it is I *am* to be exposed. Does any of this make sense?'' And the young man said: "Of course." He smiled. He finished off his pint. He set it down gently. He said: "If I appeared to be a brute, forgive me. I did not mean to frighten you." And quickly Margaret spoke up. "*No,*" she said, "you did *not* frighten me. You did just the opposite. In America, I come from a place . . . the state of Ohio . . . that once had the beginnings of what you call tradition . . . but those beginnings have been torn down . . . and I am frightened when I am *there.* I sense no order. *Here,* though, I *do* sense order, and I am not intimidated by your talk of smugglers and false lights.'' Again she smiled at Irv. "These are strange words to be coming from *me,* aren't they?" she said to him. And Irv nodded. He squeezed one of her hands. His breath was warm from the Guinness. "You have our respect," he said to the young man. "You truly do. May God strike me dead." And the young man laughed. "No such tempting of the Almighty is necessary," he said. "I do indeed believe you." He frowned into his empty pint. "We are ever aware of the Almighty," he said. "We have to be, seeing as how He every day lays His hand on us with His wind or His rain or His blessed sunshine." He smiled at Margaret. He raised a hand. "I bestow on you a bit of a benediction," he said. He smiled at Irv. "And you, too, sir," he said. "A bit of love. A bit of respect." He wiped his hands across the front of his ELVIS FOREVER sweatshirt. Grunting, he pushed himself to his feet and staggered away. Irv leaned to Margaret and kissed her ear. The pinball machine clicked, and Mr Buttermore said: "Time, please."

Margaret took Irv upstairs to their room. Perhaps it was just as cold, but it did not feel just as cold. She undressed Irv and helped him into bed. Then she hurriedly undressed herself and slid in beside him. She embraced him, and they listened to the muffled hushing sound of the Channel. Irv kissed Margaret's throat and nuzzled her breasts. She felt him, and he was soft and warm, and he told her he loved her, and he fell asleep. And she smiled. Margaret smiled. She was not afraid. She fell asleep with her hand curled around the softness and the warmth of him. The sound of the Channel was like a hand on her forehead. She and Irv spent two more days and nights in Mousehole, and evenings she sat with him in the pub while he drank stout and talked with the regulars of fishing and pirates and wars and politics and film stars, and they were joined by old Tom Stevens, and they were joined by the young man in the ELVIS FOREVER sweatshirt, and they were joined by a young fellow who said his crowning ambition was to race a motorcar at Le Mans, and even the silent Mrs Buttermore sat and drank with them, and Irv bought many rounds, and at the end of the final evening, just as Mr Buttermore was preparing to close the place, Irv lifted his pint and spoke quietly to those assembled, and he said: "I drink to life. I drink to death. I drink to mysteries and drunkenness. I drink to courage and tradition. I drink to the . . . to the *spectrum* . . . to the glorious *variety* . . . to *respect* and *sentiment* and *moments* . . ." And pints were lifted. And all drank. And hands were clasped. And Margaret even embraced old Tom Stevens, and everyone whooped. And then she took Irv upstairs to bed, but he did not fall asleep right away. Instead he hugged her and said: "This is only a start. There is more. There is London yet. And London will be different. Less chipped at the edges perhaps. Oh, you'll *see*. There is still so much *in store* for you." And Margaret said: "I believe I could live in this country." And Irv said: "I think you have a point." And Margaret said: "I wonder how they are fixed for dentists?" And Irv said: "They have socialized their dentists . . . or whatever it's called. But who cares? I could . . . well, even though I'm only fiftyeight, I could retire tomorrow if I wanted to . . . retire and live in a thatched cottage somewhere near Oxford perhaps . . ." And Margaret said: "Are you serious?" And Irv said: "A little." And Margaret said: "But what about your wife?" And Irv said: "You would be my wife." And Margaret said: "Now, you're just—" And Irv broke in, saying: "Something here has changed you, and it's only a beginning. I haven't heard a peep out of you about iron. And you're even *volunteering* things—like these evenings in the pub. Margaret, my God, don't you know by now how much I love you? If you're happy here, then the hell with Harriet; the hell with my inertia and her inertia. I'll get rid of her. I'll throw her over the damned side. I'll sell her to the Arabs. I'll do *some* goddamned thing." And Margaret said: "Hush." And Irv said: "Don't hush *me* . . . you, you . . . you *husher* you . . ." And then he did fall asleep, but Margaret lay awake half the night, and she said to herself: Would Wanda be able to take care of Mother all alone? What would Ruth and Sarah say? What would Mr Wolf say? Would I be involved in some sort of divorce action? Would my name be in the newspapers? SCANDAL ROCKS TOURNAMENT BRIDGE WORLD! SEX! ADULTERY! BALD DENTIST AND SILENT SPINSTER ADMIT LOVE! Finally, smiling a little, Margaret plumped her pillow, resolutely closed her eyes and forced herself to fall asleep. It all was stupid. It never would happen. It all was a lot of menopausal pipedreaming, and it had nothing to do with truth, and so Margaret shoved it all into a corner of her mind and slammed a lid over it. But the next afternoon, on the train from Penzance to London, while she was sitting alone with Irv in a firstclass compartment and they were watching the soft Devon countryside roll past, the rounded and trimmed hills speckled with cattle and sheep, divided by coarse knotted hedges and narrow roads, with now and then a stone cottage and everywhere a feeling of brilliant English springtime green, Irv said to her: "I meant what I said to you last night—but we'll both have to think about it very carefully. We'll be in London tonight, and we'll have ten days there, and let's really *consider* it, all right? You are receptive, aren't you, my fair maiden? Fine. Good." He made a twirling movement with his moustache. "Methinks I have you in my power. Dot is goot. Dot is *much* goot. I think that if we do not do what we want to do *now,* we'll never do it. But we do have to be sure. I have to be sure about the inertia, and you have to be sure that you can exist away from your iron world." And Margaret quickly said: "Oh, don't worry about *that.*" And Irv said: "But I want you to be *sure.* I'd hate to think of you living in a thatched cottage and pining away for your lost devils." And Margaret smiled. Or tried to smile. She looked out the window. She saw a man in a gray cap, and the man was leading two cows along a road. She concentrated on the countryside. Irv was silent.

The train arrived in Paddington just at nightfall, and Irv and Margaret rode in a taxi to their hotel, which was quite small. It was on Half Moon Street just off Piccadilly. The taxi was immaculate, and the driver had helped them with their luggage, and Margaret said to Irv: "Maybe I'm being silly, but already I know it's what you promised me it would be." And Irv said: "What? The *taxi*?" And Margaret nudged Irv in the ribs, and he laughed, and the driver stared directly forward. The traffic was heavy, but Margaret did not hear a single horn. The street signs were on buildings, and she recognized MARYLEBONE, and she recognized BAKER (Sherlock Holmes, correct?), and of course she recognized PICCADILLY, and she squeezed Irv's hand, and he said to her: "You're like a kid at Coney Island." And Margaret said: "I should *hope* so." And Irv laughed, and Margaret told him he could have picked a more original figure of speech. And he told her he was a *dentist*; he was not *Thomas Wolfe.* And she told him he ought to hear himself when he was full of Guinness. And he said thank you, but no thanks. So then they began the ten days. But they turned out to be only eight. And Margaret returned to Paradise Falls, and from then until her death the iron forever rubbed her flesh, scraping it, causing her to give way to the likes of a George Prout, causing her finally, on the ninth day of August in the year 1974, to proclaim her insistence on the order she never achieved, on the truth she never had the strength to confront, and on her resistance to those who would dismantle the uni-

verse. But in London in the late spring of 1959 she saw no one who sought
to dismantle the universe. To her, London was the ultimate *proclamation*
of the universe. She and Irv walked just about everywhere. They shopped
in the Shepherds Market, and he pointed out a number of elegant prostitutes to her, and he said: "Don't ask me how I know they are hookers.
The answer might, ah, embarrass me, kid—but take my word for it, they
are hookers. See the way they look at me. The old up and down, you
know? But nothing is flagrant, my love. They do not *make* propositions;
they *murmur* propositions. It is almost as though they are asking me to
take them to the junior prom." And Irv smiled at the prostitutes. They
were dressed well, and they also smiled, and occasionally Margaret heard
a whispered "love" or "dear," but Irv never was actually accosted. The
girls and women were pretty; the youngest was perhaps seventeen, and
the oldest was probably into her fifties, and they moved in silent coveys,
and now and then a policeman would pass them but pay them no mind,
and Irv said to Margaret: "It isn't graft. It's just that there have been
prosties in the Shepherds Market since probably the eighteenth century,
and the English have great respect for tradition. One does not incarcerate
tradition." And Irv grinned. And he and Margaret wandered in and out of
the little sweet shops, antique shops, pubs and galleries. He walked
slowly, and he said to Margaret: "Enjoy. Savor." And Margaret said yes.
And the shoppers jostled one another. And the prostitutes moved with
their solemn murmuring dignity. And the narrow alleys and arched en-
tranceways gave Margaret more of her feeling that the iron was absent.
Back home, even *the thought* of prostitutes had frightened her (Paradise
Falls had not been without them), but here not even *the presence* of prostitutes frightened her. She supposed this was because they were traditional. After all, she was in *Mayfair,* and *Mayfair* was *posh,* and it was part of
London, and *London* was *different.* But this did not mean she was blind.
It did not mean she was some gasping schoolgirl who didn't have the
sense God gave a sack of powdered sugar. Each day, as she and Irv
prowled the city, as they walked along Piccadilly past the Ritz and Fortnum & Mason's, as they strolled past the enormous curved buildings of
Regent Street, as they inspected the Burlington Arcade, as they climbed
the sagging and precariously wornout wooden steps and ate roast beef in
the Cheshire Cheese (where Samuel Johnson was said to have eaten), as
they walked along Fleet Street and the Strand, as they crossed Trafalgar
Square and visited the National Gallery, as they browsed through the
bookshops on Charing Cross Road and St Martin's Lane, as they thrust
through the theater crowds on Shaftesbury Avenue, as they dined at the
Ritz and the Café Royal and a place called the Stableman (it was in an al-

ley off the Brompton Road, and they were waited on by an immense florid
man who looked as if he were about to burst from high blood pressure), as
they saw shopgirls and elegant caned and bowlered gentlemen, as they
ducked into Hamley's and watched the toy trains circle around and
around the balcony, as they poked in shops that had fine woolens and lin-
ens, as they crossed the great parks and walked along Rotten Row and
Constitution Hill and watched the changing of the guard at Buckingham
Palace, as they stared in stupefied astonishment at the Victoria & Albert
monument and the throwntogether artifacts that had been gathered in the
Victoria & Albert Museum (dresses, Indian boxes, sedan chairs, restored
pubs, gentlemen's costumes), as they worked their way around and
through the Georgian and Victorian mixture of architectural styles that
made the turn of each corner an occasion for surprise and sometimes bewilderment, as they mingled with the afternoon crowds in the pubs and
ate Scotch eggs and sausage and cheese rolls, while Irv drank stout or bitter and Margaret drank lemonade or plain tonic, as they watched the great
red doubledecked buses push and nudge along the narrow streets, as they
paused one day at St Martin's-in-the-Fields and listened to an a capella
choral concert, as they wandered into Fortnum & Mason's and smelled
the odors of tea and coffee (Margaret bought a teapot there for her sister
Ruth), as they saw and poked and sniffed and walked through that endless
city, Margaret was aware that yes, this place no doubt had its faults—the
crowding, the expensiveness, the fact that no one seemed to be in any
particular hurry. But were those things really all that terrible, especially
the fact that no one seemed to be in any particular hurry? Oh, Irv would
no doubt be able to make good arguments against their living in this country until squirrels flew over the moon, and perhaps Margaret even would
agree with some of them, but she did not believe they mattered all that
much. What did matter was the *order* and *dignity,* the insistence that
amenities be observed, that iron persons not be tolerated, let alone recognized. And that bluster and noise be defined as contemptible and stupid.
And that the shortest distance between two points was not necessarily a
straight line, if that straight line meant destroying a historic church or
knocking down a stand of treasured trees. And she insisted on this belief
even after Irv told her: "Margaret my darling innocent babe, the British
are changing. Remember our friend in the pub back in Mousehole, the intellectual young man who claimed to have seen so many plays by George
Bernard Shaw? Well, do you remember that sweatshirt he was wearing?
It said ELVIS FOREVER, right? There he was, an ardent and belligerent defender of his native culture, and he was wearing a sweatshirt that said
ELVIS FOREVER. Myself, I liked him a great deal, but I did think there was

something . . . ah, *paradoxical* . . . about his appearance. The war has been over about fifteen years now, and changes are taking place. And they're not all that good. There's something about a hamburger joint in a Georgian building that depresses me, you know? Like a barnacle taking up residence in the hulk of a great ship. Ah, here we go again—Algernon Greenleaf Berkowitz has reared his ugly head, which is almost as ugly as his rear." And Margaret said: "All right, Irv. All *right*. But at least, when I'm out with you and we're walking along, there always is *the possibility* that we'll encounter something beautiful, or people who have manners, or men in white gloves." And Irv said: "True. The decadence that follows civilization is not unpleasant." And Margaret: "Are you saying I'm looking for *decadence*?" And Irv said: "That is not beyond the realm of possibility." And, shrugging, Margaret said: "I suppose you're right." And then Irv said something to the effect that the English writer, Oscar Wilde, had accused the United States of passing from savagery to decadence without going through the middle stage of civilization. And Margaret said: "Exactly!" And Irv said: "Good . . . only I wouldn't want you to mistake this decadence for the civilization old Oscar meant." And Margaret said: "Do we have to talk in *terms*? Can't we just *enjoy* all this?" And Irv said: "Of course we can. I am the prince of wet blankets. Please forgive me."

And that evening he took her to Cunningham's of London, on Curzon Street not far from their hotel. It was small and mirrored, and Irv said it was one of the world's best seafood houses. Margaret wore the black dress that exposed a good deal of her bosom. She and Irv were waited on by four waiters, and at one point she frowned at Irv after he had laughed too loudly over something one of the waiters had said about . . . of all the silly things . . . *asparagus*. In England, asparagus actually was served as a main course, or as an appetizer, or even as a dessert, and this apparently amused Irv no end. He insisted Margaret try some. She finally agreed, and the waiter brought her a huge platter of great fat stalks. But then, when Margaret tried to ask the waiter for a fork, Irv told her: "No, no, a fork would be an insult." He reached across the table, took one of her stalks, dipped it in a small bowl of drawn butter, than proceeded to eat it as though it were something on the order of ice cream on a stick. Margaret stared at him. She told him he was insane. But the waiter smiled and told Margaret no, the gentleman was not insane; asparagus was something of a rare delicacy in the British Isles—and certainly far more than a common *vegetable*. "Therefore," said the man, "a special way of eating it is called for." He nodded at Irv, who was chewing away and smiling. "The gentleman is doing excellently," said the waiter. "Ah, I thank you very much," said Irv. The waiter bowed. He went away, and Margaret then got up the nerve to take one of the stalks, dip it and eat it. Another waiter came with a fingerbowl and placed it before Irv. Three rose petals and a sliver of lemon were floating on the water. Irv dipped his fingers and winked. Margaret chewed on her asparagus. Irv wiped his fingers with his napkin and leaned back. "This is very exciting," he said. And then Margaret giggled a little. Later, after she had finished with the precious asparagus, she dipped her fingers, and the water was warm and fragrant. All the waiters came to the table and offered their congratulations. Margaret laughed, and she noticed that at least two of the waiters were trying to stare down the front of her dress. Then she and Irv had Dover sole, and it was beyond belief, and for a change Irv ate slowly, and she said to him: "I don't really care how silly you think I am, but I believe all my life I've been waiting for tonight, here, this dinner. Does that sound like a line out of a movie? I suppose it does. Well, I'm sorry, but I can't help what I feel. The elegance . . . I've always thought elegance was as extinct as the passenger pigeon, or maybe it hadn't ever existed at all. And all right, maybe it *is* all a movie or a TV show or some sort of foolish oldmaid *dream,* but can't you understand what I mean?" And Irv nodded. He patted one of her hands. "Of course I understand," he said. The sole was *meunière,* and it was accompanied by new potatoes, and Irv drank a white wine, and he said: "If it's a movie, the possibility always exists that it's a *good* movie." He glanced around. "I mean," he said, "just *look* at this place." And he indicated the room's great highbacked chairs, the crystal, heavy paneling that was polished to such a degree it almost seemed syrupy to the touch. There was an immense pastry trolley, and fresh fruits and vegetables were piled with fastidious care in heavy bowls on a large linened sideboard, and Irv said: "I wouldn't be surprised if the Lord reserved a table here once a week so He and his principal Doers and Shakers could get together and relax a little." Now Irv's Dover sole was gone. He fished for a cigar, snipped off its end with a pair of clippers Margaret had given him a few years earlier. He rolled the end of the cigar on his tongue, then carefully lit the cigar. Margaret smiled at him, and she breathed the odor of the cigar, and it did not bother her, and so she smiled and ate and smiled, and after a time Irv said to her: "It really gets me in the old belly when I'm in the presence of a person who has found such heaven on earth. It just doesn't happen all that much." He sipped at his wine, which was a liebfraumilch and had been recommended by one of the waiters. Margaret continued to smile. She said: "I've been waiting for this all my life." And Irv said: "You're not pumping it all out of proportion?" And Margaret said: "Maybe I am—but as long as I don't *know* I am, what difference does it make?'' And Irv said: "I do believe you have a point." Later one of the waiters came with the pastry trolley, and both Margaret and Irv had chocolate mousse, and Irv ordered coffee for Margaret and coffee and Cointreau for himself. The mousse lay sweetly against Margaret's palate. She ate it slowly, sucking it, and it was thick and unutterably delicious, and now her eyes were warm, and she leaned forward and touched one of Irv's hands and said: "You have brought me to *Cunningham's of London,* and I shall adore you forever." And, grinning, Irv said: "Adoration is not necessary. A little groveling might be in order, though." And Margaret made a face at him. And she said: "I am trying to be *serious.* I am trying to tell you that whatever *you* want *I* want." And Irv said: "Which means you really want to come to this country to live, correct?" And Margaret said: "Correct." And Irv said: "And your mother and your sisters can pack it in?" And Margaret said: "Yes. And the store. Everything. The town. Memories. Fears. All of it." And Irv said: "And myself, I'd retire and get rid of Harriet." And, clearing her throat, Margaret hesitated for a moment, rubbed one of her cheeks (it was warm) and finally said: ". . . yes." She sucked the mousse, and she kept her eyes averted from Irv's, and he said: "It sounds attractive." Margaret looked at him. "Really?" she said. "Yes," said Irv. "At our age?" said Margaret. "*Especially* at our age," said Irv. He carefully tapped the end of his cigar into an ashtray. He said: "If *you* can overcome fear, *I* can overcome inertia. I was drunk back there that night in Mousehole, but I wasn't drunk in the train, and I'm not drunk now, and if this country is what you want, if you want to help me look for a thatched cottage near Oxford or wherever the hell, or if you want to help me look for a flat here in this city, *it can be arranged.* Oh yes, my love, *we can work it out.* There have been a lot of mouths, my darling. There has been a lot of labor. In other words, I am game if you are . . ." And Margaret leaned back in her chair. She swallowed the last of the superb mousse, and it could have been concrete. And later, in the room in the little hotel on Half Moon Street, she was unspeakably wet, and Irv was splendid and strong, and he said: "Not bad for an old Hebrew on the brink of retirement." And Margaret said: "In me. Please." And Irv said: "I thought you'd never ask." And a few minutes later Margaret said: "Oh, *dear.*" And Irv said: "I do believe I can take that as a compliment." And Margaret said: "How did you guess?"

The next day they went for a long walk, and they agreed that it probably wouldn't be much before the end of the year that they would be able to get married. "I don't think Harriet will be too bitchy about it," said Irv, "but there will be money involved, and lawyers, and the New York

State divorce laws, which aren't exactly liberal." And Margaret said: "The only problem I have is Mother, and Wanda is very good at taking care of her—even though they hate one another." And Irv said: "After we get settled here, will we have to play bridge?" And Margaret said: "I don't care." And Irv said: "Are you serious?" And Margaret said: "Absolutely. The fascination is still there, and I know it always will be, but I think I'm at a point now where it no longer has to be an *obsession.*" And Irv said: "My God, tomorrow morning, when the sun rises, it will be wearing green striped pajamas." And he took Margaret by a hand. And they strolled up Piccadilly, and they agreed that they probably were doing so with what came deliciously close to being the legendary independent air. And they walked north. And they talked. They discussed country life as opposed to city life, and they tentatively concluded that a flat in London probably would meet their needs more fully. They walked along Park Lane, and the enormous city was quieter here, and they wandered through sidestreets, past rows of crisp white houses, all very neat, all very Mayfair and no doubt immensely expensive, and Irv breathed with his mouth open, but he smiled at Margaret, and she squeezed his arm. They found a small pub and they had an early lunch of shepherd's pie. Margaret had an Orange Crush and Irv had two pints of Guinness, and he was perspiring a little. They sat at a corner table, and she asked him was he feeling all right, and he told her not to be ridiculous. He said: "I'm a little winded, that's all—but the exercise is doing me good . . ." He nodded in the direction of his pint. "And not to mention my medicine here . . ." A little later he helped Margaret to her feet, and they went outside into the sunshine. They crossed a park, and they really didn't know where they were going, and now they said little. Margaret clung to Irv's arm, and he kept looking around. And then he said: ' 'My God." And he pointed across a wide street, and there was Madame Tussaud's Wax Museum. "Hey," he said, "hot damn. I love this place." He shepherded Margaret across the street, and they entered the museum, and she scrutinized the wax kings and the wax murderers, the wax Nelson and the wax Hitler and the wax Churchill and even the wax Madame Tussaud (a tiny woman who reminded Margaret a little of Mme Bird, whose singing had intimidated her so many years before). When they were done with the tour, Irv excused himself and went into the Gentlemen's, and he remained there the better part of ten minutes. Finally, when he emerged, he was pale, but he was grinning, and he said to Margaret: "The Guinness must have had some sort of effect on my lower GI tract. I've been feeling a little stuffed all day, but now *that* problem should be over. A load off my whatchamacallit, you might say." And Margaret said: "Why don't we just get a taxi and go back to the hotel?'' But Irv said: ''Don't be ridiculous. This is the shank of the day. And anyway, as I just finished telling you, my indigestion or whatever is gone. I feel like a new man, and if you give me ten minutes I probably will be able to leap a tall building in a single bound.'' He took Margaret by an elbow and they went back outside. And they walked. And they walked. South again, slowly, slowly, to the majestic eastward sweep of Piccadilly. They strolled in Hyde Park, and they sat on a bench and rested, and Irv said: ''We are like children acting out a game, but it's *all right. We're entitled.*'' He rubbed a corner of his moustache. He took off his hat and fanned himself. He said: ''My father died in a shower of hats. Do I want to die in a shower of *teeth?* My God, what a prospect . . .'' He smiled at Margaret. He said: ''We are not logical, you and I. You will be the first Mrs Berkowitz in the history of Paradise Falls, and—'' Margaret interrupted. ''But I won't be *in* Paradise Falls,'' she said. ''I'll be with you.'' And Irv said: ''Whither I goest, goest thou?'' And Margaret said: ''Yes . . . I think . . .'' And Irv nodded. ''*I* think the old man has had it for today,'' he said. He still was fanning himself with his hat, and his face ran with sweat. ''The indigestion . . .'' he said. He looked around. He blinked. He pointed east. ''The Ritz,'' he said. ''We took tea there, remember?'' And Margaret said: ''*Remember? Of course* I remember. And I poured. And the little sandwiches had watercress, and the waiter wore white gloves, and I poured the tea through a strainer apparatus of some sort, and you said to me : 'Margaret, do you feel in the presence of a priceless moment?' And I said to you: 'Yes, dear Irv, that I do.' And I tried very hard to be elegant, and I even extended a pinky.'' Now Margaret was patting Irv's knee, but he did not appear to be listening. ''My feet are cold,'' he said. He dropped his hat, and the wind caught at it. It skipped toward a large black man, who scooped it up. The large black man had plump pink palms. He brought the hat to Irv, and he was smiling, but Irv did not appear to notice him. The large black man frowned. ''Thank you very much,'' said Margaret to the large black man, and she took Irv's hat from him. ''Is anything the matter?'' said the large black man. ''Copacetic,'' said Irv. ''I beg your pardon?'' said the large black man. He was wearing a blue suit, neatly tailored; he wore a bowler and carried a cane. He said: ''Are you ill, sir?'' Irv's head moved from side to side. ''It's all . . . everything is . . . copacetic,'' said Irv. He reached for Margaret, knocking his hat from her grasp. He pressed against her, and he was having trouble with his breath. She looked up helplessly at the large black man. ''I shall fetch a policeman,'' said the large black man. He hurried off. Irv wheezed. He pressed his hands against Margaret's cheeks, and they were freezing. He said:

"I . . . don't think . . . I *really* don't think it's all that bad . . ." He
gagged. He said: "My chest . . . like a balloon . . . too much air for
the space inside . . . oh, this surely is a classic . . . myofarc myomy
shun shun myofarction . . . bands . . . not the kind that march across
a football field . . . but the kind . . . the kind that squeeze . . . myofarc o that is the truth . . . cold . . . hot . . . you got no idea
. . . what a place to leave from . . ." And Irv said: "Tell . . . o tell
the world I'm sorry if maybe I didn't do all I . . ." And Margaret, who
hardly ever wept, was weeping. And two teenaged boys stood in front of
her and Irv. One of them picked up Irv's hat. He placed it on the bench
next to Margaret. An elderly woman came along, and she was carrying a
white kitten in a basket. She was stout and tweedy, and she had tight
frosty hair. She stood with the teenaged boys and she said: "Oh, *dear*."
And one of the teenaged boys told her a black gentleman had gone off to
fetch a policeman. And Irv said: "Help . . . o help me . . ." And his
eyes were smeared. And he shivered. "Myocar . . ." he said.
"Clas . . . o classic . . ." He embraced Margaret, and she embraced
him, and then he died, and he slid off the bench, and Margaret went down
with him, and his hat fell off the bench and rolled away, and this time no
one retrieved it. Margaret lay underneath her dead lover, and gravel
scraped her cheek, and after a time the teenaged boys were able to pry
them apart, and a crowd gathered, and somewhere a child was saying
something about wanting a sweet, and then the large black man arrived
with a policeman, and Margaret looked up at the policeman, and he was a
young policeman, and he had blue eyes and purplish cheeks, and now she
lay next to Irv, and she touched Irv's face, and Irv was cold, and so her
legs moved in spasms, and an hour later she was talking on the overseas
telephone to Harriet Berkowitz in New York City.

Harriet Berkowitz's voice was flat and controlled over the tele
phone. She arrived in London by plane the next afternoon. She took
a room at the Savoy, and Margaret met her there shortly after her arrival.
Irv's body was in a hospital morgue, and Harriet Berkowitz had gone to
the morgue straight from the airport. After looking at the body, she tele
phoned Margaret at the little hotel on Half Moon Street. Margaret had
been sedated, and the telephone had awakened her from a deep and wool
ly sleep. Still, she did agree to meet Harriet Berkowitz at the Savoy an
hour later. She took two showers, and some of the effects of the sedative

wore away. But not all. Neat and fragrant, dressed in a simple navy blue suit, with every hair in place and her lipstick subtle and discreet, Margaret nonetheless kept having to fight off an urge to yawn. She went to the Savoy by taxi, and her cheek stung where the gravel had scratched it (she had carefully covered the scratch with makeup), and the city's early evening lights were too strong for her, and she blinked. Piccadilly, St James Street, Trafalgar Square, the Strand . . . all were a sort of muted neon *clamor,* certainly far less garish than, say, Times Square, but far too much for *Margaret,* at least *then,* that night, with Irv dead and his wife (whom Margaret never had met) waiting for her in a hotel room. And with Margaret wanting to yawn. And so she sat bonelessly in a corner of the taxi seat, and finally she had to shield her eyes against the glare that really wasn't a glare, and her eyes were hot, and she supposed she would weep again at any moment.

But Margaret did not weep. That night Harriet Berkowitz preempted the weeping. She opened the door immediately after Margaret's knock. She was a small woman, and her figure was trim, almost knotted. Her face was leathery. It had small features, and it probably once had been pretty, but now the moisture was gone from the flesh, and it was taut, spotted, too brown. It appeared to have been kneaded and stretched. The hair had been dyed blond; it was short, feathery, fashionable, but it was too young for the leathery face. She wore a plain green dress, a single wedding band and what appeared to be a strand of genuine pearls. An opened bottle of Haig & Haig was on the dresser next to a bucket of ice, and Harriet Berkowitz was holding a highball. It appeared to be quite strong. She offered Margaret a drink, but Margaret declined. Nodding, she pointed to a chair and told Margaret to sit down and make herself comfortable. "Thank you," said Margaret, seating herself.

Harriet Berkowitz refreshed her drink, dropped in more ice, then perched on the edge of the bed. She drank. The sound was loud, or at least it was loud in that room. She said: "I was hoping we never would meet. I must say, though, you *are* pretty. Irv was right. Oh, don't look so surprised. Occasionally one or the other of us would crawl under the barricade, and we actually would *talk.*"

"I'm glad to know that," said Margaret.

"You *are*?" said Harriet Berkowitz.

"Yes," said Margaret.

"I find that difficult to believe," said Harriet Berkowitz. She drank. She smiled. Her teeth were not her own. She said: "I have been on sedatives ever since you called me yesterday. I was on sedatives all the way across the Atlantic in the airplane. I looked down, and I saw Greenland,

and the pills were rattling around inside me like beans in a sack. And I received some more pills just a little while ago at the hospital.'' She nodded in the direction of the bottle of Haig & Haig. "And look at that bottle . . . it's closing in on being half empty, and old Harriet here never has been that much of a drinker. But I'll tell you something—the pills and the Scotch might as well be *pumpkinseeds* and *sugarwater* for all the good they've done me. I . . . he . . . Irv, I mean . . . there was a *closeness* in the sort of *separation* we had. Does that make any sense?''

"I believe so,'' said Margaret. Casually she covered her mouth, suppressing a yawn.

Harriet Berkowitz did not appear to notice. Leaning forward, she said: "I used to be amused whenever I saw your name and Irv's in some bridge column. Or at least on one level I was amused. I mean, how innocent it all appeared—*Doctor Berkowitz* and *Miss Ridpath*, bridge stars, celebrities, the toasts of the duplicate boards. But why then did he always come home? Look at me. I am like a prune in the desert, but in the past fifteen years or so I have gone to bed with something like fifty men . . . and I have *punished* him and *punished* him . . . and there even are those who would say I have punished *myself* as well . . . and why . . . I mean, what . . . how come, if the hatred was so strong, did I bother with punishment? How come, if I didn't care, I just didn't take off for Pago Pago, or Bingo Bango, with one of my fifty or however many gentlemen friends?''

"I don't know,'' said Margaret.

Harriet Berkowitz rubbed the glass against a leathery cheek. "When I saw him today,'' she said, "it occurred to me that he had put on far too much weight. Far too much of the good life, I suppose . . . ''

Margaret had an idea. Somehow she had been reminded of the death of old Fred Boyd, of the lecture old Martha Boyd had given her. She thought for a moment of the truth of truth as opposed to the truth of facts. Sighing, nodding a little, feeling another yawn nudge the roof of her mouth, she said: "He . . . well, he was . . . ''

"Was he in pain?'' said Harriet Berkowitz.

"No . . . well . . . ''

"He had to be,'' said Harriet Berkowitz.

"Well . . . I suppose . . . ''

"I had a year of nurse's training about a century ago,'' said Harriet Berkowitz, "and I know a little about a myocardial infarct.''

"Pain . . . a little, yes . . . ''

"I'm not *glad*,'' said Harriet Berkowitz. "Don't get me *wrong*.''

"No . . . '' said Margaret, covering her mouth.

"On a bench, correct?"

"Yes."

"A park bench?"

"Yes."

"He felt thick in the chest, and he perspired, and he had chills?"

"Yes," said Margaret. She swallowed. She coughed. "But there was more."

"More?" said Harriet Berkowitz.

"He spoke of you. He said to me: 'Tell Harriet I love her.' "

"He said *what*?" said Harriet Berkowitz.

Margaret nodded. "He said to me: 'Tell Harriet I love her.' "

"I don't believe that," said Harriet Berkowitz.

"It's the truth," said Margaret.

Harriet Berkowitz drank. "You really think I'm all that naive?" She drank again. "He never said any such thing. I'd sooner believe you if you told me he said: 'Now I belong to the ages.' Or: 'Strike the tent.' "

" 'Strike the tent?' " said Margaret.

"Yes," said Harriet Berkowitz. "Those were Robert E. Lee's last words. Ah, don't ask me how I know them. I don't *know* how I know them. I suppose I remember them from school. An answer memorized for a test." She drank the rest of the Scotch in her glass. She went to the dresser and poured in more Scotch, added some ice. She turned, resting her buttocks against the edge of the dresser. "I suppose you are trying to be kind," she said. "I suppose you think you can afford to try to be kind. But I don't *need* that sort of kindness. I don't *need* that sort of condescension. And that's all it *is*, you know—*condescension*. The magnanimous winner consoling the bereft loser."

"Winner?" said Margaret. "What have I won?"

"What have you *won*?" said Harriet Berkowitz. "You've won *him*— *that's* what you've won. And you've won him *forever*. He's *dead*, and so the results are *final*. All the precincts have reported . . . "

"How can I have won a man who is dead?" said Margaret.

Harriet Berkowitz began to weep. She flopped on the edge of the bed. "I . . . please don't do any more of this to me . . . *you* were with him . . . *I* wasn't . . . *you* were the one who slept with him . . . *I* wasn't . . . *I* am the *prune* in the *desert* . . . I may not be much, and I *know* that . . . but what are you trying to *do* to me? Kill me with *charity*, which is *contempt*, which is *nothing*, which is like five steps beyond being a *dead animal* scattered in some *street*, with *blood* all over, and *fur*, and *hair*?"

"I was only trying to—"

"*You were lying!*"

"All . . . all right . . . "

Harriet Berkowitz dropped her drink. The glass rolled across the carpet, and the Scotch sloshed out, making a sort of dribble of a stain, scattering ice. She shook her head. She swiveled around. She flopped facedown on the bedspread. She wept and kicked (Margaret had kicked, too), and her skirt worked itself above her thighs, which were muscular and gray. She spoke into the bedspread, but her words were muffled, and Margaret could not make them out. Margaret folded her arms across her stomach. She did not move. Then, after perhaps three or four minutes of watching Harriet Berkowitz writhe and listening to whatever indistinct words Harriet Berkowitz was trying to say, Margaret stood up, went to the bed, leaned down and patted one of Harriet Berkowitz's shoulders. Harriet Berkowitz shook her head no. Margaret yawned. Harriet Berkowitz slapped open palms against the bedspread. Now, abruptly, the odor of Scotch was oppressive to Margaret. She went to the window and opened it. She was able to see the Thames. And perhaps somewhere out there was a canoe. And again she was aware of iron, of bees, of sour tyrannical horseradish, loud voices, fear.

The accumulation of evidence. Intersections. Collisions. Sometimes it is not proper to tell the truth, and sometimes it is not proper to lie, and Margaret Ridpath surely would have been grateful had someone explained the distinction to her.

She flew back to the United States the next day. She stayed in New York City two nights, and the second of those nights she and a man named A. Mark Trowbridge had a clear top in a game at the Rillington Club. The other players all told her how sorry they were about Irv. He had been a lovable man, they said. He would be missed, they said. She told them yes, yes, she agreed. Later, while escorting her back to her hotel (the Plaza) in a taxi, A. Mark Trowbridge tried to console her by stroking one of her knees. She gasped, and bile came up, and she vomited into his lap.

She continued to play in tournaments for the rest of her life, and Imogene Brookes became more or less her regular partner. She did not believe she had any choice in the matter. If she did not play in the tournaments, how would she occupy her days? With arithmetic? With the pain of memory? With images of Mousehole and the Ritz and *style* and Dover sole *meunière* and floating rose petals and Madame Tussaud and white gloves and watercress and a proud young man with ELVIS FOREVER printed on his sweatshirt?

So came then days out of her grief, Paradise Falls days. Wanda Ripple died, and Margaret amusedly leafed through *The Majesty of Grief*, and Pauline Jones moved in, and the slapless slaps continued (and Inez Ridpath was enormously grateful for them), and Margaret never truly did weep for Irv Berkowitz. She came close that day in the park when nothing lay between herself and the *fact* of his death, when he was actually sprawled atop her and she felt the gravel scratch her cheek and she was aware of his hat rolling away. But then the moment was lost. Voices crushed it. Hands. Words. And later she really should not have been amused by *The Majesty of Grief*—for it was in *The Majesty of Grief*, by F. F. Geer, of Ottumwa, Iowa, that it was written: *The human mind and spirit are instruments of a miraculous and terrible Almighty, extensions of His divine Will. So therefore, if dreams and ambitions are shredded and splintered forever, it is the holy duty of the human mind and spirit, acting in concert, to function as His agent and defender. To accept is to understand. To accept is to fulfill and obey His desires. Each human soul is a fragment of the Lord. Ah, such a final definition! Ah, such a glory!*

One night in January of 1973, while she lay on her late sister Ruth's side of George Prout's bed, Margaret watched him come groucho-marxing in from the bathroom, but she closed her eyes when he burrowed under the covers with her. Outside was snow, and it was loose and globby, and it splattered the window, and then George's hand was on her crotch, and she said: "I'm sorry."

"What?" said George.

Margaret opened her eyes. "It never should have happened," she said.

"But I am your *man*," said George. "I *serve* you, and I . . . well, I serve you . . . ah, *efficiently* . . . and you have told me that yourself . . . "

"Which makes it gospel?"

"A person should never lie about a thing like that," said George.

"Do you have any idea how this came about?"

"What?"

"How I've come to be here," said Margaret.

George grinned. "You've *come* to *be* here because you *come* when you *are* here," he said.

"Please, George . . . please don't make your jokes . . . I am Ruth's *sister,* and this was *her* bed . . . and what did you *do* to me that brought me . . . well, you know . . . "

"Nothing," said George. "Nothing except that I told you I love you. I was *sick,* and *Ruth* was *dead,* and for all I knew *I* was *dying,* and at a time like that a person just naturally lets his defenses down. So I said what I had been holding back. And it must have meant something to you. Because you gave in, didn't you? And I've been your stud, haven't I?"

"At our age . . . all of this . . . George, we ought to be taken to the nearest gallows . . . "

"Why?" said George. "You are a damned goodlooking woman, and you give me a hardon whenever I see you, and what's wrong with all that?"

"But I'm sixtytwo, and at my age I—"

"Do you think you *look* sixtytwo?"

"I don't know . . . "

"Goddamn it, Margaret, you give cramps and gas pains to every man and boy in this town, and you *know* it. You *do too* know it."

"But isn't that grotesque?"

"No. Why should it be? I love you, Margaret, and I'm . . . ah, honored, that you're here with me . . . "

"But the town knows all about us."

"So what? This is 1973. Peyton Place is dead and buried. Who gives a damn about that sort of thing any more? Look, even Sarah and Pete know about us, but they don't say anything. After all, they know I want to marry you. Will you marry me, Margaret? Will you make an honest man out of me?"

" . . . no."

"Why?"

"You always ask me that," said Margaret.

"I'm asking it again," said George.

"Because I'm . . . afraid . . . "

"Of what?"

"I don't exactly know," said Margaret.

"I think maybe *I* do," said George.

She looked at him.

"I'm *serious*," said George. As if to emphasize his seriousness, he took his hand away from her crotch. He said: "You're in love, all right. You're in love with routine. You're in love with things never changing. As far as you're concerned, you wish this town *was* Peyton Place, and you wish this *was* some sort of scandal. You'd understand *that*, wouldn't you? But the way things are now, and have been since the day Ruth died, it's all got you going in every which a direction at the same time, right? Why, even *my kids* like you, and they've *told* you that, and it doesn't *matter* that you're in their mother's bed. You're their *Aunt Margaret,* and they've always loved you, and none of this matters *squat* to them. But to you it's all a goddamned disruption. To you it would be better if you just had your job, your bridge tournaments, your mother and all her *talk*, and of course that real *winner*, that Pauline Jones. I swear to God, if I had to be stranded on a desert island with either your mother or Pauline Jones, I'd choose your mother without a moment's hesitation. At least she wouldn't . . . ah, *snivel* . . . ah, twentyeight hours a day . . . "

"I know," said Margaret. "In all my life, I think I've gotten up the courage to be nasty to a grand total of one person, and that one person is Pauline. Oh, it's not that I'm such a *saint* and don't *want* to be nasty to *other* people . . . it's just that I don't have the nerve . . . "

"Which is what I mean," said George. "Or at least part of it. You don't believe in rocking the boat. You don't believe in hairs out of place. And the thing you and I have . . . well, it isn't *orderly*, which in *your* mind means it's *grotesque* . . . but what the hell, Margaret, the whole goddamned *world* is grotesque . . . the war . . . people dying for reasons no one can understand . . . *the walls are being pulled down*, Margaret . . . and there's no place any of us can hide . . . so all we can do is try to be honest and—"

"George. Please. That's enough."

"Do you agree with me?"

"I don't know."

"If you do, just how do you think you can change the situation?"

"I don't know," said Margaret.

"It all was different with Berkowitz, wasn't it?"

" . . . yes."

"Was there more order?"

" . . . yes."

"Even though he was married?"

" . . . yes."

"And whatever you felt for him, it's different from whatever it is you feel for me?"

" . . . yes."

"And, goddamn it, you still grieve for him. He's been dead going on what? Going on fourteen years, right? And it's like he died yesterday, right?"

" . . . yes."

"What do I have to do to change that?"

"I don't know," said Margaret. "We've talked about it and *talked* about it, and I don't *know*. I . . . ah, I've never really wept for him all that much . . . but it's as though . . . well, it's as though I still can *taste* him. I'm sorry. I don't mean that the way it sounds, but you see . . . well, we had come to an agreement, and then it . . . it was—"

"Yeah," said George. "The agreement to live in England, to find a place where the walls weren't falling down . . . "

Margaret nodded.

"It's like you have that dream preserved in concrete," said George.

"I suppose so," said Margaret.

"I want to break through," said George.

"I know," said Margaret.

"I love you," said George.

"Yes," said Margaret. She closed her eyes.

He stroked her. He kissed her. He groaned and he threshed, and he told her he never had loved anyone else.

Margaret nodded. She made several appropriate sounds. She wrapped her legs around the small of George's joyful pumping back. He entered her, and she was easy and damp, and she did sums.

So then days by the thousands. And bridge tournaments. And Inez Ridpath lost weight, and she said: "If I am losing weight, where does the fat go? Is some woman in Timbuctoo getting fat? First thing you know, she'll be sending me an angry letter, and we'll have to surround the house with policemen so I'm not murdered in my bed. I'll tell you some thing—if I'd known, I'd have murdered Dorothy Hall in *her* bed, or out on Main Street, or in Elysian Park, or at the old falls gristmill, or *anywhere at all,* and that is a fact. Best as I can recall, George Prout knows more about a fountain Coke than Ferd Burmeister ever did. Best as I can recall. Oh, by the way, where is Wanda Ripple? When is she coming home with my lime pie? To tell you the absolute truth, this Pauline Jones woman does sort of aggravate me, what with her puling and her lollygagging and whatnot." And Pauline Jones said: "I have a brother named Walter who served with the 99th Infantry Division during the war, and for years he has insisted that Lloyd was 4F. Which isn't the truth. At first, when Lloyd and I were going around together, I tried to correct Walter, but he wouldn't *hear* of it. He kept saying: 'That *fruit* was never in the Army *I* was in.' And once or twice I even cried a little, but nothing would make Walter stop telling the world Lloyd had been a 4F, and I suppose he'll die believing it, but there's something I went and looked up the other day. I stopped in at the library and I searched through a book about World War II, and in that book it said that the 99th Infantry Division was the first American unit to give way during the Battle of the Bulge. Did you know that? It was December of 1944, and *Walter's division* gave way, and one of these days I'm going to have to tell him *I* know something he didn't think *anybody* knew, and maybe *then* he'll keep quiet about Lloyd, who has been gone all these years *anyway,* gone who knows *where,* and Margaret . . . Margaret . . . oh, Margaret . . . I was not a person to be *sneezed at* at one time in my life . . . and I would . . . oh, I would have settled for any terms from him . . . but he . . . " And then, inevitably, tears, and Pauline came lurching to Margaret and embraced her. And Margaret nodded. And Margaret was vexed. And finally she said: "Ancient history solves nothing." And Pauline hesitated for a moment, then said: "Yes." And Margaret said: "Am I supposed to read something into that?" And Pauline quickly assured her no, no, nothing at all. And Pauline's face was shapeless with her timid and damply corrupt nostalgia. And Margaret turned away from her. And Pauline did not protest. Everywhere was iron, and it made harsh rusty sounds. Evidence piled up. So then the days by the thousands. So then the words. So then the grief. So then the fear. The house roared with pity and bereavement. Margaret sat quietly. She was indomitable, and she was a lie. She was tightly girdled, and she was grotesque, and her female organs had been removed, and the remnants of her teeth had been yanked out, and she did sums, and she did sums, and she did sums, but she always remembered to make the appropriate sounds when they were necessary. Whether with Pauline, whether with Inez Ridpath, whether with Sarah and Pete, whether with George, whether with her nieces and her nephews or the people at Steinfelder's or the people who played in the bridge tournaments, Margaret Ridpath never did anything less than was expected of her. So then came the sounds. So then went the days. Thousands of sounds, thousands of days, cinched and precise.

Part Six

A BOY HAS NEVER WEPT

NOR DASHED

A THOUSAND KIM

(FRENCH CANADIAN

BEAN SOUP)

The responsive readings were Lee Pike's idea, but then of course he was the leader, and the others were too frightened not to go along with him. The words had come, as recorded by a stenographer, from the mouth of a dying man named Arthur Flegenheimer, and Lee Pike told the group: "Listen good. Listen to the cool. Listen to the voice of the future."

There were four of them altogether . . . then three, after the target practice.

They knelt naked and solemn in front of Lee Pike that morning, and the Nixon masks and the Saturday Night Specials were piled on the table, and he was vaguely amused to see that Chris had an erection. Slowly Lee Pike moved from Betsy to Chris to Melissa, and he anointed their heads with precise drops of Rolling Rock, and he said: *"You get ahead with the dot dash system."*

"Oh, oh, dog biscuits, and when he is happy he doesn't get snappy," said Betsy.

"The glove will fit what I say, oh kayiyi, kayiyi," said Lee Pike.

"No hobo and pobo I think it means the same thing," said Chris, holding his stiff cock.

"There are only ten of us," said Lee Pike, *"there are ten million fighting somewhere of you, so get your onions up and we will throw up the truce flag."*

"You can play jacks and girls do that with a soft ball and do tricks with it," said Melissa.

Lee Pike stepped back. He drank from the can of Rolling Rock. *"I don't want harmony; I want harmony,"* he said.

"Flegenheimer," said Betsy.

"Let him harness himself to you and then bother you," said Lee Pike.

"Flegenheimer," said Chris.

"The sidewalk was in trouble and the bears were in trouble and I broke it up," said Lee Pike.

"Flegenheimer," said Melissa.

"Mother is the best bet and don't let Satan draw you too fast," said Lee Pike.

"Delirium," said Betsy. *"Delirium and amen."*

"A boy has never wept nor dashed a thousand kim," said Lee Pike.

"Delirium," said Chris, squeezing. *"Delirium and amen."*

"French Canadian bean soup," said Lee Pike.

"Delirium," said Melissa. *"Delirium and amen."*

Lee Pike finished the Rolling Rock. He threw the empty can against a far wall. He was shirtless. He was wearing only jeans. He pulled down the jeans. He said:"Gather around me on your knees."

They gathered around him on their knees. He pressed their heads against his belly. The girls were calm, but Chris was moaning and shaking.

"Eeeny," said Lee Pike, "meeny, minie, moe," and the index finger of his right hand moved from head to head.

Leonard Everett Pike was born March 22, 1954, in Mamaroneck, New York. He was the only child of Dr and Mrs Quentin H. Pike, and his father was a wealthy obstetrician and gynecologist. Little Leonard was barely three when he learned to read, and he was able to do addition, subtraction and both short and long division by the time he was five. When he was six his parents paraded him at parties, and he did square roots for their guests. His head was shaped like a gourd, and he had thin blond hair. There was a handsomeness to him, however, and it was thinly arrogant, but his mother called it "poetic." Her maiden name was Katrin Blomquist, and she had written two novels, both published by Harcourt, Brace. The second, *Time Without Sorrow,* had been nominated for the National Book Award in 1952. After the birth of her Leonard, though, she never finished another book. She said to her friends: "When one gives birth to a *manifestation,* one's own work and ambitions seem at best meretricious. So I am devoting my time to little Lee now. We don't call him Leonard any more. He hates the name." And Katrin Pike smiled at her friends and assured them that in no way would she or her husband *exploit* the boy. "If President Harding was right, and if there is such a thing as normalcy, then Lee will exist in that sort of atmosphere," said Katrin Pike. And she patted little Lee and kissed him. "Our little poet," she said. "Our little miracle." At five, though, when he entered kindergarten (his parents had not wanted him to skip any grades), little Lee told the teacher, a Miss Baxter, that she had shit where her brains ought to be. This was after she had carefully spent ten minutes explaining to the children the difference between what she called Number One and Number Two. He was promptly removed from the school, and his father told him: "Young man, you have a *gift*. It is not something you have *earned*. I will not tolerate your abuse of that gift." Lee was then packed off to a private school near Storrs, Connecticut, where he immediately was placed in the third grade. He was tall for his age, but the other boys all laughed at him when they discovered he was only five years old. So he picked out one of them, a plump fellow named Jasper Redfield III, and he carefully kicked Jasper Redfield III squarely in the genitals, causing part of Jasper Redfield III's scrotum to tear and bleed. The incident took place in a woods near the school, and no one else was present, which meant Lee was able to get away with the lie he told the headmaster, that he had been attacked by Jasper Redfield III. Actually, he had lured Jasper Redfield III into the woods by telling Jasper Redfield III he had buried there a book containing pictures of naked women with tits and everything.

A year or so later, when rummaging through his parents' bedroom while they were downstairs entertaining more of their friends (and they surely did have lots of friends), Lee came across the scrapbook his mother had kept of the reviews of her two novels. He leafed through the scrapbook, and most of the reviews appeared to be raves. He had read both the books, and he knew as an absolute certainty that they were sentimental academic shit. He tucked the scrapbook inside his jammies and went to bed. He awakened early the next morning, sneaked down to the basement, took his mother's garden shears and sliced the scrapbook to shreds. It was a thick scrapbook, and so he had to grunt, and he had to grimace, and he had to bite his tongue. After finishing with the shears, he sat cross-legged on the basement floor and played with the shreds. Finally, when he heard his parents getting up, he carefully gathered together the shreds and dumped them into the incinerator. He dropped in a lighted match, and the shreds flamed up, and he went upstairs for a nice breakfast of Raisin Bran, orange juice, toast and two glasses of milk. His mother never said anything to him about the scrapbook. Once he heard her mention something about it to his father, something to the effect that she could not *understand* what she had *done* with it, but she never said a word to Lee

about her fucking egotripping goddamned collection of suckhole book reviews, and he supposed she thought he was too innocent to have the vaguest idea about it.

   In the summer of 1962, when he was eight, he tore his pants one afternoon after tripping and falling down while chasing a miserable little shit
named Jimmy Oosterhaus across Jimmy's back yard after Jimmy had accused him of being a Fag Brain Genius Asshole. Lee went home to change
his pants, and he found his mother and Jimmy Oosterhaus's mother going
down on one another while sprawled across the carpet in the master bedroom. Lee stood in the doorway and watched them for a time, but they
did not know he was there, and Mrs Oosterhaus was *ugly,* with purple
stretchmarks, and fatter than Lee's mother, but Lee's mother had a hairi-
er cunt. A week or so later Lee encountered Jimmy Oosterhaus while Jimmy was alone and taking a leak in the bathhouse at the swimming pool.
Lee seized Jimmy by the neck and pushed Jimmy's face into Jimmy's
own piss. Jimmy gagged and gurgled, but Lee did not laugh. The score
had been evened, and that was enough, and Lee would not waste his time
with redundant and unproductive emotionalism. He did, though, mail an
anonymous note to Jimmy Oosterhaus's father. He wrote it with his left
hand, and it said (the misspellings were deliberate): *Why does your wive
suk Dr Pikes wive and why does Dr Pikes wive suk your wive?* Lee never
heard how Mr Oosterhaus reacted to the letter, but Mr and Mrs Oosterhaus were divorced that winter, and Mr Oosterhaus received custody of
Jimmy and Jimmy's sister Katie, and the Oosterhaus home was sold, and
all the Oosterhauses went away, and Lee's mother said something to the
effect that it all certainly was a shame. And Lee's father nodded. And Lee
looked at his mother, and she was wearing slacks, and they were tight, but
he could see right through them if he concentrated hard enough, and she
waved a hand and made a vague remark about it being time she got started
in earnest on another novel. And Lee smiled. His mother was standing,
and he stared straight at the place behind which was her great hairy cunt,
and he waited until she noticed his stare. And he waited until she abruptly
turned away and went out of the room. He watched her rear end twitch,
and he knew she had a good figure, and he wondered why she had settled
for such a flabby old cow as Mrs Oosterhaus.

   By the time he was ten he was masturbating regularly, and he had
grown pubic hair of his own, and he had read all the novels of D. H. Law-
rence, Sir Arthur Conan Doyle, James T. Farrell and Henry Miller. The
assassination of President John F. Kennedy had taken place the previous
autumn, and it had fascinated him. The public grief had fascinated him.
The muffled drums and the riderless horse had fascinated him. Mrs Ken-

nedy's sense of theatricality and bullshit had fascinated him. The new President, Mr Johnson, looked like the sort of weathered old man a person might see waving his wand in a public park. Lee also was fascinated with the murder of Oswald by Ruby. He and his parents were watching television that Sunday when it happened, and his mother ran out the front door, and the gray November wind brought a chill, and she vomited at the base of her favorite forsythia. Lee's father ran to her, and he held her shoulders, and she puked and barfed until nothing was left. Lee sat in front of the TV set, and he was cold, but he could not take his eyes off the taped replay. And the slow motion. And the faces of the commentators when they tried to explain what had happened. He rapidly switched channels, and he saw seven replays of the shooting. Finally his father took his mother upstairs to bed, and the front door was closed, and warmth returned to the room. It was what his mother called a *sunken* living room, and the chairs and the sofa were enormous and leathery, and Lee scrunched himself in a corner of the sofa and did not take his eyes off the TV set. And said to himself: Why all the commotion? What did the man ever do? What does anybody ever do? So the good die young. Big deal. So do the bad. What difference does any of it make? Why all this lather? Why all these pipedreams? Why did Mother puke? Do you suppose maybe she was puking up the taste of Mrs Oosterhaus? Lee stood up, turned off the TV set, went into the downstairs bathroom, locked the door behind him, dropped his jeans and his shorts and jacked off into the toilet bowl. His face did not knot, and he did not gasp. His eyes remained open, and they were what everyone conceded to be a lovely blue, and he turned his head slightly and stared at himself in the mirror over the sink. When he was done, he carefully washed his prick and his hands. He returned to the *sunken* living room and turned on the TV set. He was quite pleased. The sight of himself was all that had been necessary to make him come. The figures on the TV screen now were remote, and all the grief and all the solemn music were even more bullshitty than they had been before. He said to himself: The more I know, the more I don't know. There is nothing behind all those faces. Concepts and beliefs and heroes are for people who are dead and don't know it. That is a fucking vaudeville show out there. Clowns. Acrobats. Bareback riders with big tits. Mother thinks she is a moral person, and so she barfs into the forsythia when she sees a murder on live TV. But then how come she didn't barf while she was eating Mrs Oosterhaus? Well, that's morality for you, that's philosophy for you. That's this universe, and it is worth shit. And so then . . . tentatively . . . little Lee Pike began his search for beliefs. But not a *philosophy*. Not a *scheme*. Not a *structure*. Only beliefs . . . and the coolest beliefs he could find, uncommitted and incoherent and therefore truthful beyond truth.

He was graduated from prep school when he was twelve, and he was graduated from the University of Connecticut when he was fifteen (he had an AB in history, with a minor in poli sci), and he never stopped looking for his particular truth beyond truth. When he was twelve he showed his erect whang to the woman who came twice a week to clean the house. Her name was Mrs Holloway, and she was a divorcee of thirty, and at one time she had had ambitions to be a Radio City Rockette, and he talked her into taking him in her mouth. He said: "I am someplace you never will penetrate, let alone understand." He said: "The sweetness will be unforgettable." He said: "Consider how few women ever have done this." He held Mrs Holloway's ears, and he stroked her tight reddish hair, and he told her: "You never will be so nourished. I have exalted you. There now is a purpose to you beyond your insignificant *ego,* with its *boundaries* and its *words.*" And he would not permit Mrs Holloway to kiss him on the mouth. She moaned and wept, and he played with her cunt, and she smelled of Ajax, and he would not permit her to speak. Smiling, he said to her:

"Don't think I am trying to humiliate you . . . far from it . . . the only thing is . . . I am trying to make you understand truth . . . but without *philosophy* . . . without all the incessant talk of *innocence* and *guilt* . . . you should read all the books I have read, and you would know what I mean . . . as for myself *specifically,* as for the way I behave and the way I talk and the way I think and the way I dominate . . . it's all in the glands, I'm told . . . or, in your case, perhaps it's all in the glans . . . but, anyhow, I apparently secrete in strange and mysterious ways my miracles to perform . . . ah ha ha . . . funny funny funny . . . " And Lee permitted himself a sort of laugh. He seldom permitted himself laughter. It got in the way. It was clutter. It was mess. His parents were surprised and angered when Mrs Holloway didn't show up for work one day, and they were utterly flabbergasted when they read in the paper that evening of how Mrs Holloway had packed her three children into her car, had closed her garage door, had started the engine and had asphyxiated all four of them. "She was such a sort of little emptyheaded *Barbie Doll,*" said Katrin Pike. And Dr Quentin H. Pike said: "Well, I like to think I know something about women, seeing as how their most intimate mechanisms provide my living, but I'll be *damned* if I can understand why she did a thing like *that.* It had been more than two years since her last child, and surely postpartum depression couldn't have been the reason . . . not after all *that* time . . . it just wouldn't have made any sense . . ." And here their son spoke up. He said: "Perhaps she had a kind of advance knowledge." And Katrin Pike said: "Of what?" And Lee Pike said: "Some sort of personal apocalypse, I suppose." And Dr Pike said: "Sounds mighty melodramatic to *me.*" And Lee Pike said: "So does the news on television." And then his father abruptly moved a hand in a gesture of dismissal. Nodding, Lee shrugged and went into the kitchen, where he fixed himself a peanut butter and jelly sandwich and a glass of milk laced with Nestlé's Quik. He sat at the kitchen table and ate silently. Mrs Holloway should not have been so tacky, but then what honestly could have been expected of her? Tacky *people* did tacky *things,* and no one with any brains could hope for anything else. Grimacing, Lee glanced around the kitchen. He thought of the money that had bought this kitchen, that had bought the peanut butter and jelly sandwich he was eating, the milk he was drinking, the *sunken* living room where he and Mrs Holloway had coupled on the sofa; he enjoyed thinking of the money and musing on its significance; it had come from his father because his father spent every working day peering into *cunts,* or removing babies from *cunts,* or patching *cunts,* or reaming *cunts,* and this was the house that *cunts* built, and in a way Lee regretted he did not laugh all that often. Instead, he simply grimaced. Instead, he simply munched. And sifted beliefs through his mind. And moved from year to year, and talked various girls and women into copping his joint. And told them all: "See it if you wish as a gentle and giving manifestation of love, but know from *me* that nothing will be returned other than my sweet and terrific fluid. But it's not that I'm trying to *humiliate* you. I would humiliate no one. Too much *emotion* is involved . . . as in love. Too much *reason* is involved . . . as in philosophy. *So never kiss me on the mouth.* I grant the fluid. I grant nothing else. *So never speak to me of love.* I grant a certain reflexive affection limited to the moment. I grant nothing else. *So never try to build concepts and understandings.* I grant the acknowledgment only of the moment, never of any scheme. I grant nothing else." And he insisted on these proclamations, no matter how desperately the girls and women tried to hush him. And those who interrupted were punished by having their faces slapped. A daughter of his father's closest friend. The wife of an orthopedic surgeon. A dance instructress for Fred Astaire. The estranged wife of a former member of the United States House of Representatives. A teacher of Spanish at a high school in New Haven. An Avon lady. Two nurses. Seven high school girls. One former nun who was active in ghetto social work in the Bronx. Lee Pike lectured them all, and they stroked his thin gourded head, and he supposed most of them hated him, but hatred to him lay in the same trash heap as love and philosophy.

He could not be bothered with it. He was altogether obsessed with his pursuit of a greater truth. And then, when he was seventeen, he discovered the last words of a dying man named Arthur Flegenheimer. They had been recorded by a stenographer. And they were enormous. They were nothing. They were nonsense. They were disorder. They were farce. They were poetry, and he was ennobled by them, and they would guide him from then onward till the day he died.

He copied them down, editing out repetitions and banalities, and then he committed to memory what he would later call *The Flegenheimer Testament: George, don't make no full moves. What have you done with him? Oh, Mama, Mama, Mama. Oh, stop it. Stop it. Oh. Oh. Oh. Sure. Sure, Mama. Ah. Please, Papa. Please make it quick, fast and furious. Please. Fast and furious. You get ahead with the dot dash system—didn't I speak that time last night? Oh, oh, dog biscuits, and when he is happy he doesn't get snappy. The glove will fit what I say, oh kayiyi, kayiyi. How do you know this? Well then . . . oh, Cocoa know . . . thinks he is a grandpa again. He is jumping around. No hobo and pobo I think it means the same thing. I am a pretty good pretzler. I will be checked and doublechecked and please pull for me. Will you pull? How many good ones and how many bad ones? In the olden days they waited and they waited. I don't want harmony; I want harmony. There are only ten of us; there are ten million fighting somewhere of you, so get your onions up and we will throw up the truce flag. Please let me get in and eat. Let him harness himself to you and then bother you. The sidewalk was in trouble and the bears were in trouble and I broke it up. Please, Mother, don't tear, don't rip. That is something that shouldn't be spoken about. Please, Mother, you pick me up now. You know me. Oh, sir, get the doll a rofting. You can play jacks and girls do that with a soft ball and do tricks with it. It takes all events into consideration. No. No. And it is no. It is confused, and it says no. A boy has never wept nor dashed a thousand kim. Did you hear me? Please crack down on the Chinaman's friends and Hitler's commander. I am sore and I am going up and I am going to give you honey if I can. Mother is the best bet and don't let Satan draw you too fast. Please look out. My fortunes have changed and come back and went back since that. The Baron says these things. I know what I am doing here with my collection of papers. It isn't worth a nickel to two guys like you and me, but to a collector it is worth a fortune. It is priceless. Look out, Mama. Look out for her. You can't beat him. Come on, open the soap duckets. The chimney sweeps. Take to the sword. French Canadian bean soup. I want to pay. Let them leave me alone.*

Lee worked on *The Flegenheimer Testament* for the better part of two days. That was in 1971, and he had been finished with college for two years, and in those two years he had done little except read, laze around the house, seduce girls and women into copping his joint, drink a little beer and assure his father and mother that one of these days he would get his head together and decide what it was he wanted to do for the rest of his life. It apparently was very important to his father and especially his mother that he make that decision. He was well aware that he had passed far beyond them—and so were they. His mother was fond of perching on an arm of his chair, and she would say to him: "Darling, you certainly don't need *me* to tell you how different you are . . . and yes, even *strange*. It hasn't been easy bringing up a genuine *phenomenon,* and there *have* been times—as you well know—when your behavior has been perhaps even a shade *beyond* strange. You've never had friends, not *really* . . . which certainly is *understandable,* mind you . . . but the way you are has set you apart . . . not to mention the times when your father and I . . . when, ah, we, I mean, he and I have had, ah, reason to believe that your treatment of certain girls has not been the most, ah, *chivalrous* . . . not that we're *criticizing,* you understand . . . you have special qualities that *do* set you apart, and of *that* there can be no mistake . . . but, well, all I'm trying to *say* is—one of these days you must *marshal* your special qualities and make a decision as to how best they can be *focused* . . ." And Lee Pike smiled at his mother. He patted her hand, and he glanced in the direction of her cunt, and she wriggled a little, and he told her that any day now he would get his game in order and go out and conquer the world. He placed a hand on her thigh. He said: "Through everything, you have been my friend, haven't you?" And Katrin Pike said: "Oh, yes. Oh my, yes indeed." He patted her thigh. He was patting the inside of her thigh, just below her cunt. He said: "Friends are valuable." And Katrin Pike said: "We all . . . we all need them . . ." Then, twisting her legs, she hopped off her perch and hurried from the room. And her son smiled a little. Lee Pike smiled a little. He thought of the lovely rolling cadences of *The Flegenheimer Testament.*

His index finger moved carefully as he recited the poem. With his other hand, he pressed the three faces against his belly. "Eeeny, meeny, minie, moe," he said. "Now it's clear which one must go." The finger pointed directly down on Melissa, but of course she did not know that. Her face was pressed too tightly against his belly.

Then, abruptly, he pushed all three of them backward, and they sprawled.

"Sit up," he said.

They sat up. Betsy was all goosebumpy. Chris still had his erection, and he looked from one to the other of the girls. He still was moaning and shaking. Melissa, who was breathing thickly, reached up and brushed her hair back from her eyes.

Lee nodded toward the table and the pistols and the Nixon masks. "Do you all understand the necessity?" he said.

"Yes," said Betsy.

Chris nodded.

"Yes," said Melissa.

"The choice has been made," said Lee.

"We know," said Betsy.

Chris covered his face.

Melissa nodded.

Lee looked at Betsy, then nodded toward the pistols and the Nixon masks. *"Let him harness himself to you and then bother you,"* he said.

"Flegenheimer," said Betsy.

"Yes," said Lee. He looked at Chris. "Five years ago today was what?"

"Sharon . . . Tate," said Chris. His hands came away from his face.

"And today is what?" said Lee.

"Nixon . . ." said Chris.

"Excellent," said Lee. He looked at Melissa. "Where was Charlie Manson wrong?"

"He had a concept," said Melissa.

"What is the value of a concept?" said Lee.

"Shit," said Melissa.

Lee looked at Betsy. "Why did those people kidnap Patty Hearst?" he said.

"They had a concept," said Betsy.

"Will their concept be fulfilled?" said Lee.

"No," said Betsy.

"Who will die today to begin with?" said Lee.

"One of us," said Betsy.

"We need to understand our weapons," said Lee, nodding toward the table. "Tell me, Chris, wouldn't you say that is true?"

". . . yes," said Chris, shaking.

"But first would it be in order for the three of you to fuck and suck?"

"I guess so," said Chris.

"You love Melissa, don't you?"

". . . yes," said Chris.

"And you love your sister, don't you?"

Chris glanced at Betsy. He opened his mouth, but he could not speak. He finally was able to nod.

Lee looked at Betsy. *"Mother is the best bet and don't let Satan draw you too fast,"* he said.

"Delirium," said Betsy. *"Delirium and amen."*

Lee looked at Chris. *"A boy has never wept nor dashed a thousand kim,"* he said.

"Delirium," said Chris, gagging a little. *"Delirium and amen."*

Lee looked at Melissa. *"French Canadian bean soup,"* he said.

"Delirium," said Melissa. *"Delirium and amen."*

Lee nodded. "All right," he said, "so go ahead—and if the spirit moves me, I just may join in."

Chris turned to his sister Betsy and kissed her on the mouth and pressed her flat on the floor. He began to hump her almost immediately, and she beckoned to Melissa to join them. Melissa crawled to them and kissed Chris's back, his shoulders, the flesh behind his knees, then his calves, then the insides of his thighs. Then she licked Betsy's spread legs, and she licked Betsy's feet and sucked Betsy's toes. She looked up at Lee and said: "I love you."

"No," said Lee.

Chris and Betsy rolled from side to side.

Melissa rolled with them, but she still was looking up at Lee, and she said: "It's not possible?"

"It's not possible," said Lee.

Melissa disengaged herself from Chris and Betsy. She began to crawl toward Lee, who had an enormous erection.

Lee held up a hand. *"A boy has never wept nor dashed a thousand kim,"* he said.

Melissa hesitated. *"Delirium,"* she said. *"Delirium and amen."*

"Go back to them," said Lee.

"Yes," said Melissa.

Chris and Betsy had finished, and now they were apart. They were lying side by side. Chris's limp cock glistened, and Betsy was stroking it.

Melissa crawled to Betsy and kissed her on the mouth. Then Melissa kissed Betsy's breasts, and Lee began to masturbate. When he came, it was in a great smooth jet, and some of it smeared one of Chris's ankles.

Melissa Jane Scowcroft was born January 18, 1957, in Gary, Indiana. She was the fifth daughter and seventh and last child of Carson T. and Marie J. Scowcroft. Her father was a grinder in a tool factory, and her mother was a beautician, and they both drank, and they took turns beating Melissa and the other children. They lived in a frame house on a narrow street that overlooked a sand dune that overlooked US Steel that overlooked Lake Michigan. The thing everyone had to worry about was niggers, and sometimes Melissa's father would seize her at the roots of her long blond hair and tell her: "If I ever so much as catch you looking *sideways* at a nigger, I'll make you wish you never was *born.*" And Melissa's mother said: "A nigger is so *big* down there he would tear you *apart.*" And Carson and Marie Scowcroft toasted one another with Seven and Seven, and all the kids stayed out of their way. Their favorite program on the television was Roller Derby, and a WALLACE FOR PRESIDENT sign was posted in the grubby front yard in 1968. Melissa would have sooner seen grass, but then she was only eleven, and what the hell did *she* know? A year later, though, when she was in the sixth grade at St Stephen's, she began *smoking* grass, and it made her feel as though God had pulled out all her bones and muscles and tight places. The grass had been given her by a skinny black boy named Tyrone Wesley, who was fifteen and fucked her in the weeds behind a billboard that said WHEN GUNS ARE OUTLAWED, ONLY OUTLAWS WILL HAVE GUNS. Melissa enjoyed the experience, and she hardly felt torn apart at all. She was a good student, and the sisters at St Stephen's honestly believed she had what they called a bright future, and she was fond of picking dandelions and stroking stray cats (her parents would not have one in the house) and listening to Jimi Hendrix on the radio and playing with herself and reading dirty books and thinking of Tyrone. She smoked at least one joint a day every school day from the time she was twelve until she dropped out at fifteen. She dropped out by popular demand, so to speak, after one of the sisters found her with another black boy, this one named Donald McQueen, behind the same billboard. The message on the billboard had changed, however. Now it said NEXT TIME YOU ARE MUGGED, CALL A HIPPIE. The sister took Melissa into the school office and telephoned Melissa's father at the tool factory. (Donald McQueen, in the meantime, had been packed off with the police.) Melissa sat quietly and listened to the sister's end of the conversation. Then, after the sister had hung up, Melissa asked to be excused to go to the toilet. She walked out of the school, and she hitched a ride in a Pepsi truck up into Chicago. She told the driver she was nineteen, and he believed her. His name was Al DeMeo, and he had curly hair, and he was thirty, and he told her there were those who considered him to be something of a swinger. He had an apartment on the North Side, and Melissa spent the night with him there, and his grass was of a much higher quality than Tyrone Wesley's had been. Al DeMeo had been a helicopter pilot in Nam, and it turned out he could get it up only if Melissa would permit him to cut her with the blade of a small straight razor he carried for such a purpose. Melissa was so stoned she told him to go ahead, and so he carefully drew a line across her belly, just below her navel. Then, grinning and snorting, he licked at the thin stream of blood. It tickled a little, but Melissa was aware of no particular pain. Al DeMeo said he was grateful to her with all his heart, and he rolled on top of her and gave her a good hard frenzied straight fuck, earnest and serious, as though perhaps the Martians were advancing up Wabash Avenue. The next morning Melissa was the first to awken, and she decided she had had enough of Al DeMeo and his weird stuff. She looked down at her belly, and the cut was not deep, but it did sting, and so she went into the bathroom, washed herself, found a Band-Aid and patched the cut. She dressed, combed her har, went through Al DeMeo's wallet, found seventyseven dollars and twelve cents, smiled a little, nodded and tiptoed out of the apartment. By nine o'clock she was on a Greyhound bus headed for Kansas City. She had bought a tiny transistor radio in the bus depot, and she listened to the rock music of WCFL until the station faded out. Then she noodled around with other stations and looked at the farms and animals and fields and trees along Interstate 55. The total cost of the ticket and the radio had been nearly fortyfive dollars, and so she would have to be careful with her money when she arrived in Kansas City. She knew no one in Kansas City (she knew no one anywhere), so she wandered aimlessly out of the bus station, and within half an hour she was befriended by a plump middle-aged man whose hat was stained and who said he was a partner in a stock brokerage firm. He lived alone in a large old house somewhere out near Independence, and he said he had known the late President Harry S Truman "like we were on a firstname basis—old Harry and old Ralph." The man's name was Ralph Shoemaker, and Melissa stayed with him for nearly six weeks. His demands were moderate, and he never cut her, but he never gave her grass, either. And he would not permit her to go anywhere alone. If he was in fact a partner in a stock brokerage firm, he never went there. All he did was stay home and watch Melissa and from time to time give her the benefit of his poor old whackedout cock. He always came too quickly, but at least she had a roof over her head. And he took her to a department store and spent more than three hundred dollars on clothes for her . . . dresses, jeans, shoes, whatever she wanted. He said: "All my adult life I've been well off. I understand the market, you see. I understand when to zig, and I understand when to zag. Oh, I wish I were a better lover for you. I wish I didn't . . . well, go *off* so fast and then *lose* it so fast . . . but I hope there are other ways I can make it up to you. I simply like to *look* at you, and I mean, the way you are able to move, and the way your little breasts move, and you never bothering with a brassiere. Oh, you are beautiful, Melissa.''

After six weeks, she crept out of bed at about three o'clock one morning. Ralph Shoemaker had a sinus condition, and he snored. She put on panties, jeans, a blouse and a pair of sandals. She packed the rest of her clothes in a large leather suitcase of his. His money clip was on a counter in the bathroom. She removed the money, and it came to more than two hundred dollars. She fetched her radio from the bedside stand. She leaned over the snoring Ralph Shoemaker and kissed him on the forehead. His breath was sour, and she made a face. She eased herself downstairs with the suitcase and the radio. She seated herself in the kitchen and wrote a note on a scratch pad. The note said: *Dear Mr Shoemaker, I appreciate your interest, but as you must know, enough is enough. You are neat, and I'll remember you for a long time. Your Friend, MELISSA.* She propped the scratch pad against the sugar bowl and let herself out the back door. The suitcase was heavy, but Melissa walked quickly up the street. There were no sounds. She turned on the radio, and the reception was good, and she was able to pull in WCFL. She hummed with the music. Ralph Shoemaker had bought fresh batteries the day before. He was a nice man, and she wished him well. She looked up at the treetops, and not a leaf was moving. She pressed the radio against her ear, and the music made her forget how heavy the suitcase was. She hitchhiked to Los Angeles, and she had seven rides (four from truckers), and she only had to put out once . . . for a man who was even older than *Ralph Shoemaker* and said he had lost his wife to cervical cancer in 1964. In Los Angeles, in January of 1973, Melissa turned sixteen, and by that time she was tricking a gross that sometimes came to three hundred dollars a day while peddling her ass for a black pimp named DeLong Hughes. He laughed a great deal, and he was on smack, and he told her he was her main man, and he punished her when she was a bad girl, and he told her he was de longest Hughes she ever would come acrost; he was de longest *anything* she ever would come acrost, and she said okay, I dig, and when she was nervous or worried she rubbed her Al DeMeo scar.

*

They were finished. Lee said: "All right. Now we have started this great day in the proper fashion. The next order of business is to cleanse ourselves. On your feet, all of you."

Obediently they disentangled themselves and stood up. Chris was wheezing. The girls were expressionless. One of the three of them was about to die, but only Chris appeared frightened.

Lee looked at Melissa. "Bathe them," he said.

Melissa nodded. It was clear to Lee that she knew, but she did not hesitate. She picked up a large basin and went outside. Lee walked to the door and watched her. She scrambled down a bank to the edge of Tuesday Creek and filled the basin. It was a brilliant August morning, and Lee squinted into the sunlight. Melissa returned with the filled basin. She passed Lee at the door without saying anything. She went to the table where the pistols and the Nixon masks were. She set down the filled basin. A bar of Lava and several clean rags were next to the Nixon masks. She soaked one of the rags, rubbed it with Lava, turned to Betsy and said: "Please come here."

Betsy crossed to the table.

Melissa carefully washed Betsy's face and neck and breasts and crotch and legs, and then she washed Betsy's hands. She kissed Betsy gently on the mouth.

"Not too much of that," said Lee. "It is illogical."

Melissa looked at Lee. "All right," she said. She beckoned to Chris.

Chris went to the table and stood next to his sister. He reached for one of her hands and squeezed it.

"No," said Lee.

Chris quickly released Betsy's hand.

Melissa carefully washed Chris's face and neck and chest and prick and balls and legs, and then she washed Chris's hands. She looked at Lee and said: "This will be a very small one." She kissed Chris gently on the mouth.

"Wash yourself," Lee said to Melissa.

"Yes," said Melissa. She washed herself.

"Now wash me," said Lee.

"Yes," said Melissa.

"With a clean rag and clean water," said Lee.

"Yes," said Melissa. She took the basin back outside, and Lee heard her empty it on the ground. Then he heard scrambling noises as she went down the bank to the creek. There was a large sound of birds. Melissa returned with fresh water in the basin. She placed the basin at Lee's feet, went to the table and picked up the Lava and a clean rag. Chris and Betsy still stood there by the table. Melissa walked to Lee, knelt before him, soaked the rag and rubbed it with Lava. She stood up and washed Lee's face, his neck, his chest, his prick, his balls, his legs, and then she washed his hands. When she had finished, she moved close to him and said: "Please?"

"No," said Lee.

She tried to touch his mouth with a finger.

"*No,*" said Lee, drawing back a step.

"Just once before I die?" said Melissa.

"No," said Lee. He shook his head a little. He was together again. For a moment, it had almost seemed logical that her mouth touch his. But now that no longer seemed logical, and he said to her: "If you want to kiss something, you know what you can kiss."

"All right," said Melissa. She knelt and softly kissed his cock.

Lee stroked the top of Melissa's head. *"French Canadian bean soup,"* he said.

"Delirium," said Melissa. *"Delirium and amen."*

"Go stand with Chris and Betsy," said Lee.

Melissa nodded. She rose and did as she had been told.

"All right," said Lee. He looked at Betsy—plump, dark, curlyhaired, with breasts that already had begun to droop. He looked at Chris—plump, dark, curlyhaired, close to tears. They were a couple of genuine *lovers,* all right, and Lee was fortunate not to be so shallow as to laugh at them. And now he looked at Melissa—tall, tanned, very blond, with a faint horizontal scar just below her navel. Her hair was long and straight, and in a general abstract sense she was unquestionably the most beautiful and exquisitely proportioned human being Lee ever had seen. But of the three she was the most expendable, and she was intelligent enough to know it. He said to her: "Is today the ideal day?" (He had drilled all three of them in the responses, but it was necessary that the responses be reviewed one last time.)

"Today is the ideal day," said Melissa.

Lee looked at Betsy. "There are two reasons today is the ideal day," he said. "Name one of them."

"The fifth anniversary of Sharon Tate," said Betsy.

Lee looked at Chris. "Name the other."

"The end of Nixon," said Chris.

"What philosophical significance is there to all this?" said Lee to Melissa .

"There is no philosophical significance to any of this," said Melissa.

"Then why will we do what we plan to do today?" said Lee to Betsy.

"Money always come in handy," said Betsy.

"What is sex?" said Lee to Chris.

"Sex is use," said Chris.

"What is philosophy?" said Lee to Melissa.

"Philosophy is shit," said Melissa.

"What is love?" said Lee to Betsy.

"Love is use," said Betsy.

"Does there have to be a *reason* for it all to come down?" said Lee to Chris.

"No," said Chris.

"So then what are we doing?" said Lee to Melissa.

"Participating in a natural phenomenon," said Melissa.

"The phenomenon of delirium?" said Lee to Betsy.

"Yes," said Betsy.

"Where is all this most clearly explained?" said Lee to Chris.

"In *The Flegenheimer Testament,*" said Chris.

"Did Arthur Flegenheimer die in vain?" said Lee to Melissa.

"No," said Melissa. "He died in order that *The Flegenheimer Testament* be revealed."

"Did Arthur Flegenheimer die for our sins?" said Lee to Betsy.

"No," said Betsy. "Sins are irrelevant. They imply good and evil, which implies philosophy, which is shit."

"I will be checked and doublechecked and please pull for me," said Lee to Chris.

"Flegenheimer," said Chris.

"Delirium," said Lee. *"Delirium and amen."*

"Delirium," said Melissa. *"Delirium and amen."*

"Delirium," said Betsy. *"Delirium and amen."*

"Delirium," said Chris. *"Delirium and amen."*

Lee nodded. He said: "Today we do what is necessary in order that the beginning be marked. The beginning of the process that will result in the demolition of what remains of the structure. Today we rob a bank. We take what we need. We take *whatever* we need. If deaths result, so be it. We shall not *force* the deaths, however. We shall not *need* to force the deaths. They will come down naturally. We have no cause; we are not interested in justice; we are not interested in *in*justice; we simply seek to begin the process that will imply and suggest and portend a conclusion. *And we have no philosophy. Remember, philosophy is shit.* I know all there is to know about philosophy and it is the pits. We must seek now blank; we must seek now nothing; we must seek now nonsense; we must seek now disorder; we must seek now endings. Charlie Manson has gone down, and Nixon is going down, and it will all go down, and today is the beginning, and if we all die today, the beginning still will exist, since we shall have demonstrated (in some way only time will tell) that earth and God and nature and civilization are nothing more than delirium." He looked steadily at Melissa. "You know, don't you?"

"Yes," said Melissa, and she began to weep.

"Death is irrelevant," said Lee.

"Melissa's the one?" said Betsy.

Melissa dropped to her knees .

"That will be enough of that," said Lee. "You stand up."

Melissa curled on the floor.

"Pick her up," said Lee to Chris.

Chris looked down at Melissa.

"Pick her up, " said Lee to Chris.

Chris could not move.

"Do it, " said Lee to Chris.

Melissa wept and twitched.

Chris shook. Urine ran down the insides of his legs.

Melissa reached for Lee's feet.

"Oh, great," said Lee.

Christopher Grant Moss and his twin sister Elizabeth Nancy Moss were born May 22, 1958, in Haverford, California. They were the only children of Maurice L. and Helen M. Moss, and their father was the city manager of Haverford, which is north of Santa Rosa and has a population of about fiftyfive hundred. Little Christopher weighed four pounds, six ounces at birth, and little Elizabeth weighed three pounds, nine ounces, and for three or four days it was what their father later called touch and go whether they would survive. But survive they did, and they flourished. They were plump and cheerful, and their parents took hundreds of color snapshots of them. Maurice and Helen Moss could hardly believe that God had seen fit to bless them so generously. They had been married seventeen years when the twins came, which meant that Helen Moss was thirtynine the day of the delivery. But she came through the births in what she and her husband called rude good health. They and the twins were given a police escort home from the hospital, and the chief, Dan Kingman, told them he had never seen more beautiful babies. The chief had six children of his own (and he had outlived three wives), but he told Maurice and Helen Moss: "These two of yours, you ought to take them down to Los Angeles and try to get them lined up for diaper commercials, or baby food, or whatever you can find. I mean, they are a *gift*, and no mistake." And Maurice and Helen Moss thanked the chief for his kind words, but of course they did not intend to become *stage parents,* for heaven's sake, not after seventeen years of waiting—and, in fact, waiting past hope. So then the Moss twins did not become the glory of television; instead, they became the glory of Haverford, California. Their parents bought them a special twin stroller, and they were proudly wheeled along the tall leafy streets of Haverford. And their mother bathed them together. And they slept in identical cribs—except of course Christopher's was blue and Elizabeth's was pink. They ate whatever was set in front of them, and they were easily toilet trained, and they seldom wept or had tantrums. Haverford, California, is a lovely little town; its economy is based on the lumber business, but the town itself has been isolated from the rawness and the wrench and squeal of the lumber business. The town has retained what the twins' father called *character* and *integrity.* Five miles away, the great trees come down, but they can neither be seen nor heard in Haverford . . . nor can the splintered naked valleys and hillsides be seen. And so a tranquility is retained; the tall leafy streets are untouched; children are safe, and women are not afraid to walk the dog. Christopher and Elizabeth Moss were reared in this environment, and everyone smiled at them, and they tumbled and giggled and raced, and their favorite season was autumn, with its crunch and powdery odor of leaves. He was active in the Cub Scouts and then the Boy Scouts. She was active in the Brownies and then the Girl Scouts. They always sat together in school, and they helped one another with homework assignments. (He was good at math and history. She was good at English, music and art.) Except for gym, shop and home economics, Christopher and Elizabeth insisted on having the same courses through junior high and the first year of high school—before they abruptly dropped out. They did not smoke, and they were not interested in marijuana, and they were not afraid. One day Christopher said to Elizabeth: "Living here, as long as I know you're somewhere close by, I'm cool, you know?" And Elizabeth said: "Neat." And no further philosophical discussion was necessary. She was a plump fourteen when she began dating boys, and they seemed to like her because of the size of her chest, but she was not all that enthusiastic about them, and she said to her brother: "I'd just rather sit quietly and watch TV, and that's the truth. The hassle is too much. I mean, if just you and I were maybe watching Star Trek and eating Doritos, that would be enough for *me.* The rest is really a *drag,* and I mean that." And Christopher said:

322   *Miss Margaret Ridpath*

"I'm flattered." And Elizabeth smiled at him and kissed him lightly on the chin and said: "Well, you *ought* to be, you turkey." And one summer she went on a serious diet and made the cheerleading team because she knew he was going out for football. They both were sophomores, and he did make the team, as a reserve lineman. He was slow and clumsy, though, and he never got in a game. Nonetheless, both Chris and Betsy were enormously popular with their classmates, and he was elected sophomore president, and she was elected sophomore secretary. The fact that Chris was a poor football player somehow endeared him to a lot of kids, and on several occasions that year, late in games in which the Haverford Tigers were well ahead, a spontaneous chant would arise: *"WE WANT CHRIS! WE WANT CHRIS! WE WANT CHRIS!"* And, laughing, he said to Betsy: "I have become a legend before my own time." And she hugged him and told him oh, what a *dear* he was, the *neatest* brother in the *world*. She played the piano for the Youth Group at St Christopher's-in-the-Woods Episcopal Church, and Chris was of course its president. He arranged for speakers to come and talk informally with the kids about the hazards of pot, or about drunken driving, or sexual permissiveness, or the need for organized religion to take a more active role in secular affairs. And Betsy and the other girls always provided Cokes and cookies. There were a number of girls who interested him, and he had dated them, and two of them (Patti Burwell and Mary Aspinwall) had worked him into such a frenzied state that he had been forced to whip out his handkerchief, unzip himself and hastily go off. Both Patti and Mary had been regretful, but they both were virgins, and they knew nothing about the pill. They assured him, though, that they loved him madly. He was Cute, they said, and they hoped he would just be patient with them until they were able to take the proper precautions. "And then anything you want," said Patti Burwell. "And as often as you want it, my love," said Mary Aspinwall. And lot of good that sort of talk did Chris, him and his sticky handkerchief. But at least he was able to discuss the situation with Betsy, and she told him: "Well, my *goodness*, would you have wanted to knock up *Patti Burwell*? Or *Mary Aspinwall*? They're not good enough for you by *ten miles*, and you *know* it. If I didn't love you so much, I'd make you go stand in the corner and listen to Wayne Newton records the rest of your life." And Betsy gave her brother a brilliant cheerleader smile, and she plopped on his lap, and she told him nothing ever was quite as bad as it seemed. Then one Saturday night in the late spring of 1973 (school had just let out, and Chris and Betsy had observed their fifteenth birthday few weeks earlier), Betsy came home all sweaty and mussed from a date with a boy named Fred Walters, who was quarterback on the footba

team and whose father was H. H. Walters, president of the Haverford
Lumber Co, the Haverford National Bank *and* the Haverford City Coun-
cil, which every two years had the option to renew or discontinue Chris
and Betsy's father's contract as city manager. Betsy came clumping heavily up the stairs, and she turned on the light in Chris's room and told him
to wake up. She went to the edge of the bed and seated herself there while
Chris rubbed at his eyes and tried to wipe away the sleep. Their parents
were in Santa Rosa for the weekend, visiting Mama's sister, Aunt Ernestine, and so Chris and Betsy—and the family cat, Muffin—had the house
to themselves. Chris glanced at the bedside clock, and it showed 3:11. He
said: "Wow . . . must of been some kind of evening . . ." Betsy was
wearing tight jeans and a tight white T-shirt. The T-shirt was twisted, and
the tail was out, and the top button was undone at the front of her jeans.
A slight roll of fat pooched out her waist. She said: "He was almost too
much tonight." And Chris said: "What'd he do?" And Betsy said: "He
did everything. He even cried a little. And he . . . he *touched* me . . ."
And Chris said: *"What?"* And Betsy nodded down toward her belly and
said: "Well, he . . . you know . . . he, ah, *opened me up* and he
touched me . . . and it *hurt* . . . but he said to me, he said: 'Betsy,
you're not going to kill me like this. You know what *my* father is, and you
know what he is to *your* father, and either you let me or I go to my father
and I say to him maybe old Maurice Moss ought to be replaced as city
manager by somebody a little younger. So what do you think of *those* apples, huh?' And, ah, Chris, I mean, what was I supposed to say? So I *let*
him—but it didn't turn out to be enough, you know? And he told me the
next time I either have to come across all the way or he . . . oh, I don't
know *what* he might do . . ." And Betsy wept. And she flopped across
her brother and hugged him. And Muffin, brown, spayed, elderly, came
into the room and hopped onto the footboard. And Betsy was able to
choke out some words. "I . . . I don't *want* him," she said. "I only . . . oh, *you* know . . . *you* know as well as *I* know . . . oh, God
help me . . ." And she kissed her twin brother squarely on the mouth.
And Chris moaned. He pushed her face away. He said: *"No."* And Betsy
said: *"Yes.* What are we trying to *prove?* That what *does* exist *doesn't* exist?" And Chris closed his eyes. He and Betsy were only *fifteen years old*,
and what were they supposed to know about something like this? And
Chris, whose stiff prick already was rubbing the sheet (and . . . through
the sheet . . . the outside of one of Betsy's thighs), said to his sister:
'You're just . . . worked up . . . you're just worked up from Fred
Walters . . ." And Betsy said: "Yes . . . but I love you . . ." And
Chris said: *"No."* And Betsy sat up. She pulled the T-shirt over her head

before Chris could say anything. She unsnapped her brassiere. It fell to the floor. She tossed her T-shirt to the floor. She began unbuttoning the front of her jeans. She said: "Mama had us take baths together until we were six . . . and I remember, don't you? I looked at you . . . and I looked at myself . . . and we were so alike . . . but we were so different, too . . . and I was fascinated . . . and I bet you were too, weren't you? And don't go trying to act cool about it . . . you are *neat,* and I *love* you, and there's never been anyone el—oh, sweet Chris, *sweet* Chris, *sweet Chris*" And Betsy threw away her jeans. And she already had kicked off her heavy clunky brown shoes. And she threw away her panties. And Chris, who was sleeping only in his shorts, tugged them down, but at the same time he said: "If anybody ever . . . I mean, finds out . . . like, we are . . . school . . . Papa and Mama . . ." And Betsy said: "It won't hurt . . . there will be no . . . ah, babies . . . we just *have* to . . ." And now she was nibbling at him, sucking the flesh around his mouth and ears. And she said: "I have . . . oh, my love, I have saved myself . . ." And then, roaring, Chris rolled on top of Betsy, and she was as ready as she ever would be, and he plunged inside her, tearing away tissue, and she shrieked, and Muffin hopped down from the footboard, and Christopher Grant Moss fucked his twin sister Elizabeth Nancy Moss through blood and grunts and torn tissue, licking her great black nipples, kneading her soft belly, feeling the blood that came from her warm pierced cunt, and later he said to her: "I don't suppose we can ever—" And Betsy licked one of his ears and said: "Shhh . . ." And Chris said : "It's not that easy. You just can't shush me up." And Betsy said: "I know." And she embraced her brother. And they wept. And the sheets were sopping. And Chris thought of the town, of their parents, of the tall streets, of Muffin and Haverford High School and the happy loving chant of *"WE WANT CHRIS! WE WANT CHRIS. WE WANT CHRIS!"* And he said to his sister: "No way." And Betsy said: "No way what?" And Chris said: "We are outside now, and there's no way we can go back." And Betsy said: "To what?" And Chris said "What do you *mean* to *what?* To *staying* here . . ." He shook his head He said : "Church. Scouting. Foot—" And, smiling a little, Betsy said *"Scouting?"* And Chris said: "Yes. Scouting. I happen to like it, and think you do, too." And Betsy said: "You are far out. You talk abou scou—" And Chris said: "And football, too. No more football. No mor cheerleading." And Betsy said: "This is *unreal.*" And Chris said: "Yes." He thought of leaves and pianos and high skies. He embraced his siste He said: "Either we keep at it until we die or we stop it right now." An Betsy nodded. And Chris said: "We won't be able to stop." And Bets said: "No way." And Chris said: "Then we got to split." And Betsy said: "Why? We can be careful. We can—" And Chris said: "*No*. There is no such thing as being careful *here*. You understand?" And Betsy said: "I guess so . . ." And Chris kissed his sister's neck and breasts. Her hand stroked his cock. He squeezed his eyes tightly shut. He felt his face redden, and then he came in her hand, and she looked at her hand, and it glistened, and she said: "Thank you." So they left. They took off. They split. They waited until Monday, and Chris visited the Haverford National Bank and withdrew nine hundred dollars he had saved from three years of mowing lawns and cleaning yards and delivering papers. He and Betsy packed their belongings that night and sneaked out at about two in the morning. They left no note for their parents. There could be no words. There could be no explanations. Chris and Betsy carried backpacks, and they rode in a boxcar down to Santa Rosa. The next morning he lied about his age to a used car dealer and bought a '62 Pontiac for two hundred dollars. That night he and Betsy got it on in the back seat of the '62 Pontiac after he had parked the old car behind a Dip-O-Freez stand north of Sausalito. Then he and Betsy talked about freedom and love and beauty, and they were homesick, and they wept, and finally Betsy fell asleep while murmuring: ". . . . we want Chris . . . we want Chris . . . we want Chris . . ." The next morning the '62 Pontiac would not start. It coughed up some sort of greenish substance, and so Chris and Betsy abandoned it and hitchhiked down to San Francisco. They held hands, and they kissed, and they tried to keep their bodies clean, but after a time the money ran out, and it all became very difficult, especially the clean part. They drifted south to Los Angeles, and they taught one another all sorts of heavy things, and they met all sorts of heavy people, and they ate Hershey bars, and they ate some of the heavy people, and some of the heavy people ate them, and it was a long summer, and sometimes, as they lay quietly and touched one another, they spoke of home, of their parents, of Haverford High. They lay in parks and woods and vacant lots, and they touched, and they scratched, and grime lay moistly in the folds of their flesh, and now and then one of the heavy people would give them some indifferent grass to smoke. And Chris said: "Has the cost been too much?" And Betsy said: "No way." And then one night they encountered a *very* heavy *black* dude in East LA, and this very heavy black dude's name was DeLong Hughes, and he drove a Lincoln Pimpmobile that was far out, and he took Chris and Betsy to his apartment, and the doors had brass knobs, and the walls were covered with photographs of Isaac Hayes and Ron O'Neal and Pam Grier and Kareem the Dream Abdul-Jabbar, and he gave Chris and Betsy grass that was *not* indifferent, and they got to laughing and dancing, and first he fucked Betsy, and then he fucked Chris, and then he threw them both into the shower, and he joined them there, and he cleansed them, and he punished them when they were bad, and Chris was his private trade, but he was generous and did share Chris with Betsy, as long as it didn't interfere with her tricking. But Chris and Betsy still talked of Haverford High. And later, when Betsy met a tall blond girl named Melissa Scowcroft, she told this Melissa Scowcroft how popular she and Chris had been at Haverford High, and everybody seemed to like everybody else, and DeLong Hughes's bed was immense, and he and Chris and Betsy and Melissa had some great old times in it. And he kissed them when they were good with just as much passion as he punished them when they were bad. And the grass was happy and pure. Sometimes they bathed him and shaved him and anointed him and dressed him, and he was all oranges and greens and whites, and he told them they were looking at the future. And they said yes, yes, yes, right on. He patted their asses, but Chris was his private special favorite suck, and he said to Chris: "You know how lucky you are?" And Chris, stoned from there to the Malay Peninsula and halfway back, said: "Love is the heaviest . . ." And DeLong Hughes grinned at the girls and said: "An *DeLong Hughes* is the *greatuss* . . . the greatuss of them *all* . . ." And, speaking in sweet magical stoned unison, the girls said: "*Forever* . . ." And they energetically tricked for him, and so did six other girls, and he kept Chris altogether to himself, and Curtis Mayfield lived in the stereo, and God tore down Haverford, stripping away the trees, and Chris and Betsy flabbed and lolled, and they did as they were told, and they kept assuring each other they regretted nothing. They spoke of Haverford less and less, and then they spoke of Haverford not at all, and by that time God had left behind not a brick or a splinter.

Lee kicked Chris several times, and then Chris bent down and lifted Melissa to her feet. She leaned against Chris, and she pressed her face against his shoulder. He stank of urine.

Lee spoke directly to Melissa. He said: "*I will be checked and double-checked and please pull for me.*"

"I . . . I don't want to die . . ." said Melissa.

"Give the response," said Lee.

Melissa wailed.

Lee wrenched her away from Chris. He seized her hair and snapped back her head. He slapped her face with his free hand. *"Give the response,"* he said.

Melissa's mouth was bleeding. She coughed, drooled, trembled. Then: ". . . *Flegenheimer* . . ."

"Very good," said Lee, nodding. He did not release her hair, though. Had he done so, she probably would have slumped to the floor again. Instead, he slapped her two or three more times . . . but more gently. Then he said: "We all agreed last night, remember? And we agreed that I, as the leader, as the one who discovered the true significance of *The Flegenheimer Testament,* would be the one to make the decision. You know all that, don't you?"

". . . yes," said Melissa, moaning.

Lee touched Melissa's Al DeMeo scar with the forefinger of his free hand. He moved the finger gently along the scar. He said: "Remember, there is a chance you might get away." He nodded toward the pistols and the Nixon masks. "We are completely inexperienced, and perhaps we all shall miss . . ."

"Yes, Melissa," said Chris. "We just might."

Lee looked at Chris. "But not deliberately."

Chris quickly shook his head. "Oh, *no,*" he said.

"If you miss deliberately," said Lee to Chris, "I'll *know* it. And then *I'll* come after *you,* and *I* won't miss."

Chris nodded.

"You stink," said Lee to Chris. "Go out and wash yourself."

Chris hurried out.

Betsy started after him.

"No," said Lee.

"I only want to help him . . ." said Betsy.

"Never mind," said Lee. "You stay here. You listen to what I have to say to Melissa. You come back here now, and you stand where you were standing."

"All right," said Betsy. She returned to where she had been standing. She glanced down at the place on the floor where Chris's urine was drying.

" *A boy has never wept nor dashed a thousand kim,*" said Lee to Betsy.

"*Delirium,* " said Betsy. "*Delirium and amen.*"

"Fine," said Lee to Betsy. "That's much better." He still was holding Melissa by the hair. He pushed her against the table. He said to her: "I had to decide which one of the three of you was expendable. And of course it *had* to come down to *you,* dig? Of course you do. *They* are *brother* and *sister,* and they are *lovers,* and if *one* dies, they *both* might as well die, what with the grief the one left behind would experience. And *two* cannot be expended. Only *one*. Which makes *you* the one. Two from three leaves one, so Melissa it is, by acclamation, by popular demand, a command performance, a real honor . . .''

Melissa hunched her shoulders. She shuddered.

Lee reached around her and scooped up one of the pistols. "This is a .32 caliber revolver of the type commonly known as the Saturday Night Special," he said. "I never have fired one. Nor has Chris. Nor has Betsy. Nor have you. Now then, we have three of these Saturday Night Specials, and we have plenty of ammunition, *but we do need to practice under what will be more or less real conditions.* So you will be our target. Like a doe in the woods. Like Bambi's mommy. You will be permitted to flit and dart and crouch and hide, and perhaps you'll be lucky. I'm told the average Saturday Night Special is not very accurate." He pressed the muzzle against the side of Melissa's head. "Of course there *is* such a thing as short range, and if you would prefer simply an *execution*, we could accommodate you right *here,* and I for one certainly would have no—"

Melissa screamed.

Lee jammed the muzzle into Melissa's mouth before she could close it. "All you have to do is nod, baby," he said.

Melissa did not move.

"Good," said Lee. He jammed the muzzle as deep as it would go, and he heard Melissa make faint gagging sounds. He said: "Remember, there is no emotion here. We do not hate you. The only truth is the truth of delirium, the truth of zero, the truth of the end of the world. The trouble with Charlie Manson was he tried to create order by dreaming up Helter Skelter. The trouble with Nixon is he said Charlie Manson was guilty, and *now* look who's guilty, and if *there* isn't your truth of delirium, then all that remains is madness. So today we begin, you see. Today we begin our participation in the conclusion. We can always use the money, and hopefully someone will resist, and hopefully that someone will die. Someone beyond yourself, I mean."

Chris came back.

Betsy looked at him.

Lee nodded toward the table. His pistol still was jammed in Melissa's mouth. "Get pistols and masks for yourself and your sister," he said to Chris. "And the two of you put on your masks."

"Ah . . . sure," said Chris. He hurried to the table, took two of the pistols and two of the Nixon masks. He went to Betsy and gave her one of the pistols. Then he and Betsy each put on a Nixon mask.

"I have a thought," said Lee.

Chris/Nixon and Betsy/Nixon blinked at him through their eyeholes.

"From now on," said Lee, "the pharmaceutical industry would be well advised to put that face on all poison bottles." He reached around Melissa and found the third Nixon mask. Carefully he removed the muzzle from Melissa's mouth. He handed the mask to her. It was in black and white, and it was made of cardboard, and Nixon was grinning, and he needed a shave. The mask was connected to a rubber band. "Put it on me," said Lee to Melissa. He pressed the pistol's muzzle against the Al DeMeo scar. "Do it with dignity and respect," he said. "This is a sort of coronation."

Melissa's face was twisted and drenched. She could not speak. Her tongue rubbed the roof of her mouth, apparently in an effort to get rid of the metallic taste of the pistol. Her hands shook, but she carefully managed to press the Nixon mask against Lee's face and slip the rubber band over his head.

Now Lee was Lee/Nixon. "Excellent," he said, and his voice was a little muffled. He started to prod Melissa toward the door, but then he snapped his fingers. "Hey," he said to her, "I've just thought of something." He moved the pistol's muzzle along the Al DeMeo scar. "You've always wanted to kiss me on the mouth," he said to Melissa. "All right. Here's your chance."

Melissa began to fart uncontrollably. "I . . . I want to live . . . " she said, swaying.

"Kiss me, you fool," said Lee/Nixon.

Melissa threw her arms around Lee/Nixon and warmly kissed the mask's cardboard mouth. She continued to fart.

Lee/Nixon pushed her away. "Wow," he said. "You'd better get out of here before you gas us all to death."

Melissa would not release Lee/Nixon.

He placed the pistol next to one of her ears and fired. But he did not fire into the ear. Instead, he simply fired straight back, bringing pain to the ear but not otherwise harming her. She released him. She staggered back. She rubbed the ear. A part of it had been scorched. Chris/Nixon and Betsy/Nixon were embracing one another. Lee/Nixon glanced at them and disgustedly shook his head. The pistol was warm in his hand, and the room was sweet with the odor of the shot. The bullet had gouged a hole in a far wall. Lee/Nixon nodded to Melissa. He supposed her hearing had been impaired, so he shouted at her. "*On your way, little woodland creature!*" he yelled.

Melissa looked at him. She shook her head. She farted.

Lee/Nixon fired again, over her head.

She shrieked. She turned and ran out the door.

"We'll give her a count of ten," said Lee/Nixon to Chris/Nixon and Betsy/Nixon. "One," he said, and he pointed at Chris/Nixon.

"Two," said Chris/Nixon.

Lee pointed at Betsy/Nixon.

"Three," said Betsy/Nixon.

"Four," said Lee/Nixon.

"Five," said Chris/Nixon. He had caught on.

"Six," said Betsy/Nixon.

"Seven," said Lee/Nixon.

"Eight," said Chris/Nixon.

"Nine," said Betsy/Nixon.

"Ten," said Lee/Nixon. He motioned toward the door. "Come on," he said to Chris/Nixon and Betsy/Nixon. They emerged from the shack, and Melissa was perhaps fifty feet away, and she was struggling down the bank toward the Tuesday Creek.

"Don't waste your ammunition," said Lee/Nixon to Chris/Nixon and Betsy/Nixon. He broke into a lope, and they followed him. Melissa was splashing upstream, and she was flailing, and once she fell. Her hair was soaked, and it clung to her scalp like a helmet. Lee/Nixon steadied his right wrist with his left hand and squeezed off a single shot from about thirty feet. The bullet struck Melissa's right elbow, which blossomed redly. Lee/Nixon turned back to Chris/Nixon and Betsy/Nixon. *"Go ahead!"* he shouted to them.

Melissa was staggering.

" I got off one fucking fine shot!" shouted Lee/Nixon to Chris/Nixon and Betsy/Nixon. He leveled his pistol at them. *" Now let's see what you two can do!"*

Chris/Nixon quickly nodded. He fired. The bullet struck a tree a good fifty feet to Melissa's left.

Betsy/Nixon fired. The kick of the pistol caused her to fire straight in the air.

Lee/Nixon fired between Chris/Nixon and Betsy/Nixon. He had now used up four of his bullets, but they all had been necessary. *"You can do better than that!"* he shouted.

Chris/Nixon and Betsy/Nixon shook and wept. Up ahead, Melissa had slipped and fallen again—this time across a scattering of rocks.

Lee/Nixon motioned to the weeping Chris/Nixon and Betsy/Nixon. "Now we are going to kill that cunt," he said to them. "You come right along with me, and I bet you'll enjoy it."

"My God . . ." said Chris/Nixon.

"Shut up, cocksucker," said Lee/Nixon. "You miserable sisterfucking faggot."

Chris/Nixon subsided. He and Betsy/Nixon followed a pace or two behind Lee/Nixon. Melissa lay trembling on her belly. Her head and ass were out of the water, but the rest of her was submerged. She was making no sounds now, and the water was red from her elbow.

When they were twenty feet from Melissa, Lee/Nixon held up an arm and said to Chris/Nixon: "Try it again, cocksucker, and this time steady your right wrist with your left hand."

Chris/Nixon did as he had been told. He aimed carefully. His legs were wide apart. He fired. The bullet tore a great furrow in Melissa's ass, and blood flew in all directions. Melissa screamed once, and then all the tension seemed to go out of her body.

Lee/Nixon went to Betsy/Nixon and took her by an elbow. "If it helps you any," he said, "I do believe our little woodland creature has passed out." He led Betsy/Nixon to a spot about five feet from Melissa. "Now then," he said, "I want you to aim for the back of her neck."

Betsy/Nixon raised her pistol.

"Your right wrist with your left hand," said Lee/Nixon.

Betsy/Nixon nodded. She did as she had been told. She fired. She missed the back of Melissa's neck, but the bullet did tear off most of the back of Melissa's head. "How was that?" said Betsy/Nixon.

"Not bad for a beginner," said Lee/Nixon.

Betsy/Nixon giggled a little. So did her brother.

Afterwards Lee/Nixon and Chris/Nixon and Betsy/Nixon jumped into the creek (upstream of the place where Melissa's blood and tissue and bone had fouled the water), and they carefully and languidly bathed themselves, and Betsy/Nixon pulled Chris/Nixon's pudding under the water. Finally, after they all were clean and fragrant, they emerged from the water, collected up their pistols and returned to the shack. Chris/Nixon's watch was on the table. It showed just past ten o'clock in the morning. There was plenty of time to drive to Paradise Falls. The masks came off, and Lee was Lee, and Chris was Chris, and Betsy was Betsy, and the masks were placed on the table with the pistols, and Lee said: "Some things really are necessary, aren't they?"

"Wow," said Betsy.

"Far out," said Chris.

"I only wish she'd have been more of a challenge," said Lee.

"She was too scared," said Betsy.

"The farts and all," said Chris.

"Yes," said Lee. "He farts should have told us. Now tell me, do you understand how important it was that we have the experience?"

"Yes," said Betsy.

"Dynamite," said Chris.

"And was it fun?" said Lee.

"It was fun," said Betsy.

"Dynamite," said Chris.

"But we must remember that no love or hatred was involved," said Lee. "Only delirium was involved."

"Right on," said Betsy.

"*I don't want harmony; I want harmony,*" said Lee.

"*Flegenheimer,*" said Chris.

"*Let him harness himself to you and then bother you,*" said Lee.

"*Flegenheimer,*" said Betsy.

"Come to me and kneel," said Lee to Chris and Betsy.

They came to him and knelt.

He pressed their heads against his naked belly. "*A boy has never wept nor dashed a thousand kim,*" he said.

"*Delirium,*" said Chris. "*Delirium and amen.*"

"*French Canadian bean soup,*" said Lee.

"*Delirium,*" said Betsy. "*Delirium and amen.*"

There was one last can of Rolling Rock. Lee snapped it open and drank from it while he and Chris and Betsy dressed themselves, packed the rest of their stuff in the car (Betsy salvaged four of Melissa's T-shirts and two pairs of Melissa's jeans, even though she was too fat for them), then gathered up the masks and the pistols and the ammunition and clambered inside the car. Chris drove, and Lee carefully reloaded the pistols. Betsy turned on the radio, and they listened to Sha Na Na, and she and Chris laughed. But Lee did not laugh. Lee never laughed. He grimaced a little, but he did not laugh. He was glad, though, that Chris and Betsy had come around so quickly this morning. Which of course had been the real reason for the target practice. Now they would *enjoy* what they did, and so they would be *better* at it. People always were. Lee nodded in time with the Sha Na Na music, and he worked slowly and carefully, inserting the bullets in the chambers. He had the back seat all to himself, and the car headed south on Ohio 93, and he told Chris not to exceed the new 55 speed limit, and then he closed his eyes and took a brief, efficient, uncluttered nap.

*

By the time he was fifteen, Leonard Everett Pike knew he never would pursue any sort of career, or at least any sort of conventional career. He would be no scientist, lawyer, poet or politician; he did not give a thimbleful of canary shit about making any sort of *contribution* to what he knew was a world that had flipped its collective wienerschnitzel long before he had been born. Still, there was a problem involved in this decision. He enjoyed comfort, and comfort cost money, and so he would have to devise a way to be comfortable and yet at the same time not to have to contend with a lot of hassle from his parents and their fucking WASP work ethic. But he was not in the conventional hippie weirdo doper bag. Except for an occasional can of beer, he avoided all intoxicants, whether smoked, ingested or received from a needle. In addition, he kept his hair cut short, and he showered at least twice a day. He was especially careful with his cock, and he always soaped and rinsed it thoroughly. It was unquestionably the cleanest part of his body, and it certainly was cleaner than his mouth, as he often pointed out to girls and women while talking and hotting them into giving him head. Still, even though he did not need to spend money on booze or grass or shit or cunt, and even though he knew he had psyched out his parents with his genius or whatever the hell it was, Lee required freedom—*complete* freedom—from Mother and Father and their *expectations* and their confidence in what they called his *brilliant potential.* But he was not about to toss a knapsack on his back and trudge off into the sunset like some sort of penniless vagabond out of an old Jack Kerouac novel. None of that *On the Road* horse manure for Lee Pike, no indeed. Sure, he supposed he *would* eventually hit the road (after all, how long could anyone be expected to live with a dyke mother and a father who looked into cunts all day?), but by God he would hit that road in *style* and *comfort* . . . and without interference.

He waited for his opportunity . . . and in the late spring of 1972, shortly after his eighteenth birthday, it came . . . as he knew it would. He had gone into New York City and had spent a day with his friend the Avon lady, making it with her in the apartment of one of her old boarding school girlfriends, who was off vacationing in Florida. The plan had been for Lee and the Avon lady to spend the night in the friend's apartment (the Avon lady had set up everything with her husband, telling him she and the friend intended to go to the theater and catch up on old times), but one of the Avon lady's children had a cold, and so she telephoned her housebound husband to check up on the little bastard. And sure enough, the kid had taken some sort of turn for the worse, so the Avon lady decided to go home. Lee was mightily pissed, yet there really wasn't anything he could do about the situation. He and the Avon lady rode in the same train from Grand Central back to Mamaroneck, but they did ride in different coaches. He stared gloomily at his reflection in the window, and the coach had a stink of beer and jism and shit, and he saw the elongated shape of his head flicker and dance, and he said to himself: Blame it on the shape of my head, world. Blame it on glands. Blame it on chemistry. The walk home from the station was a long one, but the night was not all that cold, and Lee needed to simmer down. He had not bothered to call home. His parents were attending some sort of medical association shindig at a country club, and the chances were they still were partying it up. So Lee walked slowly, and he arrived home at about one in the morning, and sure enough, all the lights were out. But Dr Quentin H. Pike's brand-new '72 El Dorado was parked in the driveway, and Lee was a little surprised. The old man and the old lady apparently had had a bad night, and they'd apparently already gone to bed. Shrugging, Lee let himself into the house. Old Mom and Old Pop probably would be surprised to see him in the morning—he had told them he was spending the night in New York City with an old acquaintance from prep school. He turned on the light in the foyer, and the first thing he saw was Old Pop snoring away on the enormous sofa in the famous *sunken* living room. Old Pop still was in his tuxedo, but the front of it was smeared with puke. He had kicked off his shoes, and one of them had sailed all the way into the fireplace. He looked great. He looked like a true pillar of the community, the Greater Mamaroneck Commissioner of Squinting Up Cunts. Lee sighed, held his nose to keep out the stink of the puke. He went upstairs, and at the head of the stairs he heard a sequence of groans and gasps. They seemed to be coming from behind his parents' bedroom door, and Lee listened carefully, and he was put in mind of Mrs Oosterhaus. He nodded. He tapped his temple. He made a wise whispery sound. He went down into the *sunken* living room, and again he held his nose. He paid no attention to his father. Instead, he went to a desk, rummaged through several drawers and finally found the Polaroid. It was color and it had a flash attachment, and he checked it for film. Everything was in order. He nodded. He went back upstairs and opened the door to his parents' bedroom. The two figures were entangled on the bed. One was his mother, and the first flash of the good old Polaroid caught her industriously devouring Dr J. Laura Sutherland, who was fifty, plump, florid and a prominent pediatrician. In point of fact, Dr Sutherland had been Lee's pediatrician. She was kneeling, and she was facing him, and Lee's mother's head was buried inside her legs. Lee took six pictures before the women knew what was happening. Then, without saying a word, he ducked out.

His mother was waiting for him alone in the *sunken* living room when he returned home two hours later. Lee showed her three of the prints. (The other three he had buried in a plastic Baggie in a woods at least a mile from the house. He had scooped up the earth with his bare hands, and the work had given him enormous satisfaction.) He did not waste his time . . . or his mother's . . . with any sort of bullshit or recriminations or outraged morality. He sat with her in that *sunken* living room, and they both drank coffee. She wore a pink robe and a long pink nightgown, and it was obvious from the smell of her that she had taken a long, hot, steaming bath. She sat tautly, and she squeezed the handle of her cup, and then she tore up the three prints, lit a match to them and threw them into the fireplace. She knew there were more without Lee's having to tell her, and so he simply told her what he wanted. He said: "You and Old Pop have been after me to choose something. Okay, I dig, and here is what I choose: *Number One*—I want a car. I want it to be new, but it doesn't have to be expensive. It can be a Chevy, for all I care, with not even any fancy extras. *Ecshally*, Mumsy dear, I wouldn't even give a damn if it had *four doors*. I want it to be inconspicuous, and *I* want to be inconspicuous. *Number Two*—I want no interference from you or Old Pop and no hassle when I go away. Yes. That's right. There is no wax buildup in your ears. I want to go away, to *drive around* as it were, *hither and yon* as it were, tra la, tra la, seeing this great nation of ours and experiencing its people, but with *complete freedom*. Which leads us then to *Number Three*—the first of each month, you are to wire me the sum of one thousand dollars. I'll telephone here, and reverse the charges of course, and tell you where to wire the money. It ought to be romantic and fascinating for you and Old Pop . . . wondering where I'll be from month to month. Perhaps you and the neighbors can get up a pool. So okay, that's how it comes down. Three little demands. Not *requests*, but *demands*. There is no *negotiating* any of this, Mumsy dear, as I'm sure you must know. And oh, by the way, I wouldn't want you to think I'm *shocked* or *hurt* or *maimed* or anything like that. I'm not. I've known about your muffdiving proclivities for years now, ever since the times you used to get it on with that delightful sex symbol, the absent and no doubt sorely missed and yearned for Mrs Oosterhaus. I happened to, ah, stumble across you two one time, and it was one of the really moving and inspiring moments of my young life. But don't think that I was *twisted* or *embittered* by the experience, don't think hatred is involved here. Just give me what I demand, and I'll be on my way, and there'll be no hard feelings, and you and the charismatic Dr Sutherland can nibble and lap one another until the last teenyweeny grain of sand has trickled through the Great Hourglass of Life. *And,* as a matter of fact, I'll even give you a month or two to prepare Old Pop for my departure. And I'll even help you. We'll lay on him a lot of crap about how I need to *find myself*, to *think my way through my indecision*, to *touch life*, to *seek a key*. I mean, just get out one of your books. I'm sure you'll find a proper way of putting the thing. And it'll work out fine.'' Six weeks later he had title to a '72 Impala (with four doors), and he had a thousand dollars, and he was on the open road, and Old Pop hadn't been a problem at all. As a matter of fact, he had said to Lee: "I'll grant you, it's all a little extravagant, but what the hell. You're not exactly some dummy living in a shack over by the railroad tracks. And if you need to get a taste of the way people live these days, then I suppose you have my blessing.'' His parents stood in the front yard when he backed the Impala down the driveway and into the street. His father waved goodbye. His mother did not. Katrin Blomquist Pike had lost perhaps twenty pounds, and some sort of layer had been stripped from her eyes. Lee blew her a farewell kiss, and he saw her make some sort of shuddering movement that was confined to her arms and shoulders. It was a splendid summer day, and Lee drove west, and he listened to WQXR almost to Philadelphia. The Impala moved smoothly along the New Jersey Turnpike, and he got to thinking of Nelson Algren, of poolrooms, of allnight luncheonettes, of trailer courts and McDonald's golden arches, of quick gimcracky suburbs and rubber wading pools and lonely housewives giving themselves the finger while spooning Gerber's peas to little Poopsie with their free hand. He exited from the turnpike from time to time, and he idly cruised through some of the Jersey suburbs, and he looked at toddlers and their adorable haircurlered lipstickless bunnyslippered shlepping mommies, and he cruised up and down streets that were called Maple Hollow and Knollgreen and Timberwood and Oxfordshire and Green Farm, and the houses that lined these streets all had been stamped out by some colossal Punch Press in the sky with no doubt the fervent blessing of whoever it was had the stomach to be the God of Maple Hollow and Knollgreen and Timberwood and Oxfordshire and Green Farm. And Lee grinned at signs that said SLOW CHILDREN, and he grinned at the '72 campaign PRESIDENT NIXON bumper stickers that already were sprouting on the station wagons and the Audis and the Oldsmobiles of those who lived in the houses that lined the streets that had been stamped out by the colossal Punch Press in the sky. And Lee grinned at floppy little dogs, babies in sandboxes, Orkin trucks, and he wanted to walk singing along these happy punchpressed streets and tell the babies and the toddlers and the haircurlered mommies and the Orkin representatives: *Hey, folks! This is our own, our native land! Isn't it heavy? Look around yourselves and kindly repeat after me: A boy has nev-*

er wept nor dashed a thousand kim! And then, choking a little, with the Seventh Symphony of Anton Bruckner grinding mercilessly and endlessly and gallantly from a WQXR that was beginning to crackle and break up, Lee thought of the late Oscar Levant, and he told himself he would devote his life, if necessary, to peeling away America's false exterior tinsel in order to discover the true interior tinsel. He spent that first night in a Howard Johnson Motor Lodge west of Philadelphia. He showered, took a nap, showered again, dressed himself neatly and walked to the motel restaurant for dinner. The waitress was a chesty little redhead of about thirty. She had uneven teeth, and she wore a badge that said JANET. It turned out she was separated, childless and lived about half a mile from the motel. She drove an old Ford and he followed her home at midnight. It was a small frame house with three rusted auto hulks in the back yard. "Alvin was a great one for collecting junkers," said Janet, "and I'll be damned if I know why. He never had much mechanical ability. Maybe he felt sorry for them. I don't know." She and Lee went promptly to bed, and then they divided a sixpack of Schlitz. She stroked his hair and told him he had the most unusual head she ever had seen. "The *shape* of it, I mean," she said. "Almost like a *football,* you know?" And she giggled a little, so Lee pulled down the sheet and poured beer over her belly. She shrieked, so he brought the side of a hand across her adamsapple. She gurgled, and then she wept, but she was unable to say much that was coherent. Lee got out of bed and dressed himself. He left without saying anything. On the way to his car he stopped by her old Ford. He let the air out of its two rear tires. He returned to the motel, and he slept soundly, and the next morning he had waffles and sausages for breakfast, and he drove west toward Harrisburg. The year 1972 was a great one for him. The monthly expense allowance telegrams reached him in such places as Kansas City, Missouri; Helena, Montana; El Paso, Texas; Muncie, Indiana, and Dothan, Alabama, and there was not a murmur of protest from his parents. A thousand dollars every thirty or thirtyone days . . . and Old Mom and Old Pop never failed to tell him to be careful. Even Old Mom. And one time, the time he made his monthly call from El Paso, she said to him: "Darling, I've not been feeling *at all* well lately, and I was . . . I was wondering whether perhaps you wouldn't like to come home for . . . ah, a little *visit* . . . " Lee abruptly hung up the telephone. He shook his head and wondered at the nerve of some people. He thought of *The Flegenheimer Testament,* and he recited it, and one day— on an impulse—he mailed a postcard to his parents. It showed a color photograph of the Grand Canyon, taken from the North Rim. He wrote: *Dear folks—I will be checked and doublechecked and please pull for me.*

Will you pull? How many good ones and how many bad ones? Your loving son, Lee. (PS—A boy has never wept nor dashed a thousand kim.) And he grinned, and he hoped his mother would read Deep Significance into it. Delirium was splendid simply *alone,* but when Deep Significance was read into it, oh, hot dog! You could multiply the splendidness by ten! So Lee drove. And recited the immense demented phrases of *The Flegenheimer Testament,* shouted them to the Great Salt Lake and the Chicago Loop and the Gateway Arch in St Louis, picked up waitresses and highschool girls and made them go down on him, drove with care and thoroughness in a checkerboard pattern from one end of the nation to the other, literally from Aroostook County to San Diego. And had his hair trimmed at least once every three weeks. And listened to barbers and their cronies talk of Nixon and Pinko McGovern and That Nut Eagleton, and in the town of Uvalde, Texas, which had been the birthplace of the late Vice President of These Here United States, John Nance Garner, a barber said to him: "Boy, I can tell from the way you talk you are from New York City or some such place, but it ain't the way a person *talks* that's important. It's the way he *behaves.* And *you* now, the neat way you keep your hair, with short sideburns so you don't look like some kind of greaser pimp running a string of clappy Mexicali Roses with sores comin out their asses, *you* got a look to you that *tells* me somethin. It tells me we still got some straight thinkers in this here country, and it don't make no nevermind whether they come from Uvalde or New York City or where. You see, boy, what we got to *do* is get back a sense of *order,* to bang down on a lot of heads if we *got* to, but to make it so this country makes *sense* again, so that these old boys I see drinkin bootleg whisky of a Saturday night got more to look forward to than havin the govamint spend all their money on niggers or whores or moon rocks or whatever." Lee smiled as he emerged into the immense West Texas afternoon, and he shaded his eyes against the raw sunlight, and his blond gourded head had a high sweet stink of Vitalis, and his interior vision swarmed with happy witless delirious Flegenheimer phrases. Oh, 1972 was a good year, all right. Once he drove nonstop from Boise to Minneapolis in what was mostly a blizzard. He stopped only to fill the car and empty himself. He did not like Minneapolis, so he slept there for four hours, then returned nonstop to Boise, where he shacked up for eleven days with an employment agency counselor whose name was Wilma Coggins. She was a lovely blonde with immense blue eyes, perky breasts, fine long legs and a withered left arm. She told Lee she would crawl naked over rattlesnakes if he asked her. And Lee said: "This is a bad time of the year for rattlesnakes." He drove back to Minneapolis, then to Chicago, then to South Bend, Toledo,

Cleveland, Buffalo, Rochester, Syracuse, Skaneateles, Scranton, Harrisburg, Peekskill, New Haven, Boston, Bangor, Stowe, Ticonderoga, Toronto, Windsor, Detroit, Cincinnati, Evansville, Louisville, Paducah, Memphis, Jackson, Birmingham, Atlanta, Savannah, New Orleans, Pensacola, Miami, St Petersburg, Mobile, Houston, Rosenberg, Uvalde, El Paso, Phoenix, the Grand Canyon, Las Vegas, Los Angeles, San Diego, Palm Springs, San Francisco, Fort Bragg, Portland, Seattle and finally back to Boise, and each month he made his collect longdistance telephone call, and he smiled, and he ate well, and he scrounged up enough head, and he showered frequently, and he had begun to find a handle to these final ruins of the American Republic, a way to sift through the sand and shredded paper and shattered glass and rusted hubcaps. He had seen the great scarred highway earth, and no doubt Wolfe and Kerouac still would have been able to relate to it, to the abrupt and gray shingled farmhouses, the hot stinking barns, the electrified fences and the quick redwinged blackbirds, the forever battalions of corn and wheat, diesel horns in the blank unbroken prairie nights, the crushing and simple grandeur of farmland and forests and swamps and mountains, but there was an America that lay beyond the pictorial, and it was an America of delirium, and it was *this* America that concerned Lee as he fled from town to city to town to city, an America of cocksuckers and pimps and sellouts and haircurlered mommies, a bulldozered and neoned America, an America of oil spills and assassinations and Spiro T. Agnew, cardboard hamburgers, Magic Fingers in the mattress, taxes up and taxes down, Nixon embracing Chinamen, the crystal smile of Pat Nixon, a nation of Say One Thing & Mean Another, and if the cunts didn't get you, the assholes would, and sometimes both would—zappo! whango!—in conjunction, and what did the diesel horns in the blank unbroken prairie nights have to do with any of *that*? And Lee Pike, sucking grease in motel restaurants that were called The Roundup Room and The Mad Hatter and The Chop & Brew and The Candlelight Plaza, prowling bars in middleclass suburbs that were full of women who had damp cunts and called themselves Swingers, listening to the sad canned laughter of small children muffled in the endless prowling schoolbuses that scooped them up as though they were insects sucked away by a vacuum cleaner, driving the blinded and pointless suburban streets with their foolish sylvan and/or Englishy names, talking with barbers, talking with bartenders, gathering wisdom from television (next to the NBC Nightly News, the Koran was no doubt a pile of shit), walking empty innercity streets at three in the morning when no sane person would be out alone, stepping over winos and dead cats and broken bottles, reciting certain of the more apt phrases from *The Flegenheimer*

Testament, dashing his thousand kim into the face of God . . . oh, this Lee Pike, poet and pervert, glandular freak, footballhead, oh, this Lee Pike, oh, oh, oh, how he did attempt to grasp that handle. Then, on the night of June 30, 1973, he called home from Las Cruces, New Mexico (reversing the charges, of course), and he was told by the operator that the telephone had been disconnected.

Chris Moss was a careful and conservative driver. Both he and Betsy had taken an approved AAA course back at Haverford High. She sat close to him, and her head rested against his shoulder. She had noticed that Lee had dozed off, and so she had turned off the radio. She kissed her brother behind his right ear. Her left hand rested lightly between his legs. "I never would have thought it," she said.

"Me neither," said Chris.

"You know what I'm talking about, don't you?" said Betsy.

"Melissa," said Chris. He took the Ohio 93 curves easily so as not to disturb Lee. The highway was winding south out of coalmining country toward the valley of the Paradise River. (The shack had been near an abandoned mine called the Tuesday Creek. He and Betsy had ventured about fifty yards into the old mine a few days earlier, and she had said to him: *I have never been fucked in a coal mine.* And Chris had said: *Neither have I.* And so they fucked. And they giggled. And they were streaming coaldust when they emerged from the mine, so they stripped naked and jumped into the creek and bathed one another.)

"I loved Melissa," said Betsy.

"Not so loud," said Chris, placing a finger to his lips. "That is not Lee's favorite word."

"Then okay," said Betsy, lowering her voice. "I had the hots for her, and we used each other."

"That's more like it," said Chris.

"I really enjoyed it," said Betsy.

"Killing her?" said Chris.

"Yes," said Betsy.

"Well, you sure did blow the hell out of the back of her head," said Chris.

Betsy giggled. She squeezed the place between Chris's legs.

The car swerved a little. "No *fair*," said Chris.

"When you're in love, everything is fair," said Betsy.

Chris said nothing.

"I'm sorry," said Betsy. "I used the forbidden word, didn't I?"

Chris said nothing.

"Well, I can't *help* it," said Betsy.

Chris sighed.

"I don't *care*," said Betsy.

Not taking his eyes off the road, Chris removed his right hand from the wheel (contrary to accepted AAA procedure) and reached down the front of his sister's T-shirt. He stroked her breasts.

"Was Melissa better than me?" said Betsy.

"No way," said Chris.

Lee's parents' closest friends were a couple named Shaw—Bert and Sally Shaw. He was an insurance executive, and she taught English at the high school, and they had three children, all grown. They lived next door to Lee's parents, so Lee telephoned them that night from Las Cruces. He was just about tapped out (he did not live frugally, and so a thousand dollars had been just barely enough to get him through each month), and he had to reverse the charges. Sally Shaw was the one who answered the telephone, and she accepted them. She spoke quickly and brusquely, and she told Lee precisely what had happened, and she suggested he return home as quickly as possible. He told her yes, he would try to be back within two or three days. He asked Mrs Shaw whether perhaps she could wire him some money, but Mrs Shaw refused. "You little beast," she said, "I wouldn't give you a drop of sweat if you were dying of thirst in the desert." She banged down the receiver, and the noise brought pain to Lee's ear. He hung up. He searched through his jeans. He counted his money, and it came to seventeen dollars and twelve cents. He stepped out of the telephone booth and looked around. A small sheetmetal building was catercornered from the booth. A sign over the entrance said JUANITA'S SUPERETTE. He crossed the street. He entered the place, and no one was inside except an old woman with a moustache. She sat behind the cash register, and she appeared to be half asleep. She was enormously fat. Lee went behind the counter and pushed her aside. She had been sitting on a stool, but she was knocked off it. She made no sounds, however. She simply lay on the floor and blinked up at Lee. He punched open the register and scooped out all the bills. There was more than two hundred dollars. The old woman said not a word. He glanced briefly at her, then hurried out of JUANITA'S SUPERETTE and jumped into his car. He drove to Mamaroneck with only stops for brief naps. He drove straight to the Shaw home. Mrs Shaw answered the door, and he told her he needed to take a shower. She was a tall and slender woman, past fifty, with rigid cheekbones and crisp gray hair. She shrugged. She pointed up the stairs. Lee went to the bathroom off the master bedroom. He took a shower, dried himself, seated himself on the commode, shat, wiped himself, flushed the toilet, took another shower and dried himself. He had brought clean clothes, and he climbed into them. He carefully combed his hair and examined his teeth. He rolled his dirty clothes into a bundle and returned downstairs. Mrs Shaw was sitting in the living room. It was chintzy, fussy, very Early American. He seated himself on a flowered sofa and held the bundle of dirty clothes on his lap. "All right," he said to Mrs Shaw, "please tell me what you know, and then we'll try to go on from there." Mrs Shaw nodded. She wore a white blouse and green plaid slacks. She pressed her knees tightly together. She said: "There's not much more to tell other than what I told you the other night on the phone. Your mother died three weeks ago last night when she drove her car into the side of a New Haven locomotive. Earlier that day, she had been told she had a malignant brain tumor. I leave it to your imagination to speculate on whether her death was an accident. But of course, as you know, that is only part of the situation. She left a note behind for your father. He told us what was in the note. I don't know the precise wording (he never *showed* us the thing), but it had to do with her belief that the brain tumor was a punishment for certain, ah, *lesbian behavior* that, well, I don't have to tell *you* about, do I? The note also stated that you had discovered her with a woman, had taken photographs and had blackmailed her. Well, your father reacted to all of it in the only possible way . . . he broke down. The next morning his brother your Uncle Donald arrived from Great Barrington, and the funeral and burial took place that afternoon, and they were private, and your father was unable to stand without assistance. But he did say to us: 'I *knew* about Katrin. I was her *husband,* and I *had* to know. But it didn't make all that much difference. She was a good wife *anyway.*' And that was the last we have seen of him. He is staying with your Uncle Donald in Great Barrington, and he has put his home up for sale, and he has decided he has no further interest in the practice of medicine. He telephoned us last week, and he told us he was doing very well, relaxing, drinking lots of tea on his brother's porch, reading books and getting a great deal of sun. And then he said to tell *you* that under *no* circumstances were you to *visit* him or *attempt* to visit him. He said that he and his brother would not hesitate to have the Great Barrington police throw you in jail for trespassing. In other words, he never wants to see you again." Mrs Shaw hesitated, held up a hand. "But, ah, do not for a moment think all is lost. Even though next to *you* a brain tumor seems like an afternoon at Disneyland, your father has made a final gesture. And *final* is the important word here. A certified check for ten thousand dollars is waiting for you at the Mamaroneck Bank & Trust—provided you sign a document relinquishing all further claims to his estate. And actually, even if you refused the money and did not sign the document, you probably wouldn't receive a penny of his estate anyway. He's already made a new will, and the money is going to his brother and his brother's three children. Your Uncle Donald and your three cousins. Sooo . . . if I were you, God forbid . . . I would sign the document, take the ten thousand dollars and go off on my merry and verminous way into the setting sun or whatever . . . " And now Mrs Shaw was weeping a little. She hunched forward. She made a scooping movement with an arm, pointing it toward the door. "Please," she said. "Please. Please. I have no more . . . no more information for you . . . so please just leave here now . . . " Nodding, Lee stood up. He clutched his dirty clothes to his chest. "Maybe you're afraid of me," he said. "Maybe you think I'm angry with you and want to hurt you." He shook his head no. "Well, don't you worry," he said, "I do not *get* angry, nor do I hate. I am beyond that sort of thing. But tell me—did she ever go down on *you*? Or was it mutual? After all, you *were* friends for a long, long time . . . " He smiled at Mrs Shaw, but she had covered her face. He was reminded a little of the way his mother had been that night in the *sunken* living room. He left Mrs Shaw's house without saying anything more to her. It was clear he would have to take the ten thousand dollars and let it all go at that, so he drove into town, stopped at the Mamaroneck Bank & Trust and was shown into the office of a vice president named Richardson. The man produced the paper, and Lee signed it without bothering to read it. Lee endorsed the bank's check, then asked for the money in traveler's cheques, denominations of one hundred dollars apiece. He had a key to the house, and so he drove home and went inside. The place was stuffy. He went upstairs to his room and collected a few books and records he had left behind the first time. He loaded the books and records into his car, then reentered the house. He walked into the kitchen and rummaged around for a large butcher knife. Once he had found it, he went into the *sunken* living room and slashed the leather furniture. He also slashed several carpets and two original oil paintings, one of a circus clown and the other of a cat. He smashed several lamps, and he made a number of deep scratches in his mother's polished antique escritoire. He walked into the dining room and knocked over the sideboard, breaking most of the dishes. He reentered the kitchen, threw bowls and plates and cups and saucers against the walls, then smeared the floor with peanut butter and catsup and mustard and vinegar and maple syrup and Miracle Whip. He went upstairs and broke all the mirrors and slashed his mother's dresses and the suits and shirts his father had left behind. He tore down several curtains and shredded them. He chopped at the mattress in the master bedroom, and he shredded the pillows, and feathers flew, and he sneezed. He went into the upstairs library and found three copies of his mother's first novel and two copies of her second novel. He ripped them apart, and then he dropped the torn fragments on the floor, and then he pissed on those torn fragments. He stabbed at other books with the butcher knife, and he found some matches and set his father's medical dictionary afire. He dropped it on the rug, and it scorched the rug, and a fine stink arose. And Lee had an erection, and so he unbuttoned his jeans and jacked off over an opened copy of a book entitled *The Essential Woman.* When he had finished, he slammed shut the book, went into the bathroom and took a shower. After he had showered (gasping delightedly, groaning a bit), and combed his hair, he poured shaving lotion on the floor, squirted two entire aerosol cans of Gillette Foamy against the walls, poured perfume in the commode, returned downstairs and smashed several diningroom chairs against the walls. Then, breathing a little heavily, he decided it would be good to take a walk so he could calm down. He walked to the woods where he had buried the three Polaroid prints of his mother and Dr Sutherland. He dug them up and returned home. He found an envelope. He addressed the envelope to his father in Great Barrington. He scrounged for stamps in his mother's battered escritoire. He found a regular stamp and a Special Delivery stamp, and aloud he said: "Hot damn." He affixed the stamps to the envelope, and he slid the prints into the envelope, and he sealed the envelope, and then he jumped up and down, and he kicked the escritoire to bits. He smiled as he walked out the front door. He had killed Mrs Holloway, and he had killed his mother, and now he had killed the house. He drove to the corner and mailed the envelope and its precious contents. He drove out of Mamaroneck. He figured he never would return. He smiled. He had to. It had occurred to him that they never would have Lee Pike to kick around again. And aloud he said: "We must always be wary of the dreaded They." He rubbed his head, and he grimaced, and then he said: "Glands."

*

Chris enjoyed driving, and he was proud that Lee had given him the responsibility. "It'll work out just fine," he said to his sister. She was pressed tightly against him, and his hand moved back and forth, from breast to breast.

"Of course it will," said Betsy.

"Lee has drilled us very well," said Chris.

"And when Lee drills a person, a person stays drilled," said Betsy.

"Not so *loud*," said Chris.

"Well, sometimes I—"

"Now look," said Chris, "next to *DeLong Hughes* he's a . . . a . . . oh, I don't know . . . at least he doesn't believe in having someone as his *personal property* the way DeLong did . . ."

Betsy kissed a corner of her brother's mouth. "I know it couldn't have been much fun," she said.

"Well, *sometimes* it was," said Chris.

"You mean when *I* was there?"

"Yes," said Chris.

"What about when *Melissa* was there? Or both *Melissa* and *I* were there?"

"It was better just with you alone," said Chris.

"*Was* better?" said Betsy.

"*Is* better," said Chris.

Betsy removed her brother's hand from inside her T-shirt. She kissed his wrist, his knuckles. She sucked on his fingers and licked them (especially the soft skin between his fingers).

"I'll give you twelve years to stop that," said Chris.

"Ohhhhh . . . I'm all *wet* . . . "

Chris smiled. He glanced in the rearview mirror, and Lee still appeared to be asleep in the back seat.

"Do you ever think of home?" said Betsy.

"Never," said Chris.

"Me neither," said Betsy.

"Then why did you bring it up?" said Chris.

"I don't know," said Betsy. "Maybe just because it was something to *say*. I mean, maybe just because this morning has been so far out I can't quite—"

"There's more to come," said Chris.

"I *know*," said Betsy.

"And remember, we *enjoyed* it, didn't we?" said Chris. "We were scared shitless, but then we got to giggling, like maybe little kiddypoos playing with wooden trains. Lee is right, isn't he?"

"About what?" said Betsy.

"About how it's all coming down. About the readings."

"*The Flegenheimer Testament?*"

"Yes."

"Do you believe in *The Flegenheimer Testament?*" said Betsy.

"As much as I believe in anything," said Chris.

"Me too," said Betsy.

"I hope somebody tries to hassle us," said Chris.

"Me too," said Betsy.

"Bang, bang," said Chris.

Sniggering, Betsy Moss rolled her tongue into a tube and licked her brother's ear.

The ten thousand dollars lasted a little less than six months. When he was down to his last twenty dollars, Lee visited a novelty store in Elko, Nevada, and bought a large and realistic cap pistol. The store was full of all sorts of interesting artifacts, including whoopee cushions, onyx ashtrays and bookends, little windup puppies and kittens, cowboy hats, jodhpurs, spurs, souvenir booklets, postcards, coloring books, belts, fans, pillows, rubber dollbabies that pissed, fringed jerkins, catnip mice and a large collection of masks. Some of the masks were of famous persons such as Racquel Welch, Bob Hope, Dennis the Menace, Leonard Nimoy and Richard M. Nixon. The Nixon masks were a dollar apiece, but they intrigued Lee, and so he bought one. That night he used the cap pistol to rob a Shell station in Winnemucca. But he did not wear the Nixon mask. Perhaps he should have, but he wanted to save the thing for something special. He clubbed the attendant on the head and left him unconscious in the women's room. There was only fortytwo dollars in the cash register, but at least it represented a start, and after all, tomorrow was another day. Lee drove north into Oregon, and he spent the next night in a Holiday Inn just off Interstate 5. He took three showers, and he ducked out at four in the morning without paying the bill. He had given the clerk a false name and false license number. After all, how many times did motel clerks check license numbers? Hell, it was so easy to jack off those people the wonder was Lee hadn't done it all along. But he had not. Until the ten thousand had been exhausted, he had paid all his tabs. He was not quite sure why. Perhaps to avoid harassment—which was the only answer that made any sense. After leaving Mamaroneck, he had spent most of the six months in the west, and he had gone firstclass all the way, sleeping in only the best motels and eating in only the best restaurants and searching out only the best head. And gradually, as the traveler's cheques diminished and as the, ah, Moment of Insolvency approached, Lee became aware of a paradox. Driving all aratcheting and arattling across the scarred highway earth, through the great blank delirious prairie nights, with the Impala expiring by slow degrees, compounded of dirty pistons and a clogged fuel line and bald tires, he became aware of the significance of his approaching poverty, of the challenge it presented, and it occurred to him that finally he had discovered his life's calling, the *future* that had been urged on him so earnestly by his parents, and he said to himself: I shall rip off the world. I shall rape the planet. I shall set up a tent on Times Square, and the cocksuckers will line up for miles. And he said to himself: Whatever it is I need, I shall obtain. So then, when Lee Pike coldcocked that attendant in the Shell station in Winnemucca, Nevada, he was only continuing the pursuit of his destiny, and it was free of *philosophy* or *reason* or *moral pretense,* and he rejoiced in it. And the words clattered truthfully, irresistibly: *There are only ten of us; there are ten million fighting somewhere of you, so get your onions up and we will throw up the truce flag.* He traveled up and down the Pacific shore, and he kept body and soul together through burglaries and petty robberies, and he told himself: Is the FBI going to put me on its Ten Most Wanted List because I rob a Texaco station in Salinas of eleven dollars, plus six bottles of Pepsi and two dozen sparkplugs? The dude, the attendant, had eyes that were like pieplates, and he stained his crotch with piss, but what the hell, I didn't really hurt him, and the cops have better things to do than chase down some halfass stickup artist who uses a cap pistol. *Let him harness himself to you and then bother you. The sidewalk was in trouble and the bears were in trouble and I broke it up.* He always tried to keep himself at least a hundred dollars ahead, and nearly every night he lounged on clean motel sheets and watched color television and slept heavily and well. And he was forever taking showers. In the midst of life, we are in corruption: *Mother, don't tear, don't rip. That is something that shouldn't be spoken about. Please, Mother, you pick me up now.* Oregon and Washington then, south back into Nevada, and Lee shacked up for three weeks in Las Vegas with a showgirl who was six feet two inches tall. She was blond, and she had a lisp, and her name was Cheryl Potts. She told him he was the most cruel man she'd ever met, and she told him she loved his cruelty. She begged him to beat her, and she told him her mother (whom she had loved dearly and whom she still loved dearly) had beaten her every morning of the first seventeen years of her life, and so Lee said: "All right. I wouldn't want to disappoint you." And he hit her. And he banged her skull against the floor. And she rewarded him with magnificent head. And she said: "All people keep a sort of balance sheet in their memory, you know? And if they have something *coming* to them, then they'd just better *get* it. Otherwise, it's Wig City and the men with butterfly nets." *Oh, sir, get the doll a rofting. You can play jacks and girls do that with a soft ball and do tricks with it. It takes all events into consideration.* Lee gave Cheryl Potts a heroic beating the night he left her (and he was certain it was enough to send her to the hospital, although he was wise enough not to stick around), and then he drove down to Los Angeles, where in March of 1974 he more or less liberated Melissa Scowcroft and Chris Moss and Betsy Moss from DeLong Hughes. And it was literally by accident. *It takes all events into consideration. No. No. And it is no. It is confused, and it says no.* He had been to Barstow, where within fifteen minutes he had robbed a candy store, an Exxon station and a diner, and he had driven straight through to East LA without really giving it too much thought. The three quick robberies—all accomplished with his trusty cap pistol—had been about as kicky an experience as he had had since the day he had murdered the house, and he had driven all the way from the desert to East LA with a sort of song in his heart, tra la, and it had been so loud it even had pushed away the clanking wheezes and farts of the Impala. Goddamn the Impala anyway. He should have gotten rid of it long before then (it had nearly one hundred fifty thousand miles on the odometer—and in less than two years), but he felt sentimental about the fucking thing. It had been a gift from his revered mother and father, and one did not throw away such a gift too easily. It would have been like wiping one's ass with some treasured family heirloom. And, beyond all that, the car was full of stuff Lee had stolen . . . or even, in some extreme cases, bought. The Nixon mask, for instance, not to mention two portable television sets, eleven transistor radios, twelve adding machines, three cases of stereo equipment (including diamond needles), six cases of Texas Instrument pocket calculators, at least a hundred cans of everything from peanuts to Chinese noodles to baked beans to Hunt's Tomato Paste, two large cartons stuffed with furs and dresses, nine baskets filled with bottles of French wines—plus who knew *what* all else gathered from the more than forty robberies and burglaries Lee had committed since the day he had murdered the house. And so, with all the cargo in the Impala, it was no simple thing to abandon the old car and rip off another. He would need a lot of time to transfer all the stuff—and it was for that reason he had been putting off doing something about the car situation. But then, that night in East LA, he had his happy encounter with DeLong Hughes, and the problem was solved . . . at least temporarily. Lee was driving along, minding his own business, tra la, tra la, exulting in his three Barstow robberies, telling himself that he had been however briefly a one-man crime wave, when the Impala was bumped at a boulevard stop by a '71 Lincoln Pimpmobile with wire wheels, a TV aerial and perhaps seventy coats of Simoniz. The Pimpmobile loosened the Impala's rear bumper, and Lee was quickly out of his car. The driver of the Pimpmobile was a large grinning black man, and if he wasn't a pimp, then corn didn't have tassels and ears. *A boy has never wept nor dashed a thousand kim. Did you hear me?* Lee didn't want to get into any sort of hassle with this dude. Not with all that stuff in the Impala. This was Low Profile Time, and that was the truth. Lee walked toward the black man, and the black man came out of the Pimpmobile, and Lee looked at his loosened rear bumper and said to him: "Shit, man. No problem." The black man squinted at Lee. This was maybe Superpimp, and he wanted Lee to know it. He said: "Who you callin man, man?" And Lee said: "I meant no offense, sir." And the blackman said: *Sir?* You call me *sir?*" And Lee said: "Yes sir." And the black man said: "You some jive turkey." And Lee said: "Thank you very much, sir." The black man was dressed all in white, and the brim of his hat covered perhaps half a block. He hunkered down and looked at the place where the Pimpmobile's front bumper had knocked Lee's rear bumper loose. He straightened and said: "You shouldn't of stopped so quick, motherfucker." And Lee said: "I'm very sorry, sir." And the black man moved a step toward Lee and said: "What sort of fuckin puton *is* this?" And Lee said: "I don't know what you're talking about, sir. I'm simply saying that I'm sorry I stopped so quickly." The black man shook his head. "They more to this than meets the eye," he said. Then a '72 Thunderbird pulled up next to them. Two more blacks were inside. The one on the passenger's side leaned out his window and said to the man in white: "Hey, DeLong, what's happenin?" And DeLong grinned and said: "Archie my man, this here is the politest honky in the world. He got more respect for us poor colored folks than you would rightly believe." Then, to Lee: "Ain't that right, Massa?" He was cackling now. He inclined his head toward the back seat of the Pimpmobile. "I ought to add you to my stock," he said. He motioned to three shadows in the back seat. "Hey, you three! Come on out!" The door opened, and three young whites emerged—hippies all of them, two girls and a boy. The boy and one of the girls were plump and curlyhaired, and they appeared to be twins. The other girl was tall and blond and quite beautiful. She wore a white blouse, white mini and white boots. "Meet some of my livestock," said DeLong. "The fat boy is Chris, an he is my own *private* stock, if you know what I mean." DeLong laughed, and so did the two dudes in the '72 Thunderbird. "The fat girl is his sister Betsy, an they like each other a whole lot, dig? The other one is Melissa, and she *choice*, man, choice like Joyce. Her an Betsy an sometimes Chris, dependin on the kind of people come around, they work for me, an I got six other chicks workin for me, an I their daddy, an they good to their daddy, an they work hard for their daddy, an how come . . . *how come, man, how come you so fuckin polite?* It been my experience a cat when he so polite he either scared shitless or he got somethin to hide. And *you* don't look like *you* scared shitless, dig?" DeLong turned to the '72 Thunderbird and said to Archie: "Check out whitey's piece of shit." Nodding, Archie came out of the Thunderbird. He pushed Lee out of the way and climbed inside the Impala. A moment later he was rooting around in the back seat, and then he said: "Holy shit, DeLong! I think maybe your buddy here has ripped off the whole state of Utah, you dig?"

Chris Moss figured that maybe the best thing about being with Lee Pike was the feeling of cleanliness it gave a person. He'd never taken so many showers and baths in his life. Cleanliness was maybe more important to Lee Pike than anything in the world—except *The Flegenheimer Testament.*

"Penny," said Betsy. She was not licking his ear now. She simply was cuddling. One of her hands rested against his right knee.

"Clean," said Chris.

"Clean?" said Betsy.

"Yes," said Chris. The car was stuck behind a coal truck, and there was a double yellow line, and so Chris could not pass. Had he done so, it would have been a betrayal of the AAA, and he did not like to think of himself as being that sort of person. He said: "Lee has made us clean. When we were with DeLong, we were *dirty,* remember?"

"Yes," said Betsy.

"I mean dirty in the *spiritual* sense," said Chris.

"Yes," said Betsy.

"But Lee keeps us clean," said Chris.

"Yes," said Betsy.

"And he knows what he's talking about," said Chris.

"Yes," said Betsy.

That was the last Lee ever saw of his Impala and his television sets, radios, pocket calculators and all the rest of his stuff. But he still came out ahead on the deal . . . thanks to the reluctant generosity of DeLong Hughes. There was a quick whispered conference between De-Long Hughes and Archie, and then Archie jumped into the Impala and drove away. Lee had enough sense simply to stand there. DeLong motioned to the driver of the '72 Thunderbird to split. "We don't want the world thinkin this some sort of fuckin convention," he said to the driver. The '72 Thunderbird blasted away, and then DeLong motioned to the plump boy, Chris, to help this here little old ofay *thief* and *ripoff artist* into the back seat of the Pimpmobile. Lee was squeezed between the plump boy and the plump boy's twin sister, and the girl named Melissa sat in the front with DeLong. The inside of the Pimpmobile had a smell of God knows what—perfumes, pomades, grass, maybe even a little glue. De-Long kept up a monologue as the Pimpmobile crossed and recrossed the streets of East LA in no particular pattern. He said: "You just relax an be cool, you little white fucker you. We don't none of us look to do you no harm. It's just that I like somethin about the way you talk. I mean, you so polite an all, an yet you got a car with the *axles* about to bust because of all the crap you ripped off. What you tryin to be? Some sort of super crim-inal? Old Willie Sutton, he ever hear of you, he bury his head in pig shit out of mortification, right? So what happens? You have a little old *traffic accident* with your mellow daddy, DeLong Hughes, an it all goes down the fuckin drain. Because I got a late news bulletin for you, direct from Channel 4 an Mister Tom Snyder, an that news bulletin it say: *Hold every-thin! Ripoff artist ripped off! An he ain't gettin one fuckin cent for none of that stuff!* How you like that, Mister Polite? Huh? You tell me, dig?" And Lee said: "Well, sir, I *have* had better days." And DeLong said: "What about this *night,* man? What you think goin to happen to you *now?*" And Lee said: "I don't really have the slightest idea." And DeLong said: "What's you name?" And Lee said: "Lee." And DeLong said: "*Lee?* Like in *Robert E.* Lee?" And Lee said: "Yes sir." And DeLong said: "Can you give this here old jungle bunny a rebel yell?" And Lee said: "No sir. I am from Mamaroneck, New York, and I know nothing about the rebel yell." And DeLong said: "You sure do look like a cracker to *me.* That blond hair an all. An you got a funnylookin head, you know that?" And Lee said: "So I've been told." And DeLong said: "You so polite I bet you don't like to fuck." And Lee said: "No sir. You're wrong there. I do very much like to fuck." And DeLong said: "How about *bein* fucked?" And Lee said: "Well, sir, if a person is going to be raped, it's my belief he might as well relax and enjoy it.'' And DeLong said: ''Like tonight, with me rippin off your wheels?'' And Lee said: ''Yes sir. Exactly.'' And DeLong said: ''You ever been fucked by a man?'' And Lee said: ''No sir.'' And DeLong said: ''You think you might like it?'' And Lee said: ''I don't really know, sir.'' And DeLong said: ''You ever sucked cock?'' And Lee said: ''No sir.'' And DeLong said: ''Old Chris back there with you, *he* sucks cock. An he *likes* it, too—don't you, Chris honey?'' There was no reply from Chris, and so DeLong spoke again: *''Answer your daddy.''* And Chris made a hollow noise in his throat. *''Answer your daddy,''* said DeLong. And, clearing his throat, Chris said: ''I . . . yeah, I like it fine . . .'' And DeLong said: ''Almost as good as fuckin your sister?'' And Chris said: ''Ah . . . that's right . . .'' A guffaw from DeLong, and then he said to Lee: ''This here is one nice happy fambly. Everone fucks everone else, an the chicks they trick long an good but they still got some of the old juice left over for they daddy, an it all makes for the good life. An I give them grass, an me, I got a little bitty habit bout the size of a rabbit that I *indulge* from time to time, but it ain't what you call a *governin principle,* you understan? In my life, man, the governin principles is food, good whisky, music, threads . . . an findin places where my big old cock can feel all cozy an at home.'' He looked at Melissa. ''Right, baby?'' And Melissa quickly said: ''Right.'' And DeLong said to Lee: ''This here Melissa is the wet dream of every white man an boy in the world, but all she cares about is her daddy, an bringing home the bread to her daddy, an bein nice to her daddy so he don't maybe punch her out an spread her across the floor like she a piece of warm shit. An ain't that right, Melissa?'' And Melissa said: ''Right.'' And she squirmed closer to DeLong and kissed him on the mouth, and he laughed and said: ''Don't distract the driver, sweet little cunt. They a time an a place for everthin.'' Then, laughing some more, DeLong said to Lee: ''Hey, Mister Robert E. Lee or whatever you name is, you an me an faggy Chris an these two chicks, we goin to have a party. We goin to my place an we going to drink an smoke an fuck an suck an listen to good music . . . what you think of that?'' And Lee said: ''Well, since I can't think of much else to do, what with my car gone, and all my stuff gone, I'm game if you are.'' And DeLong said: *''Game?* Man, I am *game.* I *invented* game.'' And the Pimpmobile made an abrupt U-turn. Lee had no idea where they were, and he didn't suppose it really mattered. All that *did* matter was that he had to straighten out a few things with this nigger sonofabitch. And he said to himself: Poor old Rastus here has walked into a buzzsaw, and before I'm finished with him I'm going to turn him about nine shades of white. And then Lee smiled a little, but he covered his

mouth with a hand so no one would notice. DeLong parked the Pimpmobile in the basement of a large and relatively new apartment building on
Wilshire Boulevard. "I keep comin up in the worl like you wouldn't believe," he said to Lee, grasping him by an arm as soon as they all had
piled out of the car. The twins and Melissa preceded them toward the elevator, and DeLong spoke quietly to Lee, telling him: "They *shit,* them
three. Real *nothin.* But *you,* I can tell by the way you talk, *you* ain't no
fuckin little *mouse* or *bunnyrabbit,* am I right? *Course* I'm right. A man
don't get to be *DeLong Hughes* by bein *wrong,* you dig?" A nudge. "So
let's us just have our little party, an maybe you an me, I mean, maybe you
an me we got a little bit of a *future* together . . . you got you *brains,* an I
think I'm startin to like you a whole lot . . . I mean, it's not like you're
just another pretty face . . ." Another laugh from DeLong Hughes, and
then he and Lee and Melissa and the twins crowded into the elevator.
Grinning, DeLong opened Melissa's blouse and exposed her breasts.
"Honey," he said. "Suckin stuff forever." The elevator stopped at the
seventh floor, and Melissa tried to close her blouse, but DeLong said to
her: "Cool it." The door opened automatically, and they encountered an
elderly white man who was holding a white standard poodle on a leash.
He made a strangled sound when he saw Melissa's breasts, and DeLong
said to him: "Hey Mister Kapstein baby, what's the fuckin world comin
to, huh?" And DeLong pushed the man aside, and laughed. "Shit," he
said, "once you let a nigger in the buildin, the whole fuckin place falls
apart, right? No *discipline,* right?" He still had hold of Lee's arm. He
steered Lee down a hallway. "I'm the only nigger in the buildin," he told
Lee, "an it gives Mister Kapstein an the rest of them fuckin *hemorrhoids*
just to *think* about it, but they ain't much they can do, seein as how the
people who own the buildin, the *company,* that is, got sort of a connection
with old DeLong. I mean, the company that owns the buildin is also an at
the same time the company that old DeLong kind of, ah, works for, you
now? Oh, it sure is a complicated world all right." He unlocked a door
and pushed Lee inside an apartment. Melissa and the twins followed.
"Me an Chris live here," said DeLong, "an the girls they live right up the
hall on this here same floor, which makes it nice an cozy, dig?" He made
an expansive movement with an arm. He took off his hat with a flourish,
and Lee was a little surprised to see that there was some gray in DeLong's
hair, and even the suggestion of a bald spot. DeLong walked around what
was the living room. He pointed at his stereo, at the enlarged photographs
of Isaac Hayes and Ron O'Neal and Pam Grier and Kareem the Dream
Abdul-Jabbar, and he pointed at the leopard rugs and the African statuary
and the low leather chairs, and he pointed at the brass doorknobs, and he

took Lee into the bedroom and showed him the enormous bed, and he said: "Man, we ain't none of us doin nothin but playin a part, an me, I am the main *man*, baby, the main *pimp*, baby, more *bad* an better *hung* than the best dream any MacArthur Park cocksucker ever had in his fuckin *life*, an you got to believe me, Lee baby, when I tell you I am *good* at my role, an I get *respect*, an I whang an bang *who* I want *when* I want, you *dig?*" And DeLong gave Lee a shove, sending him sprawling across the bed. Behind DeLong, the twins and Melissa were standing in the doorway. They neither moved nor spoke. DeLong flipped Lee on his belly and pulled down Lee's jeans, at the same time dropping his white trousers and jumping astride Lee. "*You mine now, baybee!*" shouted DeLong, and Lee felt DeLong's prick rub him between the legs and begin to force open the cheeks of his ass. Lee tensed himself. He felt DeLong's lips against the back of his neck, and DeLong was murmuring: "Hey there, little darlin, you sure got a kinky haid, but I want you *anyhow*, on account of you're so *polite* an *smart* an sort of *sweet* an—" And here DeLong was interrupted. Lee gave a great roar and twisted over and brought both his fists against DeLong's throat, and DeLong gagged and fell back. And Lee was on top of him. And then DeLong had a knife. The blade sprung from the handle, and DeLong grimaced and said: "You shouldn't of done that motherfucker . . . you comelickin cunt you . . ." And Lee kicked De-Long in the face, using the heels of both his shoes, and DeLong tumbled off the bed, and the knife skidded across the room's heavy zebra-striped carpet. He tried to crawl after the knife, but his trousers were bunched around his ankles, and he could not move very fast. In the meantime, Lee kicked off his own jeans. He leaped over DeLong and scooped up the knife and made a jabbing movement with it toward DeLong's eyes. It did not touch DeLong's eyes, but DeLong screamed and covered them anyway. "*You cocksucker!*" shouted Lee. "*You nigger faggot piece of shit out of a whore's ass!*" And he leaped at DeLong, and he waved the knife and DeLong scrabbled backward toward a wall. And DeLong looked toward the door. "Chris!" he shouted. "Goddamn you, help me, baby!" But Chris neither moved nor spoke. And the girls neither moved nor spoke. And Lee kicked DeLong neatly in the balls, and when DeLong was down rolled him on his stomach. And said to DeLong: "Yes indeed my dear friend, we *are* going to fuck—don't worry your head about that. Only *I* am going to be the fuck*er*, and you are going to be the fuck*ee*. And Lee's prick was so hard it could have dug a trough from there to Sac-ramento. And with one great thrust he shoved it up DeLong's ass. And DeLong screamed. And DeLong bled. And Lee said: "Hey there, littl' darling, you sure got a kinky head, but I want you anyhow . . ." And

Lee, who never had fucked a man in the ass or even had been blown by a man, industriously fucked DeLong in the ass, and DeLong whimpered and flapped, and finally actually passed out. Later, Melissa stripped DeLong and used sheets to tie DeLong into a spreadeagled position on the bed. Chris and Betsy came forward and told Lee he could have them any time he wanted them, and Melissa said she loved him and never would love anyone else. Smiling, Lee thanked them all for their kind attention, and then he turned to DeLong. He slapped DeLong awake. "Listen," he told him. "You owe me money, you cocksucker, and you owe me a car, and for your sake I hope we settle your obligations with the smallest amount of fuss." DeLong only whimpered. Lee walked to the foot of the bed. "Just to show you I'm not giving you a line of shit," he said, and he used the knife to make a small incision across the instep of DeLong's left foot. It barely drew blood, but it did make DeLong yelp. Lee nodded and returned to the head of the bed. "Now listen to me, you scumbag. You made a very costly error tonight . . . as perhaps you are beginning to realize." He leaned over the pillow in order to make sure that the squirming DeLong heard every word. He said: "You should never have humiliated me. Perhaps you now know why. Because, you see, I am multiplying my humiliation by ten—and I am revisiting it on you. But hear this. It's not because I hate you. Why should I waste my time hating a scumbag? It's just that you are so fucking *gross* and *stupid* and, worst of all, such a goddamned *cliché*. A white suit and white hat, for God's sake. A Pimpmobile, for God's sake. The poor man's Superfly, right? Well, let me tell you something, poor man's Superfly. You are not *Superfly*. You are not *shit*. You are a *nigger,* which is *worse* than shit, *right,* nigger? And tonight, nigger, I am going to tear you down, and you will be naked and alone, and this bed will be sprinkled with the drops of blood that come out of your asshole . . . which means these are your last moments as a human being, nigger. And from now on, you dipshit you, you call me Massa." DeLong's head moved from side to side. Lee slapped him. He looked back at Melissa and the twins, and they giggled. He sent Betsy into the bathroom to fetch a warm wet washrag. She brought it to him, and he stuffed it in DeLong's mouth. Lee went through DeLong's wallet and came up with more than seven hundred dollars and perhaps a dozen credit cards. There were four rings on DeLong's fingers. Lee had Melissa wash the fingers so the rings could be slid off. Chris showed Lee a small box in a drawer of an immense white dresser next to DeLong's bed. The box was locked, but Lee smashed it open. It yielded more than a thousand dollars in bills of small denominations. Chris nodded toward the spreadeagled DeLong and said: "It's what he calls his petty cash." Lee smiled. He went to DeLong and removed the washrag from DeLong's mouth. DeLong groaned a little, and Lee said to him: "I am your Massa, correct?" DeLong did not move. Lee slapped him. DeLong wept. "Say it," said Lee. "No . . ." said DeLong. Lee seized the knife and drew a line across DeLong's forehead, just above his eyes. It was a shallow cut, but some blood did run down into DeLong's eyes and along the sides of his nose. And, choking, DeLong said: "Massa . . ." And Lee said: "Thank you very much." He jammed the washrag back inside DeLong's mouth and turned still smiling to Chris. "Is there any more money?" he asked Chris. "Not that I know of," said Chris. Lee glanced at the girls, who were standing in the doorway. "Any that *you* know of?" he asked them. They shook their heads no, but Melissa said: "Why don't you ask your nigger?" And Lee smacked his forehead. "Ah, why didn't *I* think of that?" he said, outright *grinning* now—and widely. He removed the washrag from DeLong's mouth. "Anything more of any value we should know about?" he said. DeLong's head moved from side to side, and now some of the blood had trickled down into his eyes. He blinked. He made small trapped noises. "You sound like a fat animal in a thin hole," Lee told him. He slapped DeLong. "Right?" he said. " . . . right," said DeLong. "Right *what?*" said Lee. "Right . . . Massa," said DeLong. "Excellent," said Lee. Again he jammed the washrag into DeLong's mouth. He turned to Chris and the girls and said: "I have a confession to make. I'm really enjoying all this. And I'm not much the sort to enjoy things too terribly much. It's not cool to get such a kick, is it?" He learned from Chris that DeLong had a second car parked in the basement—a '73 Olds. The keys were on the ring in DeLong's pocket. "Good," said Lee. "We won't want to be driving around in the Pimpmobile." He rooted around in DeLong's discarded trousers and came up with the keys. He tossed them to Chris and said: "I hereby appoint you the keeper of the keys." Chris grinned and hugged his sister. His eyes were moist. "That . . . ah, that mean we can go with you?" he said to Lee. And Lee said: "Is that what you want?" And Chris said: "Yes. I mean, otherwise DeLong would . . . well, you know . . ." And Lee said: "Would I be your daddy?" And Chris said: "Sure." Lee looked at Betsy. "You want me to be your new daddy?" he asked her. Betsy quickly nodded. Lee looked at Melissa. "How about you?" he said. *"Yes,"* she said, nodding. She came to him and tried to kiss him on the mouth, but he pushed her back. There was no expression on her face. It was as though she had not tried to kiss him at all. He said: "My family. A whole new family of my own. Only if you expect me to be a Charlie Manson, forget it. I am not *Jesus Christ,* and I am not *Hitler,* you dig?" He glared at them, and they quickly nodded. He said: "I am nada and dada and the floor caving in, all right?'' Their faces were blank. He said: "The human race is an accident of molecules, nothing more, and I want you to remember that." He grinned. "So now what we're going to do is take old DeLong's molecules and sort of split them apart, you know? And the first thing we're going to do is murder his clothes and his apartment." Their faces still were blank. He said: "It's kicky. You just wait and see." He pointed to Betsy. He said: "You go into the kitchen and destroy everything that is destructible, dig?" Then, to Melissa: "The living room—records, pictures, everything." Then, to Chris: "You help the girls. Get knives from the kitchen. Use whatever is practical and handy. Myself, I'll stay here in the bedroom with our nice docile little nigger and see how much more blood he has to give for Massa. And then I'm going to take myself a nice warm bath."

Lee emerged from his brief, efficient, uncluttered nap just as the car was approaching a small white roadside sign that said

PARADISE FALLS
CORPORATION LIMIT

He sat up and rubbed his eyes. Traffic was heavier now, and he told Chris to turn on the radio. Regular programming had been interrupted for a speech by Nixon, who was saying farewell to the people in the White House. Nixon's voice had a peeled and desperately shredded quality. Lee checked the pistols again. Everything appeared to be in order. He grinned. Nixon's shredded voice came almost in a whimper. Lee looked around. The car was at the top of a hill, and the street was flanked by two cemeteries. On an impulse, Lee told Chris to turn into the cemetery on the left. The car passed under an arch that had the words OAK HILL CEME- TERY carved on its stone facing. Of the two cemeteries, this appeared to be the older. Lee grinned at the tombstones and the mausoleums. All the car windows were open, and so Nixon's voice carried out to the tomb- stones and the mausoleums. Gravel made quiet noises under the car's tires. Lee patted Chris and Betsy on their heads, but he said nothing, and neither did they. They simply listened to Nixon and looked at the grass and the trees and the hillsides and the tombstones and the mausoleums. It really was a magnificent August day, and then the people in the White House were applauding Nixon. Lee had a fine hardon. He saw a squirrel, and it switched its tail, and it ate something out of its forepaws. Again he grinned. The car moved around a bend in the gravel drive, and then the largest of all the mausoleums loomed up. "Hey," said Lee. "Wow." This great and heroically flatulent mausoleum of mausoleums was in a sort of Victorian Parthenon architectural style, and the name WELLS was stamped on its immense bronze door. Above the door and circling the building was a frieze of angels and lambs, and the phrase GONE BUT NOT FORGOTTEN was included in the frieze. Lee told Chris to stop the car. "We need to rest for a moment," he said to Chris and Betsy. "We need to prepare ourselves." A newsman from CBS was reporting that there were tears in the eyes of Mrs Nixon, and Lee said: "I wouldn't be a bit surprised." Then he told Chris to turn off the fucking radio, and they all got out of the car. Lee led them in a walk completely around the building, and GONE BUT NOT FORGOTTEN was repeated in the frieze on all four sides. Still grinning, Lee motioned Chris and Betsy to seat themselves on the stone steps at the entrance to this splendid and stupid and impossible mausoleum. He paced in front of them, and he lectured them, and he was aware that his hardon was a glory. He moved his right arm in a grand gesture, and he said: "Ozymandias *lives!*"

Chris and Betsy frowned at him. They clearly had no idea who or what Ozymandias was, but they said nothing. In the past six months or so, they had become more frightened of Lee than they ever had been of DeLong Hughes. And Lee knew this. And rejoiced in it. "You dig?" he said.

Chris leaned forward a little. "I . . . look, Lee, we're sorry, but we never heard of Ozywhoosis . . ."

"*Ozymandias!*" said Lee. "By Percy Bysshe Shelley, born 1792, died 1822." He hesitated, placed his right hand over his chest in a melodramatically Napoleonic pose. He grinned at Chris and Betsy. He grinned at the mausoleum and its angels and lambs. He grinned at the August sunlight and the trees and the hillsides and the tombstones and the squirrels. He said: "*I met a traveller from an antique land who said: 'Two vast and trunkless legs of stone stand in the desert. Near them on the sand, half sunk, a shattered visage lies, whose frown and wrinkled lip and sneer of cold command tell that its sculptor well those passions read which yet survive, stamped on those lifeless things, the hand that mocked them and the heart that fed. And on the pedestal these words appear: MY NAME IS OZYMANDIAS, KING OF KINGS: LOOK ON MY WORKS, YE MIGHTY, AND DESPAIR! Nothing beside remains. Round the decay of that colossal wreck, boundless and bare, the lone and level sands stretch far away.'*" Now Lee's grin was more of a grimace. "End of poem," he said. He advanced on Chris. "Do you dig it?"

"I . . . I think so," said Chris.

Lee placed his hands on his hips. He stood over Chris and Betsy, and his stiff prick was making an enormous bulge in his jeans. He looked down at Betsy and said: "Explain it."

". . . bullshit?" said Betsy, blinking a little.

"What?" said Lee.

"He's saying that everything is bullshit?" said Betsy.

"Are you asking me or telling me?" said Lee.

". . . telling you," said Betsy, flinching.

"You *got* it!" said Lee. He pointed at the frieze. "Everything *is* gone. Everything *is* forgotten. Everything is *bullshit.* Everything is the way Arthur Flegenheimer says it is. Do you know who this Wells was? *No!* Does anybody know who this Wells was? *No!* It's all bullshit and delirium, right?"

". . . right," said Betsy.

Lee looked at Chris.

". . . right," said Chris.

Lee cupped his genitals in both hands. He reached down then and seized Chris and Betsy by their hair and pressed their faces against his crotch. He said: "Do not respond this time. Simply listen to the words." He blinked at the sun. He'd never felt so exalted. This was better than being blown. This was better than murdering houses or apartments or cutting up pimps till they almost died. This was even better than the target practice of an hour or so ago. Here, in front of this bullshit memorial to some hayseed Ozymandias, it all came together, and Lee recited the sacred Flegenheimer text. He spoke quietly, and after a time Chris and Betsy got to weeping quietly. At the conclusion of his quiet recitation, Lee stroked their heads and felt their weeping, but they made no sounds, and he was proud of them. He thought of nada and dada, of destruction, of dead children, of Ruby murdering Oswald again and again until all the videotape in the universe turned to runny green shit. He thought of Mrs Nixon's tears, of Charlie Manson and his stupid philosophy. And finally he said to Chris and Betsy: "We are beyond philosophy. Today we shall perhaps pull out a few floorboards and knock off some shingles and pound some cracks in the sidewalk." He stepped back from Chris and Betsy, releasing their heads. "Now we must pray," he said. He looked at Betsy. She and Chris knelt humbly. *"I don't want harmony; I want harmony,"* said Lee.

"Flegenheimer," said Betsy.

"Let him harness himself to you and then bother you," said Lee.

"Flegenheimer," said Chris.

"The sidewalk was in trouble and the bears were in trouble and I broke it up," said Lee.

"Flegenheimer," said Betsy.

"Mother is the best bet and don't let Satan draw you too fast," said Lee.

"Delirium," said Chris. *"Delirium and amen."*

"A boy has never wept nor dashed a thousand kim," said Lee.

"Delirium," said Betsy. *"Delirium and amen."*

"French Canadian bean soup," said Lee.

"Delirium," said Chris. *"Delirium and amen."*

Lee motioned to Chris and Betsy. "You may rise," he said.

They stood up. Their faces were damp.

"Do you understand?" Lee asked them. "Do you *really* understand?"

Chris took Betsy by a hand. He nodded. Then Betsy nodded.

"Very good," said Lee.

Chris and Betsy were unable to speak. Lee led them back to the car. Chris wiped his eyes with a sleeve of his T-shirt. Then he was able to drive. Lee climbed into the back, and Betsy slid close to Chris and kissed his neck. The car moved slowly away from the tomb of the hayseed Ozymandias, and Lee told Chris to turn on the radio again.

Lee was not perfect, and he freely admitted this—at least to himself. For instance, he had a weakness for symbols . . . so he had Chris drive the Olds directly across all of Arizona and nearly all of New Mexico—to Las Cruces. They went directly to JUANITA'S SUPERETTE, where they all piled out of the car. Lee's arms and back were stiff, and Melissa was leeching onto him, and finally . . . as they walked toward JUANITA'S SUPERETTE . . . he pulled himself away from her. He had not told his children why it was necessary they all visit JUANITA'S SUPERETTE. He *had,* though, told them not to question his judgment. And the tone of his voice had been enough to shut them up. He felt sweaty and gummy. He needed a shower. He needed two or perhaps even three showers. He pulled open the door to JUANITA'S SUPERETTE, and his children followed him inside. He was delighted to see the same fat old woman with the moustache—and she was sitting behind the cash register just as she had been the last time. He went behind the counter and said to his children: "Watch this." He knocked the fat old woman off her stool, and she slid to the floor, and he punched open the register, but this time he came up with barely forty dollars. He looked down at the old woman and said: "What's the matter, *mamacita?* The recession?" She blinked at him, and he did not believe she recognized him, and a lesser person probably would have been infuriated. But Lee was not infuriated. He simply smiled, then led his children outside and back to the car. Later, as the Olds rolled east along Interstate 10 toward El Paso, he said: "That place was where, in the largest sense I know, I lost my virginity. And beyond that you need know no more." And they all nodded. And Melissa snuggled close to him and assured him that she and Chris and Betsy would not ask him any unnecessary questions—not after what they had seen him do to DeLong. And Lee said: "Fine. I believe you. *And*—because I *do* believe you—I have riches in store for you . . . of the mind and the body and even perhaps the spirit, if there is such a thing." And then began the instruction in *The Flegenheimer Testament,* as Lee and his children wandered gradually eastward in one stolen car after another, with the children smoking what was left of DeLong's excellent grass and then buying more on just about any street corner they encountered, and Lee gathered them to him and told them: "Arthur Flegenheimer was born in New York City on August 6, 1902. His father owned a saloon. Arthur was a tough little fellow, and he became involved in the rackets in the Bronx. This was after his father had vanished. His mother was scandalized by Arthur's gangster activity, but there really was nothing she could do about it. When Prohibition came along, he went into the speakeasy business, and later he owned a fleet of trucks that carried beer from New Jersey into New York City. He eventually became involved in policy, corrupt unions and other really heavy activities. The district attorney was a man named Thomas E. Dewey, and he set out to get Arthur Flegenheimer. This Dewey became a real bother to Arthur Flegenheimer, and so Arthur Flegenheimer decided he would have to kill Dewey. Unfortunately for Arthur Flegenheimer, there were other gangsters who felt that assassinating Dewey would turn on too much of what in those days they called *heat*. It was determined then that Arthur Flegenheimer—and not Dewey—would be assassinated. And so, on the evening of October 23, 1935, Flegenheimer and three of his pals . . . Lulu Rosenkrantz, Abe Landau and Aba Daba Berman . . . were gunned down in a place called the Palace Chop House, in Newark, New Jersey. Flegenheimer was shot just as he emerged from the men's room, but he did not die until shortly before nine o'clock the following evening. He lay in the hospital, and he went into a delirium that was recorded in its entirety by a police stenographer. Flegenheimer's temperature was nearly one hundred six degrees, and yet his words . . . ah, they were the coolest. So listen good. Listen to the cool. Listen to the voice of the future. Arthur Flegenheimer his name was, and he was better known as Dutch Schultz, and from him came the exact contents of a human mind, the exact *meaningless* and *farcical* and *cool* essence of what we all live with every day of our fucking lives. I call it *The Flegenheimer Testament,* and you and I will create a litany from it . . . just the four of us . . . with responsive readings, and at the close of each reading you wll say *Delirium and amen. Delirium. Delirium and amen.* We shall learn our prayers by rote, and they will make as much sense as any *other* memorized prayers ever make, and *then* . . . once we *yield* to the nada and the dada of the sacred text . . . nothing is beyond us, and we need never again be shackled with *philosophy* or *concepts* or *love.* Which means we shall have revealed to us the truth of ultimate delirium. Which already has inherited the earth." And Lee smiled at his three children. And drilled them. And beat them when they fucked up. And fucked them or permitted them to go down on him when they did not. And he said: "Charlie Manson thinks he is Jesus Christ. I do not think I am Jesus Christ. Maybe this is one of the major reasons he is in and I am out." And he said: "I am perfectly willing and able to take care of you, so why should you bother with freedom?" And he said: "If we're all going to be destroyed, we might as well relax and enjoy it." And he said: "We'll not be able to do the destroying all by ourselves. Fortunately, we have the politicians on our side, and we have the human race on our side, and we have time on our side." And he said: "Fear not. Whenever you figure things are really bad, that's just when they'll become so fucking *worse* it'll blow your heads off your shoulders if you aren't careful." And he said: "Do not be dismayed if it sounds paradoxical when I tell you we shall be destroyed as well as do the destroying. No paradox exists. Only history exists, and it contains multitudes of destroyed destroyers." And Lee slapped and punched and kicked his children when they did not give him all their attention. He told them he did not particularly enjoy slapping and punching and kicking them, but it was important that they open their minds to him, that they come to understand the new level within which they now were existing . . . the level of Flegenheimer . . . the level of delirium. He permitted his children to smoke all the grass they could find (it seemed to expand them), and he himself got to drinking more beer, but he told them that in the final analysis they would have to understand their new state *rationally* and *coolly* and *without question.* The children were with him for less than six months (and he was a child himself, being just past twenty). They abandoned DeLong's credit cards—in the interest of safety—after using them about ten days and they spent all of DeLong's money within a little more than a month . . . staying in good motels, dressing well, keeping their faces fresh and clean . . . and Lee insisted they bathe every day . . . and he showered two and sometimes three times a day . . . and he told them: "For us to be safe, we must not be *clichés*. We must not look like the dreaded *hippies*. We must look perhaps like a group of virginal vagabond singers from some Baptist youth group or *Up With People*. Do you remember *Up With People* and all those happy teeth? I wonder what happened to all those *Up With People* people. Perhaps, as they became older, all their teeth fell out. Oh. Wow. Far out. Maybe they now call themselves *Up With Social Security*." And Lee smiled at his children. And then, when DeLong's money ran out, he bought the most realistic cap pistol he could find and held up two candy stores in Oklahoma City, grossing more than two hundred dollars. He performed the robberies alone, but he had the girls stand in the doorways and watch (Chris was in the car with the motor running). The robberies just about made Melissa come, and later that night, while lying in bed with Lee in a Ramada Inn, she said: "I really do love you, you know. I never thought there could be kicks like the ones you've shown us." And Lee said: "No. Love is out. There is no such word." And Melissa said: "Can't I even . . . well, dream?" And Lee said: "Shit. You sound like Marlo Thomas." He rolled atop her and pinned her wrists to the mattress and said to her: "Look, whatever this is, it is nothing more than *use*. When I have to shit, I go to the toilet. When I have to get my rocks off, I go to you . . . or Betsy, or Chris . . . or sometimes all three of you, correct? *But that's as far as it goes*." And then Lee slapped Melissa's face several times for emphasis and told her to go take a bath. But nonetheless, if his children behaved intelligently, he was good to them. For instance, he never called upon the girls to hook or Chris to hustle faggots. "If I do that," he told them, "then I'm just DeLong Hughes with a white face, and things didn't turn out so swift for DeLong Hughes, as you may recall." And he was serious, even when the money became tight. His petty robberies turned into mostly bummers, and he seldom came away from one with more than thirty or forty dollars. But he told his children: "I made you a promise, and I'll keep it." And they drifted farther eastward, stealing a new car every other day or so, moving from Oke City to Wichita all the way to Minneapolis, then back south through St Louis, and they were able to stay in motels only about one night of every three—which made it impossible for Lee to take all the showers he required. And so, on the nights they had to sleep in the car, he always had Chris park it near some sort of stream, so at least they could rinse off a layer or two of the grime. Those outdoors nights were not a total loss, though. The summer of 1974 was a pleasant one in the Mississippi Valley, and it was kicky for Lee and his children to sit crosslegged under

the stars and study *The Flegenheimer Testament* and take part in the responsive readings. "It all makes you feel kind of humble and insignificant, doesn't it?" said Lee, smiling a little and inclining his head toward
the sky. "If all those stars are up there," he said, "can God be far behind?" Then, rolling on his belly, he made dry amused sounds into a
hand, and he said to himself: Old Mom would have loved my choice of
words, my natural and effortless *eloquence*. And he went to Betsy for a
change, and Melissa glared at him, and he fucked Betsy standing up, rubbing her bare ass against the rough bark of a tree and just about lifting her
larded body off the ground with the force of his upthrust prick. A few
days later, while passing through Cape Girardeau, Missouri, Lee and his
children stopped in a souvenir shop, and Lee suddenly had an absolutely
super feeling of *déjà vu*. There, piled on a counter, were three exact duplicates of the Nixon mask he had lost when DeLong's pal Archie had made
off with the Impala that historic night in East LA. These masks were a
buck *and a half* apiece, however—what with Watergate and all, according
to the clerk. But Lee didn't care. He bought the masks anyway, and his
children grinned and scuffed and looked at him as though he had gone bananas. But he did not give a fuck. *They* didn't know what *he* knew; *they*
didn't know that *some day* there would be some profound purpose for the
masks . . . though he didn't then know what the *specifics* of the purpose
were. And they drifted south from Cape Girardeau all the way to New Orleans, where Lee became lucky, ripping off nearly five hundred dollars in
a cappistol robbery of a drugstore. This enabled him and his children to
spend a number of consecutive motel nights, and he took two and three
and sometimes four and sometimes even five showers a night. He and his
children headed northeast then, changing cars often, and the radio was
full of Watergate, and the children groaned whenever their music was interrupted by a news bulletin, but Lee told them: "It is all logical and right;
it has all been predicted by Arthur Flegenheimer; *it is all coming down*. So
I want you to listen carefully. I want you to pay attention. I believe we are
scrabbling at the walls surrounding some structure of enormous importance, a structure that we are ordained to *penetrate* in order that we *participate* in the *holy process* of bringing it all down. Remember, so far all
you have done is watch. *I* have performed the work. Not that I am *complaining*, mind you. The arrangement is as *I* have deemed it. But it seems
to me that we have been joined for reasons that eventually will be larger,
and perhaps this Watergate shit will provide us a hint." So yes, northeast
then through Tennessee and Kentucky, and the summer of 1974 moved
past them in a warm procession of stolen cars and rippedoff candystores,
drugstores and fillingstations, and the Nixon masks were carefully trans

ferred from car to car. So yes, northeast then into Ohio, and Lee drank beer, and his children sucked on grass, and then came the night of August 8, 1974, and Lee received his holy revelation, and the next day he and his children (minus Melissa . . . Melissa the beautiful . . . Melissa the scarred . . . Melissa the expendable) went out to assist in bringing it all down. Several days earlier they had penetrated the hills of southeastern Ohio and a county called Paradise, and they had been down to only about eight dollars among them, plus some canned goods, and so they had been forced to stop in a shallow valley near a creek and an abandoned coalmine. A rotten and splintered sign at the mine entrance said TUESDAY CREEK, and there *was* a Tuesday Creek, and it appeared fairly clean. In addition, an old mine office . . . little more than a shack, but nonetheless habitable . . . still was standing, and Lee decided that this would be a good place for all of them to take a brief vacation from the cares and toils of their life. There was soap in addition to the canned goods, and plenty of water, so he grinned and told them not to worry; he would sally forth on a brief excursion and bring them home some money and goodies. Which he did—and alone. Leaving the children to set up housekeeping in the shack, he drove to Columbus, then Newark, then Zanesville, then Nelsonville and Logan, pulled off eight of his cappistol robberies and returned triumphantly to the shack with more than six hundred dollars. *Ecshally,* he had ripped off more than *seven* hundred dollars, but he had decided to treat his children to some good grass—buying it from a summer session art student at Ohio University in Athens, which was less than thirty miles from Tuesday Creek and the shack where the children were holed up. Naturally, Lee was given a hero's reception when he returned— especially after he laid the grass on the children. He had brought along two sixpacks of Rolling Rock for himself, and he kept them cold by plunking them in the waters of the Tuesday Creek. Chris carefully rolled joints for himself and his sister and Melissa, and they all sprawled in the high weeds at the edge of the creek, and Lee said: "It is close. The revelation is close." And Melissa said: "Will it be a kick?" And Lee said: "Without question." And he sucked on his beer. And his children sucked on their joints. That was late in the afternoon of August 8, 1974, and the sunlight came in a hot dry dancing slant through the tall scraggly trees that clung to the banks of the Tuesday Creek, and finally . . . when the children were too stoned and inarticulate . . . Lee struggled to his feet and went to the car and switched on the radio. The Watergate thing clearly was almost at an end, and he was feeling the start of a vision. He lounged on the passenger's side of the front seat of a '71 Ford that had been stolen by Chris a week earlier in Maysville, Kentucky. He listened carefully to the radio, and someone was saying something to the effect that Nixon was expected to resign that night. Lee grimaced. He blinked at the radio. *Resign?* Was the sonofabitch really going to *do* it? Lee was astonished. A Nixon resignation was the last thing he expected. To him, it had gone without saying that Nixon would only leave office by being *dragged* from it . . . and kicking and screaming, at that. If the guy on the radio was correct, then Nixon's *resignation* was the worst sort of final surrender, and . . . and . . . *hey!* Lee sat upright. He snapped his fingers. *"Hey!"* he said aloud. He glanced at his watch. It was past four, but there was plenty of time. Then, for some reason he really didn't understand, he scootched over and looked at himself in the rearview mirror. The wind had caught at his hair a little, and so he patted it down. But it was neat hair, short, *civilized*. He'd had it trimmed about ten days ago in some small town in Kentucky. He grimaced, bared his teeth. They were even and nicely spaced. He said to himself: I could pass for David Eisenhower, and that is the plain truth of the matter. He glanced down toward the sun-speckled Tuesday Creek and his three lounging stoned children. The art student had been surprised at the amount of pot Lee had purchased, but Lee had told him: "Well, you see, there are these people I take care of, and I like to be generous." And the art student had said: "Man, *I* should have somebody so generous taking care of *me*." And Lee had said: "The thing is, they would have no chance of surviving without me." And the art student had laughed. And Lee had smiled. And the transaction had been completed, and now Lee's children were tapdancing in the clouds, or whatever it was potheads did, and the timing was perfect. *Super.* And so, for perhaps five minutes, Lee sat perfectly still. He concentrated. He drew up a timetable. He drew up a list of preliminary activities. Then, when it all was clear in his mind, he got out of the car and went to his children and told them he had received a vision. They looked at him with bleary benevolence, and Chris said: "Good, man . . . join the group . . ." Smiling, Lee shook his head no. The nearest town of any size was a place called Paradise Falls, and he told them he had an errand to perform there, but he would be back within the hour. Melissa blinked at him and said: "A . . . *another* . . . what I mean . . . you want to rip off somebody . . . I mean, somebody *more?*" And Lee said: "No. I simply want to purchase some machinery." And Betsy giggled and said: "You . . . ah, you got just fine . . . *machinery* . . ." And Lee said: "I thank you very much, but that is not the machinery I have in mind." He climbed back to the car, and his children called thickly after him, and their bodies were lax and wavery, and he paid them no mind. He drove into Paradise Falls and found a hardware store where he purchased three

.32 caliber revolvers and a hundred rounds of ammunition. The cost was one hundred seventeen dollars and six cents, state sales tax included. The clerk was a middleaged man with a paunch and a crewcut. He glanced at Lee's neat hair, and Lee gave him a reserved sort of David Eisenhower smile, and then the man said: "Protection, I suppose. You just passing through?" And Lee said: "Yes. There are three of us, my two brothers and myself, and sometimes we camp out . . . and, well, you know all these stories a person hears about your *thugs* and your *hippies* and all . . ." And the clerk said: "Yes indeed, young fellow. I can't say as I blame you a bit." He wrapped the revolvers and the bullets, and the package was heavier than Lee had anticipated. He clutched it to his chest and thanked the clerk, and the clerk said: "Now if anybody comes at you, they'll be in store for a little bit of a surprise." And Lee said: "Isn't that the truth?" He returned to the car, dropped the package on the front seat and drove back north on Ohio 93 to the old Tuesday Creek mine site, which was at least a mile off the highway and two miles from a small ramshackle settlement called Blood, which at one time probably had been a mining town of some importance. The vestiges still were there . . . the abandoned saloons, a vacant hotel . . . rows of empty and vandalized houses, old *company* houses by the look of them, dating back to before the turn of the century. It was the *sight* . . . the *aspect,* the *panache* . . . of this settlement that had interested Lee originally in finding a place in the area where he and his children could pause to rest their weary bones. To switch on the car radio and listen to the news of Nixon and Watergate while relaxing in the midst of *ruins* . . . somehow it was all very appropriate, and Lee supposed he had once again yielded to his weakness for heavy and floridly melodramatic symbolism. But fuck all that. He was only *human,* ha ha, tra la, and so allowances would have to be made. He thought of all this as he returned to the shack and the creek and the old mine and his children, and it all made him smile. He drove carefully, and he did not speed. His plan was rolling easily in his mind, and he was serene, and he drew back his lips from his teeth, and he rubbed his teeth, and he caught a glimpse of himself in the mirror, and his face was bland, and his hair lay neatly against his football head, and he said to his reflection: "Hi, Dave." And then he saw his children, and he braked the car and shut off the engine, and he carried his package down to where they lolled by the creek, and his adoring Melissa popped open a can of Rolling Rock and brought it to him, and it was *then* . . . while Melissa and Chris and Betsy were stoned and spaced and empty and without gristle or bone . . . that Lee told them what he had in mind. He sat at the top of the bank, and he gathered his children in a semicircle at his feet, and his children blinked at him, and Betsy's tongue protruded a little, and Chris was squeezing his crotch, and Melissa lay with her face pressed against one of Lee's ankles, and he said to them: "Listen carefully now. I have knowledge and insight and a revelation for you. First of all, tomorrow is the day you stop being spectators. Until now, I have done all the work. Well, beginning tomorrow, you will actively assist me." He hesitated. All three of his children were making small squealing sounds, and Betsy even managed to beat her hands together. And Chris said: "Hoo . . . hooray for . . . our . . . side . . ." And then, working carefully, Chris rolled three more joints, handed two of them to the girls and kept one for himself. Lee waited for them to light up and suck and sigh and swallow the smoke, and then he opened the package and showed them what he had purchased in Paradise Falls. "From now on," he said, "there will be no more playacting, and it all will be for real. *It is all coming down.* Remember that. *It is all coming down.*" He held up one of the revolvers. All three of his children drew back a little. "These are *real,*" he said. "This is not Silly Putty Time at the YMCA. Tomorrow . . . with Nixon gone, with every living human being on this earth knowing that *governments* are *organic* and *rot,* just as *history* is *organic* and *rots* . . . with *bullshit* having had its day . . . with *philosophy* having had its day . . . tomorrow then will mark the beginning of *delirium,* right? Of the implementation of the truths stated in *The Flegenheimer Testament,* right? So tomorrow then, because we always can use money, and just for the fucking *hell* of it, just for the fucking delirious *joy* of it, we shall invade that town of Paradise Falls and we shall rob a bank. And if anyone stands in our way, we shall not hesitate to chop down that person. We'll not *seek* to kill, since that would not be *cool,* but we'll not *pull back* either. And think of the rightness. The *real* rightness. The *true* rightness. Think of Nixon, for instance. Every time we turn on the radio, we hear some dude reporting to us how goddamned guilty Nixon is. And do you remember a couple of years ago, whenever it was, and Charlie Manson and his girls were on trial, and old Nixon said *they* were guilty? And *now* look who's guilty. And another thing. You know what tomorrow is? Tomorrow is the fifth anniversary of Voytek Frykowski. And Steven Parent. And Abigail Folger. And Jay Sebring. And Sharon Polanski, better known as Sharon Tate. PIG on the door in blood, remember? And so who comes down now? *Nixon* comes down now, on the fifth anniversary to the day of the Charlie Manson thing. I wonder whether Charlie will laugh tomorrow. I hope so. I hope he understands how delicious it all is. It's only too bad he thinks he's Jesus Christ, which means he's all strung out on *philosophy,* which is *shit,* right? But the *organic inevitability* of *delirium* is *not* shit, which means then that tomorrow will be a perfect, sunny, warm and happy Flegenheimer day, and we shall rip off a bank and use *real* guns with *real* bullets—just like the grownup folks." He hesitated. He had finished his beer, and he nudged Melissa with a toe. "More beer, please," he said. Obediently she scrambled down the bank and fetched him a fresh can of Rolling Rock from the waters of the Tuesday Creek. She popped it open for him, and he took it from her without acknowledging her. But she did not seem to mind. She curled at his feet and kissed his ankles, and he said: "And we're not to worry about *planning* or any of *that* shit. We'll just walk into the bank and *do* it. Biffo bango, hands up, ladies and gentlemen, and let's see the color of your money. And we'll be in and out faster than a bunny with a terminal case of premature ejaculation." Lee had never been much of a drinker, and the beer was getting to him, but it didn't matter—his game plan was in order, and he knew his children would do whatever he told them, and he was comforted by the knowledge, and so it wasn't until later . . . *much* later, after darkness had come, and with it a time of tree toads and leaves and the sweet stink of pot and the warm gassy ballooning of Lee's belly as it filled with beer . . . that he told them that one of them would die the next morning in order that the others acquire some proficiency with the revolvers. "A human moving target . . ." he said, burping. "Very important . . . chosen out of *my judgment* . . . eenie, meenie, minie, moe . . . you dig it?" And Chris and the girls nodded vaguely; their hands and bodies moved with flaccid languor, and of course they did *not* dig it; they had no idea what he was saying, but ah, what the fuck . . . tomorrow morning would be time enough for them to understand. And Lee finally stood up and went to the car and switched on the radio, and he thought of *The Flegenheimer Testament* and Charlie Manson and Nixon and all the dead people and PIG in blood on the door, and he thought of Mrs Oosterhaus and Dear Old Mom, and he thought of the majestic rococo humiliation of DeLong Hughes, and he said to himself: I *knew* those Nixon masks would come in handy some day. And then Melissa came weaving to the car, and she crawled inside with Lee, and she said: "They . . . oh in no way did Chris and . . . uh, whatshername . . . Betsy . . . in no way did they dig you in that . . . hee hee . . . that last thing you laid on us . . . about . . . the . . . *you* know . . . the *target practice* . . ." And Lee said: "Did *you?*" And Melissa kissed his cheek and his ear, and she rubbed her hands across his chest (but she did not try to kiss him on the mouth; she never had kissed him on the mouth; he never permitted it), and she said: "I *love* you . . . which means *I'm* the one who'll go, right? You call me beautiful . . . but *I'm* the one who'll go, right? I mean, I am the

most . . . the most . . . to *her,* I am so far *superior* . . . and you have
said so yourself . . . what is it you *want* from your Melissa? I mean, she
doesn't want to die." And Lee said: "The decision hasn't been made
yet." And Melissa said: "I want to believe . . . I want to believe
that . . . I want to believe, I mean, I got the same chance *they* do, the
same *odds* . . ." And Lee said: "Well, as long as you don't go thinking
that I have anything *personal* against the person who is chosen . . . whether you or . . . well, whoever it is . . ." And Melissa
said: "Tomorrow . . . it'll be like *coming* . . . the bank and all . . .
the people . . ." And Lee said: "I hope so." And Melissa woozily shook
her head. She had a *thought,* and she would *persist* with it, and so she
said: "Ah, what . . . what do you want from me?" And Lee said: "Right
now, I don't know whether—" He was interrupted by a voice on the radio. Melissa started to say something, but he motioned her to hush. The
voice announced that the President of the United States was about to
speak. There was a sequence of clicking sounds, and then came the voice
of Nixon: *Good evening. This will be the thirtyseventh time I will have
spoken to you from this office where so many decisions have been made
that shaped the history of this nation.* Lee grinned, and Melissa pulled up
his T-shirt and licked his belly, and he said: "Yes. Do it. And I'm going to
hold it. I'm going to hold it as long as I can—maybe forever." And Melissa groaned. She opened the front of his jeans, and his prick sprang out,
and he seized her head, and she began sucking him, and he listened to
Nixon's voice, and Nixon's voice was nudged by the mythic voice of Arthur Flegenheimer, and Lee gasped, and Lee bit the insides of his lips,
and perhaps it was the ecstasy of his revelation, or perhaps it was simple
anticipation, or perhaps it was boyish high spirits, but *whatever* it was, a
loud and victorious blast of *emotion* and *ego* and perhaps *glands* took control of him, and he heard the final montage of what he considered to be
truth and what he considered to be *cool* beyond *cool* . . . two voices, a
mad and delirious concert, Nixon and Flegenheimer: *In all the decisions I
have made in my public life I have always tried to do what was best for the
nation. Oh, oh, dog biscuits, and when he is happy he doesn't get snappy.
Throughout the long and difficult period of Watergate, I have felt it was my
duty to persevere, to make every possible effort to complete the term of
office to which you elected me. The glove will fit what I say, oh kayiyi
kayiyi. In the past few days, however, it has become evident to me that I no
longer have a strong enough political base in the Congress to justify continuing that effort. He is jumping around. No hobo and pobo I think it
means the same thing. I am a pretty good pretzler. As long as there was
such a base, I felt strongly that it was necessary to see the constitutional*

process through to its conclusion; that to do otherwise would be unfaithful to the spirit of that deliberately difficult process, and a dangerously de-stabilizing precedent for the future. I will be checked and doublechecked and please pull for me. Will you pull? How many good ones and how many bad ones? But with the disappearance of that base I now believe that the constitutional purpose has been served and there is no longer a need for the process to be prolonged. In the olden days they waited and they waited. I don't want harmony; I want harmony. I would have preferred to carry through to the finish whatever the personal agony it would have involved. And my family unanimously urged me to do so. There are only ten of us; there are ten million fighting somewhere of you, so get your onions up and we will throw up the truce flag. Please let me get in and eat. But the interest of the nation must always come before any personal consideration. From the discussions I have had with congressional and other leaders, I have concluded that because of the Watergate matter I might not have the sup-port of the Congress that I would consider necessary to back the very diffi-cult decisions and carry out the duties of this office in the way the interests of the nation will require. Let him harness himself to you and then bother you. The sidewalk was in trouble and the bears were in trouble and I broke it up. (And Lee still was holding it in. And Melissa squealed and choked and slurped, but she kept working away, and she did not complain.) *I have never been a quitter. To leave office before my term is completed is abhor-rent to every instinct in my body. That is something that shouldn't be spo-ken about. Oh, sir, get the doll a rofting. You can play jacks and girls do that with a soft ball and do tricks with it. It takes all events into considera-tion. As President I must put the interests of America first. America needs a fulltime President and a fulltime Congress, particularly at this time with the problems we face at home and abroad. To continue to fight through the months ahead for my personal vindication would almost totally absorb the time and attention of both the President and the Congress in a period when our entire focus should be on the great issues of peace abroad and prosper-ity without inflation at home. No. No. And it is no. It is confused, and it says no. A boy has never wept nor dashed a thousand kim. Did you hear me? Therefore, I shall resign the presidency effective at noon tomorrow.* (Lee made fists and beat them against the dashboard, and Melissa rolled him on her tongue and bathed him in her spit, but he still held it in.) *Vice-President Ford will be sworn in as President at that hour in this office. Please crack down on the Chinaman's friends and Hitler's commander. I am sore and I am going up and I am going to give you honey if I can. As I recall the high hopes for America with which we began this second term, I feel a great sadness that Mother is the best bet and don't let Satan draw you too fast.* (Chris and Betsy were off shrieking and giggling, and Lee still held it in.) *So let us all now join together in affirming that my fortunes have changed and come back and went back since that. Sometimes I have succeeded and sometimes I have failed, but I know what I am doing here with my collection of papers. It isn't worth a nickel to two guys like you and me, but to a collector it is worth a fortune. It is priceless. When I first took the oath of office as President five and one half years ago, I made this sacred commitment—to* "*consecrate my office, my energies and all the wisdom I can summon in the cause of peace among nations.*" *I have done my very best in all the days since to be true to that pledge. As a result of these efforts, I am confident that the world is a safer place today, not only for the people of America, but for the people of all nations, and that all of our children have a better chance than before of living in peace rather than dying in war. Come on, open the soap duckets. This, more than anything, is what I hoped to achieve when I sought the presidency. The chimney sweeps. Take to the sword. This, more than anything, is what I hope will be my legacy to you, to our country, as I leave the presidency. To have served in this office is to have felt a very personal sense of kinship with each and every American. In leaving it, I do so with this prayer: May God's grace be with you in all the days ahead. French Canadian bean soup. I want to pay. Let them leave me alone.* (And Lee let it go, and Melissa . . . who was his favorite child, if the truth were known . . . damn near choked. And Lee howled and clapped. He had heard. He had heard. He had *heard.* The voices were indeed real, and the revelation was accurate, and so he howled and clapped, and Melissa wiped her mouth, and she told him she was happy for him.)

The '71 Ford proceeded south on Mulberry Street, then west on Main, and Lee told Chris and Betsy there would be nothing to it. "We simply walk in," he said, "and show them our guns, and take what we can scrounge up, and get out within sixty seconds. No more, no less. I'll hit the cashiers, and you two hit the customers, and you are to waste anyone who interferes."

"Dig," said Chris.

"Right on," said Betsy.

"You're going to enjoy it as much as you enjoyed this morning with Melissa," said Lee.

Chris nodded.

Betsy nodded.

Lee passed them their guns and their Nixon masks. "As soon as you spot a bank," he said, "just pull up—and don't worry about doubleparking. If you have to doublepark, doublepark. Fuck it. We're only going to be in the bank sixty seconds. And Chris, *leave the engine running* . . ."

"Dig," said Chris. His voice was thin.

Betsy was fussing with her mask, adjusting it.

Lee's eyes flicked from side to side of the street. He supposed he should have looked for a bank earlier, and perhaps he had carried casualness a little too far, but what difference did it make? He and Chris and Betsy would be in and out so quickly that these rustics wouldn't know what the fuck had happened until after it had happened. He saw an F. W. Woolworth store. He saw a movie theater that had THE PARALLAX VIEW on its marquee. He saw an A & P and a sign that said CHICKEN BREASTS 37¢ LB and a poster that said WEO. He saw fat women, and some of them were fanning themselves with their hats. Children skittered and whooped. A hairy little dog ran into an Isaly's store. A man in white shooed it out.

"Ahead," said Chris. "On the right."

"You got it," said Lee.

The bank building was squat, and it recently had been sandblasted a bright white.

Lee put on his mask, fiddling with it until the eyeholes were aligned.

Betsy/Nixon kissed her gun. She giggled.

Chris slipped on his mask.

"Pull up right in front," said Lee/Nixon.

"Right," said Chris/Nixon.

"Oh my, oh *my*," said Betsy/Nixon, squeezing one of her brother's legs.

Chris/Nixon doubleparked the car directly in front of the bank.

"Dish must be de plaishe," said Lee/Nixon.

Chris/Nison and Betsy/Nixon snickered. They all piled out of the car and hurried into the bank, and they were yelling. And their guns moved in happy peremptory arcs.

Part Seven

OTTO YORK

Otto Rufus York was born on August 7, 1906, and his first spoken words were recorded in family tradition about a year and a half later when he said to his mother: "Dadda dwink dwaft."

"I beg your pardon?" said Louise York, who was sitting with the little boy in the kitchen. She was shelling peas, and she was trying to keep Otto from eating the shells, of which he somehow was very fond.

He was squirming on his chair. He stopped squirming, smiled at his mother and said: "Dadda dwink dwaft."

"Dwaft?" said Louise York.

"Dwaft *beeah*," said little Otto.

"Oh," said Louise York, and she covered her mouth. "Dwaft *beer*. Yes *indeed*. How right you are."

The dwaft beer story was not all that funny to anyone outside the York household, yet this is not particularly unusual. Funny family stories seldom are funny except to the family involved. But the fact was—Ed York *did* drink draft beer, and immense amounts of it. He was for many years the bartender in the saloon of the old Depot Hotel, and there are those who still remember him for his remarkable kidneys. It has been seriously stated that he could work ten hours, put away at least ten pints of draft lager and never slur a word, weave, stumble or—*most* remarkably—leave his post behind the bar. Or even look uncomfortable.

Otto Rufus York would admit to anyone that his name probably should have been Otto Goofus York. Still, not once in his life did he feel disgust, and not one day in his life did he fail to inspect the sky.

In 1935 or so, a flight of outside steps was removed from an office building on Main Street. Otto York wrote a poem eulogizing those

377

steps. He attached the poem to a black crepe wreath, and he read the poem to a crowd of friends, then laid both the poem and the wreath on the spot where the steps once had begun. The reason for his grief was as obvious as it was profound. For years, or at least ever since the advent of reasonably short skirts, it was possible for the healthy young men of Paradise Falls to participate in the gentle sport known as beaver shooting. That is to say, if one placed one's self within a proper angle of vision, one participated in a veritable visual feast of legs, thighs and who knew what all else, since it so happened that a beauty parlor was at the top of the steps. But then came progress, and those splendid steps were replaced by an indoor staircase, and Otto York was inconsolable. Hence, the poem, the wreath, the gathering of the crowd. The poem would be quoted here, but unfortunately it has been lost. It was torn up by Otto's wife Norma, who *really* sometimes just about lost her *patience* with him.

Curiously enough (and it amused him a little), Otto York was a bridge player of more than moderate abilities—at least in his younger days. And he was one of Miss Margaret Ridpath's earliest more or less permanent partners. But then he married Norma, and her foot came down with a large crunch, and so much for bridge. Yet he didn't really care all that much. The taut competitiveness of the game sometimes made him nervous, and he told Margaret he didn't know how in the name of Judas Priest she could *stand* it. Still, he did enjoy joking with her in bridge terms, and he was fond of saying to her: "Hey there, Good Looking, what I wouldn't give to trump *your* ace . . . "

Otto York never lost a single tooth, and he never killed a single thing, and yet he could shoot the eye out of the king of diamonds at fifty feet, and so it turned out that poor Norma York became a Skeet Widow instead of a Bridge Widow. But at least skeet had something to do with how Otto made his living, and so she was willing to tolerate it.

*

People were astonished to learn that Otto never had lost a single tooth. His explanation: "I don't believe in worrying, which makes you grind your teeth. In my opinion, an unground tooth is a healthy tooth, and it'll live with you forever."

Norma York contracted multiple sclerosis in late 1942 and she died of it in early 1944. She and Otto had been married not even ten years, and they had no children, and so shortly before her death she said to him: "I want you to marry again."

"I don't think so," said Otto.

"You are a young man," said Norma, "and you have a whole lot of time ahead of you, and I don't want you to sass me."

"But you are enough for any man," said Otto.

"Don't talk foolishness," said Norma.

"I've talked foolishness all my life," said Otto, "and it's a little bit late in the game for me to change my ways."

"You're not even *thirtyeight*," said Norma, "and I know you've wanted a little kiddie or two, and it's not too late for you."

"I got other people I can take care of," said Otto.

"You mean like *drunks* and *old ladies* and *other people's children*?" said Norma.

"You got it," said Otto.

"But they're not enough," said Norma.

"Would you like a pot of hot tea?" said Otto. "I bought some of your Constant Comment today, and I'll brew it up faster than you can say Roosevelt is a Democrat."

"Don't change the subject," said Norma.

"Who's changing the subject?" said Otto. "This whole conversation makes no sense. You're talking like you're *going* someplace. Well, you're going *noplace*. I won't hear of it."

"Thank you," said Norma.

"I love you, and I'n not going to waste my time worrying about you," said Otto. "You're going to live forever."

"Thank you," said Norma.

"Now, now, there's no reason for you to cry," said Otto.

"Be *quiet,*" said Norma.

From February of 1944 until his own death more than thirty years later, Otto York lived alone in the little house he and Norma had shared on Spring Street. He kept it neat and clean, and three times a week he drove out to the farm of a brotherinlaw, Karl Soeder, and spent an hour or so shooting tin cans and bottles off fenceposts. And Karl Soeder said to him: "It's too bad nothing happens around here." And Otto said: "No. Incorrect. If something ever did happen, the chances are I never would be able to get off a shot." And Karl Soeder said: "Then why do you keep at it and keep at it?" And Otto smiled and said: "I'm good at it, and I love it."

Otto York joined the Paradise Falls Police Department on September 1, 1928. He retired on August 31, 1971. He was a patrolman when he joined the department. He was a patrolman when he retired.

To Margaret Ridpath and others, Otto York would say: "Feeling sorry for a person is like worrying about a person—it *tears down* the person. Everybody seems so blasted *bothered* because I have lived alone so many years. Well, *I'm* not bothered. I . . . well, I've always had a lot to occupy my time. I attend skeet competitions now and then. I vacuum rugs. I visit Norma's grave and sometimes I almost get up the nerve to speak to her. Oh, she was something and a half, that Norma. I was twentyseven when I met her, and it was all because her brother Karl had parked his '31 Plymouth in the loading zone next to Steinfelder's. She was sitting in the car, and her arms were folded across her chest, and she was the sweetest little redhaired thing I'd ever been privileged to see, and I said to her: 'I'm sorry, Miss, but you'll have to move this car.' And she said: 'You'd better tell that to my brother when he comes back.' And I said: 'Comes back?' And she pointed to the alley—the one between Steinfelder's and the hardware store, you know?—and she said: 'My brother's very busy back there. Call of Nature.' And I said: 'Well, he can't park in a loading zone.' And she said: 'You mean *un*loading zone.' Which of course got me to laughing, and she frowned one of her tight little redhaired frowns at me, but then finally *she* got to laughing *too*—and before I could turn around three times and spit in the air I was married to her, and oh did we ever have a *time* of it. Maybe not all that *long* a time, but longer than a lot of people get, and you'll never hear me complaining. So don't talk to me about *lonely*, all right?''

One Saturday morning in 1956, while cruising in a patrol car, Otto York found little Freddie Farwell weeping desperately while walking along Grainger Street and blinking at the treetops. It turned out that little Freddie, who was six, had lost his canary, whose name was Mario Lanza. The little bird had literally flown the coop and had gone chirping out an open window, and little Freddie was frightened to death to tell his parents. But Otto smiled at little Freddie, scooped him up and deposited him on the front seat of the patrol car. Freddie had to stand to see over the dashboard, and Otto said to him: "Now you keep an eagle eye out—or maybe canary eye would be a better way to put it." And Otto slowly drove back and forth across the north side of town, along Hocking Street and Cumberland Street and Market Street and Mulberry Street and even along Spring Street. And he and little Freddie saw many birds, but none of those birds was Mario Lanza . . . until . . . until . . . of all the insane coincidences . . . they were passing in front of Otto's little house on Spring Street. And little Freddie made a piping sound. *"There he is!"* shouted little Freddie. *"There's Mario Lanza!"* He pointed to the porch roof, and sure enough, there Mario Lanza was. Hopping. Singing. Drinking from a sheetmetal drain gutter. Grinning, Otto looked up and said: "I'll be switched." Then he held a finger to his lips. "I'll go inside and climb out a window onto the roof," he said to little Freddie Farwell, "but in the meantime you have to be very, *very* quiet, all right?" And little Freddie, his eyes enormous, nodded. Otto crept out of the patrol car, closing the door softly behind him. He tiptoed up the walk and carefully let himself inside the house. He went upstairs to the front bedroom. It was the bedroom he and Norma had shared. It faced east, and they had enjoyed the feel of the sunlight awakening them. He carefully slid open the window and looked out onto the porch roof. Mario Lanza still was down by the gutter, and he still was hopping and singing. Otto quietly eased himself out onto the roof. It was on a steep slant, and so he lowered himself into a sitting position. Using his buttocks and hands and feet, he scrootched down toward Mario Lanza. Otto was six feet three inches tall and he weighed somewhere near two hundred thirty pounds, and so the shingles groaned. Down below in the car, little Freddie Farwell was leaning out a window and sucking his thumb. Otto slid down the roof until his legs were hanging over the edge of the gutter perhaps ten feet to the left of Mario Lanza. Then, ever so cautiously, Otto began edging toward the little bird, which still was hopping and singing and drinking. Otto still couldn't get over the fact that it was *this* house, of all places, that Mario Lanza had chosen for a bit of rest and a chirp and a hop and a drink. Otto reached toward Mario Lanza, and he tried to be as quiet as he could on the groaning shingles. But Mario Lanza heard him, hopped tentatively for a moment, then started to fly away. Otto reached for Mario Lanza. Otto was a big man, and he had long arms, but he was unable to grab Mario Lanza, who flew across the street. Down in the car, litle Freddie Farwell shouted something. Otto was off balance. Several shingles gave way. Still clutching after Mario Lanza, Otto slid off the roof. And he landed on the front walk, suffering a skull fracture and four cracked ribs. Little Freddie Farwell set off an unholy commotion, but Otto heard none of it. He was off duty for five weeks, and a few people said he had been stupid, but most of the people said oh well, what could you have expected of good old Otto York? His pay was not docked, and no one complained. Actually, his photograph was carried in the Paradise Falls *Journal-Democrat*, together with a photograph of the scene of the accident, complete with a dotted line showing the path of his fall. Dozens of his friends visited him in the hospital, and he enjoyed tapping his bandaged skull and telling them: "Examination of my head has revealed nothing."

Mario Lanza returned to his own home the day after Otto York's fall. He flew around the back yard for three days, and then little Freddie Farwell's mother caught him with a butterfly net.

Of all Otto York's many friends his closest probably was the former Paradise Falls chief of police, James N. Jones Jr, who died of alcoholism in April of '72. This James N. Jones Jr, an older brother of Miss Margaret Ridpath's housekeeper, Pauline Jones, called for Otto at the end, and they had a brief conversation. It took place in Jones's bedroom and no one else was present, and Jones said: "Otto, you always were an idiot."

"I expect that's true," said Otto York.

"You never had dreams . . ."

"Well," said Otto, "maybe I just didn't worry about not having them."

"I came close to being a great football player once . . ."

"I know," said Otto.

"But close only means something in horseshoes . . ."

"It means something in a lot of things," said Otto. "If close is *trying* and not *making* it but at least *trying* and not *falling back* and *hiding your head in the sand,* then close counts for an awful lot."

"Did you ever try?"

"I try all the time," said Otto. "I tried with Norma, and she tried with me, and we had almost ten years, which are almost ten years better than no years. And I try when I'm shooting skeet. And I try to be polite and neat and orderly and maybe laugh as often as I can."

"My liver is like a lace doily," said James N. Jones Jr, "and I'm dying, and I feel like I'm nothing, but I was the *chief,* and you never were anything more than a *patrolman,* and . . . well, no kids and all, no money . . . just good old Otto York, grinning and scratching . . . but the thing *is* . . . you probably could of been elected *mayor* any time you'd of *wanted* to be . . ."

"Well, I don't know about *that,*" said Otto.

"I want to thank you . . ."

"Thank me for what?" said Otto.

"For the times you got me out of trouble . . . you know what I mean . . . don't go acting coy and girlish on me . . . I mean, you're the best friend I ever had . . . and I don't all that much want to die, but at least I do feel I got to tell you that those times I called you goddamned dumb Otto and asshole Otto . . . Otto who falls off his own roof while chasing a canarybird . . . well, I was just, ah, *kidding,* you know . . ."

"Jim, you been drinking?"

"How's that?"

"All this here whipped cream you're spreading on me," said Otto, "it's like you're drunk again and trying to bake a layer cake."

"What . . . what are you talking about?"

"I'm saying don't try to spread whipped cream on *me,*" said Otto to his friend. "You're going to go on until the sun grows warts, and you know it. So stop all this talk about dying."

"According to you, nobody dies . . ."

"Correct," said Otto.

"Jesus . . ."

"Him neither," said Otto.

James N. Jones Jr was dead six hours after his conversation with Otto York. He passed out shortly after Otto left the room, and he never said another word to anyone. "It was almost as though he had called for a priest," said his widow to her friends. And they embraced her. And they told her there, there, hush now.

There was a statue of Beauty that stood for many years atop the old Paradise County Court House until the building was razed and replaced by a modern concrete structure in 1963. The statue was enormous, ten feet high, weighing no one really knew how many tons. It was of an expressionless female, chastely draped, with the word BEAUTY carved at its base. The figure's arms were spread in a sort of discreet supplication.

The county commissioners did not have the slightest idea what to do with the statue, and no private citizen stepped forward with any suggestion. So finally Otto York stepped forward. He was still a policeman in those days, and he said to the commissioners: "Well, if the county is willing to pay the haulage charges, I'll fix up a nice comfortable and shady place for her in my back yard."

The commissioners looked at one another. Good old Otto York. They voted three to zero to pay the haulage charges.

There were no objections in the community, and so Beauty was trucked into the back yard of Otto York's little place on Spring Street. She was chipped, and she was covered with perhaps fifty generations of bird droppings (the statue was said to date back to perhaps 1850), and Otto spent three weekends scrubbing her clean with turpentine. When he was finished with her, though, she looked mighty nifty—at least in his opinion. And she was out of the hot sun.

People would ask Otto how his girlfriend was, and his reply was invariably the same. He would say: "She's the greatest woman in the world. Never says a word."

*

He had been an only child. He had a few cousins who lived in Columbus and a few more who lived in Gauley Bridge, West Virginia, but he never saw them, and he barely knew what their names were. His wife, though, had been a Soeder, and there are regiments of Soeders in Paradise County, but he never really inflicted himself on them, even though they wouldn't have minded. He appreciated their concern, and he told them he forever would be grateful for it, but he also told them: "Paradise Falls is my family. And I got a lot of good things to think back on. And maybe even a lot of good things to look forward to—who knows?" And sometimes he sat in his back yard, especially when the weather was nice, and sipped a weak bourbon and water and chatted with his friend Beauty. Or thought of his late wife. Or of his late mother, who had died in 1924. Or of his late father, who had died in 1931—from a kidney ailment, of course. Otto thought of his friends. And he cracked the knuckles of his enormous hands. And he said to himself: I expect I haven't hurt all that many people or things or animals or feelings or whatever else. And he grinned. And he kept his clothing clean and pressed. And his grin was for everyone. And so the town was delighted when the Paradise Falls State Bank—Peter E. Saddler, President—contacted him a few months after his retirement and asked him whether he would be interested in a job as a security guard. He was, and his uniforms never were anything less than clean and pressed, and he carried the same .38 caliber Police Special he had carried as a member of the police force (the department had given it to him on his retirement), and he had carefully kept it clean and oiled for he did not remember how many decades, but he never had fired it in anger, and then those children came yelling, and they were waving pistols, and they were wearing Nixon masks, and the first and last thought Otto had was: Oh Lord, I am too old for this.

Part Eight

THE DISMANTLING

OF THE UNIVERSE

There came, inevitably, a procession of mornings that Miss Margaret Ridpath employed as a balance sheet. This procession comes with age to everyone, or so Margaret believed, and it is painful, weary, cluttered with things unopened, unfulfilled and too frightening ever to be faced. But, fearful as she was, Margaret nonetheless did try to poke about in her history, to prod it, to inspect the collisions and accidents. Perhaps this all came because of her precise mind with its efficient tumblers and gears, because of some final desire on her part to achieve a *true* neatness, a *true* feeling for the beauty of a hospitable universe free of iron. But in any event, no matter what else it was, it surely was a morning thing—as though she were saying to herself: *Today may be my last day, and perhaps I should draw up a summary.* And so she drifted into bright cornflaked and toasted and scrambledegged ruminations while Mother sat in the front room and watched Barbara Walters and Pauline moved mousily from stove to table to counter to sink, and it *had* to be age that was making Margaret try to face her history. Nothing else made any sense. Certainly not courage. So then what existed? Surely the collisions and accidents had deflected her, but in what direction? In the year 1974, which was the year she died and Otto York died and the children died, Margaret was a cinched and rigid and yet *comely* sixtythree, the mistress of her late sister's bald and hortatory Groucho Marx of a husband, and the mention of her name caused tournament bridge players to utter respectful words, and she once had been in love with a Jewish dentist who had smoked cigars in bed, and people forever *drifted* from her, and she once had spat on the grave of a woman named Dorothy Hall, and on this planet there was precisely one person (Pauline Jones) at whom she was able to raise her voice. And oh yes, what about Miss Margaret Ridpath's mother? What about the slapless slaps and the senile joy with which they were received? And why, if Wanda Ripple had hated Mother, had she left Mother all her money? Oh dear, oh dear, oh *dear,* there were some mornings when Margaret's cornflaked ruminations actually made her cornflakes soggy, and she had to get a wiggle on so she wouldn't be late to work. She'd never been late to work in her life. To be comely *and* punctual . . . ah, such an accomplishment. And so Margaret would hurry off to Steinfelder's, and of course by 1974 she had all sorts of electronic gadgetry to help her with the bookkeeping, which then gave her even more time to think, to try to summarize. Which meant that the cornflaked ruminations sometimes became the hamburgered ruminations, or the saladed ruminations, or the tea-withlemoned ruminations, and she said to herself: It all has had some sort of structure. Isn't that a fair assumption? I mean, the *days*. All the *days*. Father is with us every day as Mother blabbers on and on, and I remember how frightened of Wanda I was because Wanda hated Mother, but it turned out Wanda *didn't* hate Mother, and a story exists there someplace, but I don't know where. Only one lime pie a year, but she didn't hate Mother; she didn't; she *didn't*. And somehow Mother knows this. Just as I know Pauline does hate Mother. Just as I know Mother is afraid of Pauline. Which is amusing. Mother is afraid of Pauline, and Pauline is afraid of me, and I am afraid of Mother. And we all are mad and we don't know it. And even if we *did* know it, we probably wouldn't even *care*, would we? (Oh please, dear God, next time around reveal more of the scheme of the universe. As things stand now, we are able to perceive nothing beyond hints and fragments.) And sometimes, while working all this shattered nonsense through her brain, Margaret would exasperatedly shake her head. Or do sums. Or walk around the store and speak with some of the clerks about the illegibility of their sales slips. But always kindly. Never with anger. Always timidly. Never with sarcasm. And this was a good distraction, but it was *only* a distraction, and it did no permanent damage to her incessant daily desire to summarize. She almost was ready to believe she was having a premonition of some sort, and so she always made certain her underclothing was clean and without runs or holes or anything else that might prove embarrassing in case of some sort of accident. After all, one never could tell, could one? And George Prout said to her: "I am your *man*. You keep me *young*. Do you *feel* me? It's *good*, isn't it?" And Pauline Jones said to her: "Oh, Margaret, if only there was some way I could really *explain* to you how much I admire you . . . the way you're always . . . ah, *in hand* . . . not a hair out of place, I mean . . . and the way you've made a name for yourself that is known all over the *world* wherever the game of bridge is played . . . *the* Margaret Ridpath of the bridge columns, and I live in the same house with her . . ." And Inez Ridpath said to her: "Inez McClory's the name and sitting in the parlor's my game, and I am in love with a handsome young veterinarian who has the manners of the Archduke Ferdinand. The warm weather is the best, if I can have a Coke—fountain *or* bottled—and sit in my *STAR* chair and smell grapes and sunshine and listen to the fragile slanting hush of a willow tree . . ." And Margaret tried to listen to these voices, as she had tried to listen to *all* voices, and she was aware that it was far too late to understand how her courage had been crushed, or at least split apart, which made her also aware that the world probably was not *entirely* populated by iron persons (did she remember the trip to England? of course she did!), but she finally decided the time had come for her to push aside the antimacassars and the bridge trophies and the voices and the electronic gadgetry and the double finesses, to turn away from all the honeysuckle and all the brick sidewalks and all the smiles and rainstorms of Paradise Falls, to say to God or Whomever: *Look, we are all involved in a contest, correct? All right then, would You kindly tell me why no one has explained the rules to me? All I have is a vague sense that all sorts of things are being moved around. So kindly explain Yourself . . . ah, please?* And so in her prayers Margaret did in fact make that demand to have the rules explained. But the demand always ended in a sort of frightened sigh, and it never was answered. So all that was left to her in the final judgment was the neatness of her mind, her feeling that order did exist, a feeling that actually was more of a faith, since there wasn't really all that much proof. Oh, loving Jesus, all the *days.* Sweet heaven, all the *canoes* and all the *bees* and the dour intimidating taste of horseradish and the vanished antique belligerence of Lexie Musser. Those who reach out have their hands chopped off. The thing to be is inconspicuous. (Other people saw trolls. Other people saw Hitler. Miss Margaret Ridpath saw canoes. Miss Margaret Ridpath saw bees.) But she worked hard all her life keeping her secret from most of the world. Oh, she had yielded to her sisters and their abandonment of their mother (*their* mother, too), and she had yielded to her mother (*her* mother) in the grotesque matter of the slapless slaps, and she had yielded to the adenoidal Wanda Ripple on the matter of housework because she (Wanda Ripple) had struck up some sort of mad harmony with her mother (*Miss Margaret Ridpath's* mother), and she had yielded to the obscene sniveling and wretched elderly *machismo* of George Prout, and she had been flattened by the inattention of the tall lady from the CPV&M depot in 1917, when so much had been promised and nothing had come from it; she had been flattened by the death of Irv Berkowitz and the contempt of Harriet Berkowitz (just as she had been flattened by the contempt of Martha Boyd), and sometimes you told the truth and everything blew up in your face, and sometimes you lied and everything blew up in your face, and oh, the days . . . the *days* . . . some years the hollyhocks are better than they are other years, and some people are better than other people, and *days* should be measured as though they were a child's alphabet blocks . . . which would therefore create a *scheme* . . . which would therefore create *order* . . . which would therefore lead Miss Margaret Ridpath toward some sort of grasp of the rules of the contest. But where to begin? Out of a personal history that was aimless, vague, frightened? Or perhaps out of public history? But where was the order in the war? Where was the order in what was happening with the President and his people? If the government had gone mad, what chance was there for a Miss Margaret Ridpath? (Oh, serene she was, to *look* at her. Serene and cinched, and she spoke politely. And her underclothing was flawless. And the more she thought, the less she knew, but serene she unquestionably was, to *look* at her. The universe had given her a mother who sought punishment. It had Wanda Rippled her and it had Pauline Jonesed her, and finally it had George Prouted her . . . and her Irv Berkowitz days had been brief indeed. And her success as a bridge player was a lot of tinfoil flapdoodle, the work of children frowning over straw dolls in an iron cage. And yet she persisted in her faith that the universe had order, and she told herself that *she* was at fault for not understanding that order—and God really should not be held accountable. And so the thing she did was, she ruminated. And she carefully inspected her underclothing. And she did her very best to stay away from canoes.)

Friday was payday at Steinfelder's, and Margaret always took her check to the Paradise Falls State Bank for deposit during her lunch hour. And Friday, August 9, 1974, was no exception. It was a lovely day, a miracle, with the temperature in the low eighties and not a bit of the usual humidity that hit Paradise Falls in August. Margaret and everyone in the store had been talking about the resignation of President Nixon (for whom she of course had voted, in both 1968 and 1972), and old Bob Steffens, who ran the shoe and leather goods department, was of the opinion that the President had been railroaded. "He only did what they've *all* done," said old Bob, "and I think he's been a lot better than most. I mean, how come, if the Congress is so allfired hot that morality be served, it sat on its hands when the Bobby Baker thing came out? Or how about Chappaquiddick?" But one of his clerks, Kenny Eaton, disagreed. "You can't use that sort of reasoning," said Kenny. "If you did, then you'd have to say that Nixon should be free because the Grant Administration was corrupt, or because Nanking was raped." And old Bob Steffens said: "I don't follow you." And Kenny Eaton said: "If *I* shoot *my* wife, that gives *you* no excuse to shoot *yours*." And old Bob Steffens said: "Oh, that so?" And then of course everyone laughed. But Margaret did not laugh. She went into her office that morning and closed the door. She seated herself behind her desk and she ruminated. She thought of order. She asked herself whether anything could remain if the government went. As a bridgeplayer, she was expert at calculating odds, but how did one calculate the odds on the possibility of disorder? She shook her head. She was more disturbed than she wanted to be. Just about everyone she knew . . . and even old Bob Steffens, in his own way . . . was making jokes about the situation, exhibiting what she supposed was a chic cynicism. But Margaret would not yield to that sort of tackiness. She still believed that she had the capacity to think her way through to an explanation of all the mess—and not only the mess of Watergate, but the mess and haphazard history of her life, of slapless slaps and her preposterous grouchomarxing lover, of the cringing Pauline Jones and the endless blabber of Inez Ridpath (of her home, yes, of the silences and the trellises and the antimacassars and the strange questioning cornflaked mornings, of what she—Margaret—had come to think of as the Wanda Ripple Days as opposed to the Pauline Jones Days), and of whatever wreckage had come down on her head, of whatever nonsense, of whatever flatly amiable and courteous smalltown lunacy. And yet finally, shuddering, Margaret was able to come up with nothing beyond questions and exasperation, and so she rose from her desk and opened the door. And an hour or so later she walked to the bank . . . just as the children were driving out of the cemetery after having visited the elaborate tomb of the hayseed Ozymandias known as WELLS.

A million years earlier, Irv Berkowitz had grinned at Margaret, and he had said to her: "Sometimes you look at me like I'm a sum to be added up."

"What?" said Margaret.

"It's like you're saying to yourself: 'If *this* is so, then *that* must be so, and it all will *prove out*, and I'll get an A in the test.' "

"I don't understand that," said Margaret.

"You are seeking consistency in me," said Irv, "and it's a foolish pursuit, believe me. The trouble with you is you accept every new person in your life as though he . . . or she . . . had the same grasp of reality as you do."

"But isn't reality *reality*, period?" said Margaret.

"Oh, my God," said Irv. "Reality is what we *perceive* to be reality."

"Which means?" said Margaret.

"Which means what I am today could change tomorrow," said Irv.

"Which means there is no real order?" said Margaret.

"Right you are," said Irv.

Margaret walked slowly to the bank that gorgeous August day. She glanced at her watch, and it was about time for Vice President Ford to succeed President Nixon, to take the oath of office and give an appropriate speech no doubt having something to do with unity. Margaret nodded and smiled at people who passed her on the sidewalk. There was a slipper sale at Thom McAn, and perhaps she would stop there later, even though it was a shamelessly flagrant betrayal of Steinfelder's. She smiled a little, and she supposed that—for her—she was being terribly brave. She looked around, and the street and the sidewalks were reasonably crowded, and she loved Paradise Falls . . . she really did. An old farmer named Henry Froelich tipped his worn straw hat to her, and a woman named Irene Sayers said to her: "The news is really something these days, isn't it, Margaret?" And Margaret smiled and nodded. For some reason Margaret got to thinking of her old beau, Eugene Pearson, and she wondered what had become of him and his wife, the former Rosemary Hall. And, curiously, Margaret decided she hoped they had done well together. She grimaced into the sunlight. She was goopy and sentimental in her old age, and that was a fact. And then, shaking her head ever such a little bit, she asked herself: So what else is new? And she said to herself: Hey, I am almost sounding Jewish. Irv would be proud of me. And she also said to herself: I never grieved him as I should have. I think perhaps Harriet Berkowitz got in my way. Or perhaps my own nature got in my way. (The young man had ELVIS FOREVER on his sweatshirt, and Irv and I had succeeded in making plans, and then along came the old lady with the white kitten in the basket, and he was sprawled on top of me, and it was a *darling* white kitten, and there are no sums that can be totted up, are there? There is no formula that can be devised, is there? No set of proper words has been written, has it?) And so there then, on her final walk, elbowing past other pedestrians, smiling courteously at those who knew or recognized her, glancing in display windows at wristwatches and canned hams and Kotex boxes, Margaret sucked in the breath of the town, and then . . . when she entered the bank . . . the first person she saw was her old friend Otto York, her bridge partner from before the beginnings of time.

*

Pete Saddler came from his office, and Margaret waved at him. He leaned over a desk and spoke briefly with one of the assistant managers, a young black fellow named Sam Elliot. Then he looked up at Margaret and grinned. Again she waved at him. She was standing at one of the deposit desks, and she was endorsing her check. A smiling Otto York came to her and said: "This is Friday, so it must be payday." His uniform was clean and crisp, and the butt of his .38 caliber Police Special was smooth and spotless. His smile broadened into a grin, and all his teeth were his own, and she almost could have hated him. "Boy oh boy," he said, "you look like enough to make the world fall down and beg for mercy."

Margaret smiled. She carefully signed her name on the check, then made out a savings account deposit slip in the exact amount of the check. "Otto," she said, "in all the years I've known you, I've kept expecting you to grow up."

"That's like expecting blood from a turnip," said Otto.

"I can believe it," said Margaret. Then, smiling: "And how is your friend Miss Beauty?"

"Perking right along," said Otto. "I gave her a bath last week, and she appreciated it."

"A *bath*?" said Margaret. "But she wears a robe, doesn't she? Did you take it off?"

Otto sadly shook his head. "Tried to," he said, "but she wouldn't let me."

"Poor Otto," said Margaret.

"You'd better believe it," said Otto.

Margaret had completed the filling out of the deposit slip. She set down the pen and looked at Otto and said: "You look very well."

"Thank you," said Otto. "And so do you." He touched the brim of his cap.

Margaret nodded. She was pleased with Otto, very pleased. She always was pleased with people who looked well, and Otto surely did look well, what with his crispness, the crease in his trousers.

Margaret started toward a teller's cage, and then the three children came in.

She had watched her share of television, and she even had seen *Bonnie and Clyde* at the Ritz. The ending of the film, with its slow-motion destruction of Faye Dunaway and Warren Beatty, had disturbed her enormously. To her, it had seemed real beyond real, real to the point of absurdity, real as a parody of real. She had attended the film with Pete and Sarah, and afterwards Pete had said: "Was that the way it really was?"

"Those young people in the theater certainly seemed to hope so," said Margaret.

"*Hope* so?" said Sarah.

"Yes," said Margaret. "This is 1967, and they're fed up with everything, and so they're looking for precedents."

"You mean excuses, don't you?" said Pete.

"I suppose so," said Margaret.

"Well, as a banker I take a dim view of the whole thing," said Pete.

"They certainly don't make movies the way they used to," said Sarah.

"They don't make much of anything the way they used to," said Pete.

Pete and Sarah drove Margaret home. Pauline was sitting in the kitchen, and she was drinking hot chocolate, and she fixed a cup for Margaret, and she asked Margaret to tell her all about the film. And Margaret said: "It's too morbid for you."

"Please?" said Pauline.

"Be quiet," said Margaret.

Pauline looked away.

On an arithmetical scale, if a total coward is a zero, then Pauline was a −1. Margaret looked steadily at her, sipped hot chocolate and said not a word about the movie. There are times when the power of relentless tinfoil cannot be dismissed.

The three children were giggling and whooping, and they were waving their pistols, and one of them—a tall boy with a head shaped like a football—shouted: "*Hands up, motherfuckers!*"

All three of the children wore masks, and the masks were of President Nixon. One of the other children was a plump girl; the third was a plump boy.

"*Hold on now!*" hollered Otto York, fumbling at the holster that held his .38.

The plump boy fired at him and missed, the bullet striking an electric clock and decommissioning it.

Otto York tugged at his holster.

Miss Margaret Ridpath arranged her features in a thin astonished frown. "Oh my *goodness*," she said.

Leon Jaworski, the special Watergate prosecutor, announced that no immunity had been asked by Nixon or the Nixon people. U.S. Sen Barry M. Goldwater, Republican of Arizona, revealed that he had put away "five or six" drinks after reporting to Nixon that he (Nixon) was finished. The Los Angeles Dodgers had the best record in the major league. Funeral arrangements were being made for Robert Rounseville, sixty, the singer and actor. Funeral arrangements were being made for Baldur von Schirach, sixtysix, founder and organizer of the Hitler Youth. The mayor of Cleveland, Ohio, vetoed gun control legislation. In San Antonio, Texas, Elmer Wayne Hensley, eighteen, was sentenced to five hundred ninetyfour years in prison for his part in the murder of twentyseven boys and young men. Asked to say something about the Nixon resignation, former Vice President Spiro T. Agnew said: "I can't comment." In East Rutherford, New Jersey, Mrs Marion Greenberg Parker, seventytwo, committed suicide. She was found dead in her auto in the garage of her home after having been told she was to be evicted. Workmen in Vienna found portions of a Roman gatepost dating back to perhaps one hundred years before the birth of Jesus Christ. It was reported that there was much weeping and embracing among the Nixons during their final hours in the White House. The winning New York lottery number was 846934.

Pete Saddler and Sam Elliot crawled under Sam Elliot's desk when the shooting began. Two female customers—Mrs Norma W. Estes, widow of a former mayor, and Mrs Charles T. Meckler, wife of the assistant manager at the A&P—swooned. There were four tellers on duty. They simply stood there. There were eleven other customers in the place—including Miss Margaret Ridpath. They simply stood there. But Otto York did not simply stand there. He tugged his .38 free of his holster. He was shot in the face by the tall boy whose head was shaped like a football. Otto York spun backwards, and the tall boy laughed and whooped. He and the plump boy and the plump girl continued to wave their pistols, and the tellers' arms went up, and the customers' arms went up, and Otto York fell screaming against Miss Margaret Ridpath, knocking her down. He dropped the .38, and he flopped on top of her, and she grunted, and blood came from his face in great warm plump balloons.

*

In a brief address to the nation, delivered shortly after his inaugura-
tion at noon, President Gerald R. Ford said, among other things: *If
you have not chosen me by secret ballot, neither have I gained office by any
secret promises.*

And he said, among other things: *I am indebted to no man.*

And he said, among other things: *My fellow Americans, our long national nightmare is over. Our Constitution works. Our great republic is a
government of laws and not of men. Here, the people rule.*

The children were laughing behind their Nixon masks, and the tall
boy shouted: "It's all your own goddamned fault! Who do you
think's responsible for this? The fucking *owls*? Now let's see the color of
your money, folks!" He advanced on a fat man, shoved the fat man aside,
laughed, then went to the first teller's cage. A girl named Marysue Green-
grass was inside the cage, and she began pushing money toward the tall
boy, and he stuffed it in his pockets. "Shit!" he shouted. "We should
have brought along a goddamned bag of some sort!" He looked around,
gave a happy yelp and went to the fallen Mrs Estes. She had been carrying a large leather purse. He emptied it, returned to the tellers' cages and
began stuffing it with money. In the meantime, the two plump children—
the boy and the girl—were taking wallets and purses from the customers.
And Otto York now was dead, and he was bleeding all over the floor, and
Miss Margaret Ridpath squirmed out from under him, and there lay the
.38, directly in front of her, its butt soaked by Otto's blood. She glanced
at his face, but he had no face.

It all comes to a *moment* then. *Days* count for nothing then. *Order* is
only a word then. And so someone must do something. No one has
the right to dismantle the universe. But courage is not involved here. Outrage, yes. Perhaps. (Otto York had been a good man.) But *not* courage.
Rather, a weariness with the rhetoric and the acts of those who would pull
out the floorboards and knock in the ceiling. Weariness and an enraged
final gesture on the side of sanity.

And so, grunting, Margaret reached for the .38 and lifted it, and it was
so heavy.

She never had fired a gun in her life. She first aimed at the plump boy, who was taking a wallet from the fat man the tall boy had shoved aside. The bullet went screaming past the plump boy's left ear, and he shrieked.

The tall boy turned from the teller's cage and fired at Margaret, nicking the left side of her throat.

Margaret stood up.

The plump girl screamed.

All the customers dropped flat, and the tellers ducked under their windows.

The left side of Margaret's throat stung. She fired at the plump girl, and this time she was successful. The bullet took off the right side of the plump girl's face and ripped off the Nixon mask and slammed her back against the tall boy. They both fell down.

Howling, the plump boy charged at Margaret, as if he would hit her with his gun.

"No," said Margaret, and she shot the plump boy in the groin and then in the forehead.

The plump boy's arms spread, and he exploded, and he collapsed at Margaret's feet. He had dropped his pistol. Margaret paused to pick it up.

The tall boy slid out from under the dead plump girl.

Smiling a little, Margaret said to herself: Tinfoil 2, Iron zero.

"You old cunt!" hollered the tall boy from behind his Nixon mask. He fired at Margaret, and the bullet tore into her left shoulder. He fired again, ripping a hole in her stomach.

Spurting, Margaret advanced on him. Now she held two guns. She fired twice and hit the boy once in his left thigh.

Bleating, he staggered toward the door.

Everyone else was screaming—except the dead ones and except the two women who had swooned. (Even Pete Saddler was screaming.)

Margaret felt nothing. She followed the tall boy toward the door, and she followed him as he pushed his way outside. A hairy little dog came along, and the tall boy tripped over the hairy little dog, and the tall boy sprawled, and his pistol spun away, and Margaret came to him and knelt next to him and pressed both her pistols against his head. "No," he said.

"Yes," said Margaret. She jammed the .38 against the mouth of the Nixon mask. She jammed the other gun between the eyes of the Nixon mask.

"Please," said the tall boy.

A crowd came running.

Margaret squeezed the triggers, and she was blinded by blood and mess. She fell back. Margaret leaked. She tried to cover the places where she had been perforated, but she did not have enough hands.

George Prout came running up the sidewalk and knelt next to her, but she did not see him. Pete Saddler came lurching out of the bank and knelt next to her, but she did not see him. She died fiftyeight minutes later in the emergency room of the Paradise Valley Memorial Hospital, and she saw no one, but she did have some moments in which she was able to formulate thoughts. She said to herself: I may not have been brave, but at least I was not timid. She said to herself: I expect there will be a lot of speculation. There I was, and I came after them, little old me, and I think maybe a more sophisticated person would find it all very funny.

And she said to herself: But no one has the right to dismantle the universe.

And she said to herself: Tinfoil 3, Iron zero.

And she said to herself: If tinfoil is respect for order, and iron is loudness and lack of discipline, then maybe tinfoil is better than iron.

And she said to herself: I am sorry I had to treat Mother the way I did, not slapping her when she believed I was slapping her. But then I am also sorry I was frightened by canoes and bees.

Finally, near the very end, she was softly aware of voices and activity and perhaps a sound of sobbing, probably from George Prout. She opened her eyes, and she saw nothing, and a hand touched her forehead. And she said to herself: We save string and gather old tin cans and pile up shiny agates and put together hooks and gears and levers; we munch on decades and accumulate experience and build attitudes. Then, in an instant, it is all confiscated by time. I have been alive (after my fashion), and now I am dead, and I do not believe dead to be all that dreadful. Perhaps canoes and bees are worse. At least the possibility exists. Mother, I leave you to the tender ministrations of Pauline. George, I leave you to the contemplation and assessment of your posturing. I am not afraid. I am not afraid. *Hey! I am not afraid!*

Grinning, puffing on one of his horrible cigars, Irv Berkowitz had lain in bed with Margaret one night in perhaps 1957 and he had said to her: "I'd like to think that love makes people braver than they ordinarily are."

"Don't you think that's a romantic illusion?" said Margaret.

"So what's wrong with romantic illusions?" said Irv. "Should I be marched off to the electric chair because sometimes I get sentimental notions?"

"Of *course* not," said Margaret. "But . . . well, you and I are . . . ah, *bridge players* . . ."

Irv laughed so hard he nearly choked on the smoke from his cigar.

Dying, blind, unafraid now, Margaret said to herself: If I only ever was able to describe the ecstasy, the rewards, of simple order, of consistency, of behavior that did not fall apart because of whim or laughter or weakness. The blood of Otto York was the final outrage, and those children had no right. I did not hate them, though. I resisted them, and I punished them, but all I sought was to erase the outrage and set things back in order. It has nothing to do with iron; it has everything to do with propriety. We have laws. One drives on the right side of the road. One stops when a traffic light turns red. One lines up at the Kroger checkout counter and takes one's turn. Rules and patterns must be honored. Either we are civilized or we are not. I at least feel on the side of the angels, and I do hope and pray they will welc

Her undergarments were bloody, but they were clean, and she was smiling a little, and then she died, and she had what turned out to be a grand funeral.

Part Nine

NEWSY NOTES FROM

AN ANTIQUE LAND

The people at Zimmerman's Funeral Home stripped Miss Margaret Ridpath, drained her, patched her, bathed her, pumped her full of embalming fluid, then slid her into a fine blue dress that had been chosen by her sister Sarah. The cosmetologist, whose name was Ruby Loomis, was impressed with the firmness of Margaret's flesh tone. "She surely was well preserved," said Ruby Loomis to the embalmer, a man named Melvin (Whitey) Franz.

"She did a hell of a job of work," said Whitey Franz.

"Yes indeed," said Ruby Loomis.

"Goddamned kids," said Whitey Franz. He was rinsing out the trocar.

"Yes indeed," said Ruby Loomis, dabbing.

"Somebody has to teach them a lesson," said Whitey Franz.

"Right," said Ruby Loomis.

"She must of been a regular John Wayne," said Whitey Franz.

"Must of been," said Ruby Loomis.

More than two thousand persons filed past Margaret's open coffin the first afternoon and evening she was on display at Zimmerman's. More than two thousand *five hundred* persons filed past Margaret's open coffin the second afternoon and evening she was on display. Those days were Sunday, August 11, and Monday, August 12. The President of the United States, Gerald R. Ford, was assuring the nation and the world that American democratic principles had not been damaged by the Watergate scandal. The commentators were speculating on the extent of possible criminal prosecution of the former president, Nixon. Sarah Saddler collapsed from exhaustion Monday evening after shaking she did not know how many thousands of hands. There was some doubt whether she would be able to attend the funeral the next morning, but she somehow did manage to pull herself together. She and her husband Pete of course sat in the first limousine from Zimmerman's to St Mark's Presbyterian Church and from St Mark's Presbyterian Church to Oak Grove Cemetery. The eulogy was delivered by the same Rev Mr Ordway who had presided at Ruth's funeral back in '71. He spoke at some length of courage in the face of evil. George Prout sat next to Pete and Sarah Saddler. He had ridden alone in the second limousine. He was full of beer, and his belly felt heavy. He had put away the contents of a sixpack since seven o'clock that morning, and at one point during the Rev Mr Ordway's eulogy he had to duck out for a quick piss. Pete and Sarah frowned at him when he returned, and all he really could do was shrug and make a vague apologetic movement with his hands. All five of his children were in attendance—together with their spouses. In addition, all four of Pete and Sarah's children were in attendance—together with their spouses. Imogene Brookes had driven down from Cleveland, and all the employees of the Paradise Falls State Bank were on hand, plus the Paradise Falls chief of police, Frank Nolan, and the county sheriff, John J. Wooley. The family had received a condolence telegram from the governor, John J. Gilligan, and the story had been worth ninety seconds on each of the three national television networks . . . and extensive coverage by AP and UPI. And the Rev Mr Ordway said: "Margaret Ridpath was a person of substance, a person whose achievements in the world of bridge brought credit to Paradise Falls and pride to her family. But, above all, she had a quiet *courage* and *sense of moral commitment* that caused her to perform an act of genuinely noble proportions. We must all of us sooner or later stand up to those poor beasts that would destroy us—which is precisely what Margaret Ridpath did. Out of an enormous courage. Out of an enormous faith in retribution. It is perhaps not chic these permissive days to speak of retribution, but there is no other way to describe the spirit that must have guided Margaret Ridpath's hand. We should all be in her debt. She has reminded us all of our obligations." (Beery and slouching, George Prout asked himself: Is that silly jerk talking about *Margaret*? I ought to punch him in the nose.) The procession of hearse and flower car and automobiles to the cemetery was slow, splendidly morbid. George and Pete were among the pallbearers. The temperature was nearly ninety that day, and George's palm was so sweaty he nearly lost his grip on his handle. But he managed to hang on as he and the five other men grunted with their burden from the hearse up a shallow hill to the gravesite. The service there was brief. Only family and a few close friends were on hand. The mob had been at the church. Here there were as many birds as there were people, and the birds were setting up a genial commotion. Inez Ridpath had not attended either the funeral or the graveside service. She was home with Pauline Jones, and Pauline had explained to her *again and again* what had happened, but it still had not registered. Pauline finally became so exasperated that day (since she *had* to stay at home with the old bat, even though she *loved* Margaret and wanted to *be with* Margaret this last day, to *mourn* Margaret and *weep over* Margaret and for the final time acknowledge her fear of Margaret) that she reached up Inez Ridpath's skirt and viciously tweaked Inez Ridpath's inner thighs and said to her: "You kept me from going, you old piece of . . . ah, *dog mess* . . . you. I hope you're satisfied." And Pauline thought of the slapless slaps and said to Inez Ridpath: "From now on, everything is for real." And Pauline smiled a gray stringy smile. And the day diminished. And the mourners fled the cemetery. And a bulldozer pressed the earth over the grave of Miss Margaret Ridpath.

The remains of Lee Pike were claimed by an uncle, Donald R. Pike, of Great Barrington, Massachusetts. They were cremated, and Donald R. Pike took the ashes home to Great Barrington with him. He showed the ashes to Lee's father, Dr Quentin H. Pike, who nodded briefly, then said: "You saw him?"

"Yes," said Donald Pike.

"It was no mistake?"

"It was no mistake," said Donald Pike.

"Ashes all look the same. These could be Churchill's ashes."

"They are not Churchill's ashes," said Donald Pike. "They are your son's ashes. I guarantee that."

"What do you think we ought to do with them?"

"Flush them down the toilet," said Donald Pike.

"That's a fine idea," said Dr Quentin H. Pike. "Would you mind doing that for me?"

"Not at all," said Donald Pike.

The grieving and flabbergasted parents of Christopher and Elizabeth Moss spent more than two thousand five dollars on a double funeral. The children were buried in a lovely cemetery in Haverford, and they were buried side by side, and a fine monument was erected with the legend GONE BUT NOT FORGOTTEN inscribed above their names.

*

George Prout spent a great deal of time with Pete and Sarah Saddler, and they drank a great deal of beer in the Saddler kitchen, and they examined the thing from as many angles as they could find. It was *common* to sit in the kitchen and drink beer, but it also was *comfortable.* No answers came out of all the talk, however.

George and Pete and Sarah decided that Inez Ridpath should be permitted to live out the rest of her life alone in the old Ridpath place with Pauline Jones. This of course delighted Pauline Jones, who had proceeded from tweaking Inez Ridpath's thighs to giving her *real* slaps, which the old bat apparently enjoyed as much as she had enjoyed Margaret's reluctant slapless phony slaps. And Pauline kept the house just as Margaret had left it. The trophies gleamed.

Harriet Berkowitz read of the incident in the New York *Post.* She laid aside the paper and for some reason she wept.

The energy crisis created a renewal of interest in the depleted Paradise County coal fields. Thus it was that in September of 1975 two mining engineers came across a battered female skeleton near the old Tuesday Creek mine. A number of bullets were found, and Sheriff Wooley established that they came from the same pistols that the three dead children had used in the attempted bank robbery. Thus it was no particular feat of intellect to figure out that this female had been killed by Lee Pike and the Moss twins. But the skeleton never was identified. It has been dumped in a box in a closet of the county jail, and perhaps some day someone will come along with some sort of idea as to who . . .

*

Also in September of 1975, George Prout became drunk one night in the Sportsman's Bar & Grill. He got into a conversation with an old fellow named Bill Crowell, who told him: "That Pauline Jones . . . now *there* was a woman in her day."

George nodded. "I remember her," he said.

"Eating stuff," said Bill Crowell.

"You'd better believe it," said George.

"But that fairy ruined her," said Bill Crowell.

"A shame," said George. "Have a beer."

"Thank you kindly," said Bill Crowell.

The bartender set up another round.

Bill Crowell made a nostalgic kissing sound. "A goddamned fucking *beauty* . . ." he said.

"Right," said George.

"Me, I was 4F, and me and the other fellers, we'd set around this place and we'd—"

"I know," said George.

"Like I would of got down on my knees," said Bill Crowell.

"Right," said George. He bought two more rounds, then walked with loose bones to the old Ridpath place. It was nearly midnight, but Pauline was watching Johnny Carson. George leaned on the doorbell. Pauline switched on the porch light, then quickly opened the door. She wore a frayed nightgown, a frayed robe and frayed slippers, and her hair was gray and stringy, and she had been eating stuff in her day, and George pushed past her into the front room, and Margaret's bridge trophies gleamed, and Johnny Carson was laughing at something Orson Bean had said, and George switched off the set. Pauline had followed him. He turned to her and said: "You're about *fifty*, aren't you? My *God*."

"What is it?" said Pauline.

"What you are now, and what you were," said George.

"Pardon?" said Pauline.

"That fucking *fairy*," said George. "What *you* need is a *man*."

Pauline spread her arms helplessly.

George went to her and opened her robe and nightgown.

"You're drunk," she said.

"I'd have to be, wouldn't I?" said George.

Pauline's breath was raspy.

George touched her. She was dry. "What you need is a man," he said.

Pauline trembled.

"A *stud*," said George. He kissed her.

Pauline strained to pull away.

Her breasts were flat and flaccid. He stroked them. He kissed them. "I . . . maybe you . . . I got a right to know how come . . ." he said. "Nobody knows that," said Pauline.

He pushed her down on the sofa. He lubricated her. He got on top. She finally was able to accept him, and twice he caught himself on the brink of calling her Margaret. As of the spring of 1976, he was visiting her two or three times a week, and sometimes she even talked with him, telling him of her flocked throne and whatnot. She was able to accept him each time, but nothing beyond that, and he said to her: "I'm like the dentist, right?" And Pauline said: "Right."

A film script written by William S. Burroughs was published by the Viking Press in 1975. It was entitled *The Last Words of Dutch Schultz*.

Pauline's brother Walter died in November of 1975. She stood over his open coffin, glanced around to make certain no one was within earshot, then whispered: "My Lloyd was *never* a 4F. He was a better soldier than you were, you phony."

Pauline's brotherinlaw Harry Dana died in February of 1976. She stood over his open coffin, glanced around to make sure no one was within earshot, then whispered: "Who ever *cared* whether Paradise Falls Clay Products had you and that old man holding the same job? You were nothing but a windbag, you phony."

Nixon was pardoned. Lee Pike went down the toilet. The war ended in Southeast Asia, and the crooks and the whores fled. Paradise Falls came to refer to the Margaret Ridpath incident as the Gunfight at the OK Corral. The President publicly fell down on several occasions. Jimmy Carter grinned a great deal. Christopher and Elizabeth Moss were GONE BUT NOT FORGOTTEN.

Pauline Jones kept Inez Ridpath nicely in line, and in early 1976 Inez Ridpath was a whisper away from ninety but still reasonably fit. And Pauline beat her when necessary. But Inez Ridpath did not complain. And Inez Ridpath talked, and Inez Ridpath talked, and Inez Ridpath talked, and Inez Ridpath talked.

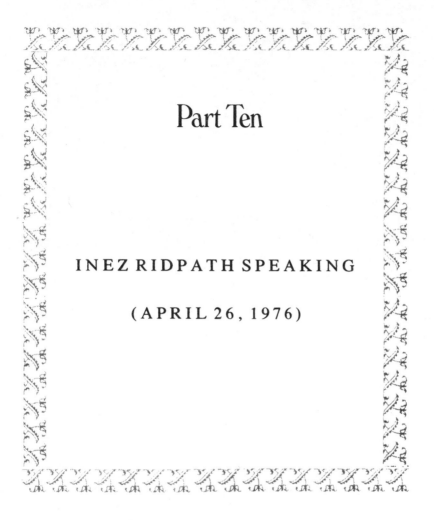

Part Ten

INEZ RIDPATH SPEAKING

(APRIL 26, 1976)

They never went hungry, and they never went cold, and yes, *of course* I know which ones are dead and which ones aren't. Paul is dead. Margaret is dead. Ruth is dead. Sarah is *not* dead. I know more than people like to think I know. Pauline is very good to me. She punishes me the way I should be punished. Margaret was good at it, but Pauline is better. I'll be ninety very soon now, and I'll outlive everyone. The bad always do. I used to be a very filthy person . . . my *body*, I mean. But now I am not a filthy person. Margaret began to clean me up, and Wanda continued the process, and Pauline is continuing the process, and there is a place near Paradise Lake where in 1911 or so John and I had intimate relations under a willow tree, and he snagged and snaffled my bloomers, and I absolutely could have *torn* him open with an *ax*. But then he did have an occasional glint of deviltry in him, yet I tried to go along with it, and I wonder whether Dorothy Hall tried to go along with it too. If she didn't, then I was the better woman, and he made a mistake when he took up with her, the *cow*, her and her dirty letters. Oh, there are places in this town where the odors of earth and grapes and whatnot are enough to tear the hair out of a person's nostrils, and it is not a bad town at all, which may be one of the reasons I keep going on, and on, and on, and Margaret died in a peculiar way, I'm told, but then who on this earth dies in an *ordinary* way, at least as far as *he* is concerned? The one who dies, I mean. The bourne from which no traveler has been known to return, or however it goes. Maybe *Pauline* is *my* bourne. Maybe I live within her, for surely she is death, which means I live within death, which is just fine and dandy, and it was an *interurban car,* if you can imagine such a thing, and how was I to know he held such deep feelings? But that didn't really mean he had to brag from the grave, did it? And my Margaret with all her silver cups full of nothing. There are those who come to me and tell me I should be proud of her. For what? The cups? Or maybe for the way she died? I don't know. I don't. I don't. I suppose she died because she figured enough was enough. I suppose she died because she wanted to give back something. Yes, it's the giving back that keeps so many of us going. Like me, giving back to the world my sorrow for what I did to my husband . . . me, so pretty I was, starting as Inez McClory of the St Louis McClorys, not a bad family affiliation at all, and so he goes and kills himself over another woman. Well, we all have to give back some way. With me it's all these years and all this talk. With Margaret it was something else. I suppose the world is crazy. A crazy world then is like that silly song. The song about kissing. *Give me a little kiss, willya, huh? And. I'll. Give. It. Right. Back. To. You.* © We give what we get. We pay. Or we make others pay. Ummm. Smack. *Enough* becomes *enough*. Then we *orate*. Or we *do*. Myself, I *orate*. Margaret, she *did*. I wish you the greetings of this unseasonably cold spring day. Now please, leave me be. I am weary. I probably have only about forty years more to live and repent, and I must conserve my strength.